The Breadwinner

Morgan True Blum

First Printing, 2018

ISBN 978-0-9980429-0-9

www.MorganTrueBlum.com

Chapter 1:
Immigrant

Hot, whiskey-soaked breath rose to the platform at the center of the speakeasy and concocted its own humid atmosphere of sweat, men, and infection. Phantom fists breached the clouds of brown tobacco smoke like shadowy islands. The gallery above the ring groaned beneath the weight of a hundred hollering drunks.

Pasha's ears rang as his head ricocheted against the maple floor. Anastas wasn't holding back any punches today. Pasha licked his frayed, chapped lips. Blood soaked his tongue with a rusty flavor. He'd been fighting for the gang known as the Breadwinners for almost four years. Three nights out of the week were spent bruising his knuckles down at the Foxhole. He'd fought some six hundred fights, and still he found the arena terrifying and grotesque.

The last thing Pasha could remember before blacking out was Anastas looming over him with bloated pride. It was embarrassing enough to lose, but to pass out? He'd be hearing about it for weeks. Someone poured their beer over Pasha's head. His limbs jolted back to life.

"Yakov, what do you think you're doing?" Klokov, Pasha's mob boss employer grabbed the bottle and tossed it aside. "Don't waste the inventory!" He snapped his fingers at Pasha. "Get up, boy!"

Pasha watched Klokov award Anastas with a fresh loaf of bread, as well as all the money gambled in their honor. Cash slipped through greedy fingers. Pennies were bitterly parted with. Many hung their heads in shame.

"I should've known better than to bet my money on some tall, skinny Ukrainian," someone complained.

"Did you get a load of those long limbs?" scoffed another. "He ain't even grown into his hands and feet yet! He's still a baby!"

Losing a fight might not have been such a heavy burden to bear if it weren't for the lives dependent on Pasha's income. He had Mama and his little sister, Katya, to think of after all. If it weren't for his family, Pasha never would have fought. He would never have stolen illegal liquor, and he definitely wouldn't have joined the Breadwinners, the gang of Slavic immigrants guarding the Lower East Side. Between bootlegging and street fighting, Pasha had done well for a Russian immigrant in New York City. Still, there were times he couldn't help but wonder if he'd made the right choice. Despite the black eyes, despite the bruises, Pasha had to earn his bread like any good American, even if it meant stealing.

Defeated and bruised, Pasha left the Foxhole and started his way home. He ducked his narrow chin into his scarf. He had a lean face with heavy eyebrows and a slim nose. His eyes weren't piercing green, or sea blue, or gray, or lavender—just plain brown, both of them. His lower lip protruded slightly in a boyish pout. As he lowered his cap the cowlick of his coarse raven hair brushed the nape of his neck and sent chills down his spine.

The filth-laden avenues of lower Manhattan were still blackened and odorous after the previous day's rain. The streets looked as though black mud had been slathered onto the pavement with a butter knife. Pasha kept his large, childish eyes trained on the sidewalk, and his broad shoulders hunched forward.

Ahead of him, the purple horizon was heavy with nightfall. Along the East River, a belt of the atmosphere had yet to darken and glowed like a snuffed hearth. The trees on the corners shed their flaming locks. Browning leaves crumbled beneath the wheels of passing motorcars. It was the end of November. In a month, 1924 would be dead.

When Pasha came upon his tenement building, he slipped into the courtyard. There was a flower box filled with dying pansies on the nearest windowsill. He knew without looking that blood covered his face. Cuts and bruises stuck out in painful contrast against his pale skin. He was as white as a birch tree these days. He plunged his hands into the decayed soil and smeared it over his wounds. The last thing he wanted was his mother to make a fuss when she arrived home. He gritted his teeth as the mud stung his open injuries.

When he finished muddying himself up, he made his way through the front door of the building and nearly ran into their landlady, Mrs. Borsuk. Pasha tipped his hat, revealing the deep bruise around his left eye.

"Good evening, Mrs. Borsuk," he greeted her in her native

Polish tongue. He looked her once in the eye, then quickly cast his gaze down again. It was a well-known fact along Orchard Street that if Pasha Chevalsky looked you in the eye longer than three seconds, you had his complete trust or else he was in a rage. Either way it was a rare phenomenon.

An assembly of elderly women had congregated on the landing above. At the sound of Pasha's voice, their eyes rolled down with pity and intrigue. He forced himself to look away.

Mrs. Borsuk patted his shoulder with an odd combination of sympathy and admiration.

"Come on in, Pavlo, better get out of the cold."

Pasha hobbled his way up the steps. He was keenly aware of each aging eye, milky or spectacled, trailing his lithe figure as he passed up the stairs. The moment he rounded the first corner they began whispering.

"Pavlo Chevalsky, such a sad, sad, story. Such a waste."

"The boy speaks three languages, you know, in addition to English. His mother is from Siberia. Married a Polish noble from Crimea, the Baron of Balalchik. You know, the one famous for making wine. My sister's niece was in his class several years back. An excellent student, she said."

"Well, what happened? Why isn't he in school now?"

"When his mother lost her job during the recession he was forced to drop out so he could help earn."

"What does he do?"

The floorboards creaked as the women leaned in closer, and the eldest whispered in a not-so-quiet voice. "He works for the Breadwinners, bootlegging and street fighting."

A gasp circulated throughout the little gathering.

"Pavlo Chevalsky a member of a street gang? Nonsense! He's such a sweet, gentle boy."

"Ah-ah, remember, Yelenka, 'it is the still waters that are inhabited by devils.'"

"Shame on you, Sarah, calling Pasha a devil. Pasha is a good boy. Besides, there are worse gangs to be a part of. The Breadwinners are practically heroes here in lower Manhattan."

"To wives and children perhaps. To mothers of sons, not so much."

Their voices died away in the greasy shadows of the second floor which hung limpid around the kerosene lamps lining the hallway. Theirs was the last door on the left, number seventeen. A sour humidity was seeping beneath the cracks and out into the passage. Pasha fished in his patched-up pockets for the key and let himself inside.

"Katya?"

"In here," she hollered from the kitchen, her voice competing with the sizzling timpani of frying meat. Pasha peered around the corner. The air was cloudy with the starch of beets and potatoes. A dewy sheen of garlicky condensation dampened Katya's heart of a face. The nine-year-old stood barefoot on a little stool in front of the stove. Damp curlicues of wavy, honey-colored hair clung to her warm, golden skin. When she thought her brother wasn't looking, she reached into a basket on the counter for something soft and brown.

Pasha's chest swelled with anxiety. He swooped forward and tucked her under his arm. He pried the mushroom from her hand.

"*Nyet*! Katya, no! What do you think you're doing? You're on a low-copper diet, doctor's orders! You can't eat mushrooms!"

She struggled to touch her feet to the floor. "How do you know I was gonna eat it?"

Pasha rolled his eyes. "Because I know you."

"If I can't have chocolate, and I can't have fish, you should at least let me have mushrooms."

Pasha set her down on the stool and tucked the basket away where she couldn't reach it.

"This isn't a bargain, *Rybka*." Little fish, he called her. "You're sick. You have Wilson's disease. There are some things you just can't have." He covered his face with one hand and sighed. "When you were born, and I got to hold you for the first time, I said 'Hello, Katya. I've been waiting my whole life for you.'"

Katya blinked her long feathery lashes. "You mean because of the babies that died in Mama's tummy?"

"Uh-huh." He pushed back her hair. "And so I would hate it if you killed yourself over something as silly as a mushroom." He tilted her diminutive chin towards the faint, yellow glow of the pendant light. "Let me see your eyes."

Pasha examined the Kayser-Fletcher ring invading Katya's silvery irises. According to the doctors, the brown ring was a result of excess copper built up in her tissues. It was the copper that was responsible for all her delusions. Wilson's disease often included symptoms of psychosis. It filled her mind with stars and light. At the age of five, she'd been released from school. Her teachers suggested institutionalizing her. Horrified by such an idea, the family decided it was best to keep Katya hidden away at home.

"Is it worse?" Katya tried not to wince as Pasha stretched open her eyelid. He sighed and bit his lip.

"I don't think so," he said, releasing her. Katya looked him over and knit her rounded eyebrows.

"What happened to you?"

Pasha rubbed at his temples.

"Don't tell Mama, okay?"

"I won't have to. When she gets home she'll see for herself."

Pasha shook his head. "Still. Don't say anything." He took the spoon from her and scooted her towards the sitting area. "Let me deal with supper. You get a jump on the piecework."

He dipped the wooden spoon into the pale, green broth and allowed the soft steam to moisten his face. For Pasha, there was something relaxing about the simplicity of making dinner. Nothing was rough or loud. Nothing was demanding or competitive. Cooking was quiet, homey, and comforting. That was how Pasha liked things.

The door opened, and their mother, Lydia, entered looking tired and windblown.

Katya hastened to her side. "Mama!"

"Katya, darling!" She pressed her nose against her daughter's cheek and sighed. Her deep-set, heavily-lidded eyes gave her a kind, dreamy expression. She was a young mother, having given birth to Pasha when she was just seventeen, but her every move was seasoned with an instinctive maternal affection.

She removed her coat and unpinned her soft, brown hair, letting it fall in waves around her shoulders. She was one of those people who seemed too good to be true, mythical almost, like a mermaid or something. Her charm often made up for her odd behavior, and even if it didn't she was tough enough not to care.

Pasha receded into the haze of boiling broth. As much as he wanted to greet his mother, he didn't want to risk revealing his injuries when it would upset her.

"*Patyula*!" She removed her gloves. "Aren't you going to come greet your mama?"

"Yeah, sorry, Ma. I got distracted with dinner . . ."

She placed her hands high on her hips. "Why are you still wearing your coat and hat?"

"I just got home, I didn't have time to—"

She pulled back his collar to kiss his cheek and jumped back in alarm.

"Pavlo," she exclaimed using his proper name. "You are covered in filth! What on earth did you get into today?"

Pasha shrugged, his cheeks filling up with his sweet, simple smile. "I got tired of being a boy and thought I'd try my luck as a mole instead." He pinched Katya's chubby cheeks, leaving behind spotty fingerprints. Katya giggled. Lydia swatted lovingly at his back with a dish towel.

"Oh, now don't do that, Pasha. You will get her all dirty, and I don't have enough water to clean the both of you! You have enough mud on you to start a garden. What were you thinking coming into the kitchen like that? You go wash up, then you come back and kiss me!"

"Yes, Mama. My paycheck is in the satchel by the way. You can go ahead and take it out."

Lydia dipped her hand into the pocket of her son's satchel and retrieved a thick bursting envelope. Inside were wads and wads of luscious green bills.

Katya peered over her elbow and gasped. "*Ochmanity*." Wow. "Pasha, what did you do to earn all this?"

But Pasha had already slipped into the bathroom to avoid being questioned. When his bath was finished he leaned over the sink and examined himself in the cracked mirror. With the muck wiped away, the bruises and cuts shined with fresh polish. Pasha combed his tense fingers through his hair. He would have to prepare himself for the inevitable interrogation.

When he emerged from the washroom, his mother dropped her spoon.

"Pavlo Ruslanovitch Chevalsky! You are cut up all over!"

As with most children, Pasha knew he was in for it when his mother doled out his full Christian name like a curse. Even more so considering how long it was.

"I'm fine, Ma," he muttered, turning to join his sister at the table. But Lydia caught him by the arm and jerked his chin towards the light. She inspected him with soft, oak-colored eyes. Her full, blossoming lips locked into a frown. He knew it didn't look good. He had a swollen black eye, a bloody nose, and a cut on the side of his head. And that wasn't including the contusion forming on his ribs, nor the one between his shoulder blades. She lowered her voice.

"Who did you fight this time?"

Pasha looked away. "Does it matter?"

Lydia relented and gently released his chin.

"When will you stop coming home to me all black and blue?"

Pasha resisted the urge to sigh. He didn't have a clear answer. Once you joined the Breadwinners, you were in it for life. Desertion was punishable by death. He looked down at his mother's long, graceful hands. Once upon a time, her fingers were decorated with dabs of paint and charcoal. Now they were marred by tiny cuts and callouses from factory machinery. He kissed her cheek apologetically. Lydia drew him into her arms, stroking his hair.

"Don't worry about me, Mama," he finally whispered. "I worry more about you and Katya."

"Sixteen-year-old boys shouldn't be worrying about their mothers. You should be out there doing sixteen-year-old-boy things." She shooed him towards the table.

***

After dinner, everyone settled into the sitting room. Lydia was bent patiently over her sewing basket by the window. Her silver needle dipped through the hem of a navy skirt, like a fish swimming upstream. Pasha flopped into an armchair while Katya brought him their father's balalaika.

"Play us some music, Pasha! Piecework goes by much faster when you play."

Lydia flashed her a warning look from beneath her lashes. "Katya, let your brother rest, dear. He is injured."

But Pasha shook his head. "That's okay, Ma. I'd be happy to." He took the balalaika and motioned for Katya to come sit in his lap. "What shall it be? *Ruslan and Lyudmila*? *The Cossack's Lullaby*? How about *The Firebird*?"

Katya beamed with a playful glow. "Play Mama's lullaby. You know, the one her father used to sing to her."

Pasha chuckled and tapped the side of his nose. "I had a feeling you might say that. *The Blind Man* it is then."

He positioned his fingers on the frets, gave the instrument a test strum, and coaxed out a moody, melancholy waltz.

"*Lucifer of the fiery coals*
had a handsome face and an ugly soul
he charmed two-thirds of the angel host
and the stars came tumbling down
An apple hung from a golden tree
to tempt a hungry wretch like me
I bit the apple and so did he
and the world came tumbling down
Trust not your eyes nor believe what you see
Visions can lie and beauty deceives
And so I see as the blind man sees
when the stars come tumbling down."

Katya laid her head against Pasha's shoulder. He couldn't help but marvel at the smile dimpling her cheeks. In a way, he envied her. For Katya, there was always something to be happy about. Even with dust on her hands and hunger in her belly, she could still see a tapestry of color others could not. Pasha couldn't understand this. Didn't she remember Papa's body hanging from the cypress tree? Didn't she remember the stern faces of the Red Army soldiers? The bullets whizzing past their heads as they ran for their lives?

Katya stroked her fingers over the body of the instrument.

"I remember when you used to play that song in Grand Central Station, and people would stop to put money in your cap."

Pasha set the balalaika aside, letting it rest against the arm of the chair.

"That was a long time ago."

"I used to love it whenever you'd take me along. We'd always stop to look at the ceiling. You would teach me about the constellations. How come we never go anymore?"

"Because we don't need to. I'm making more money now than I ever did playing the balalaika."

Katya dropped her chin to her chest.

"But you can't take me wherever it is you go now?"

Pasha sighed and leaned his head back against the chair. He pinned a curl behind Katya's ear.

"No."

Katya examined him with her peculiar stare. Pasha couldn't help but feel dreadfully exposed. Katya resented information being withheld from her. What's more, she was eerily discerning and could often dissect the truth on pure instinct. With so much to shelter her from, it unnerved Pasha to an extreme. He was struck with the urge to look out the window.

"What do you remember about Crimea?"

Katya closed her eyes and smiled. "I remember your horse,

Harpagos, and how you used to get in trouble for sneaking off to sleep with him in the barn."

At the mention of Harpagos, Pasha wanted to laugh and cry all at once. Pasha had been born with a penchant for equestrian arts, and his thoroughbred, Harpagos, might as well have been a trusty Labrador retriever. He managed a snicker.

"That happened a lot, didn't it? What else do you remember? Do you remember looking at the stars?"

Katya craned her head back and tapped her chin. "A little bit."

A smile tugged at the corner of his bruised mouth. "In those days we had a nice, wide porch to sit on. Papa would bring out the telescope and Mama would show us the North Star."

His mother drew back with a wistful breath. "How I miss that porch. Every year, after the first grape harvest, your father and I would sit on the deck and toast the season with a glass of Chardonnay."

Katya stared thoughtfully at the wall with an innocent expression seeded in her eyes.

"Do you think the soldiers kept making wine after they chased us out?"

Pasha's eyes widened. Lydia dropped her needle and thread, her full lips pressed together with severity.

"Katerina, you shouldn't speak of such things!"

"Yes, Mama." A heavy silence fell in which it was clear everyone's mind had drifted back to that horrible memory. When

Pasha closed his eyes, he thought he could smell smoke. Something heavy toppled over in the apartment above. A shower of plaster rained down from the ceiling. Pasha and his mother both gave a start. Lydia drew the back of her wrist across her forehead as though to wipe away a bead of sweat.

"Pasha," she panted, "play something else, please."

With his heart still throbbing, Pasha picked up the balalaika again and continued to play.

Chapter 2:
Two Bad Mice

Monday morning, while the sun was still struggling to get out of bed, Pasha dressed and gave a tug on the tin can phone sitting on the windowsill.

"Good morning, Miss Spichkin," he sang out cheerfully, imitating a posh accent. "I hate to interrupt your beauty sleep but you have a previous engagement with Mr. Chevalsky this morning."

Pasha leaned back against his headboard as he waited for a reply, but there was no answer. He gave the line another tug.

"Faina? Are you there? It's time to get up."

He stared at the opposite window across the courtyard, the one with the lace curtains. Nothing stirred. He cupped a hand over the receiver, mimicking a news reporter he'd heard on the radio.

"Welcome back, New York City! This is Pasha Chevalsky, your best friend speaking. Today is Wednesday, November the 26th, 1924, and it's time for Faina to get out of bed!"

Pasha pushed back his own curtains and leaned forward on the windowsill. He squinted down at the grocery store beneath the apartment. He could make out Faina's uncle and guardian, Mr. Matvei Dalka. A crate of inventory sat on the counter, labeled with the grocery's name, *Opa*. The title had suited the business far better when it was a liquor store.

He considered climbing up the fire escape and knocking on

Faina's window, but he wouldn't want to risk waking Anya, Faina's cousin. He liked Anya but she always kept a close eye on the two. They were thieves after all, and prone to stirring up trouble. Pasha always figured Anya was compensating for her father's lack of discipline. In the past, Mr. Dalka had often been criticized for letting Faina and her late brother, Leo, run wild. And it wasn't an unfounded accusation. When it came to Pasha's friendship with Faina, she was by far the rowdier of the two.

It was often said of Pasha and Faina that they were the origin of the phrase, "As thick as thieves." They were the original Bonnie and Clyde, though highly less publicized given the petty and bloodless nature of their crimes. Every morning they met up and pilfered their way through the boroughs. Faina organized the heists, and Pasha sold the goods to the Breadwinners. At the end of the week, Pasha split his earnings with her fifty-fifty, including what he'd earned in street fights.

A torrent of heavy breathing tunneled down the line, followed by the sound of someone licking their chops. An enormous, hairy dog eclipsed the window. It was Faina's Caucasian mountain dog, or *ovcharka*. He pushed aside the curtains and thrust his nose into the can.

"Mammoth," grumbled Pasha. "Get off the line!"

When the dog did not oblige, Pasha opened the window and climbed onto the fire escape. He tugged at the string.

"Mammoth, stop! Where's Faina?"

There was a terrible scratching noise from the far end of the alley as the rusted hinges of a window squeaked open. An ancient woman popped her silvery head into the alley. She was short and squat like a teapot, and she had her extensive braid wrapped around her neck like a scarf. Her large, round spectacles slid down her aquiline nose, and a chicken was shoved beneath her arm. It was crazy old Pumpkin Potemkin, better known as Aunt Poppy. Most children were frightened of Aunt Poppy as she suffered from a batty streak and talked out her head. Some even accused her of being the witch Baba Yaga, and claimed her two black cats, Ink and Iseult, roamed the neighborhood as her spies. But Pasha and Faina loved the eccentric old woman, and her cats. In turn, she doted upon them.

Pasha tipped his cap. "Good morning, Aunt Poppy!"

"Pasha," she clucked, "Faina left a message for you. She said to meet her at St. John's Freight Terminal."

Pasha fell back on his haunches, baffled. "St. John's? She would've had to be up at least an hour ago. Did she say why?"

Aunt Poppy's eyes slid from one corner of the alley to the other. Covering her lips, she bent forward and mouthed, "She went to the beach."

Pasha stared blankly at her. "The beach?"

Aunt Poppy replied with a solid wink, but Pasha remained dumbfounded. Exasperated, Aunt Poppy sighed and shooed him off.

"Oh, never mind. If you don't hurry now, you will miss her."

Pasha rubbed his hands together as he made his way down the fire escape.

"Whatever you say, ma'am. Have a nice day!"

Aunt Poppy's sleeves flailed as she shook her head back and forth. "*Patulya*! Make sure you watch out for dragons! There has been a Hephaestean Hog-Snout loose in Midtown! You don't want to go singeing your trousers! Heaven knows I have begged my nephew to speak with the authorities, but he is too busy running his company! Figures!"

Pasha tried not to cringe. Poor Aunt Poppy. Pasha had seen her threaten solicitors with an alleged unicorn horn, walk down the boardwalk with a picket sign that read "Save The Mermaids," and hand out home-made pamphlets encouraging the government to regulate aviation standards to protect the local seraph population. And she was always going on about her mysterious nephew who had bailed her out of jail several times.

"Yes, Madame. I'll be careful!" And he went on his way.

The sky was stale and pasty like an old crust of bread. Very little light made its way through the gray film of clouds. Pasha rubbed his hands together, trying to encourage some warmth into his veins. His fingers were beginning to resemble an old man's. They were crooked and knobby from bare-knuckle punches against hard, sturdy jaws, striking at muscle like a chisel on marble. Sighing, he tucked his hands away in his pockets, trying to forget.

Down near St. John's, the Rum-Runners bobbed and dipped through the harbor, their masts brushing the edge of the frayed horizon. The necrotic flesh of decaying birch trees flaked and peeled in the smoky autumn sunrise. Railroads wove Celtic chains past rotting tenements and opium-filled alleyways. Gray figures hovered in the broken windows and crumbling stoops. Cutting through Hash Square, Pasha kept his head down. Here were the poorest of the huddled masses, the most wretched refuse, the least fortunate of Lady Liberty's children. Like their mother, their complexions had succumbed to a similar green rust. Their faces eroded in a cocaine cloud.

The gravelly debris quaked against the pavement. Pasha rushed towards the freight yard. The mouth of the long brick tunnel opened upon a trembling track.

Female laughter rippled above the steam engine. Pasha smiled and rolled his eyes. Faina's laughter never changed. As a child, she had been in possession of one of those infectious, high-squealing giggles. It reminded him of the line in *Peter Pan* describing the birth of the pixies. It was that kind of laugh, the kind that could shatter and turn into fairies. Very few children can carry this sort of laughter into their adulthood without it sounding obnoxious, but Faina had managed to pull it off.

Pulling out from the tunnel, the steam-powered leviathan swam up the iron stream. It approached with powerful strides and stretched before Pasha like The Great Wall of China. Down the line of cars, against the rising sun, he could sketch out the footloose shape of Faina. She was swinging from the door handle like a ribbon on a maypole.

"Good morning, Breadwinner!" Faina's mouth glittered into an impetuous smile. Her black hair whipped behind her in a tangled tail that at some point had been a braid. There was a messy charm to her flyaway appearance, and she was joyful to look at.

As she leaned herself further out the door, Pasha's heart lurched in his chest.

"Faina, stop that! You're gonna slip and break your neck!"

But Faina ignored him. Pasha shook his head at the uneasiness which bloomed inside him when he saw her gambling away her safety. She rode hazard and danger like a carousel ride. Recklessness was both a part of her charm and vice. To be in her company itself was a madcap gamble, for you fully expected her to eventually lose in her never-ceasing game of chicken. But that day had yet to come, and she had evaded it for years.

As her car passed, Pasha began to sprint, pumping his broad shoulders and large hands. Faina knelt over the edge with an outstretched arm.

"Come on, Legs," she encouraged, "move your getaway sticks!"

Pasha swung his arm up and seized her grasp. He flung himself over the threshold and landed with a thud upon the dusty floor of the dim car. He let out an involuntary groan. His back was still stiff from yesterday's fight, and the impact made his injuries throb.

Faina's face beamed above him. "Good morning!" She was a tall, leggy girl with a prominent aquiline nose, and bushy eyebrows. Her chin was pointed, and she had passionate brown eyes. Freckles were singed upon her skin like combustible stars of radiance.

Pasha fumbled onto his elbows. "Don't you know it's dangerous to hang out the door like that? You could've slipped and gotten yourself killed!"

Faina scoffed and threw up her shoulders. "It's impossible for me not to make an entrance, Pasha. You know that."

Pasha rolled his eyes. "Yeah, I know. Your entire ego thrives upon it."

"You're darn right it does."

Pasha stroked his chin in amusement. Ever since she'd learned English, two nations had been competing for Faina's tongue. They warred inside her. She was equal parts Russia and New York City, and the music of both could be heard in her strange blended speech.

"Tell me, Faina, what were you doing lurking around Hash Square so early in the morning?"

Faina leaned casually against the crates as though nothing were amiss. "I was headed to the beach," she could not keep from giggling.

Pasha thrust out his lip and lowered his eyebrows. "That's not funny! It's dangerous for you to go skipping around at such an hour for something as silly as beach scavenging."

"Silly, you say?" She laid back on the ground. Her legs raised over her head like a burlesque dancer, showing off her men's trousers. Pasha paid no attention.

"Yeah, silly! Only you would be crazy enough to stroll the beach alone before sunrise."

Elevating her shoulders, she reached down into each bootleg.

"Aren't you gonna ask me if I found anything interesting?" Before Pasha could answer, she grinned and slid two bottles of illegal hooch from the inside of her boots. Pasha's mouth dropped. He started to say something, but Faina stopped him with a single finger. She reached into the inner folds of her oversized blue men's jacket and produced two more. Without a stitch of modesty, she rolled her pant leg below the knee to reveal a fifth bottle. She propped herself up on one elbow and stared at Pasha as though expecting praise.

"Where?" he finally managed to sputter.

"The Rum-Runners have been dumping their cargo into the harbor and letting them float to shore. They do it early in the morning so no one will see. That's why I was on the beach so early."

"But doesn't someone come to pick them up?"

"Of course. This shipment, in particular, was for one of those cordial stores up in Midtown."

"Wasn't someone there?"

"They were there. But do you think that made a difference for someone as light-fingered as me?"

Pasha smirked. “I get it, Faina. Everyone knows you’re the cleverest, fastest, and most skilled bandit of the Lower East Side.”

Like the blue coat and cap, her reputation had been handed down to her by her late brother, Leo. Throughout high school, Leo had been a Breadwinner associate. In fact, he had been something of a legend. Leo was able to run up walls, vault down fire escapes, and swing from flagpoles. New York City was Leo’s gymnasium. Before his death in 1920, he had done his best to teach Pasha and Faina everything he knew about acrobatics.

Faina rolled onto her stomach and cocked a fuzzy eyebrow. “Don’t you mean ‘we’?”

Pasha scoffed and shook his head. “I'm afraid I'm only guilty by association.”

“Is that so?” She propped her chin on her fist and ran a proud finger over the shiny necks of the bottles. “If I remember correctly, the headline from *The New York Journal* article in 1920 said *two* thieves were responsible for stealing forty pounds of liquor stockpiled at the Yale Club. Not one. ‘A boy and a girl, able to swing through the city like monkeys, and slip through tight spaces like rodents.’ The authorities dubbed them ‘*The Two Bad Mice*,’ after the story by Beatrix Potter.”

A grin leaked into the corners of Pasha’s mouth, exposing the incisor Faina had knocked crooked when they were ten. Faina pinched his knee affectionately.

“You are the Tom Thumb to my Hunca Munca. You’re just as

much of a troublemaker as I am." She turned to her side and examined her fingernails. "I gotta say, I can't decide if prohibition is either the worst thing to happen to America or the best thing to happen to us."

Pasha frowned. "You say that like we're the only ones benefitting from the illegal sale of liquor. If this goes on much longer, the entire country will rest in the pockets of mobsters like Klokov."

"Don't be such a wet blanket. You can complain all you want, but I know you too well. You're just grateful to have a law you don't feel guilty about breaking."

"Who says I don't feel guilty?"

She swatted at him with her sleeves, which ran far past her wrist, giving her the comical appearance of an old boyar.

"What reason would you have to feel guilty?"

"Faina, have you ever seen someone make bathtub gin? People are so desperate for alcohol these days they'll mix anything together! Even paint thinner!"

"That's why you gotta make sure you buy from the right person." She pulled a box of matches from her pocket and handed Pasha a lantern. "Light this for me, will you? It's freezing in here."

There was a saying in lower Manhattan that Faina Spichkin could start a fire in a lake. Faina had been causing accidental fires her whole life and under the strangest circumstances. Anytime she tried to light a match, something would happen. The stick would break, the lantern would explode, inflammable things became flammable. It had gotten to the point where Faina was now afraid of fire. But he supposed she had to be afraid of something, and so far that was a short list.

As Pasha was lighting the match, the train hit a bump, causing his cap to fall to the floor. Pasha shrank back from the light but it was too late; Faina had already seen the bruise above his left eye. She crept forward, her voice soft.

"Let me see."

Pasha huffed through his nose as he allowed her to tilt his head back. With pitiful eyes, Faina ran her cool fingers across the shiner.

"I take it the fight didn't go so well Friday?"

Pasha tensed and looked away with silent protest as she examined him. It was the absolute worst part of losing: having everyone make a fuss over his scars and injuries.

"No," he snapped and pulled his cap back down over his eyes. "Where were you all weekend anyway?"

Faina threw back her head and snorted like a colt. "Are you kidding? Uncle Matvei had us baking all the make-ahead dishes for Thanksgiving. Anya and I made the compote, we made baklava, and all the pickles for the vinaigrette. We were exhausted."

"You're still coming over for Thanksgiving dinner, right?"

"Pasha, our families have celebrated Thanksgiving together for six years. Why would anything change?" Without pausing to let him answer, she yanked on his sleeve. "Don't forget we're going to that parade Thursday morning—that new Macy's parade, or whatever it's called."

Pasha snickered and rolled onto his back. "How could I forget? Katya has been reminding me all week."

"Well, try not to get any more injuries before then." She tapped at the corner of her mouth to indicate his bruise. "You can't eat turkey with your jaw wired shut."

Pasha smirked and folded his arms behind his head. "I'll try."

"So what's the line-up for the rest of the week? Who are you fighting today? The new boy? What did Klokov decide to call him? Timber or something?"

"Yeah, Timber, because he's good at jumping outta the way."

Every Breadwinner was given a fighting name after his first month. Some boys got their names from a physical trait, like Vitalic Kristoff who was known as "Blaze" for the pigmentation on his forehead. Alexander Karp earned the title of "Red Roan" for his strawberry-blonde hair. But most earned their names by boasting a distinctive fighting style. One such example was Grusha "The Savage" Garin, who fought dirty. Then there were the moneymakers, the favorites. These were the boys who won so often they accumulated the most bets; brawny boys like Nikita "Moneyrider" Petrov, and Ivan "Trifecta" Markovich.

"Still better than mine," Pasha confessed, covering his face with his cap.

"What's wrong with 'The Stallion'?"

Pasha grimaced. "You're joking. It's the cheesiest name Klokov could've come up with."

"He named you that because of your 'unbreakable spirit—'"

"'—and my ferocity when backed into a corner.' I know, I know. It still doesn't make it any less ridiculous sounding."

Some boys took pride in their names, especially if they were good, and preferred them to their real names. Pasha was not one of those boys. Though he supposed it could've been worse. Blaze told him once, a boy performed so poorly they called him Ridgling, another name for a castrated horse.

Faina lifted his cap to look him in the eye. "And after Timber? Who do you finish out the week with?"

Pasha pushed himself into an upright position. "It's between Cavalry and Anastas."

Faina's eyes bulged. "Anastas again?"

"He's up against Stayer Sochinsky tomorrow morning, and you know how that goes. Stayer's got a ninety-three percent winning average. Odds are Anastas is going down. If I beat Timber, and chances are I will, that will put us right back together."

Faina paused. Forcing her frown away, she clapped him on the shoulder.

"Well, no matter. Tomorrow night let's you and me go to the club at the Foxhole, and we can forget all about it!"

Pasha laid back in the shadows, dismal. "I don't wanna go to the club at the Foxhole."

"Why not?" she whined. "It will cheer you up. We'll Charleston and tango like we used to!"

He leaned against the wall and shut his eyes like an old man laying down for his final rest. "I'm too tired, Faina."

Faina sighed and crossed her arms. "You say that about everything you used to love. You won't dance, you won't play baseball, you won't go to the pictures. I never see you at the library anymore."

"What good is the library if I can't go to school?"

"So you can keep learning, smarty-pants!" Faina tossed her hands in the air. "How else could I be this smart? I've been out of school longer than you have."

"Only by a couple of months," he griped.

"Not to mention, I was expelled. You dropped out. Your teachers expected you to go to a university."

"What does it matter? I'm not going now."

Faina scooted closer and propped her chin on his shoulder with a fond smile. "You were so keen when you first came to this country. You spent hours in front of your window studying. I'd never seen someone so dedicated. When your family needed money you played your balalaika in Grand Central Station. You would say, 'I'm gonna be like Vanderbilt, I'm gonna be like Rockefeller! They worked their way up. I will too.' You were determined to have the American dream, to grow up and become a wealthy philanthropist."

"You honestly think I still believe that?" He hadn't meant to sound so cold, but he did.

Faina drew back, looking slightly offended. "I don't know. I don't know what you believe anymore."

Pasha drew up his knees and folded into his chest. "I should never have become a Breadwinner."

"You were scared. Your mother had lost her job." Her voice grew dark. "Then there was that man."

Pasha's stomach turned. Johann Piyakov. How could Pasha forget his mother's drunken stalker? Faina fingered her collar absentmindedly.

"He used to scare Anya and me whenever we heard him in the courtyard."

Pasha pinched his temples between his thumb and index finger. "Well, he's dead now. Klokov saw to that. And now I'm his servant for life." He added sarcastically, "Papa would be so proud."

Faina elbowed him teasingly and appraised him with warm radiance. "You're exactly like Nicholas Nickleby."

Pasha blinked. "Who?"

She snickered and pulled his cap down over his nose. "You know! Nicholas Nickleby, from *The Life and Adventures of Nicholas Nickleby*! When Nicholas's father dies they leave their home in the country to make a life in London. Nicholas does whatever he can to provide for his mother and little sister, Kate."

Pasha's cheeks colored. "How could I forget your favorite story? You have a Dickens character for everyone, don't you?"

She tossed her braid over her shoulder. "I'm still looking for a Newman Noggs."

He patted her hand and rose to his feet. "They should write a book about you."

Faina laughed and tossed her hand as though it were littered with jewelry. "Tell me something I don't know."

Pasha rubbed his chin. "But what to call it . . ."

Faina bounced to a standing position. "*Faina Spichkin: The Modern Thief.*"

"No, no," he teased, twirling her in place. "It has to be something bigger, something grander. *Faina Spichkin: Queen of New York's Underworld.*"

Faina fell forward and grabbed Pasha's shoulders with a dramatic flourish. "*The Keen Criminal*!"

Trying not to laugh, Pasha pulled her into a tango position. "*The Bee's Knees of Bootlegging*!"

They promenaded across the car. "*The Bootlegging Beauty Queen*!"

Pasha dipped her backward. "*The Hooch Snatching Harlot!*"

Freeing herself, Faina posed with her hands high on her hips.

"No, no. *The Hooch Snatching Sheba*!" She snapped her fingers like castanets and pirouetted on the spot. Pasha laughed and supplied her with a round of applause. Faina's foot collided with one of the liquor bottles. The booze flew across the car where it hit the lantern and shattered. A massive fire rocketed up before them.

Pasha's mouth fell open. "Faina, you klutz!"

As the alcohol leaked outwards the fire germinated. It devoured the wooden planks and gnawed at the corners of the crates. Panicked, Faina waved her sleeves at the flames, but only fanned them higher. Pasha seized her floppy arms and pulled her out of the way. He threw off his coat, hurled it on top of the fire, and launched himself onto his knees. He beat it with his fists until the little flickers choked to an untimely demise. Faina stood awkwardly to the side, as smoke billowed in the car.

"There's too much smoke," Pasha coughed. "We're gonna have to jump."

Pasha gathered the remaining liquor bottles and shoved them into his pockets and pant legs. He slid open the door and grabbed Faina's arm.

"On the count of three?"

Faina nodded with shaking hands.

"*Rahz . . . dva . . . tri*!"

They hurled themselves forward into the air and landed in a patch of dry leaves by the side of the tracks. Pasha groaned and clutched his swollen ribs. The glass of the liquor bottles hadn't broken and felt cool against his skin. He let his head fall back against the damp, swampy leaves.

Faina glanced Pasha over from the corner of her eye. The smoke ribboning up from his jacket added emphasis to the glare emanating from his dark eyes. At last, she shrugged.

"You could've used my coat."

Pasha gaped at her, offended. "I'd never do that! I know how much that coat means to you!" He dusted off his pant legs. "Although I wish you'd wear something less baggy. One of these days you're gonna trip and fall. I still don't understand why you have to wear your brother's clothes during a heist."

Faina sucked her teeth. "You try running from the police in a dress and tell me how that works out."

"We would be running from the police a lot less if you would just wear a skirt instead of pants. Half the time, the police are chasing us because some lady said you were inappropriately dressed."

Faina went on as though she hadn't heard him. "It doubles as a disguise."

Pasha raised an eyebrow. "A disguise? Faina, I hate to break it to you, but you don't make a convincing boy."

Faina cocked her hands on her wide hips, looking offended, though Pasha wasn't sure why.

"Oh? And why is that?"

"Because . . ." Pasha's eyes drew a squiggly trail down her figure. Faina was curvier than a sidewinder with scoliosis. Faina glared at him, waiting.

"Pasha?"

He drew his head into his elbow and faked a cough as he got to his feet. "We better get a move on before the police show up. Where we headed anyway?"

"To Fifth Avenue, of course. I have it on good authority that Isadore Travers keeps a fully stocked bar of Europe's finest Château. Probably should've stashed the loot first, but oh well."

Pasha assumed a dry expression. "Whose authority? *The New York Daily*?"

"No, Aunt Poppy of course!"

"Seriously?" Pasha groaned. "This morning she told me she saw a dragon in Midtown. And last week your uncle had to bail her out of prison again for unlawful possession of a sea turtle. He was wearing a little hat and everything!"

Faina shrugged. "According to her, he was dressed like that when she found him. Besides, Aunt Poppy has been good to us."

"I'm not saying she hasn't, but let's be honest. She's not all there."

"Look, you wanna know how to tell the difference between Aunt Poppy's delusions and the truth? Which sounds more practical? That some ritzy socialite is stockpiling alcohol, or that there are dragons in Midtown?"

Pasha heaved a long sigh. "The socialite."

"Alright then, let's go, Legs!" And absent of any caution, they bounded northward through the crumbling foliage into the steel wilderness of Manhattan.

Chapter 3:
The Firebird

It was a full day of thieving for Pasha and Faina. Besides the alcohol they picked up from the beach, they also stole an entire case of "medicinal" bourbon from a drugstore in Midtown. There was a bottle of Canadian whiskey, and an entire collection of fine wines and champagne gathered from the fabulously wealthy on Fifth Avenue. It wasn't hard to make a living from bootlegging. But by stashing their loot in an abandoned subway tunnel, Pasha and Faina had enough liquor to supply their own speakeasy.

To keep unwanted noses out of their hideaway, Pasha and Faina started a rumor that a murder had taken place years ago at the Heath-Coleman Terminal. As a result, a fiery Hell monster was born. They called it the Pneumatos. Faina described it to the children as, "a borough bowel-burrowing beast belching blazes by the bidding of Beelzebub." She thought it would be easier to remember that way. Pasha had fashioned a makeshift flamethrower from an old air compressor. This allowed them to literally fan the flames of their urban legend whenever anyone got too nosy.

They descended down the slippery concrete steps, their coats heavy with clanking bottles. Below them, the subway tunnel was dark and mildewy.

"Of all the schemes we've pulled over the years," began Faina, "this is the one Leo would've been most proud of."

Pasha watched as his breath curdled in a cloud before his eyes. "Leo did love a good laugh."

"Love?" Faina snickered until her freckles seemed to sparkle in the dim film of light. "Leo lived for a good laugh!" Her pomp, joyous posture wilted. "Thanksgiving would've fallen on his birthday this year. He would've been twenty-two, a man by now . . . if it weren't for—"

A horrible rasping noise scratched splits into their ears. They ducked below a fiery torrent. A burning breath hovered against their necks and cheeks. Faina let out a scream. Instinctively, Pasha dragged Faina to the ground. The heat evaporated. Lichen-ringed puddles seeped through their coat and kissed their chilled flesh. Someone gave a cold laugh.

"You were saying, Spichkin?"

Pasha got to his feet. Anastas "The Russian Rogue" Sippenhaft was a massive boy for someone who made his living off the streets. His head was wide like a mastiff, his shoulders meaty with brawn. He held the hose of the makeshift flamethrower between sledgehammer fists. His two younger brothers stood on either side of him. Fifteen-year-old Vadim was to the right, tall and deceptively strong. Alexei stood on the left. He was only twelve years old, and always had the look of wishing he were somewhere else. Besides his brothers, there was also a nameless crony from the East Village orphanage and a pickpocket who at the age of fourteen had yet to become associated with any specific gang.

Pasha and Anastas faced each other at eye level with rigid bones and a hatred so electric it was nearly tangible.

"You idiot, you could've killed us!" Pasha roared. "What do you want, *svolotch*?" Swine. Pasha's vision was still adjusting from the glare of the flamethrower. For a second it appeared as though the tunnel were empty. He rubbed his eyes. It was empty! The piles of wooden crates, pulpy with mold, that had once housed a jewel mine of forbidden liquor, were all gone. The flagstones were stenciled with their wet shadows.

Faina's voice was irate. "What did you do with our stash?"

Anastas squinted his already beady eyes into glassy, gray slits. His bruised lips sneered into a disdainful grin.

"Making the rounds, picking up the last few tidbits here and there to present to Klokov this evening."

"You can't do that," spat Faina from behind Pasha's shoulder. "You're breaking one of the most basic rules of the Breadwinners. You can't steal from another member. It's punishable by flogging."

At the mere suggestion of such a penalty, a bead of sweat formed on the back of Pasha's neck.

Anastas's head shrank between his shoulders. "What would you know about it, Big Nose? Girls aren't allowed in the Breadwinners." His eyes fell on her pants, and a nasty smile bled into his mouth. "And it takes more than a pair of trousers to be a man." He turned back to Pasha and pinched his chin patronizingly. "Besides, Chevalsky knows better than to snitch, don't you?"

Pasha shoved Anastas backward. "Get outta here! You've already taken everything!"

"Not yet, I haven't."

Anastas snatched Pasha's throat with predatory finesse. Struggling against his weight, Pasha slammed his foot against Anastas's knee. Anastas staggered backward. As Pasha was about to retaliate, two of Anastas's companions ganged up on him and forced him to the ground. He felt the sharpness of a heel embedded between his shoulder blades.

Behind him, he could hear Faina struggling with one young man, which soon grew to two. As usual, they had underestimated her, and it took more to restrain her than they had thought. Anastas knelt down at Pasha's knees.

"Let's see what Chevalsky's managed to get away with today."

He removed a bottle of liquor from Pasha's pant leg and held it up for the others to see.

"Look at that, fellas! Authentic Canadian whiskey!"

From the other pant leg, he retrieved a Château from Isadore Travers' townhouse. He read the label and flexed his lip. "Imported from Paris. Very impressive."

Anastas continued fishing around through Pasha's coat, pockets, and shirt sleeves. Once he had picked Pasha clean, he turned to Faina. Anastas took his time encircling a trail around her, giving her mind the chance to invent. The tactic seemed to have more of an effect on Pasha than it did Faina. She continued to struggle, nonplused by Anastas's elaborate vulturing. Anastas grabbed Faina's ankle and took his time peeling back her pant leg until it was below the knee. Some of the boys whistled.

Pasha snapped his head up. "Forget your manners for a second and I swear I'll tell Klokov." The warning reverberated down the ribs of the tunnel. There was a glimmer of unmistakable apprehension in Anastas's eye. Pasha held his gaze with contempt. Sneering, Anastas took the Rum-Runner spoils from Faina's boot. He jerked her pant leg back down.

Anastas continued examining her with a gentler hand. Finally, he decided to search her satchel. He slid a wrapped bottle of champagne from the pocket.

"1920. A very good year." He stopped to look Faina wickedly in the eye. "Hope you weren't saving this to toast the anniversary of your brother's death."

Pasha could practically hear the formidable sizzle of Faina's mouth as it sneered up. He imagined her freckles burning in her skin with hatred, and her eyes scintillating red. As Faina lunged forward, the boy restraining her tightened his grip. Faina was lifted off her feet. She drew back her leg and slammed her heel directly into Anastas's fleshy nose. The soundless strike seemed to echo down the tunnel like a sonic boom. The world swallowed its breath. Even Anastas's accomplices sucked in a taste of fear as they watched Anastas for what he would do next.

Pasha preyed on their distraction and broke from his captors, lunging at Anastas. Anastas's hand raised to strike Faina, but Pasha vaulted onto his back, pulling him to the ground. With her legs free, Faina managed to kick the groin of the boy holding her, sending him to the ground in anguish. Pasha and Anastas tore at each other on the floor, dampness and rot splattering everywhere.

Faina was full of pluck and grit and could hold her own pretty fairly on most occasions. But she did not last long against several brawny, young men. It took four of Anastas's cronies to get her on the ground, and even then they were subjected to a good thrashing. Finally, Anastas smacked Pasha hard in the head, and he slowed, dazed. Anastas threw him to the ground.

"Better figure out something quick, Stallion." He glanced at his watch. "It's almost six. Time to report to Klokov. And you know what the rules say about showing up empty-handed: it's an offense punishable by flogging." Anastas spat at his head, kicked him roughly in the ribs, and departed.

Moments later, in a semi-conscious state, Pasha felt Faina turning him over. She tapped his face. Her frantic countenance split and multiplied, ghosted and spun in a cloud over his head. His eyes dragged open and closed, and at last her features came into focus. Her face was panic-stricken. Even her eyelashes seemed to stand erect in alarm.

"Too bad he took the moonshine," she said, fingering a cut on the side of his head. "You could use some on your wounds."

Pasha wiped the blood from his nose on his sleeve and looked to the fading gray light upon the top stair. His soul drifted back to reality. The words of Anastas's last warning now had meaning. The slow poison of dread had at last caught up with him there in the finality of the sunset. He felt as though his lungs had been pulled shut with a drawstring. He raised himself out of the mire with shaking elbows.

"W—w–we have nothing. I have—I have nothing. *Nichoho*, nothing! He's gonna flog me!"

Faina steadied his shoulders. "Shhh, Pasha."

His throat made a strange squeamish sound as he swallowed a dry lump. Pasha had only ever been flogged once, at the final stage of his initiation four years ago when he was twelve. His back ached as he recalled the struggle to endure strike after strike. The lash had scratched away sinews of flesh. It wove a bloodstained tapestry, a depiction of his own suffering forever scrawled into his skin. Then there was the brine. He remembered the savage sting of salt motes grinding between the open lesions, nestling themselves into raw unripened tissue, throbbing with exposure.

His mind raced through the memory. Passing out on the sidewalk outside the Foxhole. Leo carrying him to Aunt Poppy's apartment. Faina screaming and crying. Convulsing as Aunt Poppy rinsed his gashes. Leo forcing Laudanum down his throat. The brown juice dribbling down his shirtfront as he struggled to fill his lungs with air. Faina clutching his hand. She was clutching his hand now. Wait, was it happening again?

Was it happening now? It was happening now!

"Pasha!" Faina splashed his cheeks with a cold puddle. The drops settled amongst the bloodstains on the bridge of his pale nose. Pasha focused on her, the sixteen-year-old Faina, and bit by bit he settled back into the present. The inevitable stretched before him like groaning floodgates. When he spoke, his voice was soft and breathless.

"The night the Reds hanged my father, Papa took me aside and said, 'Pavlo, listen to me. Get out of here. Find a way out. Get your mother and sister, and leave. Run as fast as you can. Go to America. Take care of your mother and sister. You're the man of the house now.'" He rubbed the heels of his fists into his eyes. "I try so hard, and I still fail. I am *slabyy*, weak! I've shamed my father. I've shamed my family."

He felt the gentleness of Faina's head on his shoulder. "*Nyet*, Pasha. That's not true." She squeezed his chapped hands. The black was deepening. They could hardly see each other now. Pasha fingered the button holes in Faina's wrist cuffs. A loud rocketing whistle fringed on the empty air.

"Did you hear that?" Faina scanned the dark with vigilant eyes.

"Probably a train whistle."

Again, it tripped on the wind with a pleasing trill, sharper and clearer than before.

"There it is again!" Faina leaped up and turned in circles, searching for the source.

Pasha lifted his chin. At the end of the track, a light appeared. He winced as he pulled himself up from the ground. He could feel the blood rushing towards the spots where he had taken a hit. The light was coming closer, racing as a matter of fact. Color filled in its form with blistering, vermillion blooms. It flickered and singed. Faina edged towards it, her eyes brimming with curiosity.

Pasha's eyes grew even wider with alarm. "Faina, it's a fire!"

But she kept going. Her inquisitive nature had been ignited, and there was no tearing her away. Larger and larger the fireball grew. It swelled to an enormous orb of smoking yellows, oranges, and indigos.

"Faina! Are you listening?" The bulb was careening straight towards them, faster than the brutal speed of a subway train. Pasha bolted after Faina. As the strange fire was coming between them, Pasha leaped and hustled her to the ground. Yellow sparks spat from its trail and lit up the tunnel in a sparkle of splendor.

It called out once again. It was a grand, lovely, elegant note which severed the breath of the evening in exquisite song. Ash and cinder hit their cheeks. It took off again, traveling up the staircase, out the terminal. It climbed into the cityscape and waxed into the sky. Faina took off after it.

"Wait up, crazy!" Pasha hollered, chasing after. "You don't even know what it is!"

Outside the terminal, a resplendent tapestry of fire spooled across the heavens. As they made their way out into the alley, the giant fireball turned and drew back towards them. In moments it was encircling them, encasing them in a glorious halo of fizzling light.

"What is it?" Faina gasped in wonder.

A feather spat from the festering channel and settled at their feet. Pasha examined it with cautious eyes before lifting it up to their vision. The bottom was singed black, and it blossomed upwards into an ombré of inflamed orange and red. It had more color in one wispy fiber than Pasha had ever seen in his entire life.

Faina took it from him with gentle hands, her mouth dropped in bewilderment. "It's the Firebird, Pasha!"

The spinning fire wreathed around them and cast an imprint of heated scarlets upon their cheeks.

Pasha hesitated and shook his head. "But that's impossible. The Firebird—"

"—is a fairy tale?" There was magic in Faina's eyes as she smirked over her shoulder.

The Firebird rounded them one last time. She chippered once and swept back into the sky, shrinking until she vanished completely. A sterling star hung in the place where she had disappeared.

Pasha and Faina had to pull themselves away from the black slate of evening. Their eyes caught sight of something shiny on the ground. Their faces went white. The pavement was littered with silver and gold jewelry, dazzling opals, and a milky braid of pearls extending five feet in length. Their mouths dropped as they scooped up the finery and let it run through their hands.

"Pasha, can you believe it?"

Faina could hardly breathe for all the excitement. Even in the bottomless dark, the precious jewels seemed to shine. She piled them up in his arms.

"You must take these to Klokov, now! The pearls alone are enough to make Anastas look like a fool!" She pushed him along. "I'll stop by your window this evening so you can tell me what happened! I have to get back before Uncle Matvei starts to worry." Before Pasha could answer her, she was sprinting off towards home.

At the corner, she turned and waved her cap. "*Dosvidanya*, and hurry!"

Chapter 4:
A Real Man

The Foxhole was a speakeasy and nightclub run by the Breadwinners. It operated out of a former brewery on the Bowery. It had three stories, each serving a different purpose. The ground floor was an atrium occupied mainly by men and gangsters. This was where business commenced. It was also where the black market called the Paddock was managed. At the center of the ground floor was a raised platform for fighting. Above that was a circular gallery cut into the second level. Spectators could watch from the balcony, and if they were drunk enough they could pour beer on the loser.

The far side of the room housed two long passageways. The right side was host to a chain of offices and storage rooms. The left side, however, led to a long winding staircase. At the bottom of the steps was what the Breadwinners had dubbed the Crucible. The Crucible was the place where interrogations, punishments, and initiations were carried out. Insulation had been installed around the archway to stifle the screams, but every now and then one could hear an old record playing down in the cellar, while young boys were whipped, and enemies were penalized.

The second story of the Foxhole was for cards, gambling, pool, and less riotous amusements. Finally, the top floor was for dining and dancing. It was completely shut off from the lower rooms and accessed by an outdoor stairwell leading to a porch. It catered mostly to younger patrons. Adolescent street fighters often brought their girls to the top floor to dance.

Pasha found Klokov waiting on the ground floor, cracking his knuckles and glaring at his watch. He was a squat, bald, fleshy man, with scarcely any hair on him. From the back, it was difficult to tell where his neck ended and his head began. The area was thick and stumpy, marked with several sturdy rolls of flesh. Perhaps the most recognizable characteristic of Pasha's notorious employer was the fact that he only had one eye, where most people were accustomed to two. In the unoccupied socket, Klokov had placed a Russian Kopeck with the eagle side facing outwards. Whether or not it was a feeble attempt to normalize himself or else further unnerve anyone who stared for too long, Pasha would never know.

Anastas had stuck around to see Pasha punished. A sickly, yellow bruise was forming across the bridge of his nose. Pasha thought it complimented the dark, plum-colored crescents around his eyes. He appeared both surprised and disgusted to see Pasha show up.

"You're late, Stallion," clucked Klokov. "I'd almost given up. I hope you have something to show for your tardiness."

Anastas was grinning with anticipation. He looked like a child whose mother was about to read his favorite part of a beloved story. The corner of Pasha's mouth tugged upwards.

"As a matter of fact, I have plenty." He emptied his pockets onto the table until the jewels rolled off the counter and scattered at

Klokov's feet. The sound of clattering jewels drew the eyes of the numerous patrons sitting at the bar. Much like a magician might pull a garland of kerchiefs from his cuff, Pasha fished the five feet of pearls from the inside of his jacket.

Anastas looked as though he might combust. Klokov was rendered speechless. He held the strand of pearls in his hands, counting each precious bead in his head.

"Paycheck on Wednesday, boss?" inquired Pasha, victorious.

Klokov nodded his stumpy head in a distant manner. "Yeah, Wednesday." He smiled, impressed. "Should be plenty awaiting you, Chevalsky."

Pasha turned to leave when Klokov stopped him. "Not so fast, now. You're up on the roster. You fight Timber."

Pasha's insides groaned with annoyance. After everything that had happened that day the last thing he felt like doing was fighting Timber. So beaten and worn down was he by this point, he feared poor Timber might actually have a chance.

Klokov swaggered out from behind the counter and ascended his platform over the ring. He pulled the cord on the bell over his head. The crowd of patrons hushed and pulled themselves away from the brass rail of the bar. They moved like herds of wild animals towards the arena.

Sighing, Pasha shed his coat and hat. With so many sweaty bodies crowded into the room the air wasn't cold, but the hairs still stood up on the back of his neck. Pasha rolled up his sleeves and headed for the stage.

As Klokov roared his customary intro, the crowd parted to invite little Timber onto the stage. He was thirteen, a whole foot shorter than Pasha, and not an intimidating presence. He had faint, flat eyebrows and a slim, pert nose that still looked babyish. Pasha was sure the lash marks were still fresh on his back. He couldn't help but notice Timber was tightening his knees to keep from shaking. Furthermore, he had a habit of wiping his sweaty palms on the front of his trousers. A few men laughed in the crowd.

When Klokov had finally finished building the tension with his lengthy speech, he sprinkled salt onto the floor. Pasha watched it crumble like hail between them. A moment passed, and then the sound of Klokov's shrill whistle was jamming itself down his ear canals. Shuddering, Pasha tightened his jaw.

Timber lunged for Pasha with his right hand. Pasha blocked him and took a step back, his fists up by his face. Timber rushed at him again, aiming for Pasha's ear, but again Pasha caught him. For a whole minute, Timber was blocked over and over, with Pasha keeping his guard up. Around them, the crowd grew fidgety and almost bored. Klokov turned impatient.

"Hit back already!"

Pasha kept his eyes centered, pretending he hadn't heard his boss, but Klokov was not to be ignored.

"Didn't you hear me, boy? Hit back!"

Timber went in for another and missed. He was holding his fists the wrong way. Pasha couldn't help but pity the boy. His hands were hardly bigger than Katya's, and sweat had already formed on the bridge of his nose. It wasn't fair to put a boy like this in the ring, especially up against someone older and more experienced. Did Klokov really expect Pasha to hit such a defenseless opponent? If he kept blocking Timber, maybe he could tire him out without ever having to throw a punch.

Below, Anastas chimed in. "Hit back, you pansy!"

Pasha ground his teeth together. He tried to block Anastas from his peripheral vision. Timber was waning. Now was the time. One hit, it wouldn't even have to be hard. But Timber surprised Pasha by charging at him with his full weight. Pasha dodged him. The spectators laughed as Timber's chin struck the floor. Pasha waited for him to get up.

"What are you doing?" Klokov brayed. "Finish him off!"

Anastas shook his head and snickered. "I thought fairies weren't allowed in the Breadwinners."

Pasha could feel the blood rising in his face. His muscles swelled with adrenaline. He couldn't let Anastas get to him.

Two minutes passed. He was risking Klokov's wrath, but he could do this without having to hurt Timber. All he had to do was wear him down.

Timber geared up for another charge. Pasha let the boy run into him. He wrapped him in a headlock, forced him to his knees, and flipped him onto his back.

Timber clutched his chest. Pasha had knocked the wind out of him. Timber raised a weak fist, but before anyone could see, Pasha seized him by the collar. He feigned pinching the boy's throat.

"Stay down," he whispered through gritted teeth.

Timber's eyes rolled upward to meet his. His neck was damp with sticky sweat. Pasha could feel the rapidity of his victim's pulse against his fingertips. It thrummed so quickly it was almost trill-like, and Pasha could not help but be reminded of a mouse. Timber answered Pasha with an imperceptible nod, and fell back, defeated.

Pasha's name thundered through the crowd. Around him, the rafters shook as patrons stamped the floor victoriously. The smell of yeast grew stronger still as beers were popped open, and sloshed over the glass necks of brown bottles. Someone hoisted Pasha roughly to his feet. With a fresh loaf of bread put in his hand, he was crowned the winner.

But it wasn't over. A glare burned in Klokov's eye.

***

Moments later, Pasha was standing in Klokov's office, shoulder to shoulder with Timber. He kept his hands folded behind his back.

"'No harm must ever come to women, children, or invalids,'"

Pasha recited obediently.

"Keep going," pressured Klokov, a cigar between his teeth.

Pasha massaged the space between his eyebrows. "But Klokov, that's exactly what I was—"

"I said keep going!" His shoulders seemed to take up all the space in the room.

"'Protect the widow and the orphan. Any man caught raising his fist to a woman, child, or invalid will be killed. Obey your leader, and do not forsake your fellow Breadwinner. Do not steal from another member.'" Pasha couldn't prevent the bitterness leaking into his voice as he recited this last one. But as much as he hated Anastas, he couldn't bear sentencing anyone to his own worst fear.

Klokov's nostrils flared. "You're avoiding it on purpose."

Pasha drew a long sigh, and at last uttered his own sin. "'A man must be tough and strong for his family. Weakness is not tolerated.'"

Klokov bobbed his head, satisfied. "Exactly. You've been violating that rule as of late, Stallion. What's worse, you tried to fake me out today. You tried to deceive me!"

"*Nyet*, I didn't," he argued.

"Lies! Don't you know what the other boys are saying about you? Didn't you hear the Rogue while you were in the ring? A fairy, he called you!"

Pasha's blood boiled at the memory. The subtlety of the

reaction did not go unregistered by Klokov. He paused, appreciating the effect.

"I wasn't being weak," Pasha bit back finally. He gestured to Timber. "Look at him! Doesn't he count as an invalid?" He regretted having to say this in front of Timber, but it was for his own good.

Klokov jabbed at the air with his cigar. "Small is not the same as sickly."

"He's a *dziecko*," Pasha sputtered.

Klokov cocked an eyebrow. "What?"

Pasha shook his head. He often slipped into the wrong language when he was nervous or flustered.

"*Rebenok*," he corrected himself. "A child."

"You forget, you yourself were only twelve when you joined. I made an exception for you. He's thirteen. He's old enough to make his own choices. By going easy on him, not only have you shamed yourself, but you have robbed him of the opportunity to prove himself."

"Klokov, it was just one time—"

"It has not been one time. We've struggled with this from day one." He shook his head with regret. "Look, you're a good kid, Chevalsky. On the whole, you've been a great example to the other boys. You're a hard worker, a gentleman, a stand-up guy. You're more willing to put your family first than half the bucks here. And you're a talented thief. But you've always been too soft, too gentle. It's written on your face every time you get up there. The only time you ever fight with any real conviction is when it's personal. Thing is, that ain't what you signed up for."

He turned and strode along the back wall thoughtfully. "My father came to this country to create a better future for his family. As a boy, I watched him toil in the sweatshops to put bread on the table, like so many others. Freedom, opportunity . . . for people like us, they were empty promises. Where was freedom when my father was working twelve-hour shifts seven days a week? Where was opportunity when employers refused to pay him fairly? When managers deemed him too foreign for a better job, a higher paying job? The *Malchiki*, the Breadwinners, was created so the American dream would be available to all people. It was forged by the blood and sweat of family men. Family. The very reason you're here.

"I'll admit I had my doubts when you first came to me. You were lean, delicate. The other boys said you were studious, and quiet, a White Emigre raised in the lap of luxury. Your father was a baron of all things. Then you told me your story. Ma lost her job, couldn't find work because of her Russian background. She was forced to get a stint in a speakeasy. Not ideal but it paid the rent. One night some two-bit Johnny followed her home, even tried to grab her. 'Please,' you begged, 'I'll do anything. Just make that man go away. Make him leave my mother alone. Let me become a street fighter so she won't have to work in that awful speak anymore.' You were prime material, a perfect candidate. I want you to keep that in mind as you do what I'm about to tell you to do."

Pasha's brows drew together in confusion. "What is it you want me to do?"

Klokov snapped his fingers at his lackeys and gestured to Timber. They swarmed on him, pinning his arms back and pushing him towards Pasha.

"You're gonna prove to me right now you're tough enough to do this."

Timber let out an involuntary whimper. His breath grew so shallow it was clearly audible. Pasha's lips fluttered in a soundless plea. The blood drained from his cheeks as he looked back from Klokov to Timber.

Klokov stamped his foot. "Prove to me you haven't gone soft!"

Pasha stared at Klokov like a cornered rabbit.

Klokov shook his head in disappointment. He didn't appear surprised. He drew a gun from his coat pocket, cocked it into place, and held the barrel against Timber's skull.

"You have two choices, Stallion."

Timber let out another cry, louder this time. Pasha felt as though his lungs were being pressed between two slabs of concrete. The room floated before him like a separate scene. He took a step forward.

Klokov gritted his teeth. "Do it!"

Squeezing his eyes shut, Pasha unloaded his strength. The first hit knocked a hard squealing yelp from Timber's lungs. Pasha tried not to think about it. He had to get through it for both their sakes. He struck without thinking, without discrimination. He couldn't bear to look at his victim.

"Open your eyes," ordered Klokov. "Look at him when you punch! Be a man!"

Pasha opened his eyes and tried to un-focus them, willing them to ignore the mangled boy at the end of his fist.

Klokov wrenched Timber's head back by the scruff of his hair. "Go for the face! Hit him in the mouth!"

Timber's voice cracked in two as the impact forced his head up and back.

"Wait," he choked. "Wait, please!"

Klokov gave the boy a hard shake. "Shut your mouth!"

Timber's eyes were as helpless as a lamb's at the slaughter. Pasha's chest burned. His arm sprang back mechanically and jammed his fist into Timber's teeth.

"Again! I wanna see blood this time, Chevalsky! Blood!"

Pasha wound his fist back for another blow when Timber interrupted them again in a faint voice.

"Wait! Wait! I—I can't hear outta my ear! I can't hear anything!"

Pasha froze with his fist in the air.

"What are you hesitating for?" roared Klokov, causing Pasha to flinch. "You don't stop until I tell you stop!" Again he pushed the barrel up against Timber's head. "Either you take him out or I do."

What could Pasha do? With no other choice, he drove his full weight into the punch. Slippery blood smothered Pasha's fingers and spattered against his cheek. Timber gagged and a thick syrup of blood drooled from the corner of his lip.

Klokov ordered his cronies to release Timber. He rounded on the boy with a swift kick, sending him to his knees.

"Finish him."

Timber's mouth continued to move as he whispered pleas.

"Just stop . . . No more . . . Please, Pasha, stop."

Hearing his own name uttered from the bleeding mouth was almost more than Pasha could take. He gaped at the shredded form crumpled on the floor. What was left to finish? He looked back at Klokov, grasping for words, shaking his head in uncertainty.

"Kick him!"

Pasha rammed the toe of his boot into Timber's side until the boy choked on his own spit. Tears collected in his eyes. Pasha edged away. He couldn't stand it.

At length, Klokov nodded, his thirst for blood satiated. "Toughen up."

Pasha nodded emphatically to show he had understood.

Klokov gestured to the door. "You're dismissed."

Pasha tore from the room and ran out of the Foxhole. He didn't want to be seen, didn't want to be stopped. When his feet had carried him as far as the alleyway behind his tenement, his legs refused to move any farther. He staggered against the wall and pressed the heels of his hands against his eyes, trying to dam the flow of tears. Something warm and slick smeared in his vision. He drew back and looked down at his bruised knuckles. Timber's blood covered his flesh. Pasha recoiled from his own hands. He feverishly wiped them on the pavement until his skin felt raw and worn. His breath slowed.

He didn't want this. He didn't want any of this. It was one thing to throw a punch here and there for money, but to be forced to cause someone lasting injury? Someone who was weaker, younger, and more vulnerable? He couldn't bear it. He couldn't decide what he was more ashamed of—what he had done to Timber, or the fact that he was crying about it. He had responsibilities, after all; a duty to his family.

But didn't they all? Wasn't that the point? Would a boy like Timber be fighting if he didn't have something at stake?

Chapter 5:
The American Dream

With his tears finally stemmed, Pasha forced himself up the stairs and through the front door of their apartment. He stormed past the toasty, lingering fragrance of the kitchen. He thundered past his worried mother and sister, ignoring their cries of "Where have you been?" "Are you alright?" and retreated straight to his bedroom, slamming the door. He dove, lifeless, into the bedcovers.

"Pasha, my darling," his mother hollered at the door. "What is wrong?"

"I don't wanna talk about it!"

"*Patulya*," she crooned, softening her voice, "at least come out and eat something."

Pasha forced a lump down his throat. "No thanks, Ma."

Sensing the anxiety collecting at the door, Pasha cleared his throat and tried to add more cheerfully, "I'll get some later. Faina and I went over to Brooklyn and split a hotdog."

There was hesitation in his mother's voice. He hadn't convinced her.

"Okay," she at last conceded. "Let me know if you need anything." Her footsteps died away.

Pasha propped his chin on the pillow. His eyes roved the wall over his bed where newspaper clippings of his childhood heroes were taped in a collage of dreams. There was a picture of Vanderbilt, a headline about Rockefeller, and an article about Sophie Tucker. But above all, there were scads of entries about the Russian-Jewish immigrant Irving Berlin. To Pasha, Irving Berlin's music was the anthem of his first summer in New York City when Faina had taken him to Tin Pan Alley. Together they had loitered beneath the open windows while New York legends gestated in their stuffy tenement wombs. Things had seemed so simple then. He couldn't remember the last time his hands didn't hurt. He groaned and plastered his face against the sheets.

Outside there was an echo of singing above his window.

"*Some of these days*
you'll miss me, honey
Some of these days
you'll feel so lonely . . ."

Faina was traipsing over the edge of the roof, making her way down the fire escape.

"*You'll miss my hugging, you're gonna miss my kissing. . . .* Pasha, I know you're in there! Come on, you're supposed to join in!"

Pasha didn't move. The metallic clang of the steps rattled louder as she stopped outside his bedroom. He heard her hands press against the glass.

"You are in there," she exclaimed cheerfully.

Pasha remained motionless.

"Pasha?" A cool breeze skimmed across his back as the

window was slid open. He could feel her eyes on him, the faintness of her smile. The mattress groaned as she let herself in and closed the window. Her hair brushed his arm as she leaned over him, scanning for signs of floggings or beatings.

"What's the matter?" she asked finally.

Pasha did not answer but continued to play dead.

"Was Klokov pleased?"

Silence. Faina flopped playfully to a seat, making the bed bounce.

"Come on, Pasha!" He could hear her grinning. She scratched the back of his neck to make him shiver, and he swatted her hand away. The floorboards creaked as she stood and admired the hodgepodge of inspiration cluttering his wall.

"I see you added Dorf." She was referring to the clipping of the Russian Major League player, Eddie Ainsmith. "And a picture of Fifth Avenue. At the rate we're going we'll be there soon, won't we, Pasha?"

At last, Pasha grumbled into his pillow. "We're immigrants, Faina. The American dream doesn't apply to us."

She ruffled his hair. "What are you talking about? You know that's not true! Look at old Izzy, look at Dorf!" She laughed. "Pasha, we've seen the Firebird! That has to be some kinda sign, a blessing—"

Pasha rose up on his elbows, his face pained and sour. "You're the one who told me that!"

Faina leaned back, jarred by the edge in his temper.

"When I was eleven years old. I was playing my balalaika on the sidewalk, trying to earn money. You looked at me like I was an idiot, like everybody else, like all the kids at school! And you told me that!"

Faina's tone fell deep within her chest, like the rumble of a volcano moments before it erupts. "That's not what I said. You asked me why the other kids made fun of you for wanting to be like Rockefeller. And I said, 'The general idea around here is that the American dream doesn't apply to people like us, to immigrants.' I didn't say it was true. I didn't say it's what I believed."

"You thought it. You thought it like everyone else! I could see it in your eyes!"

"That's ridiculous," she sneered as she got to her feet. "If that were true, why do I still have dreams of becoming an actress?"

Pasha flew up from his bed, tossing his hands in the air. "I don't know! I don't know why you do what you do! I don't know why you continue to entertain these fantasies!" His eyes cut across her with a cold, condescending glare. "And what do you mean, 'we've seen the Firebird'? That wasn't the Firebird, Faina! I mean, listen to yourself, you sound like a baby! The Firebird is a children's story, it's a fairytale! It's not real! Face it, Faina! People like us don't get fairytales. We don't get the happily ever after. Our lives don't change. We're raised in the slums, and we die in the slums. We're worthless, we're nothing!"

Faina gaped at him as though he had struck her. One look at the ache in her eyes and Pasha was punctured with shame and regret. He opened his mouth to apologize, but Faina's foot broke forward, and she gave him a hard shove.

"I am not worthless! What happened to you? You're supposed to be sweet and kind! That's who you were! What are you now? You let them change you. You have no joy. You won't allow yourself the pleasure of it! You see only what's in front of you, like a mule with blinders, and you think yourself superior for it, not realizing how foolish it makes you look! Never have I seen someone so in love with their own bitterness! You are so proud, you can't even accept blessings when they literally fall at your feet! You think you're doing yourself a favor? You're not! You're isolating yourself!"

She swallowed audibly. Tears stained the corners of her eyes. "Maybe I am foolish about some things. I was foolish to think Klokov couldn't break you. I was foolish to think you'd never lose hope, that you'd stay that innocent boy, fresh off the boat, my best friend."

Pasha moved towards her, his arms reached out in sorrow. "Faina, I'm sor—"

"You do what you want!" She staggered away from him. Her mouth was a hearth, her tongue like flint, and he could've sworn sparks spat off her teeth. "But I will not accept unhappiness."

She rushed past him towards the window, but Pasha dashed in

front of her.

"Move," she ordered, ducking around him, but he caught her by the arm and pulled her back.

"Faina, I'm sorry! I'm so sorry! I don't think for one second you're worthless! I didn't mean for it to sound like that."

She continued to tug against him, but Pasha held on to her hands.

"You're my best friend." He wrapped his arms around her, hugging her closer, and felt the heat rising from her skin. "Without you, I would have lost hope a long time ago. Remember how lonely I was my first night here? You saw me lying here, sulking—"

"You were crying, not sulking."

"Alright, alright!" He plopped down on the bed. "I was crying. You saw me through the window and tried to make me laugh by popping out from the curtains."

She was helpless against the smile creeping back onto her face. "You were pretty pathetic."

He pulled her to a seat on the edge of the bed and leaned his head, puppy-like, on her shoulder.

"I was miserable. And if you never speak to me after this, I'll be miserable all over again. You'll be a big star, and I'll be some sorry sap that made you cry."

"Is that right?" She propped her chin in her hand.

"It is. And every night I'll stand across the street, staring at your stage door, waiting for you to come out, hoping, 'this will be the night she forgives me.'"

She nudged him with her shoulder. "Okay, you can stop groveling now. I forgive you. Shine my shoes some other day."

"Promise me you'll always tell me when I'm being stupid."

Faina snorted, and let her head fall against his shoulder. "Now, honey, you know that's a promise I can keep!"

Pasha hugged her and laughed, burying his nose in her hair. "And promise you'll never get rid of me."

"Only if you promise me the same."

Pasha leaned back and stroked his chin. "Thieves' Honor?"

Faina covered her mouth and laughed. "May I, Faina Adrianovna Spichkin, never enjoy liberty if I ever forsake Pasha Ruslanovich Chevalsky. Your turn."

Pasha held up his right hand. "May I, Pasha Ruslanovich Chevalsky, die in the slums if I ever forsake Faina Adrianovna Spichkin."

***

That night, Pasha was plagued with a vivid, peculiar dream. It was midnight, and he was somewhere in the countryside, hopelessly lost in the woods. Craning his neck, he made a slow turn in the middle of the path. The tips of the fir trees brushed the sky like paintbrushes, blurring the stars into a swirling galaxy of color and confusion. His heart felt claustrophobic inside his ribcage. His eyes fell upon the

North Star, Polaris. He breathed a sigh of relief. It would guide him home, even if he did not know where he was.

While he was plotting his bearings, he realized, to his horror, that Polaris was falling, dropping from the sky like an injured bird. In a blinding ball of white light it streamed past him, close enough to touch, and then it was gone.

Above him, the constellations shifted and rearranged themselves into a new pattern of asterism. Draco, the serpent constellation, began to move. It slithered across the ceiling of the heavens until its eye, the red star called Thuban, stood in Polaris's place.

***

Pasha awoke with a terrified start, the red light still glaring in his eyes. He winced and reached for the chain of his lamp on the nightstand. In the blunted cylinder of yellow illumination, Pasha spied Katya crouching by his door. The crimson gleam was radiating from something in her hands.

"Katya," he admonished, rubbing his eyes, "what are you doing?"

As the sting cleared, he realized she was holding the Firebird's feather he had stashed away in his coat pocket. Katya gasped and let the plumage drop to the floor. Pasha stumbled out of bed, catching it before it hit the ground, and hid it away in his hands. The glow turned the outline of his fingers pink.

"I'm sorry, Pasha," sputtered Katya. "I was worried about you after you skipped dinner, so I came to check on you. I saw the light coming from your pocket. I didn't know what it was. I'm sorry!"

"It's fine," he insisted briskly. He hadn't meant to scare her. He stuffed it back into his pocket.

A tight silence passed between them. Katya leaned forward with enlarging pupils.

"W—what is it?"

Pasha regarded her from the corner of his careful eye. What should he tell her? He had to be careful about what he said in front of Katya. Her mind was fragile.

"I don't know. I found it in the city." It wasn't as if he was really lying. After all, he wasn't going to believe it was the Firebird. But if it wasn't a feather from the Firebird, what was it?

The innocence fell from Katya's face, and she turned upon him with a penetrating look. "You're lying."

Pasha shifted uncomfortably. He tried to stare her down. He did not dispute her, but he didn't offer an explanation either. It was never any use lying to Katya. She'd look up at you with those strange eyes. You would sense she was unraveling you, like plucking stray threads from a carpet.

At length, she sighed. She looked as though she were taking a moment to collect her thoughts on the tip of her tongue.

"It reminds me of a dream I had."

Pasha patted the mattress, indicating for her to lay down. If he tried to sneak her back into their mother's room, Katya would wake her up, and Mama had to get up awfully early to be at the factory.

"Why don't you tell me about it?" he suggested, pulling the covers up to her chin. If he got her back to sleep quickly enough, maybe she would think she had dreamed the whole encounter.

Katya laid her head against the pillows, trying to recall the scene. "I was walking through Central Park when I saw a shadowy figure standing on the stairs of the Terrace. He had a long walking staff with one of those funny globe things on top. You know, the one with all the rings."

"You mean an armillary sphere?"

"Yeah, that's it. When he saw me watching him, he turned and smiled at me. He was tall, skinny, and bald, and he had a short, gray beard. He had lovely blue eyes and long eyelashes. He held out his hand to me. I was gonna take it, but a giant blind man wandered out of the archway playing Mama's lullaby on the accordion."

Pasha couldn't help but laugh as he slipped under the covers and settled beside her.

"A giant blind man playing the accordion? That is a wild dream."

"But that's not all," she rambled. "A curly-haired man was dancing on the edge of the fountain and playing along on the violin." She yawned and rubbed her eyes. Her voice slowed.

"And . . . and then . . ." she struggled, "I saw a fire-breathing man with a scruffy red beard dancing with a mermaid." Her little arms began to fall, then, at last, came to rest below her chin. Pasha waited anxiously. She didn't stir. He breathed a sigh of relief. At last, she had fallen asleep.

Pasha smiled. Even when they were closed, her eyes seemed wide and overstimulated. Pasha couldn't help but be reminded of a kitten. Careful not to disturb her, he laid down beside her and slid under the covers. As he was shutting his eyes, Katya jolted back to life.

"And then a bright, yellow gypsy wagon came flying across the sky!"

Pasha jumped so high he almost fell out of the bed. He clutched his chest.

"A flying, yellow gypsy wagon?"

"Bright yellow!"

He sighed and smoothed back her hair, forcing himself to bury any signs of frustration.

"And how was it flying?"

"It was pulled by a team of flying horses, of course."

"Flying horses?" he repeated, burrowing back under the covers. "That is quite a dream. Now, go to sleep. Maybe you'll have even more."

He felt her chin on his shoulder.

"Pasha, may I ask you something?"

Would she ever fall back asleep? Pasha rolled over to face her.

"You know you can. But after that, you have to go to sleep."

He covered her eyes playfully, and Katya began to giggle.

"Shhh, don't start that or you'll never stop." He smiled, genuinely this time.

Her voice was soft. "Do you ever wonder if our dreams are real?"

Pasha made a show of putting on a serious face. He leaned down to her ear and whispered, "I sure hope not, because sometimes I have this dream where I'm standing in the middle of Times Square in nothing but my underwear."

Katya burst into squealing giggles, infecting Pasha, who was trying very hard not to laugh. He pressed a hand over her mouth.

"Shhh, alright," he chuckled, "I'm getting you wound up."

"I mean it though, Pasha. What if our dreams are more than dreams? What if they're trying to tell us something?"

Pasha scratched his chin. "That sounds like a heavy subject to tackle before bed. Why don't you let me sleep on it, and I'll tell you what I think in the morning."

Katya cuddled her head against her brother's chest and shut her eyes. "Okay, Pasha."

Pasha watched as his sister's breathing slowed to a nice even pace. He kissed her forehead. For a brief moment, the idea of being a

Breadwinner actually seemed tolerable.

Chapter 6:
The Caravan

The following morning was difficult. Pasha and Faina no longer had a place to hide their loot, so they kept everything stashed in pant legs, in bootlegs, up sleeves, and in pockets. The more liquor they accumulated, the more fatigued they grew from the weight of the bottles. Jumping from freights was troublesome. Once a bottle broke, soaking through Pasha's clothes and cutting up his leg. Worn out and aggravated, they decided to take a break and sat leaning against each other's backs near Gothic Bridge in Central Park.

"How's your leg?" Faina asked.

Pasha shrugged. "Not so bad. I'm used to a lot worse, you know."

"I see. Tough guy."

Pasha shut his eyes and rested his head against the back of hers.

"Pasha," she wondered aloud, "why didn't you turn in Anastas yesterday?"

Pasha sucked on the inside of his lip. "No one in the underworld likes a canary, even when you're in the right."

"But it's Anastas. Nobody likes Anastas. I doubt even Klokov likes Anastas." She paused. "You don't feel sorry for him, do you?"

Pasha's sweeping nose wrinkled in a sneer. "Of course not! I'm the last person who would feel sorry for Anastas! It's because of people like him that others are afraid of immigrants!" He lowered his voice. "*You* used to feel sorry for Anastas."

Pasha felt her spine stiffen. When she spoke, her words had an acerbated bite to them. "That was a long time ago."

"I'm sorry he called you 'Big Nose' again, by the way."

Out of nowhere, a small, flat rock struck Pasha on the side of the head. He winced and swiveled around.

"Look who it is!" Anastas swaggered forward, his entourage in tow.

Faina and Pasha scrambled to their feet. Pasha threw back his shoulders. "What do you want, you big jerk?"

"Yeah," agreed Faina. "Leave us alone, and do your own work today."

Anastas ignored her and bumped chests with Pasha. "Where'd you get the goods at the last minute?"

Pasha's eyes bore into his with acrid loathing. "None of your business."

Anastas's eyes slid over Pasha's shoulder and narrowed, hawk-like, on Faina. "No? Perhaps Faina 'the Hyena' would like to tell me."

His coterie made a move to close in on her when Pasha pushed Anastas back.

"Like I said yesterday, you touch her, and I have no qualms about turning you into Klokov."

Anastas's broad shoulders shook with laughter. "Pavlo

Chevalsky, ever the noble guardian! Must be all the bourgeois garbage your father filled your head with."

"Yeah, the apple never falls far from the tree, does it, Anastas?" He stuck his lip out in a mocking gesture. "You gonna grow up to build bombs one day like your old man?"

He might as well have slapped the snicker off Anastas's mouth. His gray-green pupils simmered like a boiling storm, yet Pasha kept twisting the knife.

"But your ma was in on it too, wasn't she? You gonna carry on the family business?"

"At least my parents believed in something!"

"Your parents believed in murder! They were terrorists! Isn't that how they met? When your father was kicked out of Germany?"

"Careful, Chevalsky," Anastas warned, leaning in closer.

"Then he wooed your ma with recitations of Marx and Nietzsche! How sweet!"

Slowly, achingly, they circled each other, veins trembling, complexions saturated with the red flush of adrenaline. Anastas jabbed a finger into Pasha's chest.

"You know what you are? You're an insignificant piece of rubble from an empire that did nothing but sit around and take! Lazy, inbred dogs! You come here bragging about all the things you're gonna do. How you're gonna be like Vanderbilt, like Rockefeller, like J.P. Morgan! More blithering capitalist pigs this stupid country builds altars to."

"If you hate this country so much, why don't you leave? There are plenty of women and children back in Russia right now who would love to be in your place. But they can't, thanks to the Immigration Act! They don't want any more of our kind coming to the U.S., and why is that? Because people like your parents decided to plant a bomb on Wall Street!"

"What do you mean our kind? You filthy *Khokol*!" Ignorant Ukrainian.

"I'd rather be a filthy *Khokol* than a savage, anarchist swine!"

"I bet you got that necklace from your whore mother!"

At the mention of his mother, Pasha could hold back no longer. His reserved shell fissured open like porcelain. He seized Anastas by the collar and ripped back his fist.

"Don't you dare say a word about my mother!"

Faina was tugging at the back of his jacket, hanging on his elbow, trying to put away his arm.

"No, Pasha! Leave it! Let's go!"

Anastas snorted. "You know, after she found out about your initiation, she went to Klokov and begged him to let you go. I heard she offered herself to him."

Pasha's ears rang.

"Liar!" he roared. They wrestled to the ground. Pasha jammed his fist into Anastas's teeth. Anastas kneed Pasha in the hip and tossed him back over his head. The bottles of alcohol Pasha had stashed in his clothes shattered. Motes of glass embedded into his skin.

Meanwhile, Faina was running from Anastas's legion of disciples, springing under the bridge and across the lawn.

Finally, Anastas pinned Pasha by the neck. His thumb and index finger pressed into the tender muscles of his throat. His eyes glimmered with delight as he savored the sound of Pasha's chokes and gasps. Across the way, Faina shrieked. The boys had caught her. They pulled the bottles of alcohol from the inside of her boots and pant legs.

Anastas rose and kicked Pasha in the groin, ensuring he couldn't interfere. He strode to the place where Faina lay pinned to the ground.

"Take off her coat," Pasha heard him order.

The boys forced her arms out of the sleeves and handed it to their superior. Anastas gave it a shake. Bottles tinkled musically in the pockets. One by one he culled the goods.

Looking back at her, he sneered. "Nice coat. I think I'll keep it for Klokov."

Faina shrieked in horror. "No! No! No!" With savage rage, she jumped up from the ground and vaulted onto Anastas's back, tearing his face with her fingernails. He grabbed her arm, and throwing himself forward, flipped her off his back. Faina winced and cried out. Her shoulders tensed. She stayed down, and laughing, their tormentors disappeared.

Pasha tried to raise up. He gagged with pain. Trembling, he fell back onto the grass and looked out at Faina. She sat bewildered amongst the fog, wearing a look of true horror. The material of her shirt was rather thin and hardly enough to keep her warm. Tears stung her face, and she choked on her own sobs.

When at last Pasha's pain had subsided into something manageable, he staggered to Faina and sat beside her.

"They took his coat, Pasha! They took Leo's coat!"

Pasha shed his own seedy jacket and draped it over her shoulders. "I know, I know," he soothed, but she could not be consoled.

Her sobs seemed out of place in the manicured perfection of the park. She crumbled into his shoulder. Pasha hugged her close.

"I'll get it back, I promise. Thieves' Honor!"

Faina sniffed and wiped a tear from her eye. "Pasha, you can't use Thieves' Honor on something uncertain. What if Anastas was lying about taking it to Klokov, and he burns it? Then you would have broken your promise, and I'd have to name a punishment."

Pasha smirked and shrugged. "If that happens, go easy on me. That is, if you think I deserve it." He was trying to make her laugh, and it seemed to be working, for she brightened somewhat.

At the sight of Pasha's pant legs, her mouth fell open.

"Pasha, you're hurt!" She leaned forward and plucked the glass from the material of his trousers. "All those broken bottles, you're gonna bleed to death!"

"I don't know about that," he chuckled. "But I have a feeling I may smell like I took a bath in bathtub gin."

Faina struggled to hide her amusement as she unlaced his boots. "I think you should go home."

"You know I can't."

"Why not? You need to make sure you wash all the grains from your skin. You don't wanna get an infection. I can steal more alcohol, and you can take it to Klokov this evening."

"I'm not gonna do that. You, however, need to get home before you catch a cold."

Together they shook the remaining shards from his shoes and brushed the tiny grains of crushed glass from his elbows and knees.

The vacuum of silence was ponderous. It made Pasha feel incredibly helpless. But the hush was broken by a whistling sound whittling its way through the park. The noise stretched in a long narrow stream, like the tail of a firework. The Firebird had returned.

Her wings beat overhead, fanning their faces with intense heat and turning their skin red. She twisted a winding ring of fire around them. As little sparks darted from the trail and spat on their faces, they became hard, and even gave a faint sting.

The friends squinted their eyes in the blinding light. The sparks were specks of topaz and emeralds!

The Firebird spiraled upwards, leaving a corkscrew trail of

glitter behind her. They watched her tail bob amongst the treetops. She raced for the horizon and was lost somewhere over the harbor.

"Where do you think it's going?" Faina wondered in amazement.

"A better question would be where did it come from? And why is it coming to us?"

"One version of *The Firebird* says she flies around dropping pearls from her beak to needy peasants, so they can trade it for goods and services. Sounds a lot like us if you ask me."

"'She?'"

Faina rolled her eyes. "Everyone knows the Firebird is female!"

"Whatever you say, Faina. It's just a fairytale."

Faina dropped her mouth open and stared at him incredulously.

"How hard did Anastas hit you? Do you even remember what we're talking about?"

"I'm just saying, there has to be a logical explanation for all of this."

Faina sighed. "Sure, whatever you say."

"You wait and see. Tomorrow it'll be in the papers, along with a perfectly sound explanation. I mean, we can't be the only ones who saw it. This is New York City, and it's the middle of broad daylight!"

Pulling Pasha into the shelter of his coat, Faina nodded her head sarcastically.

"Uh-huh. Well, we'll see, won't we? Come on, let's go home. Now that we've got all these jewels, let's not wait around for Anastas to steal them. And we can clean you up."

They made their way across Central Park, sharing the coat, Faina occupying the right sleeve and Pasha the left. The weather had taken a peculiar turn, and a small, silver cloud now hung above them.

The breeze picked up, and out of nowhere snow began to fall, accumulating rapidly. Despite it being late November, it hadn't snowed in New York since the first of April, and yet a thick blizzard was now eddying around them.

"I'm freezing, Pasha!"

"Faina, no matter how many times you say that, it's not gonna make you less cold. But you might stay warmer if you stop squirming!" Pasha tugged the jacket closer around them. "You're letting in a draft."

"Well, we'd get there faster if you wouldn't walk so slow! Where did all this snow come from, anyway?"

"I don't know. Maybe it's fake. Part of a gimmick or something."

"Feels pretty real to me."

A peculiar sound caught Pasha's ear. He closed his eyes, straining to listen. It was hardly uncommon to hear music in Central Park, or anywhere in New York City really. That's not what intrigued him. It was the familiarity of the tune that tugged at his ear.

“Do you hear that?” Pasha halted, nettling Faina. She was in too much of a bothered state to be very attentive.

“No, I don't hear anything.” She began to tug forward, but Pasha yanked her back, wrapping his elbow around her and slamming his hand over her mouth.

“You will if you be quiet!”

She rolled her eyes. Pasha drew back as he felt her opening her mouth to lick his hand, but she stopped. The notes had caught her attention as well. They were floaty, incandescent sounds from far away. It was rather hard to place what the music sounded like, for it seemed a million things all at once. The louring of a violin ribboning through the trees, accompanied by an accordion. The bash of tambourines clattering and rolling towards them like debris spat from an old truck. It marched and swaggered, it danced and tumbled, it rejoiced and yet it cried.

It advanced up the road with grim dignity. The blizzard clouded the ambling shadow, turning it gray. Beyond the falling icicles of lace, circles of soft, diaphanous light bobbed from lanterns.

“They’re gypsies,” whispered Faina, as the voices began to take shape.

“*Lucifer of the fiery coals*
had a handsome face and an ugly soul
he charmed two-thirds of the angel host
and the stars came tumbling down. . . .”

Pasha couldn't believe it. His whole life the only person he'd ever heard sing *The Blind Man* was his mother. Yet here he was in Central Park hearing it played upon a violin and accordion. Recalling Katya's dream from last night, Pasha almost laughed out loud. All he needed now was a bright yellow gypsy wagon flying across the sky.

No sooner had Pasha thought this than the enormous shadow emerged from the fog. Pasha's mouth fell open. His knees weakened. It was a bright yellow gypsy wagon hauled by a team of four beautiful horses.

The first person to emerge from the snowy cloud was a short, stocky man with a ginger beard and a hard, ruddy face. His pink complexion was scorched with rusty freckles from the tip of his snub nose to his broad forehead. A short, fat cigar was pinched between his teeth, and his coat was unusually thin given the state of the weather. He looked out at them from beneath the brim of his dingy leather Panama. His intense russet eyes glowed like the mercury of a thermometer.

As the second man approached, Pasha made himself small against the trees. The stranger was by far the largest person Pasha had ever beheld, standing about seven feet tall. His arms were round and solid. His calves were so wide and muscular that vesicles had formed in the leather of his boots from nearly bursting. His blanched jaw was broad, and blocky, and formed a perfect capital "L" shape from the side. Close-cropped curls of mousy brown hair topped his head and matched his thick mustache and bushy, low-set eyebrows. A German accordion was draped from his neck. He played his instrument almost lovingly, with a tender touch, gently guiding the muscles as though soothing its parched bellows.

Pasha was afraid he might catch him staring at the enormity of his silhouette, but the man's empty eyes fixated on the distance before him. He gazed into it as if seeing nothing at all. Could it be he was really a blind man like the one in Katya's description?

"*An apple hung from a golden tree*
to tempt a hungry wretch like me
I bit the apple and so did he
and the world came tumbling down. . . ."

Atop the yellow wagon, a gangly man played the violin. It was hard to place his ethnicity. He reminded Pasha of a friend he'd had in school from India, but there was more of a gold undertone to his skin, like that of the Turkish. Thick curls of long dark brown hair bounced against his chiseled face. A faint five o'clock shadow lined his tapered chin. His sharp, bright eyes were like two halves of a kiwi, colorful and lively. As the group passed, he flashed them a tight-lipped smile. His was a broad, almost musical grin that for some reason reminded Pasha of the long keyboard on a piano.

The caravan rolled on ahead, exposing the open back of the wagon. Peeking out from the warm, burnished curtains was an attractive young woman in her early twenties. She was at least partially black, with skin like the warm pages of a book. The kaleidoscope of soft shapes making up her figure gave her a hazy, unreal appearance, like a cloud, or a mirage. She had muscular arms and sturdy, plump thighs. Dark helixes of black walnut hair fell softly down her back, and her large, dreamy eyes moved in a balmy, pensive manner. Something about her presence was quiet and comforting and mirrored the gentleness of Pasha's own soul. Against her chest, she held a scrubby orange cat with fluffy cheeks.

"*Pray for blindness, and don't trust your eyes*
Better a wise man than a fool made of lies
for the blind shall live in Paradise
when the world comes crumbling down."

The girl caught Pasha's eye and smiled. There was something familiar about the box-shaped pout to her lips and the rounded clip of her dimples. It was as if she knew him, and the two had been friends for a very long time, maybe even family, as odd as that seemed. When he smiled back at her, it felt as though they were bonding over some shared secret, yet Pasha did not know what it was.

"*Trust not your eyes nor believe what you see*
Visions can lie and beauty deceives
And so I see as the blind man sees
when the stars come tumbling down."

As quickly as they came they vanished, and became a shrinking light drifting away into the fog. It seemed to Pasha they would keep going on, rolling across time like a road paved with stars. The surrounding air grew silent once more.

"Pasha," Faina finally whispered, "who were they?"

The sound of her voice startled him and caused him to jump. "You said they were gypsies."

"Well, yes, I mean, at least I think they were."

Something in her voice sounded unsure.

It seemed as though it had never happened. Such a spectacle it had been, yet it disappeared so fast. Were it not for the ribbons of tracks they left on the ground, it would've been easy to believe they'd never been there. And those too were fading quickly in the falling snow.

"When I look at them," Faina wondered aloud, "I feel as though I've forgotten something."

Pasha silently agreed. He was chilled by the words, an echo of his sagely sister. Upon seeing them, he had acquired an uncomfortable feeling of ambiguous loss. The conclusion was still too broken in his mind to be spoken aloud. He decided not to mention his sister's dream.

When Pasha and Faina stepped onto Fifth Avenue, the sky was colored with autumn again, and the temperature was mild. Not a single trace of a snowflake clung to their hair. Stranger still, as they looked back, the park itself was completely dry, showing no signs of having had a blizzard in months. Astounded, and somewhat frightened, Pasha and Faina returned home.

Chapter 7:
The Blood of Leo Spichkin

The white signet of the moon stamped a seal of nightfall across the horizon. Pasha returned to the ground floor of the Foxhole to report to Klokov while Faina headed upstairs with Anya for Tango Night. As before, Anastas was waiting, hungry for Pasha's blood to spill on the whipping post.

"You look empty-handed, boy," observed Klokov.

A smug grin stained Anastas's lips. Pasha lifted his chin high and dumped the jewels onto the table.

"Looks are deceiving."

Pasha could have laughed out loud for the dumbfounded expression on Anastas's face. Klokov did laugh.

"You're full of surprises, Chevalsky." He turned to Anastas, still chuckling. "You're gonna have to step it up to keep up with this one."

Pasha wasn't certain how Anastas restrained himself from jumping over the table and slamming him to the ground. He only stood there with a stony face, more ominous than if he had erupted. His eyes bore into Pasha with a baneful hatred that promised violence. Pasha was inclined to get as far away from Anastas as he could, but he still had to get Faina's coat.

Pasha would have to tread carefully. If he revealed Anastas had stolen the coat from his friend, his female friend in particular, not only would they flog Anastas, but he could easily be sentenced to death. As much as Pasha disliked Anastas, he would much rather have seen him succumb to his own consequences. Few people are comfortable with blood on their hands, after all. Pasha cleared his throat.

"Before I go, I have a favor to ask of you, Klokov."

Klokov actually smiled. "What is it you need?"

"I'd like to trade for that coat." He pointed to Faina's dingy hand-me-down overcoat tossed across the counter.

Klokov looked as though he hadn't heard Pasha right. "You wanna trade one of your priceless jewels for this old coat?"

Pasha felt stiff. He forced himself to maintain eye contact. "Yeah."

But Klokov was shrewd. Something ominous pooled in his eye. He turned to Anastas.

"Did you steal from him?"

Pasha shook his head. "*Nyet*, no. I—"

Klokov stabbed a cigar in Pasha's direction. "Quiet! Let him answer." He swiveled back to Anastas. "Did you steal this coat from him?"

Anastas did not quaver. He stared Klokov in the eye, his shoulders thrown back, his hands folded cooly behind him.

"No."

But a fellow street fighter piped up from the back of the bar.

"Yeah, he did! That's Leo Spichkin's old coat. I see his little sister wearing it all the time."

Pasha's heart throbbed wildly in his chest. Klokov bit his cigar into two pieces. He rose to his full height and leaned into Anastas's face.

"Not only did you steal from one of your own, but you stole from the dead? Leo Spichkin was an honorable associate of mine!" His voice grew louder until it seemed the shot glasses would shatter on the shelves. "That boy came to me at sixteen years old, looking to help his poor uncle when the Bowery Butchers came harassing him for money."

"Like he cares," snarled another. "Anastas's parents were anarchists, remember? Just like those guys who blew up Wall Street. Killed thirty people, including Leo Spichkin!"

Anastas was cornered. The entire bar was in an uproar.

"I didn't kill Leo Spichkin," he spat. "As for my parents, they were already in jail when the Galleanists targeted Wall Street. Since their arrest, I've worked to distance myself from their reputation. I've renounced my father and mother. When I came looking for employment, did I go to the Butchers who armed my parents' union in the first place? No, I came to y—"

Anastas was cut short as Klokov struck him across the face. Pasha's breath stole away. Anastas was not a small boy, and now he lay clutching his face on the floor. Klokov yanked him up by his collar.

"What is the number one rule in this brotherhood? Tell me the rule!"

Anastas spat blood from the inside of his cheek. "Protect the widow and the orphan."

"You stole from this girl! You stole from the deceased Leo Spichkin's orphaned little sister! You realize I could have you killed for that? Huh? Tell me, did you raise a hand to a woman?"

Anastas started to answer, but Klokov pivoted to face Pasha. "Did he raise a hand to her?"

Pasha stammered. Technically, the answer was no. Anastas hadn't tried to hurt Faina, he only threw her off his back when she attacked him. As for the rest of his entourage, Anastas was the only Breadwinner, the only one bound by the rules of chivalry.

"No," Pasha finally managed, "but Klokov, do we really have to go through all this? He's just a stup—"

Klokov held up his hand. "As for you, Chevalsky, you need to do a better job of protecting your girlfriend."

"She's not my . . ." Pasha sighed and scratched the side of his head. "Yeah, okay."

Klokov returned his attention to Anastas. "You see him? You see your brother over there? That's honor. He has every right to order your head on a silver platter, but he decided to spare you. You're lucky I don't have a bullet lodged in your worthless skull. As it is, I think a flogging will suffice. Take him downstairs."

Pasha was hit with a wave of nausea. The others cheered and dragged Anastas on his knees towards the Crucible. Klokov tossed Pasha the jacket and jerked his thumb to the door.

"You're dismissed, Chevalsky, unless you wanna hang around and watch. Wouldn't blame you if you did."

Trembling, Pasha ran out the door. His hands pressed against his ears as he tried to drown out the senseless jubilation of carnage pouring from the cellar. He scrambled up the stairs to the restaurant on the top floor. Beaded shadows flounced to a phonograph in the window. He halted at the entrance and clung to the railing. The muscles of his jaw forced open as he leaned over the balcony and gagged. He pinched his eyes closed until the urge to vomit had passed. At last, he opened the door.

The space was overcrowded with young men and women tossing shots. Bodies danced a little too close. Fragments of disillusioned rants spun through his ears. He spied Faina sitting at a table with Anya. She was dressed in one of those tasseled, sequined numbers with the hemline drawn up short. It was clear she had spent some of her bootlegging money, for there was no other way she could've afforded such an outfit. Her hair was curled into ringlets. A flashy headdress topped off the ensemble.

Anya spotted Pasha from the table and pointed him out to Faina. Faina bounced to her feet and scurried across the room to meet him.

"How did it go?" Her smile faded as she neared. "Pasha, you don't look so good."

Forcing a smile, he motioned her to follow him outside to the porch. Together they withdrew into the cool night air, the pounding music fading behind the doors.

"I have something for you." Pasha took the coat from his satchel and laid it in her arms.

Faina gaped at it in disbelief.

"Surprised?" chuckled Pasha.

Faina came back to life and wrapped her arms tightly around his neck. Pasha couldn't help but laugh.

"You didn't think I would break my promise, did you?"

Faina shook her head. Tears soaked into his shoulder. Pasha pulled away to look her in the eye with his easy smile.

"Now don't cry. You don't wanna walk into the Foxhole with damp cheeks."

Faina nodded and sniffed. "Did you turn Anastas in?"

Pasha bit his lip. "I didn't . . . technically. Klokov kinda figured it out." He drew a hand across his forehead and turned away.

"They aren't gonna kill him, are they?"

Faina's face was impassive. Pasha couldn't tell if she was concerned or vindicated.

"No, but he's getting flogged."

Faina lowered her eyes. She crossed to the railing and faced out over the Bowery. Her hands flexed open and closed on the bar. Pasha rounded his shoulders and leaned against the post.

"I don't know. Maybe I should have handed him over. Klokov asked me if he raised a hand to you, and well, he did hurt you."

Faina laid a comforting hand on his arm. "No. Not exactly. I'm glad it wasn't you that turned him in. Why don't you stay, Pasha? Stay and dance like you used to."

Pasha smirked and looked up at her with her strange, imperfect beauty.

"Nah, I gotta get home to Mama and Katya. Go have fun okay? I'll see you in the morning."

And holding open the door, he watched her disappear into the fog of flappers.

Chapter 8:

The Fire Breather in Central Park

The next morning, Pasha awaited Faina at the Conservatory Water in Central Park. His head was buried in a newspaper.

"I don't believe it!" He flipped to another page. "This is crazy!"

"What's crazy?" Faina asked, plopping herself on the bench beside him.

Pasha's eyebrows pushed to his hairline. "Nothing. No mention of a freak blizzard in Central Park anywhere, or a giant flaming bird for that matter." He crumpled the paper and slapped his knee.

Faina leaned forward with a smug expression. "What did I tell you?"

Pasha thrust out his lip and pointed the paper at her. "That means nothing. I'm still not convinced."

Faina threw up her arms and slumped across the back of the bench. "Give me a break, Pasha!"

Pasha got to his feet and tugged at her hair. "You're crazy, you know that?"

"Yeah, and it's a lot more fun." She hooked her arm through his elbow. Together they strolled beneath the carapace of ginger foliage.

"You know what we should do?" Pasha rubbed his chin. "Next time we should bring a camera. That way we can snap a picture and sell it to *The New York Times*."

Faina's face fell. "Sell it? And let everybody in on our secret? Have you lost your mind?"

"What do you mean our secret?"

"Well, the Firebird brought us all sorts of valuables. You really wanna share that with the whole of New York? Thanks to the Firebird, we'll soon have enough money to move out of the Lower East Side! Maybe we could even buy your freedom from Klokov!"

"Keep dreaming, Faina."

"Oh, I will."

They followed a path lined with black cherry trees. The cordial, valentine fragrance summoned thoughts of candied fruits bleeding from chocolate shells on the backs of their tongues. It was a beautiful day. Pasha longed to stop and lie in the grass. In a perfect world he and Faina would be salivating over Thanksgiving plans. But Pasha was a Breadwinner. They had work to do. They had to get on with it.

Pasha bounced his chin. "Hit up anything good this morning?"

Faina held out a leg. "Three bottles of Busch in the old bootleg."

"Isn't that some kind of saying?"

She shrugged. "How should I know?" She gave her foot a shake and the bottles clinked together. They passed beneath Glade Arch.

"Hey," an authoritative male voice hollered. Pasha's shoulders jumped to his ears. Two uniformed police officers approached them. The shorter one pointed to Faina.

"It's the girl with the pants again!"

The taller one threw up his hands in aggravation. "Come on, lady, not this again! We've told you before. . . ."

Pasha's instinct was to act natural. They only had three bottles of beer, and they were stashed in Faina's bootleg. All they had to do was apologize and say they would go home so Faina could change. Pasha turned to whisper his reassurance to Faina, but she had already made a dash for it.

"Hey!" the officers growled.

Pasha hesitated, took one more glance at Faina over his shoulder, then bolted to catch up with her.

"*Chort voz'mi*, Faina!" Confound it. "Was that really necessary? It's not like they were gonna check your bootleg or anything! Now they'll have us for running from law enforcement!"

"You forget, smarty-pants, we have warrants!"

Behind them they could hear the shiny heels of the policemen striking the pavement.

"Ya no good *bohunks*!"

"The term you're looking for is *katsap*," Faina corrected them. "We're Russians, not Czechs!"

Pasha swatted at her. "Don't help them!"

"Hey, I got a reputation to think about!"

They headed towards the tunnel of the Greywacke Arch. Their strength waned. With every slam of their feet, blood was beaten into their cheeks and sweat poured from their brows. Unfortunately, the scenic woodland path lent nothing to their trademark get-away skills. There was nothing to knock over, or slide under. All they could do was run.

At the entrance to the passage, Pasha tripped over his own legs and fell forward on the asphalt. Faina ground to a halt.

They were doomed. The police slowed. Then, out of nowhere a turbulent gust of fire ignited over their heads in a blinding, burning stream. A smoldering wall of combustion barricaded them from the two officers. Beyond the wall of flames, the taller one shielded himself from the dam of fire. He stumbled backwards. Pasha and Faina covered their heads. After a moment, the burning stopped.

They peeked open their eyes. The wall of fire had evaporated. The two officers ran in the opposite direction. Their hands clutched the pistols on their hips.

"That's it, we gotta go for backup! That ain't natural!"

"Looks like you could use some assistance," said a voice from behind Pasha. They turned to spy the stocky, ginger-bearded gypsy from the day before. He rubbed his thumb and index finger at the bottom of his cigar. A flame struck up through his flesh, lighting the tiller until it glowed orange. He took a drag, puffed a little cloud, then turned and spat on the ground. A small torrent of sparks streamed from his mouth.

"Now, I've had my run-ins with the law, believe me, and I gotta tell you mates, that was just plain terrible."

His speech was tinged with an urban British inflection, a Londoner perhaps. Patches with strange symbols were embroidered on his leather aviator jacket.

"It's never a good idea to cut and run," he went on.

He sucked in a little too much of his cigar and turned to cough. Fire spewed from his throat. Faina covered her mouth with her sleeves, suppressing a shriek of bewilderment.

The man eyed Faina's pant leg, which had become soaked with amber liquid.

"I think you broke your bottles."

***

Moments later, they sat outside a bakery on Forty-Second Street, encouraging the stranger to try his first bagel. He removed his weather-beaten panama, showcasing his wild, red hair. Instead of combing it sideways he brushed it upwards like a wavy flame. Not wanting to be caught staring, Pasha's eyes darted downwards.

He tore into his bagel. The slick sliver of salty lox slipped between his lips. His eyes shut. He hummed with satisfaction as he tasted the sweet red onions, the tart capers, and the buttery cream cheese. When he opened his eyes again the man was staring at them with a fuzzy raised eyebrow.

Faina glanced up at him, and covered her full mouth.

"Do you like it?"

The man turned over the soft, dense pastry and nodded. "It's good."

"You should try it with the *losos*. Cured salmon, that is."

He flexed a frown. "No thanks." Pasha could've sworn he heard him mumble, "I'm not into mermaid food," but immediately dismissed this as ludicrous.

"So is your name really Pyro Anomaly?" asked Faina, her mouth still stuffed with bagel.

"Of course not." He leaned back in his chair. "It's a non de plume."

"A what?"

"*Psevdonim*, a fake name," Pasha explained between bites.

"So what's your real name?"

"Never you mind." Pyro huddled down into the collar of his coat. "Pyro is what you'll call me."

"And you said you're part of a traveling gypsy circus?"

He bobbed his head and, taking a flask from his hip, unscrewed the cap and downed a drink of liquor.

Pasha and Faina glanced at each other. Faina cocked her head.

"You're awfully brave to drink that in public."

Pyro threw her a questioning look.

She hastened to explain. "You know, with Prohibition."

He steadied his gaze on her, and took another swig.

"Alcohol is illegal."

Pyro jumped, spewing whiskey everywhere. Faina blinked and wiped her cheek in disgust.

"It's what?" he thundered. "You've got to be kidding me!"

"I know, it sounds like a joke, but it isn't. That's why we ran from the police. We're bootleggers, and we didn't wanna get caught."

Pyro turned his head curiously. "Bootleggers . . . Oh! I get it now! That's why you had the bottles in your—Got it! But, wait a second, aren't you kids a little young to be drinking?"

"We don't drink it," explained Pasha, "we sell it."

"Haven't you heard all this?" blurted Faina. "It's been in effect for four years now."

Pasha elbowed her in the ribs and leaned tactfully forward. "But you're not from here, are you?"

Pyro's eyes bulged as he shifted in his seat.

"Yeah, that's right. I'm from Can . . ." He scratched his scruffy chin. "Candida . . . no, no that's a fungus. Canader! No, wait. Uh, Canadia! That's it, I'm from Canadia!"

Pasha and Faina stared at him in astonishment. Faina repressed a snort while Pasha tried his hardest to keep a straight face.

"You mean Canada?"

"That's what I said, Canadia."

Pasha sucked in his upper lip and nodded. "Right. That's what you said."

Faina propped her chin up with her elbow. "I would have thought with that accent you came from London."

"Oh, we all talk like this up there."

Before Faina could utter another breach of etiquette, Pasha steered the conversation in a new direction.

"So about this gypsy circus, you said you're putting on a show tonight?"

"That's right. You two oughta come up and see it. I insist. Besides, it's free."

"But in Grand Central Station? How did you get permission?"

Pyro waved an airy hand and pulled a cigarette from his pocket. "My employer, he knows a guy."

Faina looked him over incredulously. "Who's your employer?"

"Staccato Nimbus."

Pasha huddled down in his seat with a hand over his mouth. "This man is crazy," he hissed to Faina in Russian.

Faina shook her head. "*Tufta*," nonsense. "Staccato is probably another *psvedonim*."

Pyro snapped his finger beneath the edge of his tiller. A spark flew past Faina, causing her to shudder. Pyro took notice.

"What's wrong with her?"

Pasha rolled his eyes. "She's afraid of fire."

Pyro's face remained impassive but his voice seemed to soften.

"Why is that?"

"She's clumsy with it."

Faina elbowed Pasha roughly. She did not like him answering for her.

"Hm," Pyro grunted. "So was I when I was your age, but look at me now. Funny how your fears become a part of you, isn't it? The thing you're most afraid of can be the very thing that makes you great." He put out his cigarette. "Here, let me show you something."

He fumbled in his pocket for a box of matches. Why a fire breather would carry matches was beyond Pasha; his mouth was effectively a blow torch. Without igniting it, he instructed Pasha to hold the match between his fingers. He motioned for Faina to scoot closer.

"I'm going to teach you a trick that may help you feel less afraid."

He lit the match with his thumb. Faina's eyes glowed with a blend of fear and fascination.

"Now, wet your thumb and index finger in your mouth."

Faina did as told.

"Give me your hand."

Again she obeyed.

"You're gonna snuff the match with your bare hands."

Faina recoiled.

"It's an easy trick, Faina," Pasha assured her. "You won't hurt yourself." Though to be honest, he wasn't quite certain. Faina's fiery mishaps often seemed beyond rational control.

Bit by bit she returned her hand to the gypsy's. Before they reached the flame, Pyro paused to stare her in the eye.

"I'm not gonna let it hurt you." His eyes were sincere. "All you're going to do is pinch the wick very quickly. As soon as you've touched it, release it, or else you'll burn yourself."

Faina hung her fingers over the match. Pyro dipped her hand down. Pasha didn't even blink. As the heat caressed the tips of her fingers, Faina reared back her chin. She pinched her eyes closed. For a moment, the fire appeared to be swelling, drawing towards her fingers like a magnet. Faster than their eyes could calculate, Pyro opened and shut her fingers on the tip. An easygoing stream of smoke replaced the feisty little flame.

"You can look now."

Faina peeked out of one eye. She threw her hands up in excitement. "I did it!"

Pyro couldn't help but smile at her delight. "See? What did I tell you?"

"I can't believe it." Pasha shook his head, astounded and pleased. "Nobody died!"

Pyro reclined against his chair with a smile. "Now, you gonna come see our act tonight or not?"

Faina turned to Pasha with pleading excitement.

"Let's do it, Pasha! We can take Katya! Anya and I finished up most of the baking over the weekend."

"What time does it start?"

Pyro checked his watch. "Eight o'clock."

He shrugged. "Alright, I don't see why not."

Faina clapped her hands together as though she were a small child, while Pyro packed away his things.

"Excellent. Well, I better be off. Got a show to get ready for, after all."

They said their goodbyes, and soon Pasha and Faina were making their way towards Fifth Avenue. Faina shoved her hands in her pockets and glanced sideways.

"Do you think Anastas will try to steal from us again after last night?"

Pasha took his time with his reply. The simple answer was no. Yet he couldn't shake the feeling that Anastas posed a new threat—a deadlier threat.

"I doubt it. I didn't stick around to watch him get flogged, but after seeing how worked up everyone was, it had to be bad. He was lucky they didn't kill him."

"You don't think Klokov will make him go in the ring, do you?"

There was a cynical edge to Pasha's laugh. "Of course he will! Klokov is brutal, Faina!"

She pursed her lips. “Everyone will be expecting you to unleash your vengeance on him in the ring today. Are you gonna go easy on him?”

Pasha came to an abrupt stop. He hadn’t thought about it before. There was no way Anastas would be in any shape to fight, but Klokov would know if Pasha tried to give Anastas a break. He couldn’t risk faking him out a second time. Before he could make a decision he realized Faina was tapping him on the shoulder.

“Pasha, look! It’s one of those advertisements you like so much. You know, the ones that remind you of Harpagos.”

She pointed to a Yellow Chariot Cigarettes poster pasted to a drugstore window. Charging across the headline was a chiseled gladiator in a chariot drawn by a dappled gray horse.

Faina nudged his side. “You were really into the whole equestrian thing, weren’t you?”

“How could I not be? My family bred racehorses for generations.” Pasha ran his fingers over the bridge of the horse’s nose. Behind the driver, the sun shone like a bright yellow flame. His smile faded.

“Do you know what my mother told me when we had to sell Harpagos to gypsies before leaving for America? She said every horse is born with a pair of wings inside them, and only gypsies know the secret to unlocking them. They teach them how to fly, and they travel around the stars.”

Faina's voice lowered to a hush, and he knew she meant what she said next. "What if that were true?"

Pasha didn't dispute her this time. He only forced a scoff. "Wouldn't that be something?"

Chapter 9:

Khleb Da Sol

The final stretch of citrine sun throbbed upon the horizon. Pasha braced his muscles and set out for the Foxhole with a good fifty pounds of liquor cached in his clothes.

The basement pulsed with anticipation. People crowded around the ring, dragging on cigarettes. Money was tossed into the pool like tokens in a wishing well. All attention turned to Pasha as he wandered through the door.

Anastas stood at the edge of the counter with his arms crossed and his sleeves rolled up. At the sight of his injuries, Pasha almost gasped out loud. His left eye had been swollen shut. A thick bruise had formed where Klokov had struck him. Mauve stripes licked his arms. They feathered into blue and green at the edges, and crossed like bolts of lightning.

At the sight of Pasha, Anastas's gray eyes ignited with a hatred so pernicious it bordered on the perverse. There was a sick purpose in his glare, as though the flogging had been a religious cleansing.

Klokov turned his single, beady eye upon Pasha. He gave no words, but gestured to the skinny, young man. Pasha unloaded nine bottles of gin, three decanters of vodka, four flasks of whiskey, a container of Kentucky Southern Comfort, and twelve medicinal bottles of bourbon.

Klokov's stony mouth crackled and fissured until it burst open with joyous laughter.

“You never disappoint, do you, Stallion?”

Dusting his hands on the knees of his trousers, he stood and directed the two boys towards the ring. They removed their outer clothing. Pasha’s ears thrummed with a flume of adrenaline. He took his place across from Anastas. His opponent appeared all too eager for an opportunity to lay his hands on Pasha’s throat.

The crowd hushed as Klokov ascended the squat little podium. He held the trophy of mouthwatering bread in his right hand. With his left he sprinkled salt onto the floor. At last he blew his whistle.

Pasha threw himself into Anastas, unloading his full weight, driving his opponent backwards. Anastas charged back with equal strength, neutralizing the blow. Then something strange happened. Without so much as a touch, Anastas weakened and toppled beneath Pasha.

Something was off. He had overpowered Anastas much too quickly.

Anastas swung from below. With a hulking fist he struck Pasha on the side of his skull.

Pasha retaliated and broke his balled hand across Anastas’s plump mouth. Blood pinched from the corners of his already-sore lips. He raised to shove Pasha away, but Pasha caught his fist and sent another blow hammering across his cheek.

Something was definitely not right. Anastas was barely putting up a fight. Pasha's instincts swore it wasn't from weakness or injury.

He finished Anastas off with an uppercut through the chin. Anastas went limp. Blood pooled in the ring.

"The winner!" Klokov boomed, yanking Pasha to his feet and raising his fist high in the air. Klokov placed the bread in Pasha's hands. It was heavier than usual.

Anastas remained rooted to the ground and let out a dramatic groan. Klokov smacked him on the back of his head.

"Get up, Rogue! He hardly grazed you." It was true, and puzzling. Pasha had only given a couple of hits, hardly enough to take down someone of Anastas's size and skill. With the fight over, the two competitors followed their superior to the bar.

"You boys order yourselves a drink," Klokov mumbled. "You've had a hard week, the both of you. Let's do our best to move past it. Wait right here while I go grab your pay."

A slim, needle-nosed man whom Pasha knew as Vasily, the bartender from Saturday nights, pushed through the crowd and tapped Klokov on the shoulder.

"Someone outside to see you, boss. Said it's urgent."

Klokov knit his brows together in surprise. He rapped his fist on the counter.

"Wait here." Popping a cigar between his lips, he slipped outside. Vasily turned to Pasha.

"Oh, and Faina's waiting for you in the back hall. She looked upset, like she was trying not to cry or something."

Pasha drew back in concern. "Is she okay? Did she say what was wrong?"

Vasily shook his head and scratched at his greasy scalp beneath his cap. "Nope. You better go see."

Pasha flexed his hands as he got up from the stool and set out down the hall.

"Faina?"

But no one was around. He ducked his head through the empty rooms but there was no sign of Faina, or any girl for that matter. He walked up the short stairwell to the back alley. He looked around. She was nowhere to be found. Maybe she had gone upstairs? He'd check after Klokov handed him his pay.

When Pasha went back to his seat at the bar, Klokov was returning from outside. Pasha looked for Vasily to tell him he hadn't seen Faina, but he had vanished.

Pasha chewed on his lip. It wasn't Vasily's day to be working anyway. Folding his hands on the counter, his eyes followed Klokov as he made his way to the back room down the hall where the cash was kept. It took a solid effort not to notice the bruised and battered Anastas flanking his own left side. Pasha had expected him to say something, taunt him, make some kind of rude remark, but he was quiet. Pleasantly quiet, in fact.

Klokov seemed to be taking his time. Pasha was thinking he

might order a glass of water, when a horrible, thunderous roar made him jump in his chair.

The bar went silent. A door slammed so violently down the passage, Pasha thought it had splintered. Klokov came rumbling into the open.

“Someone’s stolen from the cashbox!”

Gasps and whispers circulated up and down the bar.

“The lock was clipped,” he went on to explain. “All the money, gone!”

“When could this have happened?” cried a lackey.

“It had to have been done overnight,” observed Anastas, finally speaking. “Otherwise one of us would’ve seen it happen.”

Klokov shuffled back behind the bar and took to whispering in anxious trills with his crony. Anastas glanced down at Pasha’s loaf of bread sitting atop the counter.

“What’s the matter, Chevalsky, you couldn’t wait till you got home?” He spoke so loud he actually caused Klokov to jump.

“Geez, Rogue! Tone it down a bit! You don’t have to scream.”

Anastas pointed to his ear. “Can’t help it. My ears have stopped up from the swelling.” He gestured to his eye.

“Your eyeballs connected to your ear canals now?” Klokov rolled his eyes. “Yeesh!”

Pasha cocked his head at Anastas. “What are you talking about?”

"You took a chunk outta your bread. Geez, can somebody get this sap a bag before he eats the table?"

Pasha glanced down at the loaf of bread. Anastas was right. There was a perfect, finger sized hole drilled into the side.

"I didn't do that."

As Klokov reached for a paper bag, he noticed it too. He paused and stared, unflinching.

"Boss?" Anastas snapped his fingers. "You alright?"

Klokov picked the bread up between his muscled hands and ran a finger over the incision. He held it to his ear and shook. Pasha's blood was cold and metallic in his ribcage. Klokov's nostrils flared. He dug a meaty finger into the sliver, raising his head towards Pasha with a savage grimace. With an irate thunder, he broke the bread in two. Crisp, green, hundred dollar bills fluttered in a shower around them. Quarters, nickels, and dimes bounced with metallic clangs.

"You!" Klokov reached across the counter and seized Pasha by the collar.

"Klokov, I didn't do it! How could I have done it? When would I have had the time?"

Klokov let him go. Pasha's cheek collided with the marble surface as he fell to the floor. He scuttled back against the nearest table.

An adolescent voice piped up from the back of the room.

"That's baloney! I saw him go back there while Klokov was

outside."

Pasha swiveled around in horror. It was the fourteen-year-old pickpocket who hung around Anastas.

So he had been set up. It had all been thoroughly and deviously premeditated. What argument could he make?

Before another word could be said against him, Pasha sprang up from the floor and bounded out the door.

"Bring him back here," cried Klokov.

Pasha sprinted down the alleyway. His knees felt like they were burning and disappearing at the same time. His legs itched from pumping adrenaline through his veins. The road seemed to grow longer and narrower as he felt the hot breath of mortality on his neck.

He ducked sideways into an alley, turning over trashcans and swinging from fire escapes until he reached a deep passage. They would've been expecting him to cut across to the street adjacent. This way he could avoid them. Pasha made himself flat against the wall and waited for the commotion to pass up the street.

He peeled himself from the wall. A breeze skimmed the end of his nose as something silvery whistled past him. A knife embedded itself into the side of a dumpster.

Pasha's breath caught in his throat. Klokov was barreling towards him like a train, his hand reaching for his pistol. Pasha leapt atop the dumpster and reached for the fire escape over his head. He swung his legs onto the landing and charged up the steps.

Klokov was much shorter and stockier than Pasha. It took him considerable time to lumber onto the dumpster. After a few jumps, he managed to grab the bottom rung of the fire escape, but pulled the rail right from its hinges. Pasha did not stop until the edge was within his reach.

He rolled onto the cemented rooftop. Behind him, Klokov managed his more stately henchmen up the dumpster. Shots fired, ripping chunks from the brick wall. Pasha ducked and scuttled to the opposite side.

He had driven himself into a corner. There was no way to climb down, only a seven-foot gap between him and the next building. He looked to the right. The roof of the adjoining establishment was a good ten feet high. Furthermore, there was nothing Pasha could boost himself up on. He recalled how Leo had taught him to run up a wall, but ten feet was a long way to go. Was it even possible?

There was a loud clamor as Klokov's cronies successfully made it to the top. Pasha had to decide.

He dashed towards the wall of the building attached. Someone fired a pistol in his wake. Pasha leaned back. He flattened his left foot against the wall and pushed. He pulled his chest forward, and quickly stepped with the other foot. His hands reached upwards and found the ledge.

Heart thundering, Pasha scurried over the side. Shattered cement pelted his face as bullets broke through the stone. He sprinted across the line of connecting structures until he came to a narrow alleyway on Grand Street. Pasha hopped off the edge of the roof and between the windowsills in a zigzag pattern towards the ground. At the second story, he leapt onto a dumpster and bolted down a row of trashcans, coming out on the sidewalk.

Pasha pulled his cap down over his face. He may have lost them, but he wasn't going to take any chances. He had to get home and warn Faina.

Chapter 10:
Staccato Nimbus's Singing Circus

Pasha did not risk going through the front door of his tenement house. It wouldn't be long before Klokov came knocking on his door, demanding his mother hand over her son. As he reached his window, Mammoth barked across the way. Faina drew back the curtains and poked her head into the courtyard.

"Pasha! You're back! Did you win?"

Before he could answer, Katya opened his bedroom window and threw her arms around her brother's neck.

"Pasha!"

Pasha cocked an eyebrow. "Katya! What are you doing in my room?"

"I had a feeling you were coming in through the fire escape."

Pasha's eyes glazed over skeptically. "Uh-huh, a feeling. I see." He ran his hands over his face, pressing his fingers into his temples. "Uh, go back inside. I'll be right there, okay?"

But Katya didn't budge. "Pasha, something is wrong."

He groaned. Now was not the time for her to unravel him.

Faina nodded her head and knit her eyebrows together. "Katya is right, something is wrong. What happened?"

Pasha buried his head in his hands. Faina huffed.

"That's it." She swung her leg out the window. "I'm coming over!"

While Pasha waited for Faina to make her way over, he slid through his bedroom window and turned to Katya. He forced a lightness into his face.

"Katya, sweetheart, I need you to go into Mama's room and put on a nice dress."

Her oddly chromatic eyes penetrated him with an infallible sense of knowledge.

"Why? Pasha, what's going on? You're scared, I can tell."

Pasha exhaled through his nose. "Tonight, we're going to a circus in Grand Central Station."

Her face lit up. "Really?"

"Yeah, *Katenka*." He scooted her towards their mother's room. "There's gonna be a man who breathes fire, and tightrope walkers, and all kinds of music, I'm sure."

Katya resisted him. "But, wait, Pasha, that doesn't explain what's really going on! There's something you're not telling me!"

He opened the door to their mother's room and forced her inside. "Go get ready. We don't wanna be late!" Without waiting for her reply, Pasha shut her in. He turned and leaned against the door, sighing and massaging his fingers through his hair. The handle wrenched. With lightning reflexes, Pasha grabbed it and held it in place. Katya beat her fists against the door.

"Pasha! Let me out!"

"Drop it or else you're not going!"

There was an exasperated huff on the other side of the door, then footsteps as Katya walked away.

Faina appeared in his doorway across the hall.

"Are we still going to Grand Central? I was thinking we should ask the gypsies about the Firebird. Something tells me they know what's going on."

"You're right," Pasha groaned. "In fact, I'm gonna do more than that." He walked past her and sat on his bed. "I'm gonna ask if I can join them, wherever it is they're headed. I need to leave town."

Faina shut her eyes. "Did I hear you right? Did you just say you're gonna join a band of traveling gypsies?" She sat next to him, shaking her head. "Pasha, what's going on?"

He glanced across the hall, making sure Katya was out of earshot. Without thinking, he began babbling in Ukrainian. Faina slammed a hand over his mouth.

"English or Russian. I don't speak Ukrainian, remember? You need to calm down." She released him. "Take a deep breath, and try again."

Pasha swallowed and tried to get a hold of himself. "Anastas framed me."

Faina's eyebrows drew together in disbelief. "Framed you? How?"

"It's a long story. They think I stole money. Some of his pals were in on it. Vasily too, I think. Anyway, I gotta find a way to leave the city."

"You're serious?" She stared at him, searching for the joke in his eyes.

"Faina, if I stay here they'll find me, and they'll kill me. They know where I live. It's like you said, whatever is going on, the gypsies know something. And if I go with them I'll be outta harm's way."

Faina looked puzzled. "Go with them? And do what? Are you just gonna leave your mother and sister behind to fend for themselves?"

"Of course not! I'll earn money somehow, and I'll send it back to them. People do it all the time. They won't try to harm Ma, or Katya, or you. It's against their code so I don't have to worry about that. I'll do whatever the gypsies want. I'll shovel horse manure, hang up fliers, anything. Or else I'll go somewhere where I can make money." He leaned back against the wall and rubbed his temples.

Faina stood and turned away from him, her arms crossed.

"And when I can," continued Pasha, "I'll come back, and we can start over somewhere else."

Faina's head sank as she lowered her voice. "What about me?"

"By 'we', I meant you and me!" He twitched and coughed into his hand. "And my family, of course."

Faina looked surprised. "You mean run away?"

Pasha gave a playful smile. "It's only running away if your uncle says you can't come. And if he says no, then I'll just have to climb up the fire escape and kidnap you." He snatched her around the waist, but Faina shrugged him off. Her eyes bore into him with frightened uncertainty.

"Take me with you now!"

Pasha squeezed her hand.

"Faina," he began softly, "it's safer for you in New York. What are you worried about? The Breadwinners aren't gonna come after you."

"I'm not worried about the Breadwinners, stupid! I'm worried about you! You need me."

Pasha dragged his hand over his forehead and sighed. "I do need you. But this is for your own safety. You don't need to be trekking all over the country with me."

Faina rolled her eyes. "And what am I supposed to do while you're away? I can't sell to Klokov because I'm a girl. I'm dead weight to my uncle. I can't work in the grocery because of my reputation, and no other places will hire me."

"You can help me by taking care of my mother and sister."

Faina growled and walked away from him, throwing her hands in the air. Pasha chased after her.

"Come on, Faina. I mean it. You're family to us. My mother, she loves you like a daughter. For goodness' sake, you've been calling her 'Mama Lydia' since we were ten years old! You never call her 'Mrs. Chevalsky.'" He grabbed her hand. "Please. Take Katya to the parade for me tomorrow. Stay here and watch over them for me. Faina, look at me." He propelled her chin towards him. Faina scowled at him through her tears.

"You're my best friend! Don't leave me behind!"

"Everything is gonna be fine."

"You're abandoning me!"

Pasha gave a soft laugh. "Why would you think I would do such a thing? When everything is safe and settled, I'll come back for you. We'll go somewhere beautiful. Some place with mountains and trees, and you and I can have adventures every day. I promise."

Faina sniffed and brought her eyes up to meet his. He was getting through to her. He took both her hands in his.

"Thieves' Honor?"

Faina gave a limp nod and tried to smile.

"May I, Pasha Ruslanovich Chevalsky, never enjoy freedom if I ever forsake Faina Adrianovna Spichkin."

Faina took a deep breath.

"And may I, Faina Adrianovna Spichkin, lose all my liberty if I ever forsake Pasha Ruslanovich Chevalsky."

***

Pasha left a note on the kitchen table for his mother, and together he, Faina, and Katya rode into Grand Central. During their journey, he kept his cap low over his eyes and his collar turned up. Faina scanned the crowd like a machine, eyeing every passenger who boarded.

When they got off the train, the crowd shrank and constricted into a tightly knit channel. It pushed them towards the main concourse like wild rapids. Neither Pasha nor Faina knew what to expect. Pasha clung to his little sister's hand in the overwhelming bustle. What if there was no gypsy circus? What would he tell her? It could've easily been a trick, or the imaginative prattle of a half-crazed hobo with a panama hat . . . who also happened to breathe fire.

A din of pounding orchestral music walloped over their heads like a giant dancing bear. Up ahead the golden concourse ebbed with its usual warm glow of gold and granite. Gasps ran down the line as the patrons wandered into a dazzling macrocosm of splashy fantasy. Mammoth-sized paper flowers polka-dotted the walls. They shuttered and bloomed of their own accord. Tropical birds—many of which they had never seen before—zipped through the trapezes, perched on the high wire, and whistled popular tunes of the day. Pasha halted as a punchy, taffy-colored canary whipped past him singing *Alexander's Ragtime Band.*

Faina leaned over to Pasha and whispered from the side of her mouth, "How are they getting away with this?"

The concourse was so crowded with sensory gaiety, Pasha almost forgot to answer.

"Normally, I would say they had to pay someone off but . . . they're gypsies. Gypsies who travel in an old, horse-drawn wagon of all things! They can't have the money to put the entire station on hold."

And yet policemen walked about as though it were just another day. Now and then one would stop to admire the paper flowers, or tap their feet to the rhythmic music.

Faina scratched her chin. "You would think for something this big we would've seen advertisements."

Two women swaggered past them, linked arm in arm.

"Look at this, Dianthe. Makes you homesick, doesn't it?"

"It does, Chloris, it does."

A bird brushed by and knocked Dianthe's hat from her head. Pasha hastened to pick it up.

"Excuse me, ma'am, you dropped your—" As Pasha looked up, all speech left him. The woman had an entire garden blossoming through a fade of grassy hair. Dianthe blushed green.

"Thank you, sweetheart."

She took the hat and hastily shoved it back on her head. As the two women hurried away, he could hear the lady whispering, "That's what I get for not weeding today!"

Katya and Faina struggled not to laugh. Pasha tried to quell the enchantment bubbling up inside him. He reminded himself it was all part of an illusion, but it was becoming harder and harder to keep that in mind.

Circular stands had been erected around the center of the room.

They took a seat in the front row.

Katya tugged on Pasha's sleeve and pointed towards the middle of the concourse. "Pasha! Look!"

A live orchestra had been set up towards the far wall and, to Pasha's astonishment, was playing by itself. Faina flashed him a smug look. He shrugged and tried to appear nonchalant.

"There's probably a band playing behind a wall somewhere."

"Okay then. How do you explain the fact that the bows are moving themselves? Or that the woodwinds are floating in midair?"

Pasha opened his mouth and snapped it shut. He had no explanation. Fortunately, the lights dimmed, excusing him from supplying an answer. A man in a green station master uniform walked to the center of the ring with a microphone in his hands. He appeared to be Italian-American. An enormous pair of golden wings crowned his back, and matched the uniform splendidly.

"Hey, it's Angelo!" someone in the crowd yelled. A few others waved and called Angelo's name. Angelo gave a sheepish smile and put up his hand.

"My fellow New Yorkers, as Head Guardian of the Grand Central Gateway it is my pleasure to introduce you to tonight's entertainment." He spoke with a thick Bronx accent. "Now before we go any further, I must remind you for the safety of our performers that, should you need to exit the stands at any time, please refrain from flying or levitating."

A few people in the audience groaned.

"As for any esperites joining us tonight, you may now take this time to please turn off your lights."

A woman a couple of rows back let out a sigh. "Guess that's me."

Pasha glanced over his shoulder in time to see her body glowing with a bright golden light. Pasha elbowed Faina hard.

"Faina . . . Faina, that woman was glowing!"

"Calm down," she hissed.

"But that woman was glowing!"

"Well, then don't stare."

She forced him back around. Angelo dusted off his hands. "Without further ado, I give you the Singing Circus!"

The station erupted into a round of applause. Angelo made his way towards the stands and took a seat next to Pasha. Katya leaned across her brother.

"I like your wings. They're very pretty."

Angelo smiled a broad, genial smile. "Thanks, I just molted."

There was a heavy click as a broad spotlight came to life. It highlighted the figure of a lanky man on a tightrope, poised with his violin. Pasha's brain gave a throb of recognition. It was the same gypsy who had played atop the caravan the day before.

With solemn reverence he dragged his bow across the silver strings. Out spun a tune so vibrant it was like language. The music was layered with a tapestry of conflicting emotions. There was dignity mingled with grief, hope fused with melancholy, and grandeur courting humility. The violinist raced through the notes until he came to one final, suspenseful chord, and tore his arm away. Turning towards the audience on the high wire, he bowed and made a sweeping gesture towards the floor.

A salvo of snare drums rippled. The arena erupted in an explosion of light and color. The unmanned orchestra struck up once more, and a menagerie of animals made of pure golden light stampeded through the air. There were cranes, winged horses, swans, and even dragons flying through the room. It was as though the station housed its very own biosphere in which living creatures of myth and legend came alive. It was enough to turn the adults into children. Their faces grew younger and brighter.

When the parade of creatures had faded, the music beat out a regimental march well-suited for the entry of a magi. The snap of a cymbal turned their attention to a well-dressed bald man standing at the center of the ring. He appeared to be in his early fifties and wore a satin waistcoat with an expensive-looking purple cravat. He was a sleek, broad-shouldered fellow with an elegant, haughty bearing. His face was angular and chiseled, and he was rather fiendish with his default expression of scathing contempt. A sweeping nose poked out over a dark silver beard, and there was condescension in his sunken, heavily-lidded eyes.

His long fingers wrapped around the neck of an ebony staff topped with a silver armillary sphere. Beside him, Katya was kicking her feet.

“Pasha! Pasha, it’s him! The man from my dream!”

“Shhh, Katya.”

The man gave a gallant bow as the music came to a close and the audience applauded. He gestured to the gypsy looming above the crowd on the high wire.

“Thank you! Thank you, everyone for such a warm and lovely welcome. Special thanks especially to our violinist Skelter up there amongst the constellations tonight!”

Skelter bowed clownishly with his knobby knees poking out in opposite directions.

“Allow me to introduce myself.” The man turned the rings of the armillary sphere three times. The staff shortened to the length of a ruler. He scribbled his name in midair, the letters shining with glittering, golden light.

“My name is Staccato Nimbus. I shall act as your host for tonight, and welcome you to our humble show.”

Pasha leaned into Faina’s ear and scoffed. “Listen to his accent.” There was no mistaking the British inflection in his voice, which was far more proper-sounding than Pyro’s.

Faina giggled and nodded. “And Pyro tried to convince us they were Canadians.”

"They're obviously not from anywhere on this continent."

Faina beamed as though he were about to suggest something truly exciting. Pasha crossed his arms.

"They're obviously from England!"

Faina's smile dropped. She rolled her eyes. "Yeah, that's it, Pasha. England. England is full of fire-breathing gypsies. They're like double-decker buses." They returned their attention to Staccato.

"Tonight you will feast your eyes on a multitude of spectacular sights and visions, all which defy explanation. Well, unless you're Voilerian."

The audience giggled but the joke was lost on the three in the front row.

"Before we venture any further, I feel it is my duty to remind you things are never quite as they seem."

Staccato threw his staff into the air where it hovered into an upright position. As the rings of the armillary sphere turned backwards, the staff elongated.

"Eyes are tricky things which tend to deceive. Funny we should rely on them when, in fact, they are infamous for their lies." Staccato reached out and touched the tip of his staff. It melted into a black serpent and wrapped itself around his arm.

Several members of the audience shrieked. Staccato ignored them. "We say seeing is believing, and therefore we are inclined to make swift judgements about everyone and everything."

The snake dripped like molten tar from his wrist and grew rigid again.

"Our eyes constantly command our attention, telling us what to think and feel, what to glorify and what to recoil from." A ribbon of yellow light leaked from the armillary sphere and coiled in the palm of Staccato's hand. "Tonight, I implore you to free yourself from the tyranny of sight. Defy the logic of your vision, and decide for yourselves whether or not what you see is real . . ."

He tossed the light in Pasha's direction where it exploded into a shower of glittering golden particles.

" . . . Or illusion." Twirling his staff in a silvery arc, he vanished on the spot.

The lights darkened to a shade of blue. A singular, disembodied voice floated out of the shadows to serenade them. It did not form words but remained a vague vocalization. Pasha leaned forward. Even he was not immune to the electric pull of the mystery which beckoned them all forward.

A drum struck. A flame ribboned in the center of the room and vanished. From the front row, Pasha could see an abstraction of Pyro's face in the flashes of light. His fist pounded the instrument a second time. The singing poured into the spaces between the percussion like water pooling between stones. All at once the drums exploded into a frantic stomping rhythm accompanied by bursting fireballs.

Pyro picked up his speed until enough light was generated to see his acrobatic form.

His bare chest was painted with vivid shapes of curling gold. A long pink scar ran down his right arm. He must have burned himself at some point. It had to be an occupational hazard, after all. Surrounding him was a wall of different types of drums, all suspended in midair. Pyro was using his entire body as an instrument. He threw himself against the pulsing surfaces. He beat with his fists, heels, and arms. He pounded the drums with his elbows until sparks shot across the room.

His shadow bashed and crackled. Pasha half-expected him to explode and ribbon away into empty smoke. As Pyro gave one last savage trill upon the drums, he jumped to a halt, and the fire consumed him. His silhouette was stiff, as though he had hardened into diamond. Katya tugged on Pasha's sleeve.

"How did he do that, Pasha?"

"Some sort of special effects, I'm sure."

Faina glared at him from the corner of her eye. "Really, Pasha?" Her voice was full of sarcasm. Pasha ignored her.

Wistful notes from a violin flowered into the music and swayed across the floor. They wrapped themselves around Pasha's skin like living creatures. Red sheets of silk dropped down from the ceiling in long, flowing strips. The fire enveloping Pyro snuffed out. The drums floated off into the darkness.

With his shoulders thrown back, Pyro wrapped his arms in the red silk and hoisted himself off the ground. Once he had attained some height, he pumped himself back and forth, building momentum. As he swung higher, he flipped his legs over his head and leaned back until he was suspended upside-down. He looked like a bird diving through the air.

The audience doubled over in awe as fire ignited down his spine. It spread through his arms, flickering and feathering like flaming wings. Pyro had become the Firebird. He soared over the audience, performing acrobatic tricks. Meanwhile Skelter continued to play his violin.

Clouds formed on the opposite sides of the floor and eddied like ocean waves. Gold flecks glittered in the mist as the vapors crept towards each other to the center of the ring. As the atmosphere evolved, Pyro let go, falling through the air and vanishing in the clouds.

Pasha jumped as Faina elbowed him in the ribs. “Uh, Pasha?”

He followed her finger towards the ceiling. Pasha had to clench his seat to keep from falling over. The constellations, which had been painted on the ceiling over a decade ago, now moved and rearranged themselves into new patterns.

A bolt of blue-green silk tumbled down from the ceiling. The young woman who had been sitting at the back of the wagon appeared in the folds. She tangled herself from the waist down in the material and hung cradled over the long empty space in an artistic pose. Her coils of brown hair rippled as she swung herself back and forth, turning over, flipping, and performing amazing aerial tricks.

The lights dimmed so her body became a simple silhouette. A hoop lowered down in front of her. She climbed into the sphere and draped herself in various hanging positions. As the lights came back on, she pulled a cord of her dress. Her skirt unraveled into twenty feet of shimmering, champagne satin. It faded into brilliant gold glitter, and split like the fluke of a tail. She pumped herself back and forth in the hoop, allowing the light to play with the sheen of her skirt. Skelter picked up his violin once more, and the girl began singing about a mermaid queen named Evangeline.

The music sank into Pasha's bones and took him away. It took him back to his dreams. Everything went blank in front of him. The sceneries evaporated and all before him was darkness. He could hear the music, closer now, unaccompanied. A white light burned his eyes. His fingertips came into focus. He became aware of himself. The glimmering enveloped him and stretched into an explosion of imagery. Everything in the circus became real.

Mermaids sifted their tails through the waves. The girl stood in the surf, and bent over him with a sweet, loving smile.

"Are you ready to come home, Pasha?"

Chapter 11:
The Bargain

When Pasha opened his eyes, he was lying on his back in the middle of Grand Central Station. The cerulean tapestry of inverse constellations floated miles above him. There was no high wire. There was no trapeze. There were no skeins of silk draped like frosting. Ordinary people buzzed in and out of terminals like honeybees. There were no wings, no flowers, no mermaids. He could hear whispering on either side of him. Katya and Faina's faces loomed over him.

"Pasha, are you awake?" Faina whispered.

Pasha rubbed his forehead with the heels of his hands. "What happened?"

"You fainted right in the middle of the performance."

Pasha sat up on his elbows and looked around him. "The performance! Where did it—? It was right here! There were stands, and birds, and acrobats!"

A shadow fell over his head. Someone stood behind him. Pasha's eyes traveled up the long arms of Staccato Nimbus, who was now wearing an overcoat and bowler hat. His gloved hands rested on the head of his staff, which had been shortened into a fashionable walking stick. Pasha pushed himself into a full, upright position.

"Not too quickly now," Staccato warned. "I know this is a lot to take in, but you're going to have to bear with me for a moment." He held out an elegant hand to help lift him to his feet. "Go slower."

After a moment of hesitation, Pasha took it. With Faina's help they lifted him onto his own two feet. Pasha stood at eye level with Staccato. He was even more intimidating and mysterious up close.

"So," Staccato began, meticulously adjusting the cuffs of his sleeves, "you're the boy I've heard so much about."

Pasha drew back. "I wasn't aware I was that famous. What is it you've heard about me?"

"Quite a lot. You're Pavlo Ruslanovitch Chevalsky, heir to the title of the Baron of Balalchik. You're descended from a long line of Polish nobles who were famous for making wine. In 1918, you fled Crimea with your mother and sister after the Bolsheviks killed your father. You booked passage to New York. You were screened at Ellis Island, and made a citizen of the United States of America. In 1920, you joined the Breadwinners to save your mother from a stalker. Afterwards, you and your little friend here made a name for yourselves by using jumping, climbing, and gymnastics to evade the police. And as of this evening, you're a man on the run."

Pasha glanced at Katya. He had not wanted her to hear this, however, she gave no reaction.

Staccato glanced slyly over his shoulder. "And that's not all."

"It isn't?"

"You've seen the Firebird."

Pasha froze. His hand lingered outside his pocket.

Staccato nodded his head. "Go ahead. Let's have a look."

The room lit up as Pasha presented the feather, confirming what Staccato had guessed at. The host leaned in closer for a better look, the plume lighting the hollowed orbits of his eyes.

"Yes, there's no mistaking that, that's for sure. An authentic tail feather from the Firebird."

Faina stirred to life. "Where does it come from? Why has it come to us?"

"Because something big is about to happen," said Katya, in a voice much older than she. "Something important."

Staccato folded his long fingers together.

"Your sister is right. There is something much larger happening here. Things never happen without purpose. Nothing is without purpose, really. Every grain of sand in the hourglass is a crucial moment for someone, and Pasha, this happens to be your hour."

Pasha's eyes fidgeted around the room as Staccato fixated on him with a meaningful gaze.

"Everyone at some point in their lives has considered the possibility that there's more to the world, more to it than the eye can behold. After all, how do we get such phenomenon as magic and miracles? A great deal of these things come from the heavens."

He bounced his staff upwards in his hand and pointed at the constellations in the sky. They began to move again. Pasha wheeled around to observe the people hustling through the concourse around them. No one was reacting.

"Don't they see what's happening?"

Staccato shook his head. "They don't see it because I do not wish them to. It's easy to manage on people unaccustomed to magic. Even more so when one considers I'm not the only miraculous in New York City."

Pasha squeezed his eyes shut and shook his head. "What do you mean 'miraculous'?"

"Miraculous: one of the seven Fay races; a person with the ability to cast illusions, interpret and induce dreams, and move things with the power of their mind."

He stretched his hand towards Pasha. Without touching him he lifted the cap off his head. Katya giggled as Pasha's eyes crossed. He snatched his cap from the air and shoved it back down over his head, irritated. Staccato smiled as though he hadn't noticed.

". . . And of course, almost always originating from Voiler." It sounded like he had tried to say the word "Voila."

Pasha gaped at him. "I'm sorry, 'Voiler'?"

Staccato pointed back to the ceiling. The night sky mural faded away. The outlines of the constellations became borders, and the blots of stars became cities. Painted mountains, islands, and seas replaced the twilight. The river Eridanus became an actual river which emptied into Cetus, now an ocean. Argo became a seafaring island. Virgo was a breadbasket of golden grains. Aquarius was a massive waterfall. And then there was Polaris, a city seated in a country called Ursa.

"It's a map," exclaimed Katya, "and the constellations, they're kingdoms, countries!"

It wasn't a perfect fit. Some of the constellations had been absorbed into each other as landmarks rather than countries. Many had changed sizes such as Cancer, which had been stamped with the Greek translation of the name, *Karkinos*. It was now an ocean and spread much farther than the original asterism, one side making it all the way to the edge of Ursa Minor.

"Voiler is where all magic originates," Staccato explained. "And now it is almost the only place where you will find it. Or at least, out in the open. Your world, 'the Other' as we Voilerians call it, once had magic too."

"What happened to it?" asked Katya.

"People stopped believing. Magic takes faith, you see, and without faith it becomes powerless."

"But I believe in magic."

Staccato looked upon her with a strange fondness.

"Yes, and that gives you power. Don't ever stop believing, Katerina, or else you will lose your connection to all the wonders and miracles life has to offer."

Pasha waved his arms. "Wait, wait, hold on a second. You're telling me there's a whole other world out there in the stars? And there are people there who can move things with their mind, and cause visions, and make paintings move around on ceilings?"

"Well, yes," said Staccato, as though this were a stupid question. "That's exactly what I just said."

Pasha drew a long exhale. "Okay, I don't know what you did to me while I was out, whether you poisoned me, or drugged me, but I don't have time for this nonsense." He grabbed Katya by the hand and whirled Faina towards the exit. "I have a family to take care of."

Faina resisted and whispered through gritted teeth, "Pasha, stop!"

"Not to mention, I'm a little preoccupied with trying to figure out how not to be murdered in my sleep tonight."

Katya wrenched away from him. "Pasha, let go!"

He reeled her back in. "Come on, Katya. Faina's gonna take you home."

"No, Pasha! You have to listen to him!"

"Listen to him? Katya, he's *bezumets*, a crazy man! I know it's hard for you to understand, but magic and firebirds aren't real! Life isn't like a storybook. Things in the real world are complicated. Things for people like us . . . well, they just don't work out, okay?"

Katya stared at him with ashamed disappointment.

"You don't really believe that, Pasha! You're just saying that to make yourself feel better!" She had pierced him with keen accuracy.

"It's true, Katya! That's life! It's a cold, dark, horrible place where everybody suffers! It's time you learned that!"

Wrinkling her nose, Katya shoved her brother with a wrath Pasha had never detected in her before.

"You're a liar, Pasha! Stop lying! You lie to everybody! You try to lie to Mama about the Breadwinners! You lied to me about the Firebird feather! You even lie to yourself every day because you're afraid of getting hurt!"

Pasha stepped back in shock.

"You know the Firebird is real," she thundered.

Faina put a comforting arm around Katya and pulled her back a step. She narrowed her eyes on Pasha.

"Pasha, we saw it twice, on two separate days! We weren't poisoned, we weren't drugged. What about Pyro? What about the snowstorm?"

"What about my dream?" reminded Katya.

"How can you be so stubborn?" Faina persisted. "You're working so hard to deny the existence of something you know to be true! Given everything we've seen in the past week, it would take more faith to believe magic isn't real than it would to accept it."

Pasha stared at the ground. He sank his teeth into his bottom lip. Maintaining the scowl on his face, he turned back to Staccato and said in a low voice, "Alright. What is it the Firebird wants with me?"

Staccato rested his hand on the head of his staff. "She wants you to catch her."

"Why? Why me?"

"Presumably because Voiler is in great danger. Do you remember the dream you had the other night, Pasha?"

His neck stiffened. He'd shared this dream with no one. "Yes."

"You saw Polaris fall from the sky. In Voiler, Polaris has been the most powerful city for several generations, just as it has been the pole star for several generations. But it wasn't always that way. Before Polaris, Thuban was the brightest star in the sky. Do you know the constellation where Thuban resides?"

"Thuban is a star in Draco, the serpent."

"Correct. There was a time, long ago, when Draco ruled all Voiler as a tyrant, enslaving Fay and using their power to create all sorts of suffering and torment."

"What are Fay?"

Staccato waved his hand. "'Fay' is the term used to describe all magical peoples. Anyway, that's ancient history. Draco was overthrown centuries ago. Voiler was given its freedom, but not its safety, not in its entirety. For years now, Draco has been working to reclaim its position as the most powerful kingdom in existence."

"And what is it that's so awful about these people?"

"Draco is host to a most terrible people. Ophidians, they are called—notorious blood drinkers and cannibals. They are beautiful in both form and figure, but deadly, and powerful too. Their king, or 'the Cobra' as they call their ruler, is an ophidian known as Samael, who wishes to cleanse Voiler of all magic and to slay anyone who wields supernatural power, which happens to be a significant portion of our world."

"And he's overpowering this city of Polaris?"

Staccato nodded his head. "When the King of Ursa died, thirty-five years ago, Draco was given stewardship of the country."

"Didn't the King have an heir to succeed him?"

"He did."

Pasha glared at him impatiently. "Well, where is he now? Did he die or something?"

"No. He's standing right in front of me."

Pasha looked over his shoulder. Faina and Katya stared back at him. He turned to Staccato, whose gaze was fixed on Pasha. Pasha's eyes grew wide.

"Wait, no, no, no! I'm an American! We don't do monarchies. Besides, I know my father. He was a baron, not a king! You said it yourself, my father's family goes back generations!"

Staccato examined the armillary sphere of his staff in a bored manner.

"Your mother grew up as an orphan in Siberia. What do you know about her family?"

Pasha blanched. The circumstances of his mother's childhood were complex and clouded. What little she had shared, Pasha was sure she had made up to amuse him and his little sister.

"She wasn't an orphan; she had a father, an English man. His name was David Kingsley."

"An adoptive father. Do you know anything about her real parents?"

"Well, her mother's name was . . ." Pasha stopped.

"Go on," Staccato prompted him.

"Evangeline."

"Precisely. Lydia Chevalsky née Kingsley was born Lydia Northstar. She is the only child of King Bruin and Queen Evangeline. After the death of her parents, Lydia's family decided that, in order to keep your mother safe from her enemies, she had to leave Voiler. Lydia was taken to Russia and put up for adoption, while the Voilerian public was told she'd died. You are her firstborn son."

Pasha swept the hat from his head and squeezed it in his hand.

"So the Firebird wants me to catch her because I'm supposedly the heir to some ancient throne? What happens if I catch her?"

"If you catch the Firebird you will be granted one wish. It doesn't matter what you wish for as long as Samael doesn't catch it."

"Why can't someone else catch it?"

"The Firebird has chosen two competitors. You and Samael. Only one of you can catch her. Only one of you can make the wish. That's how it works."

Pasha's brain felt like a lead weight inside his skull, and it was troublesome to keep upright. He wished he could sit, or better still, lie down. There was too much to think about: firebirds, magic, and kings.

Klokov was probably waiting outside his tenement building with a revolver. Pasha didn't even know where he would sleep that night. He couldn't go home.

Staccato cleared his throat.

"Pasha, I'm here to make you an offer. I believe the two of us can help each other, provide each other with something the other one needs. You see, the whole circus business, it's actually a front for something much more important. In reality, I'm the head of a resistance. The band of gypsies are really a band of government-hired mercenaries bent on stopping Samael from slaughtering the Fay. To do that, I need you. And you need to find a way to disappear. If you agree to come with me to Voiler and catch the Firebird, I will pay you, and far more than what you're used to getting paid. And at the end of this endeavor, should you wish to relocate your family to Voiler and take back the throne, we will arrange that. Or if you'd prefer, you can pass up the throne and start over somewhere in America, or Voiler, or anywhere in the world."

Faina and Katya anchored their eyes on Pasha. At last he sighed.

"Alright, when do we leave?"

Staccato's mouth slid into a furtive but satisfied smirk.

"Meet us here at Grand Central at eight tomorrow. I'm sure I needn't warn you not to share any of this with your mother."

Pasha scoffed. "It goes without saying."

"Don't forget to pack. Oh, and don't worry about Klokov finding you tonight. We've taken care of that."

Pasha's eyes bulged.

"Taken care of?" How many times had he heard that phrase? "You didn't—"

Staccato threw back his head and laughed. "He's not 'sleeping with the fishes,' if that's what you mean. Still, you will need to be careful on your way over in the morning. Go home and rest, you have nothing to fear."

Chapter 12:
The Mermaid in the Wheelchair

The platform was unusually desolate as Pasha, Faina, and Katya awaited the train home. They spoke very little and when they did, it was in hushed, quiet tones.

"I know you can't say anything about Voiler to your mom," hissed Faina. "But what are you gonna tell her about the Breadwinners?"

Pasha rolled his neck. The thought made his head ache.

"I don't know, but I guess I better come up with something quick."

"Why not tell her the truth?"

"You want me to tell my mother that the Breadwinners are trying to kill me because they think I stole money?"

The corners of her lips wrinkled cynically. "What's the big deal? She already knows you're a Breadwinner."

Pasha looked back at Katya. She was happily occupied watching a bat circling the rafters.

He exhaled. "I know." He threaded his fingers through his hair. Katya gave his sleeve several frantic yanks.

"What is it, *Rybka*?"

"My locket," she cried. "It's gone!"

Pasha dragged his hand across his forehead. "What locket?"

"The locket Papa gave me. I put it on so I'd look nice for the circus, but now it's gone! It must've fallen off!"

Pasha sifted through her curls, thinking it might have gotten stuck in her hair. He pulled back the fold of her collar. Sure enough, it was gone. Pasha felt sick for her.

"Aw geez! Katya is right."

She pulled the hem of his coat back towards the concourse. "We have to go look for it!"

Pasha pinched the bridge of his nose with his fingertips. This was New York City; they would never find it.

A figure appeared over his shoulder at the bottom of the ramp.

"Are you looking for this?"

It was the girl, the aerial ballerina, holding the locket in her right hand. She was sitting in a wheelchair. Pasha glanced down at her wheels in confusion. Without thinking he raised his eyebrows. The girl was a double amputee—her legs stopped below the knee.

Katya sprang towards her. "Yes, that's my locket! I was so worried about it. Thank you!"

The girl placed the necklace gently into Katya's open hand.

"You must be very careful with that. It was given to you by someone very special, wasn't it?" Her accent was very similar to Staccato's.

Katya whipped her head up and down. "My papa. How did you know? Are you a miraculous like Staccato?"

She shook her head 'no' with a modest smile. Her eyes

sparkled with kindness.

"I'm a mermaid," she said at last. "I have a gift called psychometry. It means I can read the history of objects. I can feel the energy coming off of them."

Familiarity came into Katya's eyes. "Of course! You're the mermaid from my dream!" She glanced down at her amputated legs. "But where are your fins?"

"I'm in my human form at the moment. Mermaids can change from one to the other, you see."

As Pasha edged closer, the girl's lips parted in alarm. "Your arm!"

Pasha looked down to the place she was gesturing and spotted the cuts from his brawl with Anastas.

"Oh." Pasha's cheeks colored as he fumbled for an explanation. "It's nothing . . ." But the words faded away as she took his hand and ran her finger over the long, faded ripples of skin. The scars vanished with a faint greenish light.

Pasha's mouth dropped open. His fingers trembled. He tried to speak, but his throat had become so dry he had to peel his tongue from the roof of his mouth.

She noticed the black bruise circling his eye. Gingerly, she reached up and stroked her thumb beneath it. Her fingers were smooth and consoling, like the hands of his mother. As her nail traced his skin, Pasha's muscles un-tightened and the soreness left him. Finally she cupped his cheeks and absorbed the last of the pain.

Pasha touched his face. He felt around for the dried cuts and scabs. They were gone.

"H—how did you do that?"

"Mermaids have healing powers." She smiled simply. "I'm Princess Sonata Soter, by the way, of Karkinos. Your cousin."

Pasha's eyes popped open. "My cousin?"

Sonata giggled with a sheepish grin. "Well, second-cousin. Half-cousins. Your grandmother, Evangeline, was my father's half-sister. They had different mothers."

Pasha flexed his lip. So they were related! That feeling of strange kinship, that familial sensation in his chest, it was as though something inside him had known. Pasha laughed.

"Well, I guess you know who I am then."

She shrugged. "I wouldn't be here if I didn't."

Pasha went on to introduce Katya and Faina. Katya, of course, was enamored with Sonata.

"You have dimples, just like me!"

Sonata's eyes lit up with amusement. "That's right, I do."

Katya glanced down at Sonata's knees, and before Pasha could stop her, she was asking the dreaded question.

"Sonata, what happened to your legs?"

Pasha's face turned bright red as he yanked Katya back and slammed a hand over her mouth.

"Katya! You can't ask her that! That's rude! I'm so sorry, she hasn't had much social interaction before now."

Katya pried Pasha's hand off her mouth.

"Don't talk about me like I'm crazy!" She turned back to Sonata. "I didn't mean to be rude. It's just, you had legs during the performance when you were sitting on that hoop."

Sonata threw back her head and laughed. It was a simple, pleasant sound for a princess, absent of superiority and airs.

"It's quite alright." She took Katya's hand once more. "When I was fourteen, I was kidnapped by some very bad men, and they cut my legs off."

Pasha hadn't expected such a brutal explanation.

"Why?" inquired Katya.

Pasha squeezed her shoulder. "Katya . . ."

But Katya ignored him. "Were they ophidians?"

Sonata nodded. "Some of them were." She addressed Pasha and Faina now. "They were a band of radicals from Draco, followers of Samael. They call themselves the Children of Nachesh, or, the C.O.N."

An intense breeze stirred up around them as the train came barreling into the station. Sonata backed up her wheels.

"Well, you three better get home. You'll want to rest before tomorrow."

She bade them each goodnight, and wheeled herself back

towards the concourse. She looked back at them over her shoulder and gave a wink, her lips glowing with an unconditional sweetness. She disappeared around the corner.

Chapter 13:
A Little Faith

"I promised Papa I would take care of you and Katya!" Pasha's voice rang through the thin walls as he slammed the door to his bedroom.

Lydia pounded down the hallway, swung open the door, and pointed an irate finger in his face. "You are my son! It is my job to take care of you, not the other way around!"

Pasha threw out his arms in exasperation. "Well, what are you gonna do? Lock me in my room so they can come and shoot me?"

Lydia's hands shook up around her head as though she would tear her ears off.

"Don't—don't say such things!"

She collapsed to a chair and bawled into her arms. Pasha wrung his hands through his hair and knelt at his mother's feet.

"I'm sorry, Ma!" He reached for her hands. "I know you're scared something is gonna happen to me, but that's why I gotta leave."

Lydia wiped her tears with the back of her hand and looked down at her son. Pasha hugged her legs. He laid his cheek on her knees and smiled up at her. Apparently, this was too much for her to bear. To Pasha's surprise, she shuddered away from him and fled the room in a second wave of tears. Her door slammed. Pasha could hear her wailing into her mattress. He cradled his head in his hands and dug his fingernails into his temples to keep from crying.

When he was sure he had composed himself, he climbed onto the fire escape. Faina was waiting cross-legged in front of her window.

Pasha covered his eyes. “Did you hear all that?”

Faina rested her chin on the bar as she popped her lips. “Yeah. She didn’t take it very well, did she?”

Pasha slumped against the wall with his face buried in his hands. “She’s crying.” He hugged his knees to his chest. His shoulders heaved. He listened as Faina climbed down into the courtyard and ascended his side of the building. He felt her presence beside him. She put an arm around his shoulder.

“I didn’t want to believe the Firebird was real.” He lifted his head slightly. “Why? It’s not that I find it hard to believe . . . it’s that I didn’t want to. I didn’t used to be that way.”

“No. You didn’t used to be that way.”

“What happened to me?”

Faina hesitated. He could sense the pages of her mind turning. At last, she spoke.

“You’re protecting yourself from being disappointed. If you don’t expect anything good to happen you can’t be hurt when things go wrong. Trouble is, I think we all have the power to fulfill our own expectations, whether good or bad.”

“You think I’m cursing myself by having so little faith?”

“No, I think you’re cursing yourself by putting your faith in the wrong things. No matter what, you always have faith in something, even if you put your faith in nothing."

"That's assuming faith has the power to do anything at all."

"It does. Haven't you ever heard of a self-fulfilling prophecy?"

Pasha scrutinized her with a hard eye. "So, you're saying if you believe in something hard enough it's more likely to happen?"

Faina shrugged. "That's what faith is, it's confidence in your expectations. So, as long as you expect things to go wrong, they will. I'm not saying it's that way all the time, but I do think it's possible some people work themselves into that situation, and I believe that's what you're in danger of."

Pasha sat up. They leaned on each other's shoulders.

Faina's voice grew softer. "When will you be back?"

"I don't know." Pasha rubbed his chin. "I won't let it go too long without coming back to see you."

Faina reached into her pocket and placed something small and cool in Pasha's palm. Pasha looked down. He threw back his head and laughed.

"Our lucky penny."

Faina managed a faint smile. "Mhm. The one we found flattened by the train tracks in Grand Central. I want you to take it with you."

"For luck?"

"For luck, and so you'll remember to come back for me. Call it a symbol of your promise. I'll be sure to leave you some baklava on the fire escape tomorrow morning to take with you, since you have to miss Thanksgiving and all."

Pasha tugged a lock of her hair and pulled her into a tight hug. "I'll miss you while I'm away."

Her answer was muffled into his collar.

"You'll take Katya to the parade in the morning?"

He felt her nod beneath his chin. Faina sniffed. Her shoulders trembled. Tears flooded onto his clothes. Pasha's lips parted to say something but he could not think of any words. He laid his cheek on the top of her head and let her sob.

Chapter 14:
The El Train

When it was time for Pasha to leave, his mother was reluctant to let him out of the apartment. She would hardly let go of him all through breakfast.

"Ma, I'm gonna be late," Pasha insisted as Lydia continued to pin him to her chest.

"Now you know it is bad luck if you don't take time to sit down before a journey."

"But we've been sitting here for ten minutes!"

It was just the two of them in the apartment. Katya and Faina had already left to snag a place at the front of the crowd for the parade and had taken Mammoth with them. Pasha had said farewell to his sister, but Faina did not come to say goodbye a second time. Pasha didn't mind. Knowing Faina, it would've been too painful to go through it again.

He finally managed to wriggle out of his mother's grasp and put his dishes in the sink. "It's a traveling gypsy circus, what's the worst that could happen?"

As he began rinsing off his plate, he glanced back at her over his shoulder. If he had to lie to her, it was best to tell as much of the truth as possible. She wasn't looking suspicious so far. Her eyes remained far off and sad, and he wasn't altogether sure she was paying attention.

"And after I've helped them out for a little while," he continued, "I can go off and find a suitable place to settle. Somewhere we can start over, and I'll send for you."

The chair scraped the floor as Lydia rose and turned him around to face her.

"And how long will that be?"

Pasha shrugged hopefully. "Not too long."

Lydia sighed and raked her fingers through his bangs. Pasha didn't stop her. Instead he closed his eyes and savored the moment. It would be a long time before he felt her soothing touch again. At last he sighed.

"I gotta go, Ma." He retrieved his coat and hat from the hook by the door, and hastily threw them on. Lydia followed staring at him in pained silence.

"I'll be fine," he reassured her as they stood in the doorway. Pasha threw his arms around her neck. He could feel her hands shaking. He squeezed her tighter. "I love you, Mama."

"I love you too, my sweet boy."

Lydia brought both his hands up to her face and kissed the inside of his left wrist. Pasha knew it was silly, but he couldn't help but feel incredibly happy whenever she gave him this special kiss.

Pasha set out for Grand Central with his cap pulled down low over his brow. The platform at Bowery Station was crammed with people eager to reach the Macy's Parade. Pasha felt both exposed and protected. It would be easy to go unseen amongst so many bodies, and yet anyone could've been a part of the crowd.

As the thought passed through his brain, a terrible blast split the air. A lightbulb shattered overhead. People screamed and shoved each other out of the way.

Pasha wheeled around. There was Anastas, wielding a revolver in his direction.

"There he is," he shouted over the din, "get him!"

Pasha's knees kicked into action. He ran up the wall of the staircase, swung over the banister, and headed left down Bowery Street. He made a beeline for every obstacle to slow down his pursuers like Leo had taught him. He vaulted over every trashcan. He ran down every bench. He jumped onto the hoods of cars. Guns fired in his wake.

When Pasha made it back to the sidewalk, a stray bullet struck a streetlamp, encasing him in a shower of broken glass. Covering his eyes, Pasha tripped backward into the open window of the Sweet and Savory. His legs flew up over his head as he somersaulted beneath a table. His head slammed against the spiky red heel of a woman's shoe. Pasha's ears stung as the lady let out a shriek. He tripped out from beneath the table, nearly turning it over.

"Excuse me, ma'am!"

Outside, a crowd of Breadwinners dominoed at the door as the manager barred them from entering.

"You're trespassing on Butcher territory! No Breadwinners allowed!"

Pasha swung up the stairwell, his heart twisting inside his chest. He needed to get to a fire escape or rooftop. As long as he stayed off the streets, he might lose them.

He launched himself through the first unlocked door he could find, and straight into a brothel. Paying no mind to the scantily clad ladies, he frantically searched for a window.

"Where you going handsome?"

"Yeah, what's your rush?"

"Sorry, kinda busy." He ducked beneath a canopy of lace. The room shook as a stampede of pursuers pounded up the staircase. Doors slammed below. It was only a matter of time before they found him.

Pasha spun in a circle. Curtains and sheets plastered the walls. Where was the window?

A shawl roped around his neck, and his head fell into the lap of a woman caked in rouge.

"Is there something I can help you with?"

Pasha shrugged. Might as well ask. "Yeah, can you take me to the roof?"

She tossed her head and laughed. "Adventurous, aren't we?" She traced a fingernail beneath his chin. Pasha turned bright red and tried to raise up.

"No, you don't understand—"

"That'll cost you five extra." She pushed him back down.

"No, you don't get it, I don't have any money."

The woman flung Pasha out of her lap with disgust. With her painted talons she latched onto his ear and dragged him towards a window hidden behind a pink curtain. She opened the latch.

"No money, no deal." She pushed him onto the fire escape and slammed the glass.

Pasha's head hung out over the alleyway.

"Well, that worked out." As he stood, his hands felt strangely empty. His face went white. He turned around and banged on the window.

"Wait, I forgot my—" The glass swung open as he was almost knocked in the head with his suitcase. "Thank you!"

Above him, the metal beams of the El Train track began to rattle. He climbed to the rooftop. At the top of the Sweet and Savory, the wind plowed across Pasha's cheeks and tugged at the tail of his coat. The Third Avenue El Train chugged over the Bowery one story below. He lifted his foot over the railing.

A force knocked him off his feet and sent him sailing onto the landing beneath him. Pain throbbed through his back. He tried to get up but winced.

The fire escape shuddered as someone large and monstrous bounded over the hem of the rooftop and landed with his boots framing Pasha's head. Pasha squinted his eyes. There, eclipsing the bright morning sun, was the figure of Anastas. He pointed the barrel of his revolver at Pasha's forehead and cocked the gun into place.

"Anastas," Pasha's chest pounded with dread, "don't do this."

Anastas gave a crude snort of a laugh and inched the barrel closer.

"Aren't you sick of getting compared to your parents?" The metal felt cold against Pasha's forehead. "You said it yourself, you've tried to distance yourself from their reputation. That's why you joined the Breadwinners and not the Butchers. If you kill me, then people are gonna say you're just like them."

"You wanna know something funny, Chevalsky? I am like them! You've said it all along. Now it's the truth."

Anastas dug his finger into the trigger. Pasha grabbed him by the wrist with both hands and, mustering all his strength, pushed up. The sound of the gun split his ears. Anastas stumbled backward, and the revolver went flying into the streets below. Without thinking, Pasha rolled off of the fire escape and slammed onto the tracks of the approaching El Train. The shrill whistle set his teeth on edge. He got up to run, but Anastas sprang on him from above. He throttled Pasha to the ground. Anastas jammed his hand around Pasha's throat with unbearable pressure.

"You think you can guilt me into letting you walk free?" His teeth ground shut. He spat as he hissed. "Believe me, it will be a pleasure to have your blood on my hands."

Choking, Pasha thrust his fist upwards across Anastas's nose. Instinctively, Anastas recoiled and let go. Pasha wasted no time. He ran in the opposite direction. But Anastas was determined. He dove for Pasha's ankles and dragged him to the edge of the track. Pasha could feel the earth quaking beneath him as Anastas pinned his head to the outer rail.

"Are you insane?" Pasha's voice competed against the roaring volume of the locomotive.

There was a violent sheen filming Anastas's eyes. Pasha struggled to get lose, but Anastas was too strong. As the train drew closer, the jarring of the tracks banged Pasha's skull and rattled his teeth.

For some reason, Pasha felt the tail feather of the Firebird calling to him from his pocket, begging to be released. It burned through the fabric of his coat and heated his skin. He didn't know where the impulse came from, but he had to retrieve it.

"It's in my pocket," Pasha blurted.

Anastas did a double-take, looking him up and down as though he had lost his mind.

"What?"

"The name and address of the place where I got the gems after you stole our stash, it's in my pocket!"

He stared into Anastas's eyes, willing him to take the bait. There was a glimmer of relent. Sneering, Anastas kept his dominant hand pinned to Pasha's throat and reached into his pocket. Pasha's heart pounded in horror as the monstrous silhouette of the train appeared in the corner of his eye.

An anguished cry ripped from Anastas's throat as he wrenched away from Pasha. The Firebird feather had burnt a perfect impression into the back of his hand. His skin pulsed with the odor of burned flesh.

Pasha rolled off the track just as the train came barreling towards them. He ran after the locomotive. Grabbing the handle of one of the cars, he swung his foot onto the coupler and pulled himself up. He climbed to the roof.

At the top, Pasha looked out over the adjoining track. He expected to see Anastas on his knees, swearing revenge, but he was nowhere to be found. Maybe Pasha had missed him. They were moving at an awfully swift pace after all.

As he was turning around, a fist swung into the side of his face. Pasha went sliding across the top of the car. The Bowery stretched below him in a generous and unforgiving drop. Anastas made his way over the top of the train.

A familiar face popped over the side of the roof and smiled at Pasha.

"Hello, Pasha! Happy Thanksmitzvah!"

Pasha jumped. It was Pyro Anomaly.

"You know, you really shouldn't sit so close to the edge." Pyro pushed Pasha up to a seated position. "That'd be a right nasty fall." Clinging to the edge of the train, Pyro ducked down and called to someone in the streets below. "Sonata, I found him!"

Before Pasha could reply, he was seized by the ankles. Anastas hurled him to the end of the car. His chin struck metal. Anastas grabbed him by the back of his collar. He hooked his arm around Pasha's throat. A knife pressed against his neck. Pasha clawed at his arm.

Pyro swung himself onto the roof, his shoulders thrown back, ready to fight. He took one look at Anastas and frowned.

"Aw, hellfire, Pasha! When Staccato said you might be in trouble, I was expecting experienced thugs! I can't strike a kid, that's a serious offense!"

"*Yemu vosemnadtsat'*!" Pasha sputtered.

Pyro cocked his head to one side. "What?"

Pasha cringed. "He's eighteen summers!"

Pyro gaped at him. "What in the blazes are you talking about?"

"He just turned eighteen!"

Pyro shrugged his shoulders. "Fair enough." Reaching into his coat, Pyro retrieved a chakra—a sharp, metal disc. He flexed his arm and a flame ran up from his hands to the weapon. He chucked it at Anastas's arm, leaving a fiery incision in his sleeve. Anastas dropped the knife, which skidded off the side of the train and onto the tracks.

Anastas was defenseless, his sleeve ablaze. He flailed about desperately, slapping his arm, snuffing out the charring flare. Pyro surged across the car. He grabbed Anastas by the scruff of the neck and tossed him off the train.

Down through the air Anastas flew. There was a terrible ripping noise as his body tore through the awning of a flower stand, and he landed safely in a pile of chrysanthemums.

Pyro's hand flinched over his mouth. "It didn't break for that fella in the pictures!"

Pasha shrugged. "He's alright."

Before Pyro could reply, a bullet ripped past their heads.

Klokov had latched onto the side of the train and was now climbing over the roof of the engine. He took aim again. Pyro threw himself in front of Pasha. With supernatural precision, he blocked the hit with the rim of his chakra. Pyro tossed the ring at Klokov. The firearm knocked from his grasp.

Klokov lurched into a standing position. Pyro lunged across the car, chakra raised. Klokov blocked him and, with his free hand, forced his fist into Pyro's abdomen. Pyro staggered but soon recovered. He fell back on his haunches, rocked back and bucked Klokov in the stomach. Klokov stumbled backward, clutching his injury. Pyro sprang back to his feet.

"Pasha, I need you to jump!"

Pasha's eyes bulged. "Jump? Jump to what?"

"The horse!"

"What horse?"

"Pasha," a feminine voice called from down below. Pasha peered over the edge. It was Sonata, clinging to the back of a white mare, a pair of diamond-like prosthetic legs on each side. Pasha's eyes came alive with fear.

"It's too far! There's no way—"

A pair of enormous feathery wings emerged from the horse's shoulders, and they lighted into the air.

Pasha's jaw dropped. "You have a pegasus." He shrugged. "Never mind."

The moment Sonata was close enough, Pasha dove over the edge of the cart and landed in the saddle. A little girl pointed at them from the street below.

"Mommy, look! It's a flying horse!"

The girl's mother patted her head and smiled. "I see, dear, it must be from the Macy's Parade."

Pasha's eyebrow crept up his forehead in a comical expression. This woman thought it was all part of the parade. A flying horse! It had been so easy for her to dismiss the spectacle as an illusion! His cheeks burned with shame. How silly he must have sounded to Faina when he dismissed the Firebird, the snowstorm, and everything that had followed.

He watched as Sonata leaned down and whispered something into the horse's ear. The mare swooped back down to the pavement below.

Pasha looked back at the train. Pyro was about to throw another chakra when Klokov came barreling towards him like an angry rhinoceros. He thrust his head into Pyro's skull, propelling him backward over the edge of the train.

Pyro caught himself on the ledge. He hung suspended over them. Sonata spurred her horse to keep up.

"Let go!" she hollered. "We'll catch you!"

Pyro shook his head. "No way! It's personal now!" He swung himself upward in an arc to the roof.

Sonata sighed and shook her head. "Show-off!"

A shrill police whistle sliced through the air, causing them to jump.

"Hey, you two!"

Pasha and Sonata tensed with fear as she forced the horse to a stop and turned around. Their breath dammed at the back of their throat as a smart-looking officer on a chestnut Clydesdale trotted towards them.

"Ain't you two with the parade?"

Pasha felt the tension coil down Sonata's muscles and release her. Lifting her chin a little, she cleared her throat and looked him in the eye.

"Yes, as a matter of fact, we are."

"Well, I hate to break it to you, ma'am, but the parade has

already started. I'm afraid you're gonna be a little late. But if you want, I can offer you a police escort to Herald Square."

Pasha looked back at the El Train. He could make out the remnants of Pyro's flames as they headed up Third Avenue. Sonata tossed her hair over her shoulder and put on her most winning smile.

"That would be wonderful! Thank you so much, Officer!"

"My pleasure. By the way, that's a fine horse you got there. Makes a very convincing pegasus. She an Arabian?"

Sonata waved a hand. "Why yes, as a matter of fact, she is! Her name is Scheherazade. You must have an eye for breeding."

Turning his head away, Pasha leaned forward and whispered, "What about Pyro? That track runs out at 129th, you know."

"Relax, he'll catch up, trust me."

Herald Square was jammed with a collage of cloches and fedoras in autumnal shades of scarlet, goldenrod, and beaver. Mothers bounced little girls in their arms. Fathers carried sons on their shoulders. The parade was still somewhere up Broadway, but Pasha could hear the joyous shouts and pounding music thundering across the crowd. Sonata thanked the officer and, pulling on the reins, led them into the crowd on the corner of Sixth Avenue.

Pasha reached under his cap to claw through his bangs. "What do we do now?"

"We have to get to Grand Central. Staccato is waiting for us."

A massive shadow of a man in a fedora eclipsed them,

blocking the sun and turning the air to a bitter, stone chill. Pasha gasped in fright, but Sonata, unfazed, nodded her head and smiled.

"Hello, Melodious."

The man removed his fedora. It was the seven-foot-tall accordion player, the one that in Katya's dream had been blind.

"When you did not arrive at Grand Central, Staccato sent me out to look for you." His accent caught in Pasha's ear and took him by surprise. He was a German. "Is Pyro with you?"

"I'm afraid not. Got caught up in a bit of a challenge, as usual. He'll be fine."

"But you have the boy." Melodious strode forward, his enormous hand stretched out in greeting. "Forgive me, Pasha, I do not think we have formally met. My name is Melodious Krüner."

Pasha's hand felt infantile as Melodious encased it in a hearty handshake. His small, narrow eyes hid beneath a pair of bushy eyebrows. They were pale, unfocused.

"Pleased to meet you."

Melodious doffed his fedora once more. "Well, we'd best be on our way before Staccato worries anymore."

He reached for the reins of Sonata's horse, but Pasha stopped them.

"We can't just walk out into the street. Not without a police escort." Pasha pointed to a man with a fur hat across the road. "You see that man? That's Boris Smirnov, the big guns. He works for

Klokov. By the looks of it, he's armed and keeping an eye out for me. I bet you anything there's another right across from him. Three total is the standard."

He squinted farther down the street, and there, as he'd guessed, was a young Breadwinner right in front of Macy's multi-story window display.

"Ah, see? That's Anton Solokov. He's new, but they say he's one of the best foot soldiers of the Lower East Side." Bending his head around the corner, he spied the final predator. "Denis Moroz. These days he's not as threatening as Smirnov or Solokov, being an older man with a family and all. But his history serving the Breadwinners is legendary."

Sonata bit her lip. "And we can't fly out in front of all these people either. We may have been able to get away with it on the Bowery, but there are reporters and photographers here."

As Pasha settled himself into a spell of dire contemplation, someone smacked him on the back of the head. It was Faina, dressed for the parade in her nice coat and red tam. Beside her was Katya, dwarfed by Faina's fluffy, six-foot, bear-like dog.

"What are you doing here? You were supposed to be at Grand Central Station an hour ago! This place is crawling with Breadwinners, all on the lookout for you!"

"Well, Happy Thanksgiving to you too," Pasha spat sarcastically. "I hope you're enjoying the parade, because for the past hour I've been running around trying not to get shot!"

Faina's cheeks blanched. "They shot at you?"

"Yes!" He glanced at Katya. "And for goodness' sake, cover her ears!"

Faina rolled her eyes and muffled Katya's hearing with her jacket cuffs.

Pasha pointed into the crowd. "To get to Grand Central we have to cross through here without being seen by Klokov's sentries."

"We'll arrange a distraction. Let me be a decoy."

Pasha gave a cynical scoff. "You're gonna distract all three of Klokov's guards stationed on different parts of the street?"

"Not all three," insisted Melodious. "Allow me to assist. Give me 'the big guns,' as you say."

Faina rubbed her hands together. "Leave Solokov to my feminine charms. As for Moroz, let Katya and Mammoth deal with him."

Pasha gawked at her. "Have you lost your mind? We can't involve my little sister! She's nine years old!"

"Pasha, she said herself she knew about the Breadwinners. Besides, it's expressly forbidden for a Breadwinner to harm a woman or child. Add to the fact Moroz is just an old grandfather now, and Katya's the perfect fit! He'll be a sucker for her!"

Sonata prodded Pasha with her elbow. "Faina is right. At this point, it's our best bet."

Pasha drew a long sigh through his nose and pinched his forehead. “Fine. Just don’t do anything reckless, okay?”

And huddling together, they concocted a diversion. Minutes later Melodious was sidling next to Smirnov, his hands folded calmly in front of him. Faina sauntered girlishly past Solokov and pretended to trip into his arms. Solokov swung to catch her, resting his hand on the small of her back.

“You alright, Miss?”

“Oh my,” she exclaimed, “I’m so sorry, I didn’t see you there.” Faina tilted her head and put on a smoldering Clara Bow pout. “But, to be honest, with a face that handsome I’m not sure how I missed you.”

Pasha resisted the temptation to laugh out loud as he watched Faina slip her hand into Solokov’s coat pocket and retrieve his pistol. He never noticed a thing.

Meanwhile, Katya and Mammoth approached Moroz with wide, innocent eyes, and a scroll of crocodile tears.

“Excuse me, sir? Can you please help me? I can’t find my Mama.”

Moroz whipped out his handkerchief and knelt down to dry her tears. Sonata whispered to her horse, and the wings shrank back to invisibility. She swept her eyes across the street one last time.

“Alright, let’s go.”

Pasha turned up his collar and pulled his cap down low. The slow clip-clop of Scheherazade’s hooves seemed to beat out the rhythm of an executioner's march. They grazed past Faina and Solokov.

"Wait a minute!" The rise in Solokov's voice sent a current of chills through Pasha's veins. "You're that broad who's always hanging round Chevalsky! Hey, wait a second—"

There was a flurry of motion as Faina shoved Solokov away. She ran towards Pasha, holding the pistol aloft.

"Pasha! Catch!"

Everything seemed to move in slow motion as the firearm tumbled carelessly through the morning breeze. Pasha reached for the gun. He caught it in his right hand.

"Smirnov!" Solokov hollered. "Look alive!"

Peeling back his trench, Smirnov uncovered a shining, polished twelve gauge. He took aim at Pasha's head. The moment he laid his finger on the trigger, Melodious ripped the gun from his hands and twisted the barrel like a balloon animal.

"Tell me, *mein* friend, have you made your peace with God?"

Smirnov stared at him in disbelief. "No."

"Then I suggest you stay out of my way."

Melodious conked him over the head with the firearm, knocking him out cold. Katya's voice rang over the din.

"No! That's my brother, you bully!"

Moroz was barreling towards them, clutching a revolver. Katya was hanging from his elbow. Before Pasha could react, Mammoth sprang forward and latched onto Moroz's right arm. The revolver shot into the sky. Spooked, Scheherazade reared up on her back legs, causing Pasha to fall from the saddle and onto the pavement. Solokov's gun spun across the asphalt and fell down a storm drain.

Solokov spotted Pasha and bolted towards him. Faina dashed down the sidewalk, grabbed Katya's arm, and reached for Mammoth's leash.

"Heel, Mammoth! That'll do!" She turned to Pasha. "What are you doing? Run! Run!"

Solokov was mere feet away now. His hand reached for Pasha's collar. The air began to sparkle with an illuminating, red heat. A stream of feathery fire came whistling down Broadway. It was the Firebird.

The crowds clapped and shouted in awe, mistaking the phenomenon for fireworks. The Firebird seized Solokov's collar with her talons and carried him thirty feet down the road, depositing him in a dumpster. Pasha scrambled to his feet. Melodious reappeared, threw Katya over his shoulder, and spurred Pasha and Faina forward.

"Run, children, run!"

And with Melodious prodding them along, they left Herald Square and sped off towards Grand Central.

***

The clock above Grand Central Station ticked in the shadow of Mercury's enormous wings. Sonata stood beneath the viaduct.

Scheherazade was absent.

"What happened? I thought you were right behind me."

Melodious urged them through the sparkling glass doors. "No time to explain." They made their way through the foyer and out into the gilded concourse.

Sonata removed her gloves one finger at a time. "I had Scheherazade escorted to the gateway, and it's time we do the same." She stopped in front of an empty ticket booth. "We'll let you say your farewells, Pasha."

Pasha kissed his little sister goodbye, reminding her that the morning's events were to be kept a secret from Mama. When he finished, he turned and embraced Faina.

"Promise me you won't do anything dangerous or stupid while I'm gone." He struggled to laugh. "I don't want anything happening to my best friend."

Faina squeezed him tighter. "Be safe. You better come back for me."

"You know I will."

"Thieves' Honor?"

Pasha leaned his cheek closer to hers. "Thieves' Honor."

As they pulled away, a light flickered on inside the ticket booth and the bars of the window grew to the size of a doorway. It was no longer a ticket counter but an elevator. The door rolled back, and an odd-looking porter with great flowery horns stuck his head out.

"All set to go, Your Highness?" He directed his gaze towards Sonata.

Pasha's eyes snapped open. He looked around. None of the pedestrians seemed to notice the newly materialized lift or the horned man awaiting them.

"Why, thank you, Mr. Oakley. I believe we are."

Sonata took his hand as he slid the gate open further. Faina and Katya gaped in amazement. Melodious and Sonata took their places inside the lift. Mr. Oakley looked expectantly at Pasha.

"Well, kid, you coming or not?"

Pasha balked for another moment or two. Blinking, he nodded his head with his mouth open.

"Uh, yeah, yes, sir."

He stumbled onto the platform. Mr. Oakley shook his head.

"Kid acts like he's never seen a sylph before."

Pasha gave Katya and Faina a little wave as the sylph rolled back the panel, and they disappeared.

Chapter 15:
The Gateway

It was the longest elevator ride Pasha had ever taken. The air grew frigid as they descended deep into the cold, coppery depths of Manhattan Island. Two minutes passed before the lift finally slowed to a halt.

"Soter Hall," announced Mr. Oakley. "First commissioned in 1890 by King Thessalos of Karkinos for Voilerian migration."

Sonata touched Pasha on the forearm. "That's our Uncle, Pasha. My father took the throne after Thessalos stepped down in 1894."

Pasha flexed his lip. "There's something you don't hear on the walking tours."

The gilded bars drew back upon an enormous three-story platform. Four blown-glass chandeliers hung from the scaffolding. Each was the size of a taxicab. Numerous Voilerian travel posters plastered the pillars. Pasha's eye drew to the advertisement for Monoceros. In the picture, a herd of unicorns in soft pastel colors stampeded through a white meadow scintillating with snow.

Staccato was standing with his back turned before an elephantine locomotive. Meanwhile, two porters loaded up the last of the luggage. The first had wings like Angelo, only smaller and of a silky, black color. The second was an ordinary-looking man who moved things telekinetically with the aid of a staff.

"Is that everything, Mr. Nimbus?"

Staccato's attention was fixed in the direction of a large opal clock a few feet away. The timepiece was flanked by four mermaid statues hewn from limestone. Two were women and two were men. Pasha watched as Staccato's eyes snagged on the hand of the mermaid with long, wavy hair resting her chin on the outside of the clock. His lips pursed into a hard line. A muscle in his eyebrow twitched. He tore a handkerchief from his pocket and chafed it across an invisible spot of dirt on the mermaid's fingernails. The porter raised an eyebrow.

"Mr. Nimbus?"

Staccato jumped and turned. "Hm? Oh, uh, yes, yes. That will be all, thank you."

Reaching into the folds of his jacket he handed them each a generous tip. He caught sight of the three over his shoulder.

"Ah! There you are! I was beginning to worry." He squeezed Sonata's hand and drew her forward. "When you didn't show up with Pasha I sent Melodious out to look for you."

Pyro jumped down from the observation deck where he had been lurking. "There's an idea! Send the blind man to go looking for someone!" His tie was undone, and the top buttons of his shirt and waistcoat opened upon a fresh bruise. His face was marred with a few bumps and scratches but for the most part, he was unharmed.

Melodious crossed his heavily muscled arms. "I am a Moira, endowed with superior senses and short-term foresight. Loss of vision is of little consequence to me. After all," he knit his brows together and raised a philosophical finger, "God uses the weak to shame the strong—"

Pyro waved his hands. "Yes, alright, Preacher Man, I was only teasing."

Staccato lifted his nose into the air. "I wouldn't have had to send Melodious out looking, Pyro, if you hadn't lost focus. Your instructions were to find Pasha and deliver him safely to Grand Central. And what do you do instead? You get caught up in a showdown with some thug!"

Pyro rolled his shoulders. "Aw, come on, Staccato! You should've seen that coming. You know I can't resist a tussle."

Sonata circled him like an upset mother hen.

"Just look at you!" She snatched Pyro's arm and set to work absorbing his injuries. "You're bruised all over!"

Pyro thrust out his chin and smiled. "Adds to my roguish good looks, don't you think?"

Sonata smacked the back of his head.

"Ow!" Pyro pushed out his lower lip. "Well, what about Skelter? Why didn't you send him?"

Staccato heaved a sigh. "Skelter had his own problems, I'm afraid."

Skelter popped his head out the window of the car and looked around. His bright, curious eyes flew towards Pasha. His mouth spread into a jubilated grin as he wagged his hand back and forth like the tail of an overly excited puppy. He was in such a hurry to get out and greet Pasha, he turned and slammed his head into the window.

Pyro rolled his eyes. "What happened, Skelly? Did you see another dog?" He glanced back at Pasha. "He likes dogs. Well, all animals really."

There was an odd sense of grace in the way Skelter staggered towards Pasha on his long legs, constantly tripping but never falling. Skelter grabbed his hand and yanked him forward in an exuberant handshake. He was the type of person who loved everybody no matter who they were. You could see it in the way his eyes collected in your every detail. His long, thin fingers spread wide when he waved, just like his smile, as though they could hold all the joy in the world.

Staccato cleared his throat. "He said he ran into a Horologium Hearth Winder."

Skelter zipped upright and gesticulated wildly. Pasha cast a confused glance towards Staccato, who covered his eyes in an exasperated manner.

"I'm sorry, a Hephastean Hog-Snout."

Pyro threw back his head and sputtered. "A Hephastean Hog-Snout? Here?"

Skelter crossed his arms and gave an emphatic nod. Staccato threw up his shoulders.

"That was precisely my reaction! Everyone knows if you want

to find a Hephastean Hog-Snout you have to go to Oyster Bay, not Manhattan of all places!"

Pasha scratched his chin. It appeared Skelter was mute.

Angelo poked his head out from a booth near the opal clock.

"All set, Mr. Nimbus?"

"Yes, Angelo. You can go ahead and set the dial."

Angelo leaned forward in his chair and reached for a large lever attached to the wall. Pasha turned his head towards the opening of the train tunnel. His pupils shrank as he stumbled backward. It was as though the mouth of the passage had transformed into a window overlooking the heavens. Angelo pulled the lever and the stars spun until they arranged themselves into the pattern of Cepheus.

"You want the station on the north side of Errai?"

Staccato rubbed his handkerchief over the head of his staff. "South side, if you please."

Sonata hooked her arm around Pasha's elbow and led him towards the car.

"We better go ahead and board."

Pasha's eyes darted around the platform. "But what happened to your pegasus? And the wagon?"

A whinny from an oversized carriage at the back of the line answered his question. Sonata giggled and spurred him forward. "Staccato always sees that the pegasi travel in style."

"Pegasi?" Pasha repeated in wonder. "You have more than

one?"

"Well, something has to pull the caravan. We have four in all. Staccato's Aquarian Star Trotter, Lancelot; Pyro's Miranian Blue, Brash; Melodious's Herculean Musclehoof, Shmetterling; and Scheherazade who is in fact, not an Arabian, but an Altairian Shooting Star."

They each took a seat inside the first compartment. Pyro reached over Pasha's head and pulled a hand grip down from the ceiling.

"You might wanna hang on to one of these."

Pasha hesitated. "Why? Does it get really rough?"

Before Pyro could answer, Staccato rounded the corner of the compartment. "Alright, everyone brace yourselves." He took the seat beside Sonata.

Pyro dropped his voice lower. "It helps to close your eyes too."

Skelter's lips slid into a cheeky grin as he signed. Pyro knit his eyebrows together.

"I am not a giant-yellow-candied-chicken-liver! Sonata, Skelter is being mean to me!"

Staccato pinched the space between his eyebrows and heaved a sigh. "Oh, do stop whining, Pyro!"

Pasha cocked an eyebrow. "Geez, how bad could—"

The train lurched forward and Pasha's head hammered against his seat. The windows outside went dark and the locomotive ripped upwards at a severe right angle. Pasha shot his hand over his head and seized the handle.

"They call it 'the Leap of Faith,'" explained Melodious.

"Honestly, I think 'the Leap of Terror' would be more appropriate," quipped Staccato.

Pasha sucked in a terrified mouthful of breath and squeezed his eyes shut. Everything went silent.

Chapter 16:
Something Wicked

A moment later, Pasha's nose and head stung with pain. His body felt odd, weightless. He could feel his clothes dragging behind him. He tried to take in a breath, but all he got was a mouthful of salt water. Pasha forced his eyes open. His heart nearly burst from his chest. He didn't know how or why, but he was floating underwater, completely alone. The compartment and his new companions were gone. The train had vanished. The very seat he had been sitting in had disappeared. It was as though he had awoken from a dream only to find himself trapped in a claustrophobic nightmare. And the worst part? Pasha could not swim.

Down through the bubbling, green water he sank. Salt stung his eyes. He reached for the rippling light of the surface suspended over him. He thought he could hear music but he was sure he was just hallucinating in the last moments of his life. Pasha plowed his arms through the space, trying to work against the force, but it seemed of no use. The water was too heavy, too strong, and he feared he had finally come to his end.

As his last bubble of hope was about to burst, the ceiling of water became shaded with red, sparkling radiance. The waves above him shattered into millions of confetti-like bubbles, as something rough and round came racing towards him. A heavy stone rippled past, followed by a rope. It was an old anchor. Pasha grabbed ahold of the cable, and unable to swim his way to the top, he began to climb.

Pasha broke through the waves with a gasp, panicked for air and grateful to see the light again. He spun in a circle, looking for the train, for a ship, for the person who'd saved his life, but all he saw was a vast ocean. As for the anchor, it was fastened to an old, dead tree jutting out from the cliff face. It looked as though it had hung there for a hundred years. Pasha craned his head, trying to see over the top of the bluff.

"Hello?" he called out. "Is anyone there?"

The rope creaked in the wind. No one answered him. He recalled the red light, the subtle whisper of music. Had the Firebird saved him again? Over the course of three days, she had rescued him from several dire situations. A thought occurred to him as he clung shivering to the rope. If the Firebird would go to so many lengths to save Pasha, would she do the same for Samael?

Pasha's teeth chattered. He needed to get out of the water and find shelter. The air was frigid, and at least ten degrees cooler than it had been in New York. Unfortunately, the lower shoreline was too far for Pasha to try and swim to. Instead, he climbed the rock face, using the rope to get him halfway.

At last, he rolled over the ledge and into the grass. All around him was beautiful countryside and shadows of blue mountains. Towering fir trees rose above him with fresh, mossy tree trunks. Strange blue lights hovered in their feathery branches. It was one of the most beautiful places he had ever seen, but still, he was alone.

Pasha sat up and trembled. Further along the coastline was the shadow of a palace. If he could make it there, he could make it to civilization.

He rose to his feet, the weight of his coat resisting the will of his knees. He took one look back at the ocean. It fed endlessly into the horizon without a soul to disturb it.

***

Pasha made it to the city quicker than he expected. With the cold clinging to his shoulders he may have walked faster. Shortly upon arriving, it became clear the town was desolate. There was no sound save for the waves crashing up against the seawall. The gabled windows of the townhouses were dark. The waters in the canals remained still. Scalloped shells tiled the roofs. Many lay broken in the street.

As Pasha observed the motorcars deserted in the road he scratched his head in confusion. Unlike most abandoned cities, this kingdom was far from ancient. The titles displayed in the bookshops were only a decade or so old. Now and again he would come across something magical like a poster advertising dreams, or a trident repair store, but never any people. He pressed on towards the castle.

Several chunks had been ripped out of the filigree domes. Many of the floating blue lights flickered. One side of the castle sank into the ocean so it appeared to be leaning. The gates stood open and unguarded as he entered the rotting estate.

He made his way up the crumbling front steps, stopping to look back at the vast ocean stretched out below him. Amongst the frothing landscape of blue peaks was something he hadn't noticed before. Not far in the distance was a second kingdom, almost Greek in appearance. The castle was filled with open-air pavilions and sturdy Corinthian columns. It had flooded nearly to the top, for several of its towers barely poked up from the waves. Stacks of empty buildings faced each other in a series of drowned roads.

Shrugging, he returned his attention to the front door. Something about the place had an odd sense of familiarity. For a moment Pasha felt as though he were walking through the ashes of the estate in Crimea. The knockers at the entry were shaped like large bear heads and held blue lights in their mouths. A giant gash in the door rendered them useless. Pasha crawled through.

The stone floor of the interior had preserved the frost like a tomb, but at least there was shelter from the wind. Pasha's hands brushed across something shaggy and soft as he breached the threshold. It was an animal skin rug. He crumpled his face against the wooly pelt and felt instant relief from the cold. He watched his sigh billow in an opaque cloud and looked up at the ceiling.

The grand buttresses stretched like branching birch trees over his head. Pulsing, white stars peppered the ceiling. Shredded tapestries of silver bears on a hunter green backdrop dangled from the rafters.

His eyes widened. This was Polaris, the North Star, the capital of Ursa.

But why was it empty? Why was the door ripped to shreds? Why had dust collected on the marble banisters? Why was the city abandoned? According to Staccato, Ursa was supposed to be under Draco's stewardship. So where were they? Hadn't they taken care of it? Wasn't that the job of a steward?

Pasha rose up from the carpet shivering and desperate to explore. He shed his heavy, sodden coat and trembled in the wet linen shirt plastered against his skin. He would dry quicker this way and avoid any rashes.

He took his time up the grand stairwell, leaving a trail of icy water droplets behind him. He wandered down a corridor on the second floor. At the end of the long hallway, the path forked in two different directions. Pasha decided to explore the room at the far left, the one with the enormous double doors. The cherrywood was so dark it was almost black. His reflection appeared in the shine. He brought his thumb down on the latch of the bear-shaped doorknob and pulled open the door.

Inside was a luxurious bedchamber with the lush grandeur of a king. The wide mattress was covered with fur throws. Weighty curtains circled the bed. A side door left ajar drew him to an adjoining dressing room. To Pasha's delight, it was stocked with heavy clothes for a wintery climate. He stripped off his garments. Unfortunately, there wasn't anything less grand than a stiff-collared shirt and an evergreen waistcoat with buttons depicting the national seal. Everything looked as though it were dated thirty years, and the clothes were much too big for him. But he didn't care, he wanted to be warm and dry. He threw on a pair of black trousers and slipped his shoes on over that. He glanced in the mirror. He looked decidedly Victorian.

A familiar song caught in his ears. It poured through the cracks in the windows and seemed to light up the lifeless, old building. Pasha's heart danced inside him. It was the Firebird.

He ran from the closet and looked about. There she was, sitting on a branch outside the window, pecking at the glass with her glowing, golden beak.

It was the first time she had been still enough for Pasha to get a good look at her. Her neck was swanlike, and she was surprisingly tall with long, thin legs. Bright plumes sprouted from her head, and a fan of fiery feathers draped behind her like the train of a dress. She stared at him, absolutely motionless. This was it, this was his chance!

Pasha curled back the latch on the window. The bird cocked its head and hopped farther away. She ruffled her feathers and chirped in a fussy manner. Pasha stuck out his hand.

"Come here, girl. I'm not gonna hurt you."

But the Firebird whipped her flaming tail. She looked out over the courtyard and flapped her wings. Her head turned back to Pasha as she tweeted. It was almost as though she were trying to speak.

As Pasha was placing his foot on the roof tiles, he heard a

voice outside which made him jump.

"I know I heard it, Pythius," exclaimed a raspy male voice. Pasha fell back inside on his bottom. He needed to get out of sight.

"You needn't go shouting about it, Jormum," snapped another, "lest it hear you and fly away!"

Were these ophidians? A knot formed in Pasha's chest. Perhaps they wouldn't harm him. After all, Pasha wasn't a Fay, and it wasn't as if they knew who he was. He listened to the front door slam. There was no sound to their footsteps! A feeling of dark foreboding fell upon Pasha's lungs like an anchor. Traces of voices whistled in the wings below. Wisps of words tiptoed past the shadows, almost like rattling, almost like snakes.

"A presence has been here," said the one called Pythius. Pasha could almost feel the drenched weight of his sopping coat being lifted from its puddlesome form on the threshold.

"A mermaid perhaps?" mused the one called Jormum.

"Dear brother, you forget. Never again shall the fishtails pick up and leave the water, not since Samael's curse. As for the mermaids left to tread the sand, seawater would extinguish their souls from their loathsome bodies."

Curse? What curse? Staccato had never mentioned a curse before. And what did they mean the mermaids couldn't leave the water? Sonata was a mermaid, wasn't she? She could walk around on land. Something told Pasha these were not the type of people who could be reasoned with and he needed to get out as quickly as possible.

He looked towards the way he had come. Pasha's heart sank as he realized he had left a trail of water leading straight to the shadow he was now cowering in.

No sooner had the realization entered his mind than he heard one of them hiss, "Looks like they left us a trail."

Pasha dashed from the corner and slipped down the narrow hall. He tried to remain as silent and as light-footed as possible. He felt a shimmer of anxiety run up his ventricles as fear flooded his heart.

A slender wooden door beneath the steps caught his eye. The servant stairwell! Pasha fled to the door and swept behind its sanctuary, trying with all his might to steady his shaking hands. The dread fogging up his chest informed him the pursuers were approaching up the main steps. His breath coiled at the tail of his throat as pure animal instinct took over. Flat silence fell upon his ears in a dense sheet.

Through the keyhole, Pasha could make out two figures in white gossamer robes drifting past the door. Veils saturated with pungent perfume covered their heads. An overpowering fragrance of floral musk seeped through the cracks. Their backs were turned.

"Remove your veil, dear brother, and perhaps we can follow its scent."

Pasha leaned away from the keyhole and looked himself over. Could they smell him? "The trail leads us hence," purred

Jormum. Silence lingered at the entry.

"By my third eye, I sense a corporeal life," remarked Pythius.

"Yes, dear brother, and the water drops lead us to it."

"My perceptions stretch, they defy what I see on the ground. They tell me it dwells there beneath the stairwell."

Pasha had pasted himself to the corner of the nearest landing. Long, triangular shadows eclipsed the vapors of gray light leaking beneath the door. He could hear their voices drifting further towards the bedchamber.

"It is this glacial air which clouds your judgment, Pythius. Cold freezes the juice in the veins of the fruit, but put it out to sun and it will sweat. The hearth would do you good. Come, let us catch our game, and we shall enjoy a nice meal by the fire."

They drew away. Pasha could feel it in the lightness of the air. A heavy door thundered shut behind them. They were gone.

Pasha vaulted over the railing to the first floor. He had to get out. He grabbed hold of the door handle and pushed his thumb down on the tab. There was a deafening, metallic scratch. Flakes of rust crumbled between the pistons with ear-splitting friction.

Pasha bit his lip. There was a disturbance overhead. Pasha lashed up the stairs, swinging up the railing, determined his feet should never touch the ground.

Someone threw themselves against the door below, plastering their face against the wood.

"I knew it," shrieked Pythius, his breath stringy, "there is deceitful flesh behind the bones of this door!"

The jiggling of the iron handle haunted Pasha up the stairs as he sprinted past the fourth, the fifth, the sixth floor.

"It is ground shut!"

"Come away, Pythius! You are allowing your passions to run away with you!"

"I know what I am about, Jormum!"

Pasha did not stop running. He had no idea how many flights he had gone up. He lost count after ten. The terror raging through his bloodstream transformed the simple halls into sinister labyrinths. He threw himself out the servant's stairwell. Not sure where else to go, he headed for the west wing. He bolted down murky passages, beneath scourged pillars and frayed banners. A door opened and shut close by. Pasha spurred over the gallery railing and lowered himself to the ground.

He slipped behind a pair of oak doors and bolted them shut. He had barricaded himself inside a tremendous library. Outside, he could hear the hiss of the serpentine men approaching.

"Do you smell it, Pythius? The fragrance of a bloody broth boiling!"

"I can almost taste it, dear brother."

"Good for the vertebrae, good for the senses."

"Good for the taste."

Pasha scrambled to find another exit amongst the myriad of crowded shelves. There had to be another way out! Something struck against the door. Pasha grappled up the side of the bookcase. The bolts clanked with the rattle of keys. Balancing on the top of the shelf, Pasha leaped to the banister of the gallery and climbed over the edge. There was a dumbwaiter near the sitting area. Below him, the doors burst open. Pasha made for the dumbwaiter. He threw open the door, grabbed the pulley, and squeezed inside. Curses filtered through the library. Sliding the door closed, Pasha let go of the rope and rocketed down the shaft.

Down Pasha traveled with nightmarish speed, packing his screams deep inside his lungs. At last, he squeezed the rope. The box yanked like an elastic band. His head collided with the roof. He slammed to a halt. His muscles felt slingshotted.

For a moment, he sat in the darkness, leaning his head back against the wood and allowing his tendons to throb. He listened. Nothing. He lifted up the door and rolled out of the cubby. Total darkness. He must have come upon the cellar. An odd, metallic odor hung in the air. He felt for a lamp on the wall. His fingers came to the knob. He turned the dial until a low, blue light came on. Pasha stumbled back in horror.

It was a kitchen of terror. Jars of blood lined the shelves, labeled like containers of olive oil. Dead bodies wrapped in gauze hung from hooks in the ceiling like flies caught in a web. Their lacerated arms dangled over their heads, allowing their blood to collect in tubs below them. The ophidians were harvesting it. Pasha had to wedge his fist between his teeth and bite down on his knuckles to keep from crying out. He forced his eyes to the floor, wishing he could forget what he had seen.

A light reflected from a puddle on the ground. It was coming from a long, lit passage. Pasha drew closer to the tunnel. He could smell salt. He could hear seawater roaring through a drain. Perhaps he could follow it out. He raced down the vault.

Before he could go far, a whip ensnared around his ankle, knocking him off his feet. Water seeped through his clothes. His cheek struck against a rock. Blood trickled down the side of his face. Rolling over, he found himself faced with the shadow of an imposing ophidian woman. Pasha went white.

Her strange beauty bordered on the perverse. It turned his stomach. Her features had such precise symmetry it was unsettling, inhuman even. White, satiny hair rippled over her thin shoulders. Her flesh was so pale and bloodless that the flush of her cheeks was a dusty sepia color.

With a wrench of her whip, she dragged Pasha closer to her feet. She swept down and wiped a smear of blood from his face.

"Now, there's a drop of blood I'd like to swill."

As she sucked the blood from her finger, her pupils rolled back into lifeless, black marbles. The waterline of her lid was so florid against her ashen skin that her eyes became two solar eclipses. She hummed with satisfaction.

"Delicious!"

A shudder came over her body. A network of parchment brown veins appeared beneath her skin. Buxom lips peeled back over tusk-like fangs unsheathing themselves from her pale gums. Her jaws unhinged as she opened her mouth and threw back her head. Her throat had become a vacuous hole.

Pasha lashed his hand across a puddle, spraying the ophidian's eyes with salt water. The ophidian recoiled, dropping her whip and clawing at her eyes. Kicking up his legs, Pasha bucked her in the abdomen. The woman stumbled onto the stone floor.

Pasha was trembling so violently he wasn't sure how he made it to his feet. He soared down the passage without looking back. He turned every corner, desperate to get far away from the ophidian woman.

Footsteps echoed behind him. He sprinted faster. She was catching up.

He slid down an incline and stopped. A thought struck him. Ophidians didn't have footsteps. It was impossible to hear them approaching. Who was chasing him?

"Wait! Boy! Wait," a soft, feminine voice called out. He swiveled around. A diminutive shadow filled the passageway. A woman bloomed in the flickering light. She had a dirty kerchief tied around her dark red hair and was dressed like a servant.

"I won't hurt you, I promise," she insisted. "I'm here to help you, to get you out of here. You're Pasha, aren't you? Your friends are looking for you."

"How do you know that? Who are you?"

"My name is Madrigal Moon, former captain of the Ursine Search and Rescue. I'm a slave here to the Stewardess of Ursa, but that doesn't matter."

Pasha inclined his head. "The Stewardess of Ursa?"

"The woman who attacked you. You needn't worry. I'm on your side. Word was sent out amongst the rebels this morning that a member of Staccato Nimbus' company was lost, a young man. Surely, it must be you."

Pasha's heart flipped inside his chest. "Yes! It's me! Tell me, please, how do I get out of here?"

She grabbed his arm. "Come with me. We have to get you out of here before they summon the C.O.N." She led him down the damp passageway. "You were on the right track heading towards the well. It used to be a secret entryway for the monarchs of Karkinos back when they were allies. All mermaid kingdoms are a joint rule. And before Draco took over, Karkinos and Ursa ruled land and sea together."

Pasha nodded his head. "So, the well is a passage to open sea?"

"Yes. The ophidians don't come near it. They must be very careful when dealing with salt water after cursing the mermaids. The passage in the well will lead you out of here, but you won't go very far without a way to breathe." She reached into her pocket and took out a folded kerchief, damp with brine. She unwrapped the bundle. They were olives. She placed one of the shining berries in his hand.

"Eat one of these, and you'll be able to see clearly under the water and hold your breath for hours at a time. This will get you through to the other side. Staccato and the others are waiting for you in Errai on *La Sirena*."

"On what?"

"It's a ship, you'll see it once you get into open water."

She led him down another hallway towards the music of rushing water. They descended a shallow set of stairs into a small, dome-shaped room. In the middle of the floor was a circular pool ebbing with seawater.

"Go ahead and eat the olive," Madrigal instructed. "Once you're down there just follow the passage out. There are mermaids outside to help you should you need it. Now go, hurry!" She corralled him towards the pool. Pasha dug his heels into the ground.

"Wait, aren't you coming?"

"Of course not, I can't. Not until the curse breaks."

"What curse?"

"Didn't Staccato tell you? The Land Lock Curse! Years ago, the C.O.N. stole a trident from Karkinos called Sea-Splitter, and made it so no mermaid in the sea could leave, and no mermaid on the land could return. If I entered seawater it would kill me. Now hurry, you must go!”

“B—but I can’t swim,” Pasha sputtered, half embarrassed.

Madrigal shook her head, fighting against her worried expression.

“Never mind that. The passage is shallow, and you won’t need to breathe. Just wait at the end of the tunnel for the mermaids to come find you.”

Angry whispers echoed along the tunnel, and Madrigal turned to him with desperation in her large, wet eyes.

“Go, now!”

Chapter 17:
Primal Instinct

With a long breath, Pasha plunged himself into the salty pool. A breaker of icy water enveloped him. He squinted his eyes. When he realized there was no sting, he allowed himself to gaze fully into the water. There was a roof above him and a floor below him. He couldn't free fall to the bottom of the ocean. What's more, he didn't have to worry about breathing. His fear left him. He pushed on through the tunnel.

The underwater hall was lined with strange, starry shapes of phosphorous light. Pasha reached out to touch one of the soft glowing masses. An arm curled inward. They were starfish. Feathery seagrass brushed beneath his chin. Ahead of him, bushels of iridescent anemones billowed in the current. Sparkling, lavender bubbles of foam floated about him like fairies. He'd never known how beautiful the ocean could be. It wasn't long before he could make out the natural light of day shining in dappled surges at the end of the tunnel.

Outside, the passage opened upon a lush coral reef teeming with color. The water was clear, but there were no mermaids. Beyond him was open water. Places below him extended past his sight. Trenches and crevices blurred into obscurity where the light was too far to touch. Where could they be? How long did he have before the effects of the olive wore off? What if something went wrong and it didn't last as long as Madrigal had said?

Something sparkly emerged from the velvety shadows below. Pasha peeked out over the edge and squinted his eyes. Light danced in the watery fog. Long, fluid shadows formed, waving like banners in a breeze. The light grew stronger, and soon he could make out three mermaids swimming up from the bottom of the ocean. Tridents were slung across their backs, and each wore a large pendant stamped with an official-looking crest. Pasha felt his body relax. There was something comforting about watching them, as though their presence had tranquilizing power.

"Pasha," the young merman in the lead called out to him with a smile. He was heavily muscled with a golden tail, deep, suntanned skin, and metallic bronze eyes. A crown of long, thick dreadlocks floated around his shoulders. "Pasha, is that you?"

Unable to give a verbal reply, Pasha waved awkwardly from his place inside the tunnel. The two female mermaids giggled, and Pasha couldn't help but blush.

"Come on out," the merman laughed, beckoning him forward. "This is the L.A.S.A., you have nothing to be afraid of."

The mermaid with the coral tail elbowed him in the side. Her pretty black braids were coiled in a bun on the top of her head.

"Coast, you silly flounder, he doesn't know what the L.A.S.A. is!"

Coast tapped his forehead forgetfully. "Right, we're with the Lost At Sea Assistance Squad, Stella Real, Karkinos division. We've come to rescue you, so there's no need to be frightened. You can come out now."

Pasha hesitated. Without speaking, how could he convey he couldn't swim? One of the mermaids swept close to him, the blonde one with the green tail, almost poking him in the nose with her own. She looked him up and down. Her eyebrows knit together in concern.

"Coast, he's frightened, poor thing. Don't you feel his energy, Aqua?"

The other mermaid swished her tail and swam up to his right side.

"I do feel it, Briny! Oh, darling, you don't know how to swim, do you?"

Pasha shook his head. Without hesitating, they each took an arm and slung it over their shoulders.

"Well, never you mind," chirped Briny on the right. "We're here to rescue you."

"That's right," agreed Aqua on the left as they towed him into open water, "just relax and let us do the paddling. We'll have you reunited with your friends in no time."

"I suppose we could always teach him to swim on the way there. It's quite simple, Pasha, all you have to do is kick your legs while you hold on to us."

Coast hastened alongside them. "Now, now ladies, let's try not to overwhelm him. Don't worry, Pasha, now that you're in the hands of the L.A.S.A. you have nothing to fear. Just sit back, relax, and allow us to escort you to Errai."

***

Pasha was surprised at how quickly the journey to Errai passed. He had been so absorbed with the spectacles around him, time seemed to fly away. Furthermore, the mermaids were able to swim at an impeccable pace without tiring themselves. Soon they drifted in the shadow of a modest-sized ship. The mermaids carried him towards the glass ceiling of rippling waves.

Pasha gasped for breath as he broke the surface. He slicked his bangs back and rubbed his eyes. Sonata was leaning over the side of the ship. She looked back over her shoulder.

"He's here!" She waved down to him. "Hang on, Pasha! We're on our way!"

Staccato's voice overpowered her.

"Sonata Ondine Soter, you step away from that railing this instant!"

Ignoring Staccato, she tossed Pasha a life preserver, nearly hitting him in the head. Pasha clung to the side, and the mermaids let go. They would not breach the surface but looked up at him from beneath the water.

"Thank you," Pasha choked. "You saved my life."

Coast shook his hand, and Pasha took this to mean they had understood him. He smiled.

Overhead, Pyro and Staccato were lowered down in a rowboat. Briny and Aqua jumped out of the water and kissed Pasha's cheeks. They disappeared in an instant. Pasha felt his face turn scarlet.

"Watch out there, Pasha," Pyro laughed. "Mermaids are downright aggressive flirts when they take a liking to a man."

Staccato leaned back and called to Melodious.

"That's enough! You can stop now!"

They hovered a few feet above the water. Pyro leaned over the boat.

"Alright, Pasha, give me your hands." Pyro hunched over the side and hoisted Pasha into the raft. "Take her up, Reverend!"

Melodious saluted and wrenched the pulley. As Pasha collapsed on the bench, Pyro eyed his clothing and snorted.

"So, what happened, Pasha? Did you fall through a wormhole and get stuck in the nineties?"

Pasha lifted his head. "What?" He sighed and shut his eyes. "It's a long story."

"Well, you don't have to explain it all at once," reassured Staccato. "Get some rest first. I'm sure you've had an exhausting morning."

Once the boat leveled with the deck, Pyro hopped over the railing and dusted himself off. At the sight of Pyro, Sonata crossed her arms as though Staccato had offended her.

"You let Pyro help, but not me?"

Pyro rolled his eyes. "*Oi*, what's wrong with me lending a hand?"

"You're an igneous. If you fell into the water, your powers wouldn't work until you were dry again."

"Yeah, but unlike you, it ain't gonna kill me."

Staccato stepped over the railing and sighed. It was clear from his expression this was not the first time they'd had this conversation.

"Sonata, dear, you can't go near seawater, it's too dangerous. And for goodness' sake, stop standing so close to the railing! You shouldn't even be out here. I told you to stay inside until we reach land."

Pasha raised an eyebrow as Melodious helped him on deck. Staccato spoke to Sonata with the authority of a father, and Sonata was not a child. She lowered her eyebrows.

"That's over a week's journey! I'll lose my mind! I'm a mermaid, you could at least let me look at the water!"

Staccato rolled his eyes. "Don't be so dramatic, Sonata. Your safety is a priority. And don't you give me that look, young lady, or I will be writing to your parents!"

"I am twenty-four years old, thank you! You can't order me about like a child!"

"No, but I am the head of this expedition. I say who stays and who goes, and if you can't do as I say, I have no problem sending you straight back to Ascella to stay with King Thayer until the curse breaks! Is that understood?"

Sonata bit her lip and wrinkled her nose. "Yes, Staccato."

Staccato tilted her chin up. "Regardless of your age, you are still my responsibility. Your parents would skewer me if I let anything happen to you, and they would be right to do so." He straightened his shoulders. "Now, I would like you to please escort Pasha upstairs where he can change into some dry clothes. Get him something to eat. We'll join you in a minute."

Sonata nodded, and taking Pasha by the arm, led him gently up the stairs.

"Sorry you got into trouble," whispered Pasha. "Are they always so protective of you?"

"Only around seawater. Staccato is my godfather, you see, and my father's best friend. I was separated from my parents during the Land Lock when I was fifteen. I stole Sea-Splitter back from Samael and threw it into the ocean where he couldn't retrieve it. That's when I got kidnapped by the C.O.N. and had my legs amputated."

Pasha's eyes grew wide. "You took on Samael when you were fifteen?"

Sonata glowed with pride. "I saw an opportunity, and I took it. I'm sure you would have done the same."

Pasha could hardly contain how impressed he was. "How did you escape?"

"Staccato rescued me, risking his life in the process. He's taken care of me ever since. He even designed a pair of enchanted prosthetics especially for me."

She held out one of her shimmering diamond legs. Pasha had wondered about that. Where he came from, if people lost both their legs they never walked again. Not only could Sonata walk, but her gait was the most natural thing in the world. What other explanation could there be but magic? She smoothed her skirt down and continued on.

"They were so advanced, a prosthetist offered him an incredible sum of money for the patent. Now, mermaids all over Voiler with similar injuries don't have to lose hope of ever walking again. It's wonderful, isn't it?"

Pasha's eyebrows stretched in amazement as he agreed. He thought about all the wounded soldiers that had come back from the war. How many had he seen with missing limbs? It so happened one of his friends had been forced to become a Breadwinner after his father lost both legs in the trenches.

Sonata led Pasha through the entryway into the warmth of a luxurious cabin where coal burned in a furnace. Pasha shivered against his wet clothes.

"So, what happened? How did I become separated from you?"

Sonata sighed and frowned. "I was rather hoping you might hold some sort of clue."

"Me?" He rubbed his hands up and down his forearms. "I'm the last person who would know. I don't even know how it was supposed to work in the first place."

Pasha's suitcase was stowed away on the window seat. He opened the latches and fumbled around for something suitable. One of the buttons fell from the old waistcoat and rolled onto the carpet. Sonata bent down to pick it up. As she held it to the light, her eyes grew wide with horror.

"This is—where did you get this?"

"Polaris."

Sonata stared at him, mouth agape.

"You were in Polaris? Is that where you ended up?" Her questions came pouring out one after the other. "Pasha, if you were in Polaris you need to tell me, it's very important. If you ended up in Pol—"

"It wasn't like that exactly."

Pasha explained how he had ended up in the water and how he had headed towards the city in search of shelter.

"What shelter? Where did you go?"

"The castle."

"The castle?" There was hardly any sound to Sonata's words. "You mean you actually went into Alfbern Hall?"

Pasha glanced back and forth. "Uh, Alfbern Hall?"

"That's the name of the palace! Were you in the palace?"

"Yeah, I was inside the palace."

It took Sonata a moment to compose herself. She pressed her

fingertips to her lips and leaned against the desk with her eyes closed. It was some time before she spoke again.

"Go back down the hallway to the door on the right. You can dress in there, and when you come back we'll discuss this further. I'll make us some tea and set out some sandwiches. You need to eat."

Pasha thanked her and headed down the passage. When he returned, Sonata was removing the kettle from the heat. She motioned to one of the armchairs before the furnace.

"Come sit down, Pasha. Make yourself comfortable."

As he was lowering himself into the chair, something small and fuzzy hopped into his lap. Pasha gave a start. It was the orange-and-white cat Sonata had been holding when he first saw her in Central Park.

"Don't mind Cello," Sonata giggled. "He's very friendly."

Cello kneaded his paws into Pasha's legs and purred contentedly as Pasha stroked him behind the ears.

"You bring your cat with you?"

Sonata shrugged. "Where else is he supposed to go?"

Pasha smiled, amused. "A cat for a mermaid. Who would have thought?"

"Oh, he thinks he's a mermaid too."

Pasha gaped at her. "He likes water?"

Sonata shrugged. "Happens when you grow up in a mermaid kingdom, I suppose."

She poured the tea into both cups and handed one to Pasha. She offered him his plate.

"Go ahead and eat, Pasha. I know you're starving. You don't have to mind your manners in front of me. I'll explain as much as I can while you have your fill."

With her permission, Pasha dug in voraciously.

"As you know," she began, "the gateway in Grand Central took us to Errai. You, however, vanished into thin air and ended up right outside Polaris. My fear is that somehow Samael might have tampered with the system."

Pasha forced down a bite. "Can he do that?"

Sonata thought for a moment, frowning in concentration.

"I don't know. I hope not. But Draco has become very powerful. I don't know if Staccato explained it to you or not, but Samael is sort of a beloved public figure in Voiler."

Pasha choked. "Beloved? I thought Samael was some crazy, cannibalistic dictator who wanted to cleanse Voiler of all magic."

Sonata bit her lip and shrugged. "Well, he is, but it's a bit more complex than that. Some people love him, some people hate him. The problem is, Samael's more villainous agenda is carried out in secret by means of the C.O.N., though he claims to have no affiliation with them. The C.O.N. does all the dirty work, and Samael's public image remains untarnished so he can go on manipulating the masses. Draco even has a seat on the Ecliptic Council now."

Pasha cocked his head. “What’s the Ecliptic Council?”

“Voiler’s international peace courts.”

Pasha brightened. “Oh, so kind of like the League of Nations?”

“Yes, exactly like that!”

Pasha smiled secretly to himself, grateful he didn’t look like a complete idiot. “When you say Samael manipulates the masses, what do you mean exactly?”

Sonata set aside her teacup. “Samael claims ophidians have been the victims of prejudice for centuries because their ancestors once enslaved Voiler. Several decades ago, he decided to do something about it. He began teaching people about Draconian culture, why the ophidians embraced such a violent way of life, and what the benefits of such a lifestyle might entail. He wrote books, he held rallies, he did seminars. Soon people began adopting his doctrine. Primal Instinct, he called it.”

“And what is Primal Instinct?”

Sonata hesitated, searching for the right words.

“An old ophidian principle, also known as ‘the Heart’s Desire.’ On the surface it appears harmless, good even. It claims human desires are based on a need which must be fulfilled in order to live a healthy life. But Primal Instinct takes the idea to an extreme. Ophidians believe no desire is wrongful. They would have us give into our every impulse no matter how immoral or unjust. It’s survival of the fittest, putting your own needs and desires before others in order to be happy."

"Don't people realize how wrong that is?"

"Many do, but Samael has made it so it's taboo to criticize their practices."

Pasha stared at her in disbelief. After what he'd seen in Alfbern Hall, it seemed impossible people could be fooled by such evil.

"Is everyone aware ophidians eat people?"

"Well, not exactly. It's known they like to drink human blood, but only consensually."

Pasha gaped at her, baffled. "What? Who consents to having their blood drank?"

"Not many people, unless they're desperate for money. You see, ophidians will pay handsomely for human blood, that's why Draco wanted ahold of Ursa in the first place. The more poverty Samael can create in a population, the more people are driven to sell themselves. Meanwhile, their more violent appetites are kept secret from the Ecliptic Council. But there is more at stake than people realize. As you know, Samael has secretly been planning a genocide of the Fay and all their kin. He's using Primal Instinct to turn people against us."

Pasha raised an eyebrow. "But what does Primal Instinct have to do with the Fay?"

"As you can imagine, Voiler is heavily populated by the supernatural, mermaids in particular. Because of this, many Fay hold seats of high power throughout our world. They have their own kingdoms, hold positions in the government. Samael blames the Fay population for imposing laws prohibiting the practice of Primal Instinct. He believes any law preventing people from living out their passions is discriminatory towards their culture. For example, laws which outlaw child sacrifice, or cannibalism, or homicide. He says the Fay are abusing their power, and so he wants us out of the way."

"Don't people question his sanity when he advocates genocide?"

Sonata shrugged. "Samael keeps his ideas of genocide separate from his public image. It's like I said, he lets the C.O.N. take care of that so he can avoid taking the blame. The things they do to people . . ." She put a hand to her lips and looked away.

"I know. I saw it for myself."

She shook her head. "I can only imagine. It must've been terrible at Alfbern Hall. You must share with me all you've been through."

Before Pasha could go on, the door flung open, and in came the rest of the company.

Staccato adjusted his cravat. "Is it time yet?"

Sonata glanced back at the clock. "Two minutes 'til one."

Staccato opened the doors of a wide cabinet in the wall to reveal a radio. He flipped the switch and began cruising with the dial.

Melodious laid a hand on the back of Pasha's chair. "Samael is in Capricornus today. He is presenting a lecture about Primal Instinct at the College of Capadacius. They are broadcasting it live."

Sonata snorted. "Now, you'll get to see how he operates."

"*Oi*, Sonata!" Pyro crouched down beside her chair. "Skelter and I thought of the perfect way to let you go out on deck."

Without waiting for a reply from Sonata, Skelter threw a tarp over her head and bundled her up. Pyro threw out his hands.

"Ta-da! See? It's waterproof!"

Sonata glowered at the two from the recesses of her makeshift cocoon. "Melodious, hand me my trident please."

Pyro and Skelter fell back on their haunches guffawing.

Melodious shook his head and chuckled. "Do not pay them any mind, Princess. We are all concerned about your safety. After all, 'a friend loveth at all times.'"

Sonata rolled her eyes with a sarcastic flair. "Oh, yes, they're very loving."

"Aw, come on, Sonny," Pyro persisted. "It's not that bad! You could start a whole new trend. Maybe we can make it into a raincoat."

Sonata pushed out her lip and whined, "Staccato!"

Staccato threw up his hands. "Alright, everyone hush, it's starting!"

The fuzzy grains of static sewed together in a smooth, scintillating, smoky voice that coiled around the room.

" . . . It's our way of life, that's all. The Fay have looked for ways to excuse their prejudices. For centuries they've condemned us, and I suppose that's understandable to an extent. I can't argue, they did suffer greatly under my ancestors' regime. But history functions as a way to learn. I believe Voiler is in a time and place where we can gather together peacefully and learn about one another's heritage. That is why we're here today!"

There was hopeful laughter in his voice as all around him the audience applauded. Pasha raised his eyebrows. Samael didn't sound at all like he'd expected, and he wasn't like the ophidians at Alfbern Hall with their odd, antiquated way of speaking. Instead, he was personable, friendly even.

"It's an ophidian virtue that to live well one must nurture the desires of the heart and follow where it takes you. No doubt all of you have experienced strong desires. Some want passion, others, material wealth." He laughed. "Ah, I see many of you nodding your head in agreement. See? It's a familiar experience! We've all shared these feelings, and that is because we all share a primal instinct."

He was involved with his audience, even silly at times. It was easy to look past the things he was actually suggesting and fall for that charisma.

"What if I told you you could have it all? You need only to reach out and take it! There is no disgrace in self-service, my friends! Shame is a learned behavior, a conditioned response. Shame is a tool used to defy our own nature, to rob us of the very things that fulfill us.

We all have impulses. It's universal! It's natural! If it's natural, how could it be wrong? It's a simple matter of listening to your heart. What could be purer, I ask you? What could be nobler?

"We've all been taught to glorify discipline, moderation, temperance. But when something is good, why restrict? I say, celebrate it! There is no such thing as too much of a good thing, and our bodies know this. It's biological. That's why when we see something we like or even something we dislike, we respond physically. It's our body's way of trying to speak to us, and we need to listen!

"Men, if you desire a woman, take her! Do not let anything stand in your way! And women, I implore the same of you! Do not take 'no' for an answer! If anyone should try to stop you, eliminate the obstacle. Take their life if you have to! You owe it to yourself to be happy. Protect your happiness! Do not stand by idly! Do not let sentimentality affect your judgment! It is this way in the animal kingdom, and so it was meant to be with us!

"Finally, brothers and sisters, whatever is modern, whatever is expedient, whatever feels good, whatever makes you happy, whatever guarantees your success, remember and dwell on these things, for they are the desires of your heart. Practice them at home, recite them before you go to bed at night, whatever you need to do to change your way of thinking, and you will find peace."

The crowd was in an uproar of praise and admiration. Staccato flipped the dial and turned it off. Enough had been said. Pasha's mouth dropped open.

"How can they fall for that? Weren't they listening? He just told them to go rape and murder!"

"I suppose," began Staccato, "it's easy to accept because in truth it really is what the human heart desires. He's clever, Samael. He's playing into the darkest part of mankind. He's telling people what they've wanted to hear since the dawn of time."

Sonata sighed. "Now you see what we're up against."

After a long stretch of solemn silence, Pasha sighed and ran his fingers through his drying bangs. "Where are we headed?"

"To Cortijo Del Mar in Aquarius to speak with Mother Genesis," replied Melodious.

"Who is Mother Genesis?"

It was Sonata who answered Pasha this time. "The oldest tree in existence, the tree of all knowledge and wisdom, guardian of the sylphs and esperites."

Pyro nodded. "She's going to tell us where we can find the Firebird."

Pasha's mouth dropped open. In his memory, the Firebird sat on the rooftop of Alfbern Hall.

"I saw it! The Firebird! It was outside the window at Alfbern Hall. If we wanna catch it, we gotta go back."

Everyone gasped and exchanged worried glances.

"Not to Polaris." Sonata shuddered. "It's too dangerous! Isn't it?" Her eyes were uncertain as she looked back at Staccato.

Pyro threw up his arms. "Well, of course, we have to go back! How else are we supposed to catch it? We have to follow it!"

Staccato shook his head. "I think it would be wise to apply a little more strategy in this situation."

"Strategy?" Pyro choked. "Here's the strategy: It goes to Polaris, we follow it, we catch it. What more strategy do you need?"

"The Firebird wants to be caught by either Pasha or Samael. No matter what we do, she is going to stay within reach of both, providing each with equal opportunity. But when she isn't following one of the two, she is tending to her own needs like any other living creature. There are places she likes to go. Mother Genesis is the most likely to know where these places are, where she nests, where she drinks, where she sleeps. And those are the places we'll search."

Chapter 18:
Desperation

It had never occurred to Faina after Pasha was gone to cease her bootlegging activity. It was good money after all. Uncle Matvei may have leased half the building and owned the grocery store below their apartment, but they were not wealthy like they once were. *Opa* had earned more in its former life as a liquor store than it ever did as a food market. But bootlegging was a highly lucrative trade, and the money Faina made selling illegal liquor to Klokov through Pasha was a considerable prop for the family's finances.

Unfortunately, without Pasha, Faina had no middleman to peddle to Klokov. Girls were not permitted to become Breadwinners or associates, and to sell to the Breadwinners you had to become one or the other.

Three days after Pasha left, Faina was inspired to apply a little creativity to her plight. She tucked her abundant hair into her brother's cap, slipped on his clothes and set out to the Foxhole to do business with Klokov. In the mornings, the venue was not particularly crowded as long as a Bread Fight wasn't scheduled. She found Klokov unaccompanied at the long table in the back where Paddock business was usually conducted. He hunched low over his accounting book, calculating sums and costs. There was an enormous shiner on his bald scalp, and his left hand was heavily bandaged.

Without a word, she took the large wooden crate she'd carried from home and set it on the table. Klokov dabbed his pen on a scrap piece of paper without looking up.

"Looking to do business, pal?"

Faina dared not risk a verbal answer, so she grunted and nodded her head. When she did not respond, Klokov glanced up. His good eye glazed over skeptically as he reached up and tilted the bill of her cap away from her face.

"Miss Spichkin?"

Faina's spine unwound from its coil of knots as she sighed, defeated.

"Yeah, it's me."

"You know if you didn't dress that way all the time that disguise might have served you better."

She removed the cap and shook out her hair.

"I wanna become an associate."

Klokov snickered and shook his head.

"Uh, no."

Faina leaned over the table with an iron tenacity. "And what am I supposed to do with all this, eh? Let it go to waste?"

"You know the rules. No women."

Faina refused to give up. She fished through the crate until she unearthed a bottle of fifty-year-old Château and thrust it under his bump of a nose.

"If you'll look at what I brought I think you might reconsider."

Klokov drew his eyebrows together in astonishment. "Where did you get this?"

"A townhouse on Fifth Avenue. And that's not all I got." She lifted four bottles of genuine, high-end, French champagne out of the box. Klokov turned the bottles gently in his hands, appraising, evaluating, dissecting.

"You aren't stealing from rival gangs, are you? Because you know that's dangerous—"

"I know better than to do something so reckless. My brother was one of your greatest colleagues, after all. He used to let me help him sometimes. . . ."

Klokov jerked his head and snorted. "Yeah, Chevalsky too I hear."

The veins branching around Faina's heart grew cold. Her shoulders tensed. Klokov glanced up at her with a cocked eyebrow.

"Relax, I'm not gonna ask you any questions about the boy."

"You're not?"

"Nah." He frowned. "He may be a treacherous, thieving, little rat, but we don't harass family members. We'll find him on our own. Why make you suffer for his sins?"

Gathering her courage, she pressed her fingertips to the end of the table and forced the words from her throat. "Pasha didn't steal the money."

Klokov reached into the crate for another bottle, unfazed by her plea.

“Uh-huh. And how do you know that?”

Faina opened her mouth as if the answer had been on the tip of her tongue waiting to spring forth and clear Pasha’s name. But she did not know. Pasha had never explained to her what happened.

“Anastas framed him.”

Klokov rolled his shoulders as though trying to relieve himself of a nagging crick.

“Look, normally, I would believe you. But the proof is against him this time. Anastas came up clean.”

“That can’t be! There has to be something you’re overlooking! You know what type of boy Anastas is, and he’s always had it out for Pasha!”

Klokov pinched the space between his eyes and held up a hand. “Enough. I said I wasn’t gonna harass you about the boy. This has nothing to do with him—”

“It has everything to do with him! You see, Pasha was my family’s breadwinner. When Leo died, Pasha split half his pay with me, including what he made street fighting. When you chased him off, you robbed me of my family’s main source of income. You owe me some kinda assistance.”

Klokov leaned back in his chair and lit a papery cigar. “First of all, I didn’t rob your family of anything. It was Chevalsky who robbed you when he decided to steal—”

“But he didn’t—”

Klokov held up his hand again. Faina grew still. She watched him pick up the bottle and eye the label greedily. Slowly, his gaze fell to the scorch mark on her sleeve.

“I remember when your brother got that burn.” Klokov leaned back and scratched his chin. “He was lifting from some fed’s wine cellar when the sap walks in the front door with his lady friend all liquored up and hot to trot.” Smoke chugged from the corner of his mouth as he chuckled. “Kid had to duck behind this oriental dressing screen and lean up against an old sideboard, and the whole time his elbow is in this ashtray. Now he swore up and down the thing was stone cold while he was sitting there but somehow, next thing he knows, his sleeve is on fire . . .” Klokov trailed off with a hoarse laugh, pinching the space between his eyebrows.

A proud smile crowned Faina’s lips. People who knew her brother were always stopping her to share some wild story about him that had earned an honored place in their memories.

At last Klokov regained his composure and was able to finish. “Boy, I would’ve given anything to have seen the look on your brother’s face! And still he gotta outta there without raising any eyebrows! He was an excellent man to do business with. Loyal, hardworking—”

“Yes,” she interrupted. “Leo worked hard to take care of his family. After our parents died he felt it was his personal responsibility to do everything he could for me."

Klokov stared at her long and hard for a moment. There was an unmistakable softness in his eye. Faina would've thought perhaps he was noting the resemblance between Leo and herself, had there been any resemblance to note.

"I get what you're saying, kid," he at last admitted. "I'm willing to lend you a hand. However, if I consent to take you on as an associate, you can't go running your mouth around town. No one can know! You breathe a word about this to anyone, and I will not hesitate to blacklist you without assistance! You may be a special circumstance, but I've got a reputation to uphold."

Faina was giddy. She pressed a hand over her mouth to cover her smile. "I promise! Believe me, Klokov! No one will ever know!"

"Good. In that case, you can have the job. I'll have my men arrange something where you don't have to come down here to make deliveries. I'll let you know when we've got it set up. We'll find you, got it? You're dismissed."

Faina was quick to leave the Foxhole. She couldn't wait to return home and cuddle up with Mammoth. At the end of the street, a crowd had gathered outside Blum's Financial Trust. There was nothing particularly remarkable about a crowd forming outside any establishment in New York City, but the black and white throng of suits and policemen assembled in front of the bank had none of that modern, eclectic vigor which normally peppered the city's masses.

Instead, Faina felt an old sense of sickening familiarity.

She was well-acquainted with murder. Not only had her brother died in a terrorist attack, but she'd lost her parents to Red Army terror at a young age. She could recognize its approach the way cats divine oncoming storms.

She drifted dizzily through the multitude. She could hear Anya's anguished sobs competing with the whistles and sirens. She pushed through the crowd. Anya was bent over Uncle Matvei's bloodied form on the pavement.

"Papa!" Anya threw back her head and wailed. He had been shot several times. Anya reached a devastated hand towards Faina. "Papa is dead!"

Chapter 19:

The Cobra

"Dinner will be served in the courtyard, Your Majesty." The Sultana of Capricornus was beaming from ear to ear. Her blush was like the desert sunset outside the large bay window of Samael's accommodations at Tamal.

"Thank you, my lady," Samael crooned. "I'll be along shortly."

"Please, dear Cobra, do call me Charmion."

The final rays of sunlight danced off her dangling gold earrings and cast sparkling stars on her lovely brown neck. Samael warmed his eyes to her as he smiled.

"Charmion. I'll be with you shortly."

Her back bent in an alluring arc as she bowed low and backed towards the exit. Her enormous shimmering eyes lingered upon him until the door shut completely. Samael's facade evaporated in an instant. He took three aggressive strides towards the window. Below him, the courtyard was lit with ornate glass lanterns. Servants in white veils set the banquet tables with all sorts of exotic finery. He crossed to the vanity and continued preening.

It was easy to see why so many women found him attractive. There was an architectural quality about his face, as though his features had been well thought out like some tedious piece of artwork. The high seat of his cheekbones seemed measured and perfected. His nose was artisanal and straight. Two sleek but heavy eyebrows balanced his delicate features with a seductive thread of masculinity. His short, dark beard made an excellent frame for the exquisite shape of his fine lips. They were not necessarily full, but they were striking and well-defined, crowned with the sharp pinch of a cupid's bow.

What's more, there was something tranquil and angelic about him that fooled people into thinking he was gentle or kindhearted. How deceiving looks could be. He supposed it was the eyes. They were rounded, doe-like, and prismatic blue. They added to his perceived divinity like a pair of angel wings.

He dipped his hand in a basin of water and slicked back his long hair. He glared at the clock on the wall. Where was his report? At last, there came a knock.

"It's Xylophis, my liege," announced a thin voice from the other side of the door.

"Enter."

The man who appeared in the doorway was light and delicate and his skin was nearly translucent. The trappings of a government official decorated his flowing white robes. It was so easy, Samael thought, to underestimate his people. An ignorant person might take Xylophis's sophistication for fragility. One might even go so far as to say he was rather dandified. And yet Samael knew his appetite for human flesh to be insatiable, with a violence about him. He carried a leather portfolio filled with notes and memos.

Samael smoothed the front of his robes. "So, Staccato Nimbus is back in town, is he?"

"He was sighted by a C.O.N. member in the Cepheus District."

"And he's brought some gangly boy with him?"

"That's the report, Sire. He infiltrated Alfbern Hall. We believe he was after the Firebird."

"What?" Samael's voice crepitated off the tall ceilings. "Are you certain?"

Xylophis's blonde curls seemed to tremble. "That's what the reports say, Your Majesty. She was sighted outside the palace just before the boy was. Then he reunited with Staccato Nimbus and his companions off the coast of Errai."

Samael's nostrils flared. He struggled to take even breaths. His anger was about to bubble over when his fury washed away with a delicious realization.

"They know who the other competitor is!" Samael's perfect lips split into a sickening grin of gorgeous, white teeth. "That's who he's brought back with him! The other catcher! Xylophis, I have an assignment for the C.O.N. I need an interrogation. We must find out from the Fay who my opponent is. I know they know. They're greedy with their secrets. Tell the C.O.N. to do whatever it takes to make them speak. Take them to Crux if they have to! Sacrifice them on the altar! Bleed them out! Put the fear of me in them! Can you remember all that?"

"Every word, Your Majesty."

He clicked his tongue. "Dear Xylophis, you have my deepest gratitude." He turned to the vanity and reached for the sheer, glittering robe on the hanger next to the mirror. He removed his dressing gown and replaced it with the princely attire. He left it open at the collar, exposing his well-defined chest. He continued to address Xylophis while primping in the mirror.

"I need to know where Staccato and his rebels are. Where were they headed?"

"East, Your Highness, in an Aquarian ship."

Samael draped himself with a string of glittering jewels across the shoulders.

"Find them. Follow them. Sink that ship. And we'll go out and meet them."

Xylophis bowed accordingly. "Yes, my prince."

Samael inclined his handsome head towards the window with a furtive smile. "Has the delicacy arrived yet?" He looked down into the courtyard.

A young woman in a silken robe was waiting at the end of a long table where a chef arranged lobelia fronds on a platter. A team of assistants brought forth a rolling cart of needles, sutures, and broth bowls. After adding the final touches of garnish, the chef helped the woman onto the table. Samael watched as she cast off her robe and laid down on the platter. The attendants set to work covering her unmentionables with flowers and lettuce leaves. She presented the cook with the pale flesh of her inner arm, ready to receive the needle.

"I see it has." Samael flicked his thin tongue across his long canine teeth. "I do love a good *saignant*. The girl from Kochab, just as I requested." His palette watered as he recalled the flavor of her velvety blood, aged to a fragrant gourmet perfection. "Did you try her at the Baroness's Banquet in Aigle Piliar?"

Xylophis closed his eyes with satisfying memory. "Mmm. Yes, I remember, *un petite morceau splendide*!" A splendid little morsel. He joined Samael at the window and watched as the chef marked off the places for biting. "An excellent choice, I must say, Your Majesty!"

"I better go down before the blood cools." Samael reached for his bejeweled circlet and mantle. "It never does taste quite as good after the first bite."

Chapter 20:
The Oldest Tree in the Forest

As the company departed the harbor, the vast green rainforests of Aquarius rose up before them like the gates of the Emerald City in *The Wizard of Oz* books.. Massive blue butterflies nested upside-down from the towering violet canopies. Flowers the size of ponies opened and shut their petals like wings, and emitted a soft, dreamy perfume. Pasha closed his eyes and allowed the fragrance of coconut and sandalwood to fill his senses.

"It is a good thing we stopped in Alshain." Melodious stroked the muzzle of his gargantuan, winged draft horse. "Schmetterling's shoe was nearly gone."

Staccato breathed a harried sigh and raised his eyebrows. "We didn't have much of a choice. We have to stop wherever there's a Fay Financial, since the Land Lock put all my savings underwater."

Pasha scratched his chin. "You went bankrupt from the Land Lock?"

"No, I mean they're literally underwater. All my finances were handled in Stella Real where the vaults are kept in the ocean."

Pasha shrugged. "What's stopping you from going down and making a transaction?"

"Just as no mermaid in the sea is able to leave it, no mermaid-forged objects can be taken out until the curse is broken. The Land Lock locked everything into place. That which was outside the water was confined to the land. All that was inside was confined to the ocean. My savings were in darions, a currency fashioned by mermaids. Now all my money comes from what I earn working for government rebels. Our division was organized by Thayer, King of Sagittarius."

"So King Thayer funds all your expeditions?"

Staccato bit his lip. "Partially. A great deal of it comes from Aries."

Sonata came stumbling after them, trying to rid herself of Pyro and Skelter. Her eyes burned as she faced her godfather.

"Was having Pyro and Skelter carry me down the gangplank really necessary?"

Staccato paused and lifted an eyebrow. "Pyro and Skelter carried you down the gang-plank?"

"In a tarp!"

Skelter and Pyro snickered over Pasha's shoulder. Staccato shrugged and rubbed at his beard.

"Huh. Not a bad idea. Glad they thought of it."

Sonata growled as she retreated into the wagon and pulled back the curtain. Staccato paid no mind and together the company forged ahead.

The path was so overgrown that Staccato and Pasha had to help guide the pegasi on foot. Pyro sat in the driver's seat steering the reigns with Skelter by his side, while Melodious kept close to the front should they need a log pulled out of the road.

Winter may have been growing closer, but in Aquarius, it already felt like spring. In the shadows, the moss glowed with a faint periwinkle light. Something like lightning bugs circulated lazily above the lichens. Several times Pasha thought eyes were blinking at him from the shrubs, but it always turned out to be some strange toad or a funny polka-dotted bird.

It soon became evident that no matter where they were in Aquarius, they could always hear the sound of rushing water. Sometimes it was near, sometimes it was far, but the noise never evaporated completely. When the trees began thinning into a smooth road, an overwhelming stench stained the air. It could only be described as moldy laundry mingled with sour dog. Pasha discreetly hid his nose in his collar, but Pyro made no subtleties about it.

"Ugh! Crikey, that's unbearable! Staccato, don't tell me you had to grow up here amongst this stench!"

Pasha's voice was small and timid. "What . . . what is it?"

Staccato rolled his eyes. "It's the dye pits."

"Like where things go to die," Pyro teased.

"Very funny, Pyro." Without another word, Staccato wandered off the trail and pulled back a curtain of moss. Beyond was a bustling outdoor workspace cluttered with round holes of foaming blackish-blue mixtures. The workers were mostly female and were plunged to the elbow in the brackish concoction.

"They're indigo pits. One of our most valuable commodities in

Aquarius. Kings and queens will pay exorbitant prices for a bolt of Aquarian indigo silk." Staccato fingered his own silken, indigo cravat as though in a trance. "Not that the laborers see much of it." He stared for another moment or two, then turned and forged ahead.

"The smell comes out eventually," remarked Sonata from the back of the wagon.

Melodious sucked his teeth. "That is what you think."

Pasha hastened to keep up with Staccato's pace. "So, how far do we have to go before we reach Mother Genesis?"

"We'll have to get farther away from civilization." Staccato pushed aside a vine with the end of his staff. "You can find a Sylph almost anywhere there are trees, but they prefer to colonize in secluded areas."

"Can't we just fly there?"

Skelter shook his head and pointed to a sign off the side of the road with a large "X" painted over a pair of wings.

"This is a no-flying zone," translated Staccato. "Here and there you'll come across them, particularly in localities where dragons are known to frequent. But not to worry, that isn't the case here. There's a Mermaid Bath House nearby, and it's closed off for privacy reasons."

Skelter and Pyro exchanged furtive grins.

Sonata stuck her head out out the open hatch behind the driver's seat.

"I saw that, you two!" She crossed her arms and muttered to

herself, “If I did go back to Sagittarius, at least I wouldn’t be surrounded by men twenty-four seven.”

“And anyway,” Staccato continued, “before we see Mother Genesis, there’s something of yours we need to pick up, Pasha.”

“Something of mine? As in me?” Pasha hastened to get a good look at Staccato’s expression. Staccato did not smile, but there was a glint in his eye that seemed to want to.

“Yes, you.”

“What is it?”

Staccato shrugged. “Something useful in a place like this. I’ve no doubt you will be very happy to see it returned to you.”

Pasha’s eyes dilated. “Returned? Is it something I lost?”

“Lost?” Staccato appeared to be feigning distraction. “Yes, you could say that. But no more questions, you’ll find out when we get there, and we appear to be making good time.”

Pasha flashed Sonata a curious look through the hatch. She gave him a wink. Eager to know more, he ran behind the wagon where Sonata was waiting for him with a mischievous smile.

“What is it?” Pasha whispered.

Sonata leaned over the ledge of the caravan and shooed him away playfully.

“You’ll see, silly.”

It was an entire hour before they reached a sign indicating the no-flying district had ended. Pasha heaved a sigh of relief.

Staccato had never looked more sly as he settled in front of a canopy of vines drawn across the path like a curtain. "Pasha?"

Pasha's ears pricked with interest. Staccato beckoned him forward.

"You'll find him beyond this thicket."

Pasha raised an eyebrow, his mind heavy with curiosity. "Him?"

Staccato waved him forward. "Go on." He swept back the curtain of greenery.

In a moment of rapturous awe, Pasha's breath was stolen away. Behind the shrubbery was a glen of grazing pegasi, their great, feathery wings tucked over their shoulders. Pasha ducked through the foliage.

"Something I lost is here?"

Staccato nodded his head, the tiniest hint of a smile at the corner of his lips.

"Look behind you."

Pasha turned around. His mouth dropped open. For a moment, he thought his knees might give out from shock. Harpagos, his childhood horse, galloped towards him. An enormous wreath of iron-gray wings fanned from his shoulders like laurels. His charcoal mane fell loose about his broad, dappled neck. He tossed his head back and whinnied with joy.

"Harpagos!" Pasha bounded towards him, arms outstretched.

His smile was so broad it made his cheeks sore. Harpagos shoved his head under Pasha's shoulder like a dog as Pasha buried his face in the coarse hair.

Pasha was overcome with emotion. It didn't seem real that he should be feeling the warm breath of Harpagos's muzzle against his skin. The horse gave a playful snort and butted him to the ground. Pasha laughed out loud.

Staccato smiled and stroked his chin. "He's been waiting for you a long time."

Pasha tried not to laugh as Harpagos buried his fuzzy nose inside his collar. "But I don't understand. How is it possible? You weren't one of the gypsies who bought Harpagos from us, were you?"

Staccato calmly shook his head. "No, it wasn't me. But we aren't the only Voilerians out there exploring the Other, you know."

Something about his reply felt oddly evasive. It was a simple answer to a question that demanded a lot of explanation. Pasha shook the thought from his head. He would worry about that later; for now, he was just happy to see Harpagos.

"Can he really fly?"

Staccato gestured to Harpagos. "See for yourself."

Without a moment's hesitation, Pasha mounted Harpagos bareback. He didn't even have to tell Harpagos what to do. The horse took several long strides and soared into the clouds. Pasha's mouth curled into a massive grin as he clung to Harpagos's mane. The lush rainforest shrank away to a blur of green. Birds skimmed past them, flapping their wings as they chirped and sang. Mountains faced them at eye level. Pasha could feel himself hovering in his seat as Harpagos dove downwards. He tucked his chin to his chest, trying to keep from laughing and screaming at the same time. For once, he felt not a single worry about anything—not about home, not about himself—he was too happy to be anxious. Finally, Harpagos drifted back to the very place they had begun.

Sonata's shoulders wound up to her ears as she waved her hands at Staccato.

"You can't just let him fly bareback his first time! He could've broken his neck!"

But rather than apologize, Staccato appeared highly amused. "Nonsense, the boy's a natural. You worry too much."

Harpagos's hooves thumped against the ground as they slowed to a stop. Pasha dismounted, panting from exhilaration.

"All this time, I thought my mother made up those stories about gypsies teaching horses to fly."

Staccato ran a hand down Harpagos's smooth muzzle.

"She was quite right. All horses have the ability to grow wings, but only Fay know the secret to unlocking them."

Pasha laughed as Harpagos nibbled at his cowlick, but something Staccato had said struck him as curious. How did his mother know about pegasi? She'd been put up for adoption as an infant. There was no reason for her to know anything about Voiler.

"So, all this time Harpagos has been with you?"

Staccato tensed, pausing before he answered. "For six years. He usually travels along with us, but he's been on rest this past month. That's why he's here."

Pasha drew his eyebrows together. Six years? Had Staccato known of Pasha's existence for six years? How long had he been keeping an eye on him? Furthermore, how did Staccato know Harpagos was Pasha's horse?

As though sensing Pasha's oncoming questions, Staccato turned back to the wagon and dusted off his hands.

"Alright, well we better get a move on. Cortijo Del Mar is too far of a journey for you to ride Harpagos, Pasha. I'm afraid you'll have to postpone your reunion for a little while." He steered Pasha towards the back of the wagon in a hurry. Meanwhile Melodious hitched Harpagos alongside Schmetterling.

Inside the caravan, Sonata was struggling to shift a sliding drawer back into its track. The wheel gave way, and she accidentally smashed her finger.

Pyro bit his lip. "Ouch! You alright, Sonata?"

She held up her finger and winced. At the sight of the cut, Pasha's eyes grew wide. The blood trickling down her finger was so dark it was almost blue.

"Sonata—your blood, it's—"

"Oh, yes," she shrugged. "Mermaids have more copper in their bodies than other humans. It can cause the blood to have a bluish appearance sometimes, but it's nothing to be concerned about. It's perfectly normal." She pressed a fingertip to the injury and it instantly healed. "Now settle in, boys. We've got a long trip ahead of us."

***

Pasha would never have dreamed the journey to Cortijo Del Mar would span an entire day. As it turned out, continental Aquarius was massive. By the time they reached their destination, it was sunset. The woods below them were illuminated in a soft, sapphire light.

"We're here!" Sonata beckoned Pasha to the window as she pulled back the curtains and pointed into the valley. There, at the tip of her finger, was the most enormous, the most titanic, the most elephantine waterfall Pasha could ever have perceived with his eyes. The sheer height was so overwhelming he could scarcely see the bottom through the dense mantles of glittering mist.

Pyro yawned and stretched in his bunk below. "Well, if you've got anything important to say, you better say it now."

Pasha tilted his head. "Why? What do you mean?"

"You can't hear a blue blazing thing over those falls! Not until you're behind the barrier anyway."

When the wagon finally landed, Pasha realized Pyro hadn't been exaggerating. They had settled a considerable distance from the waterfall, and the effect was still deafening. Pasha trotted after his companions down a path of crowded greenery. The trees seemed to be watching them; they compressed the company on either side until the tops of their branches knotted together in one canopy.

At the end of the path was an archway of beaded vines. Staccato held it open, and they filed in. The roaring was muffled to a soothing flood. Staccato massaged his ears.

"That's much better, don't you think?"

There was no question now that the trees were watching them; the feeling was unmistakable. A patch of moss peeled back from a limb. Pasha craned his head back. A greenish-colored girl with flowers in her hair, or perhaps growing from her hair, scurried barefoot across the treetops. Noises like split wood echoed around them as tree trunks unraveled into torsos. Roots pulled up from the soil and transformed into flowering feet and ankles.

At the bottom of the path stood a ginormous silk cotton tree with thick torsions of soft, pale wood. Its limbs reached outwards with a spray of carmine, honeysuckle-shaped blossoms. A breeze coiled up its trunk, and the tree sprang to life. A branch drew itself away to reveal a wooden face with bark so soft it became flesh. The features shifted into focus. A bend in the trunk became the powerful thighs of a woman. The supple curve of a bud became fingers, and the smooth pith of a knothole transformed into lips. The luscious green foliage fell across her pruned shoulders in cascading tendrils. She stretched her arms over her head.

"I was wondering when you'd come wandering back into my woods, Staccato Nimbus." She threw him a playful wink. "Many a spring has passed since you sat beneath my shade. Many more since you swung from my branches and slept in my canopy as a boy."

"Come now, Mother Genesis, if it were that long you would have forgotten me by now."

She leaned forward, resting her carved chin upon delicate, flowering hands.

"You silly creature! Even if I weren't the tree of all knowledge I could no more forget you than I could forget any of my sons or daughters."

"That's saying something," whispered Pyro to Pasha. "She has a million!"

Mother Genesis rose to take them all in. "What a treat you have brought me! Everyone's here! Sonata, Melodious, Pyro, and oh my! Skelter, darling! How I've missed your company! I do hope you'll be playing some of your music during your stay."

Skelter came forward to brush his lips against the back of her blossoming palm. Finally, she settled her gaze on Pasha. Her vibrant eyes grew wide as a smile dimpled her wooden cheeks.

"Oh, my . . . So, you've brought him at last! Come here, little one."

Pasha's knees trembled as he stumbled forward. He did his best not to stare, but she was so extraordinary, so beautiful, so unlike anything he had ever seen. Her branching fingers caressed the space beneath his chin.

"How sweet you look, my love! Look at those big brown eyes! Oh, he's absolutely precious!"

"That's a great feature, isn't it?" teased Pyro. "You know, you just don't see enough preciousness in kings these days—ow!"

Sonata elbowed him in the ribs.

"And so much of his family in his face!" She pushed his hair back. "He has Evangeline's chin, and his grandfather's nose."

Staccato examined his fingernails in a disinterested manner. "Does he now? I never noticed."

Mother Genesis smirked at Pasha and lowered her voice. "He never does."

Pasha tried not to laugh. At length, she turned a wary eye upon the miraculous.

"I hope you haven't brought him here for the reason I think you have."

"And what reason would that be?" Staccato preened the collar of his shirt in feigned innocence. Mother Genesis turned to Pasha with a protective glow in her verdant eyes.

"Has he brought you here to catch the Firebird?"

"Yes, ma'am."

She threw Staccato a look of grave disappointment.

"And no doubt you've come to ask me how to catch her!

Whenever you need answers, you always come looking for me!"

Staccato threw up his shoulders. "Well, where else would I go? I thought you'd be flattered. It should please you that I come seeking your advice first."

"It might, if you ever listened to what I had to say! I know you, Staccato. You only take my advice when it's convenient. If you don't like what I have to say, you get upset and question my credibility! You've done the same thing since you were six years old! Many things have changed about you as you've grown older, Staccato, but the one thing time has not altered is your stubbornness!"

"Now, Mother Genesis," interceded Sonata, "I hardly think that's fair. You know in the end Staccato always comes to respect your advice. And who knows, perhaps he'll follow it this time."

Staccato glared at Sonata, nettled. Mother Genesis unfolded her branches and heaved a long sigh.

"Well, you're not going to like what I have to say."

Staccato leaned forward. "I would still like to hear it. Come, Mother Genesis, how could I question the tree of all knowledge? You know everything!"

Mother Genesis groaned and dropped her shoulders.

"Alright, fine. Don't say I didn't warn you. The victor of the Firebird has already been determined, and you are not the winner."

"What?" Staccato's staff gave out beneath him and he almost fell over. "How do you know?" He shot Mother Genesis an accusing glare.

Mother Genesis shook her branches. “See? What did I tell you!”

Sonata nudged Staccato aside. “Please, Mother Genesis, do explain.”

“Samael was always meant to catch the Firebird because it is the will of the bird herself. Do not ask me why, for you will know in time, but it is not your hour.”

“Not our hour?” echoed Pasha. “What do you mean? Why can’t you tell us?”

“My darling boy, so much you have still to learn about this place. It has been this way from the moment of my conception. It is contrary to the rules of my being. I am the tree which possesses all knowledge, but not all knowledge is meant to be possessed by mankind. And some knowledge must occur in its own time. If I told you something before you were ready to hear it, you would drop down dead on the spot. That’s simply how it works.”

“I see.”

“But I can tell you this,” she turned to Staccato with a motherly vengeance, “forget about that blasted bird and let this poor boy be!” Her booming voice sent a bevy of sparrows flocking from their nests.

Staccato’s knuckles grew white as he clenched his staff. “But why? Can you at least tell us why?”

“I did! Besides, there are more important things you can be

doing to help the world at large."

Staccato looked as though he might tear his hair out, if he had any hair to tear.

"If Samael catches the Firebird, she will grant him one wish, and he'll wish for the power to conquer all of Voiler again! What could be more important than keeping him from catching that bird?"

"You ask all the wrong questions! You're putting your faith in the wrong answers! You're falling into someone else's trap!"

Staccato threw his hands up. "Whose trap?"

"You will know in time! Until then, stop chasing the Firebird! You are not meant to catch her. Instead, focus your efforts on breaking the Land Lock Curse and freeing all the mermaids."

"Freeing all the mermaids?" Staccato's voice cracked. "What good will that do?"

Sonata smacked his arm, looking wholly indignant. "Excuse me! Mermaid goddaughter here, waiting to be reunited with parents!"

Staccato pinched his forehead. "Sorry, dearest, you know I didn't mean anything by it."

Meanwhile, Mother Genesis had had enough.

"I knew this would happen! Didn't I say it? Didn't I say you wouldn't listen? My warnings mean nothing to you when you have a mind to do something. Well, it's no use beating around the bush. You're obviously not going to change your mind. I'll tell you where the Firebird nests. Do you remember how the Phoenix Islands got their name?"

Staccato's eyes glowed with an epiphany. "Of course! Why didn't I think of it before?"

Pasha glanced from Staccato to Mother Genesis. "What? How did they get their name?"

Staccato turned to Pasha with such excitement it was almost frightening. "The Phoenix Islands are ruled by the mermaids of Cetus. The ancient Cetaceans predicted one day a phoenix, or in this case, the Firebird, would rise up in a time of great divide and drink the lava running through the heart of the volcano Fornax! So, they built a nest to accommodate her! That's where she's staying!"

Mother Genesis looked somewhat annoyed. "I'm surprised at you, Staccato. Did you really need my assistance to figure that out?"

He turned to Mother Genesis and clasped her branches. "Dear Mother Genesis, I could never have done it without you! You know you've always been my chief source of inspiration!"

"Yes, yes, well, all the same, I am glad you came because I have something to give you. Despite what you may think, I am not in total contradiction with your efforts. You all have a great task set before you, and so I have a contribution to make."

"A contribution?" Staccato leaned closer. "I'm listening."

"What I'm about to entrust to your care possesses great power. You must promise to regard such power with the utmost care and respect."

"You have our word."

Mother Genesis clicked her tongue. "You can be foolish at times, Staccato Nimbus, but I know this is a matter I can trust you with. Go down into the glen. I'll meet you there." She closed her eyes and twisted back into a tree once more.

Pasha froze, fascinated. Staccato had to prod him along with the tip of his staff.

"Come along now, Pasha, this way." They walked down the pathway descending into a bluish glen on the west side of the falls.

Pyro seemed restless with agitation. By the time they made it halfway down the hill, he could hold his tongue no longer.

"We aren't really going to stop chasing the Firebird, are we?"

Sonata ground to a halt. "Are you saying you don't trust Mother Genesis? How could you, Pyro! She's the tree of all knowledge!"

"Oh, come on, you don't buy that, do you?"

"Of course I do! Mother Genesis has never been wrong! It's historical fact! No self-respecting Fay would ever question her!"

Pyro threw up his hands. "Look, regardless of your faith in Mother Genesis's infallibility, letting the Firebird go would be too much of a risk."

Sonata swiveled around to her godfather. "Staccato, do you hear him right now?"

Staccato turned and sighed. "Pyro is right. I'm afraid the stakes are too high to take such a risk."

Sonata dropped her mouth in disbelief. "You can't be serious! Staccato, shame on you! You should know better!"

Melodious nodded in agreement. "Listen to Sonata, my friend. You are leaning too much on your own understanding."

"Precisely! Mother Genesis has never been wrong. What reason do you have to doubt her?"

Staccato groaned and rubbed the space between his eyebrows.

"It's not that I doubt her, I'm merely covering my bases. With so much hanging in the balance, how could I, in good conscience, abandon the chase for the Firebird?"

"For someone who doesn't doubt her, you sure do seem to be showing a lack of faith."

Skelter rose up behind Sonata's shoulder and nodded, claiming his allegiance. Pyro drew back in shock.

"What? Skelter! Not you, too!"

Skelter pointed to Sonata and tapped the side of his head. Pyro stamped his foot.

"What do you mean, Sonata is always right? I can be right too, you know!"

Skelter crossed his arms and shook his head.

Pyro's eyes fired with indignation. "How can you all be so stubborn? It's not like we're doing anything criminal! Like Staccato said, lives are at stake here! It's a matter of caution, not doubt!"

But Sonata remained unfazed. She placed her hands coolly on her hips.

"If Mother Genesis says give up the Firebird, I say we give up the Firebird, and if you won't heed her instruction, I refuse to go any further! You can send me back to Ascella if you wish. I'll have Thayer assign me a new task, one where I can focus my efforts on freeing my people!"

Pyro's mouth nearly hit the floor. "This is ludicrous! Have you lost your mind?"

Staccato rolled his eyes. "Now really, Sonata, don't you think you're overreacting a little?"

Sonata did not answer. She merely stared them down, boiling with her mighty will. Staccato folded his hands behind his back with a smug, yet level-headed expression.

"Fine. You're going to travel all the way back to Sagittarius by yourself?"

Melodious spoke in her place. "Not by herself. I will accompany Sonata if she chooses to leave."

Skelter beat a fist on his chest and placed his hand on Sonata's shoulder, asserting he would do the same. Sonata gave a satisfactory smile.

"It seems you're outnumbered."

Pyro bowed his head in defiance. "Oh, I don't know about that. Pasha, what do you say?"

Pasha's insides groaned. He winced apologetically at the three companions united in opposition and took his place between the stately miraculous and the combustible igneous.

"Sorry, Sonata, but I have to go with Pyro and Staccato on this one."

Pyro didn't bother to hide his jubilation and pumped his fist into the air.

Sonata regarded Pyro with a superior-looking jeer. "What are you so excited about? We're at a stalemate."

"*Oi*, considering Pasha is the one who's supposed to catch the Firebird, his opinion should count twice!"

"What does that matter to us? We're not interested in catching the Firebird!"

Finally, Staccato threw down his staff. "For the love of stars! Mother Genesis is waiting for us down in the glen! Can we at least postpone this decision until after she's shown us whatever it is she wants to show us?"

Sonata swept her nose into the air. "Fine!"

She marched past Pyro with an impenetrable sense of dignity. The gesture nearly drove him mad. In many ways, Pasha was relieved not to be opposing Pyro, whom he feared might not be so forgiving.

But he didn't feel good about disputing with Sonata, either. Despite her composure, she was very passionate when it came to her opinions. He liked Sonata. She was quiet, motherly, peaceful. It was easy for him to believe they were cousins. In no way did Pasha wish to disrupt that relationship. For now, he kept his distance.

Chapter 21:
Cicada Hatches

Down in the glen, Mother Genesis was possessing the body of an erratic-looking live oak. A coat of Spanish moss traveled down her back. Though the effect was somewhat different than the silk cotton tree, the body still retained her more dominant features.

Pasha was impressed. “How did you do that?”

“A simple act of transferring the spirit. That’s how I get around. Not that I make a habit of leaving very often. I am a tree, after all; I like to keep my roots.”

Nearby, a golden light emerged at the roots of a sycamore tree. Pasha approached it with caution. “What is it?”

Mother Genesis pushed him forward.

“This is what I’ve been waiting to show you. It’s been a full eighteen years now. She’s about to hatch any moment!”

Sonata leaned over Pasha’s shoulder. “It’s an esperite!”

Staccato’s eyes grew wide. “And not just any esperite, a child of Mother Genesis, a first-generation esperite. Twelve total are born each year, and they all go on to serve great purposes.”

There was a cracking noise as the roots retracted like long, bony fingers, and the wood split open and dilated. The branches trembled above them until leaves rained upon their heads. The hole in the tree stretched open, exposing a ray of yellow light. Pasha could make out the form of a glowing leg.

Sonata crossed her fingers and chanted under her breath. "Please be a girl, please be a girl . . ."

The bark peeled back further. Two hands curled beneath a chin. There was a bare shoulder, soft knees. Finally, the trembling stopped, and the hole in the tree ceased expanding. Inside was a slender girl with long, pale blonde hair as fine and as silky as a newborn infant's. Sonata pumped her fist into the air.

"Yes! Finally! I'm not the only woman anymore!"

The esperite's body glowed with golden light like a fairy. Pasha didn't immediately notice her state of undress, with all that long hair covering her. She wasn't a baby, but a young woman, only a few years older than Pasha. She blinked her wide, glowing eyes at them like a newborn kitten.

Before the girl could move, Mother Genesis shielded her with her branches, as several sylphs came forward to dress her.

"If you'll wait one second, gentlemen, we'll have her presentable."

Pasha turned away. He could hear a twinkling noise over his shoulder like soft wind chimes.

Sonata tapped him on the shoulder. "You boys can look now."

The sylphs had robed the esperite in loose-fitting dungarees made from a soft green material. She did not walk or crawl. Instead, she floated languidly on the air currents as though she were a breeze herself. As she went along, her body faded into a golden cloud from the waist down. It was she who had made the twinkling noise with a toss of her hair. Pasha eyed her in fascination.

"So, she's been in there for eighteen years?"

"That's how first-generation esperites are born," expounded Sonata. "They develop and gestate inside the tree after they're planted, and are born full-grown."

The esperite drifted low into the bushes, where she observed Pasha with her vivid green eyes.

Mother Genesis waved her out impatiently. "Come out of those shrubs, dear, and say hello. There's nothing to be afraid of."

The esperite looked back at her mother, never removing the scrutinizing expression from her face. She floated cautiously towards the group, still focusing on Pasha. She swam around him in a circle, playing curiously with the buttons on his sweater. Pasha didn't mind; in fact, he found it rather amusing.

Pyro, on the other hand, was confused. "What is she doing exactly?"

"I'm afraid you'll have to bear with her for some time." Mother Genesis twiddled her twigs. "She was only born a minute ago, after all."

Pasha stepped in with his conclusion before Pyro could employ his lack of tact.

"So, what you mean to say is, even though she's eighteen years old, she still hasn't learned everything yet?"

“Precisely.”

“And she’s supposed to go with us to Cetus?” Pyro bit his lip in concern.

Mother Genesis bowed her head. “That is her purpose. You may have to help her now and then as she develops. Eventually, she must learn to use her legs rather than float about constantly. But you’ll find she’s quite handy in a tight situation. She will give you both guidance and protection when you need it.”

Pyro thrust out his lip. “If you say so . . .”

The esperite moved onto Pyro and studied his hands with intense interest. Pyro didn’t appear altogether comfortable with it.

“She can still talk and stuff, can’t she?” he inquired hopefully. But the esperite answered his question for him.

“What are you?” She leaned into Pyro’s face so suddenly, he actually stumbled backward. Sonata stifled a laugh.

“An igneous. Do you know what you are?”

She blinked. “No.”

Pyro rubbed a hand over his eyes. “Brilliant.”

She turned to Mother Genesis. “Mother, what am I?”

“You’re an esperite, dear.”

For the very first time she smiled, and her light ebbed brighter.

“Oh, yeah! I’m an esperite!” She looked down at her glowing hands as though seeing them for the first time. “But who am I? Don’t I need a name? What should I call myself?”

“How about Cicada?” Pasha suggested.

“Cicada?” She hovered upside-down, inches from Pasha’s face. “What’s a cicada?”

“It’s an insect that hatches inside a tree and doesn’t come out until it’s fully grown, kinda like you.”

Her eyes studied him in deep contemplation, then exploded with strange, unsmiling excitement.

“Cicada! I like it! I like you!” If she hadn’t said so, Pasha would never have guessed, for she looked so intense he thought she might hit him. Cicada looped back into an upright position and turned again to Mother Genesis, her face still serious. “I like him, Mother! He thinks of good names!”

Mother Genesis stroked her flowering fingers through Cicada’s hair. “Well, perhaps you should ask him his name, like a proper young lady.”

Cicada swung back to Pasha in a golden arc, continuing to poke her nose too closely in his space.

“What’s your name?”

“Pasha.”

“Pasha! I’m Cicada.”

Pasha contorted into a simper of amusement and held out his hand in greeting. Unsure of what to do, Cicada took a small pebble and enclosed it in his palm. It was all Pasha could do to keep from laughing.

“Uh, thanks.”

Cicada threw up her shoulders. “Don’t mention it.”

“We’ll have to work on that,” groaned the matriarchal tree. “For now, why don’t you all make camp here and allow her to get acquainted with you for the rest of the day. I’ve already made up accommodations, and I won’t take no for an answer.”

***

Hours later Pasha was lying in a bed of flowers beneath a canopied glade. When he first saw the pillow resting in the patch of poppies, he assumed they were going to sleep in sleeping bags. But the moment he laid down he realized these were no ordinary flower beds. The ground was softer than any mattress and so comfortable he’d already fallen asleep once.

Everything was quiet. Sonata reclined nearby in her wheelchair with Cello, reading. Most everyone else had gone off to shower. There was a rustling noise as Pyro pushed back the curtains and entered, rubbing a towel through his damp hair. He held out his hand for Cello to sniff.

“Whatcha doing, Cello, old boy?” But Cello turned up his whiskers. Pyro sniffed. “Torches, Sonata, you’ve turned him against me!”

Sonata rolled her eyes. “I did no such thing. Cello has his own opinions about how you turned down Mother Genesis’s advice.”

“Alright, if Mother Genesis is so wise, why did she think

sending us a baby would help us?"

Sonata closed her book. "She's not a baby, Pyro. She's eighteen years old."

Pyro glanced back at Cicada through the trees. She appeared to be playing some primitive form of peekaboo with a patch of sunflowers.

"She's a baby."

Sonata flared her nostrils and turned to Pasha in astonishment. "Can you believe him?"

How many times was he going to be dragged into an argument today? Pasha shrugged with his chin to his chest.

"Well, actually I kinda agree with Pyro. I mean, don't get me wrong, I like her, but she does seem like a liability."

Sonata looked from one to the other, astounded. "Do either of you realize how powerful she is?"

"Not really," retorted Pyro dryly.

"For your information, esperites can be downright dangerous at this age. She's still discovering her powers, still learning her place in the world."

"Then why the bloody heck do they wait so long to wake 'em up?"

"That's how it works, Pyro! They need that time to develop."

"Well, what are we supposed to use her for? A flashlight?"

"If we run into a coven of liliths, or a band of furies, or even a brood of ophidians, you might think differently. Besides, some female companionship may enable me to maintain my sanity in the testosterone mobile over there."

"How is she going to fight off an ophidian? They like the sunlight, don't they? They sit around and lay in it all day."

"You forget how easily their senses can be overwhelmed. Too much light can cloud their judgment. She can blind them, and what's more impressive, she can tamper with their thermal detection."

"Really?" Pasha leaned forward, intrigued.

"Yes. Esperites can make light and heat appear where there is none, enabling them to send ophidians off on false trails. In many ways, they are quite similar to igneous."

Pyro snorted and folded his arms across his chest. In all the excitement Pasha had forgotten about their previous quarrel; Pyro, however, had not.

"Wait a second! Now that we've got Cicada, we have a tiebreaker, don't we?"

Sonata lifted her head. "What are you so excited about? You really think Cicada would go against her mother's wishes?"

"Not all children are goody-two-shoes, you know. She could have a rebellious side, maybe some resentment after being locked up in a tree for eighteen years."

"How many times do I have to tell you? She couldn't leave the tree, she would have died! She was still developing!"

Pyro and Sonata continued their bickering, while Pasha checked on Cicada. He found her still engrossed with the sunflowers. As he neared her, he realized she was staring them down as though they had offended her dignity. Pasha's eyes darted back and forth between Cicada and the yellow blossoms.

"What are you doing?"

Cicada threw down her fists. "They won't stop following me! See, watch!" She drifted past the sunflowers. They turned their petals to follow her. She looped backward and hovered above them. Again they tilted their haloed faces in her direction. She zoomed back and forth and still the sunflowers hastened to keep up with her.

"Why do they keep following me?" She buried her reddening face in her hands. Pasha tried to hide his amusement.

"It's because they think you're sunlight."

Cicada sniffed. "What?"

"Sunflowers like sunlight, they follow it around with their heads. It helps them grow."

Her face illuminated with clarity. "Oh! I get it now!"

"They won't hurt you. They just like you."

Cicada's frown grew to a smile. "They like me! That changes everything." She pressed her face to the center of the flower and inhaled the summery fragrance. Despite the fact that she was eighteen years old, there was still something quite babyish about her features. Her eyes were wide and overstimulated, her mouth was small and pink, and her face was perfectly round. She had tiny hands, little shoulders, a thin neck, and a childish figure. Pasha wondered how much she already knew. What would they have to teach her? How long would it be before she attained their level?

"So, you know how to talk. Do you know how to read?"

She cocked her head like a puppy. "Read?"

"You know, like written words, books, that kinda stuff."

"Show me."

"Uh, okay, wait right here."

He ran back to the yellow caravan and looked for something she could read. He spied a newspaper lying on Pyro's bunk. He grabbed it and returned to Cicada.

She unfolded the thin, pulpy sheets of paper and held them far away from her as if adjusting her eyes to the size of the text.

"*The C.O.N. Invades Sheretan. On Tuesday, the second of December, a coven of liliths confirmed to be affiliated with international terrorist group the C.O.N., or Children of Najash, interrupted a local Christmas festival and took twelve igneous hostage. The victims of the kidnapping were subjected to water torture. Many were injured, and one was confirmed dead at the scene of the crime. All were branded with their birth names on their arms.*"

Pasha was so engrossed in the story, he completely forgot the purpose of the exercise. He had only wanted to see if she could read; he hadn't been expecting the article to be so interesting.

The leaves rustled and Pyro burst from the glade looking rather irate.

"*Oi*!" He pointed an accusing finger at Cicada. "What are you doing with my newspaper?"

Cicada soared high into the air out of Pyro's reach, clutching the newspaper to her chest.

Sonata wheeled after him. "Pyro, calm down, it's just a newspaper. Anyone can read it."

But he wasn't listening, he was jumping for the newspaper, waving his arms trying to grab it from Cicada's grasp. Cicada stared at him with curiosity.

Pasha grabbed Pyro's arm and pulled him away from her.

"Wait, Pyro, it's not her fault. I wanted to see if she could read. I saw the newspaper lying on the bed. I didn't know it was personal. I'm sorry."

But Pyro seemed determined to fault Cicada.

"I just want it back!" He leaped higher, his arms flailing. Cicada's eyes sank down to the newspaper and back to the crazed Pyro. With two fingers she held the paper within his reach, testing him. Pyro leaped for it. She drew back. She held it out again. Pyro hopped. Again she pulled it away. An impish smile grew on her face until finally, she had driven Pyro mad.

"Give it back!"

Cicada threw back her head and laughed. She skidded off

through the trees. Pyro ran after her.

"Come back here, you bloody fairy, and give me back my newspaper!"

Pasha was weak in the knees from tearful hilarity while Sonata gaped in alarm.

"Pyro! No! You'll scare her!" She thrust her wheels forward. A surge of overpowering, spectral light exploded through the trees. Instinctively, Sonata and Pasha shielded their eyes. Next thing they knew, it was gone, and Pyro was panicking at the top of his lungs.

"She's—she's blinded me! I'm blind! I've been blinded by a bloody fairy!"

Sonata shook her head. "Oh dear, we better go help him."

They entered the woods. Pyro was rolling on his back, pressing his hands over both eyes.

"She's blinded me! I can't see nothing!"

Sonata halted with Pyro wallowing at the foot of her wheels. "Can't say I didn't warn you. Come on, get up. It's not permanent. It only lasts an hour."

Pyro groped to a standing position. Pasha spied Cicada hiding amongst the branches of a maple tree, watching them like a frightened cat. He beckoned her down but Cicada shook her head. Pasha shrugged and helped Sonata lead Pyro back to the glade where he could lie down and recover.

"There, there, now," soothed Sonata as she pulled Pyro's

blanket up to his chest. “It’s not that bad.”

“I’ll be lucky if I ever see again!”

“Really now, Pyro, that’s ridiculous. Would you like me to get your stuffed dragon?”

Pyro’s mouth fell open. “You promised you’d never tell anyone about Torchy!”

Sonata shrugged. “I don’t know what you’re so upset about, nobody’s around except you and me.” She winked at Pasha.

The newspaper floated back into Pasha’s memory. Pyro must have forgotten about it in all the chaos. Without anyone noticing, he snuck out of the canopy to go look for it.

He was eager to finish the article. Why was it so significant that the liliths tattooed the igneous’ names on their arms? What did it mean? Cicada was still sitting up in the tree when he returned.

“Will you come down now?”

Cicada poked her head out of the branches. “Is he gone?”

“He’s in bed now.”

Cicada drifted to the ground as though she were being deflated. “Thank goodness! I think he’s crazy!”

“You wouldn’t be the only one. Do you still have that paper?”

“I hid it there.” She pointed to a squirrel’s nest in the trees.

“May I see it, please?”

“Sure!” She flew into the canopy and retrieved the article, smoothing it out into manageable sections. She handed it to Pasha, who thumbed through the pages looking for the original piece.

"We should probably return this to him, you know."

"Will it make him stop acting so crazy?"

"It'll help." He opened back to the column and began reading again, but it was quite dark now. "Cicada, can you do me a favor and shine your light on this?"

"Absolutely!" She hovered above him and placed her elbows on his head, cupping her chin in her hands. Pasha read aloud to her.

"*Many were injured, and one was confirmed dead at the scene of the crime. All were branded with their birth names on their arms.*" He stopped. "You wouldn't happen to know why liliths would tattoo people's names on their arms, would you?"

"Nope!"

"Do you even know what liliths are?"

"Nope!"

Pasha chewed on his lip. "Me either. I just know they're bad news." He cleared his throat. "*Such occurrences are not uncommon in the kingdom of Aries. Attacks of a similar nature are quite frequent in Ram Country. Due to the high population of igneous, water torture is always a recurring theme. Many remember the 1901 Hostage Crisis when three hundred igneous were taken prisoner during the Thaw Moon Festival and held inside St. Pyre's Fort. Among the captives were the King's three children. As many of you may well remember, the eldest of those offspring, Prince Arson, did not make it out alive.*

To this day the 1901 Sheratan Hostage Crisis holds the record for the largest number of victims taken captive by the C.O.N. at one time."

Cicada clicked her tongue. "Sounds horrible."

"Did you understand most of that?"

Cicada leaned back and hovered over his shoulder. "I know what hostages are, and what igneous are, and what Aries is."

"How is it you know all that but you don't know what liliths are?"

"I don't know. But they couldn't be a race of people, because I was born with a knowledge of all races in Voiler."

Pasha redirected his attention to the newspaper. Why would an article like this be so important to Pyro? Maybe it wasn't. It wouldn't be unlike him to grow possessive around the new member whom he considered babyish. But something told Pasha this wasn't the case. There were connections, after all. Pyro was from Aries. Pyro was an igneous. All this had happened in 1901—how old would Pyro have been? Had he been there when all this had happened? Could he have been one of the three hundred igneous held hostage?

Pasha folded up the paper. "Come on, let's take this back to Pyro. It's getting late."

At the mention of Pyro, Cicada whipped around his shoulder and shrank before his very eyes.

"If it's all the same to you, I'll just hide here."

She curled up until she was no bigger than the palm of his

hand, and tried to pull his collar over her head.

"*Blin!*" Pasha shook his head. "I mean, gosh! You can change sizes?"

"Well, I can shrink. I can't grow myself larger than my natural size."

"That's amazing!"

She swam back into the open air, restoring herself to her proper measurements. "Do I really have to hand-deliver it to that crazy person?"

"Nah," Pasha laughed. "I'll do it. We both should be getting ready for bed anyway. Sonata is going to stay with you down by the willow trees so you won't have to sleep alone."

Cicada clapped her hands together and looped backward. "I love willow trees, they're so ... willowy! Come on, I'll light your path back to camp."

Cicada walked him the short distance back to the glade and floated away to the willow coppice. When Pasha went inside, Pyro had yet to fall asleep and was lying in his flower bed with an arm thrown over his eyes.

Pasha cleared his throat. "I got your paper back."

Pyro groped clumsily through the air for the newspaper. After several attempts, he managed to catch hold of it and stuff it under his bedcovers.

"Thanks, mate."

"Can I ask you a personal question?"

"Depends on what it is."

"How old are you?"

"I'll be thirty-three next March. Why?"

"Just wondering."

Pyro grunted and rolled over on his side with his back towards Pasha. If Pyro was thirty-two years old now, in 1901 he would have been nine. There were so many questions Pasha was dying to ask, but he wasn't going to bother Pyro with them. Sonata would know. She would be willing to explain everything to Pasha. Perhaps he would ask her tomorrow.

"I'm gonna go wash up." Pasha dusted his hands. "Where do I go again?"

Pyro jerked his thumb over his head. "Follow the path past the meadow of bluebells, and you'll see it on your right."

Gathering up his toiletries, Pasha set out down the path. Along the way, sylphs crept amongst the branches, whispering, laughing, sleeping. Some eyed him flirtatiously. Pasha bent his head low and blushed. Overall, he liked the sylphs and the esperites, and Mother Genesis was incredibly kind, but it all made him feel rather paranoid about trees.

Chapter 22:

A Nice Girl with a Lot of Charm

Faina huddled beneath the door of the Foxhole where long-tapering moisture sucked off the black awning like barnacles. A black cloche shielded her cheeks from the wind, and her kitten heels clicked on the pavement. She had come directly from the funeral. She braced herself against the chilly breeze, eager to escape inside where she could force herself to do the unthinkable.

She was exhausted with grief and harried with desperation in a way that made her lungs ache. The grocery had gone up for sale, the remainder of the building sold to Mrs. Borsuk, and their apartment had been put up for rent. Faina, Anya, and Mammoth were now living with Pasha's mother, sharing Pasha's room. Faina regretted that now, after her son had gone, Mama Lydia had found herself supporting two more children in his place.

As Faina entered the ground floor of the Foxhole, she found Klokov preoccupied with two young associates. She sat at the bar and waited. Nearby, a gaggle of mobsters discussed what they had seen in Herald Square Thanksgiving morning.

"I am telling you, it was the Firebird! The very same from myth and legend!" Obviously this man was still in touch with his Russian heritage, unlike some of the others.

Another man laughed. "Yeah, Anatole, you sure you weren't hitting the bottle that morning?"

"No, I swear! It attacked Solokov, dragged him across the square!"

"Yeah, yeah, I heard about that. Look, it was just a firework gone astray. No big deal, the kid was even alright!"

"The Russian Rogue, Anastas—he saw it too, down near the Bowery! He even has a feather-shaped scar on his palm."

"You mean the big blonde kid whose parents were the anarchists? Come on, Anatole, you know better than to listen to him. Poor kid," the man shook his head disgracefully, "he's one troubled soul. Probably looking for attention."

Faina watched as Klokov shook hands with his suppliers and dismissed them through the door. Without wasting a moment, she scooted back her chair and advanced towards the table with her head bowed and her hands folded together. Klokov's expression softened with pity.

"Good morning, Miss Spichkin. What can I do for you today?" There was grave respect in his voice which told Faina he'd heard about her uncle. She glanced around at the sweaty congregation of men occupying the room, leaning back in their chairs with cigarettes and noisily poking at billiards.

"I wish to discuss a private matter."

Klokov bobbed his head and, getting up from his seat, gestured to his office down the hall. It was not unusual to see Klokov approached by grieving women looking for assistance, so little attention was given to the pair as they retired to a discrete setting.

Klokov shut the door behind them, and offered Faina a chair. "So, what did the police say about your uncle?"

"They think it was the Bowery Butchers," she knit her brows together, "and yet they would have no reason to attack him. My uncle never crossed the Butchers—I mean, there was that whole deal with the extortionist, but that was six years ago."

Klokov shook his head. "That was dealt with. Viktor Volkov and his racketeering was what compelled your brother to seek me out in the first place. We took care of it. That's no reason for them to come after your uncle now. You sure he didn't have any secret dealings with anyone? Anything suspicious?"

She shook her head. "My uncle was . . . *Nevinny*, um," she tapped her forehead searching for the translation, "naive that is. I probably knew more about the street gangs of New York than he did by the time I was ten years old."

"He was an upright man. I respect that. Just so you're aware, I have a few of my men looking into it. We'll let you know if any leads turn up."

Faina bowed her head with solemnity and mouthed a phrase of gratitude. Klokov poured a glass of water from the sideboard and offered it to her.

"Where are you and Miss Dalka staying? Did you remain in the apartment?"

She shook her head. "We couldn't afford the rent. Mrs. Chevalsky took us in. Now, she has two more people to take care of in addition to Pasha's little sister. And our landlady, Mrs. Borsuk, raised the rent yesterday. Anya and Mrs. Chevalsky both work in factories, and are paid next to nothing. I know I'll be getting my paycheck from you in a week, but I'm afraid it might not be enough to take care of all of us."

Klokov drummed his fingers on his cigar, searching for a solution. "Why can't you just get a normal job in a shop or something?"

Faina lowered her eyes. "You know why I can't do that."

There was pity and maybe even something akin to guilt in Klokov's expression.

"I've got a reputation. No one will hire me." She fought against the tears flooding into her eyes. "I've already tried."

Klokov stared unblinkingly at the wall for several moments. At length he snuffed out his cigar and steepled his fingers with an air of contemplative tranquility.

"Look kid, you're going about this the completely wrong way. Instead of trying to compete with my boys, why don't you try dating one instead?"

A bitter taste stained Faina's tongue. "I don't have time to date one of your sweaty racehorses. I have a family to take care of."

Klokov knit his brows together. "That's the point!" He leaned across the desk and made an attempt to soften his voice. "Listen, you're a nice girl with a lot of charm. You could easily find a reasonable young buck with a steady job, decent income, and stability to take care of you. What's so bad about that? I don't understand you, kid. Wouldn't you rather be at home where it's quiet and safe than some drunken speakeasy? Wouldn't you rather be loved and supported than constantly running from the police and getting knocked around all the time?"

Faina stared silently at her hands, the thrill of victory stolen from her lips and replaced by a horrible sense of helplessness.

"You're not gonna change your mind on this, are you?"

Klokov frowned and shook his head. "I can't encourage this situation forever. Not only is it against my principles, but it's risking my reputation."

Sighing, Faina got up from her chair. "Well, a girl can try." She shrugged. "Thank you for your time."

The moment she exited the door, she ran smack into Anastas who was leaning against the wall, smoking. He eyed Faina and plucked the cigarette from his mouth.

"You're in a rush, Spichkin."

Faina ignored him and made to pass by, but Anastas blocked her path.

"Any word from Chevalsky?"

"If there was, I wouldn't tell you."

She made to pass him a second time but he grabbed her firmly by the forearm.

"You really think Klokov's gonna let Pasha set foot back in the city? He's gone, Faina, and he ain't coming back for you." He lowered his mouth to her ear. "Come on, Faina. We could make it fun."

Faina batted her eyes sarcastically. "Oh, yes, Anastas, every night I dream of you whispering sweet nothings in my ear. Things like, 'Big Nose, Ugly, Hyena, Tart,' oh, and let's not forget how you mocked my brother's death!"

Anastas waved his hand. "Look, I know I said some things in the past, but you know I didn't mean any of it. Things haven't exactly been easy for me, you know that."

Faina rolled her eyes. Anastas frequently tried to excuse his behavior by trying to make people feel sorry for him.

"I was just sore at you for hanging around Chevalsky all the time. He turned you against me. He made you hate me."

"You did that yourself."

Anastas chuckled as he bracketed her against the wall. "You don't mean that time I offered you a little cigarette in the alleyway, do you?" He took another drag and blew the smoke in her face.

Faina felt sick. She wrenched her arm back and shoved his chest, eager to get away. Anastas's face turned dark as he backed her into the wall. Faina stared up at him defiantly.

"You really think the Foxhole is the best place to harass me?

All I have to do is scream."

Anastas glared at her for another moment or two, and slowly backed away. Without another word, Faina ran as quickly as she could towards the exit.

Chapter 23:
The Speed of Light

The following morning, Pyro awoke with his vision restored and his attitude in full vigor. The hope that Cicada might break the tie seemed to have put him in a delightful humor. Pasha couldn't wait until the decision was made. He was eager to get it over with.

When Sonata flopped down at the table looking exhausted, Pyro couldn't help but tease her.

"How's that female companionship going? Looks like you two were up all night sharing each other's secrets."

Sonata's eyes burned with warning. "Shut up, Pyro."

Pasha offered her a weak smile. "Did you not sleep well?"

Sonata sighed and pinched the space between her eyes. "Not exactly. Cicada is still a little excitable, having just entered the world, and didn't fall asleep until very late."

Pasha bit his lip. "Sorry to hear that."

"It's alright, I'm used to babysi—Skelter! That better not be goat's milk I see you sneaking into Pyro's coffee! You know what happened last time!"

Foiled, Skelter set down the creamer of goat's milk and shoved his fist under his chin. He pointed a finger at Pyro, then at the pepper shaker. Sonata shook her head.

"I don't care if Pyro put dragon freckles in your milk! I will deal with him! Alright?"

Skelter nodded and grinned, but the moment Sonata turned her head, he stuck his tongue out at Pyro. Staccato appeared at the open space in the back of the wagon where he began brewing a second pot of coffee.

Lately, Pasha had noticed Staccato had a habit of humming to himself when he thought no one was listening. It would have been a perfectly ordinary ritual if not for the fact he was always humming the same scale. He may have rearranged them into different patterns but the notes stayed the same: F, G, A, Bb, C, D. If Pasha hadn't been forced to take private music lessons as a child, he might not have noticed.

When Staccato was finished, he sat at the table with his plate.

"Sonata, sweetheart, could you please pass the orange juice?"

Without so much as looking at Staccato, Sonata took the pitcher of orange juice and smiled angelically at Melodious.

"Dear Melodious, let me top that off for you there." Before Melodious could stop her she poured the last bit of juice into his glass. Pasha bent his head down and stifled a laugh. Melodious thanked her under his breath, and sheepishly pushed his glass towards Staccato. The miraculous was wholly unamused.

"Do you plan on letting this grudge of yours go anytime soon?"

Sonata straightened her shoulders. "I might if you gave some real consideration to what Mother Genesis suggested."

Staccato drew a slow, measured breath through his nose and

cut into his eggs with a vengeance.

"You know, if I didn't know any better, I'd be inclined to say the surname 'Soter' was Latin for 'My way or the highway!'"

Sonata glanced up indifferently. "Of course, why do you think we've keep you around for so long?"

At this remark, the boys burst into laughter. Even Staccato had to smile a bit. At the far end of the table, Cicada had been considerably quiet. Her attention was absorbed in playing with her food. As she held out a piece of egg for Cello to lick off her fork, Pyro forced his teeth into a solicitous grin.

"So, Cicada, now that you're a part of the company, I was hoping you could settle a little disagreement for us."

Cicada put down her fork. "Disagreement?"

"Yeah." Pyro rose from his seat and circled the table. "You see, half of us have our hearts set on catching the Firebird, while the other half doesn't. In fact, half of us are threatening to quit the expedition if we do continue chasing the Firebird. We hoped you could be the tie-breaker for us. So, what do you think we should do? Should we abandon the endeavor? Or should we continue our chase for the Firebird like Pasha here wants?" He set his hands on Pasha's shoulders and squeezed, driving the emphasis home. "You wouldn't want to disappoint Pasha now, would you?"

Meanwhile, Pasha cringed and tried not to cry out as Pyro pinched his muscles. Sonata slammed down her fork.

"Now that's not fair! Cicada, the reason half of us don't want to chase the Firebird is because your mother, the tree of all wisdom and knowledge, said it was a waste of time! You wouldn't go against your mother's wishes, would you?"

The tension looming over the breakfast table was electric. Cicada appeared overwhelmed. She stared blankly at the two as if it were a much simpler matter than they made it out to be. She shrugged.

"Let's chase the Firebird."

Sonata leaned back, affronted.

"What? Cicada, your mother said Pasha isn't destined to catch the Firebird. Why should we endanger our lives for a lost cause when there are more constructive things we could be doing?"

"Mother said I'm supposed to assist you while you try to catch the Firebird."

"But the Firebird is meant to be caught by Samael!"

"Yes, but Mother knew Staccato wouldn't follow her advice and would continue to chase the Firebird anyway. Staccato was always going to decide to chase it. So my purpose is to protect you against the dangers you'll face while doing so. She already knew the outcome. So in a way, you may not be destined to *catch* the Firebird, but you are destined to *chase* it because Staccato is pigheaded."

Sonata was at a loss for words. She hung over the table, defeated, groping for a piece of reason to latch onto.

Meanwhile, Pyro collapsed into a laughter of victory.

"How's that for irony? Defeated by your own sense of logic! Did you hear that, Sonata? Did you hear what she said? Destined! We may not be destined to *catch* the Firebird, but we're apparently destined to *chase* it! Case closed!"

Pasha sat back and observed Sonata's reaction. He was hoping she wouldn't be too angry, otherwise she might not answer his questions about Pyro's newspaper. But her heart and her brain seemed to have reached an impasse.

Having at last received what he wanted, Staccato reached for her hand.

"Now, Sonata, don't be upset. We all voted on it. There's no reason to run off and quit."

Sonata chewed her lip. "I will stay for the same reasons as Cicada, to protect you from your own foolishness! Now, if you'll excuse me, I'm going to go for a walk."

Finished with his plate, Pasha hastened to put away his dishes, and ran off to catch up with her in the woods. She hadn't made it very far down the path when he found her.

"Hey, Sonata! Mind if I join you?"

Sonata stopped and turned with a dignified sweep in the road.

"You may." She waited for him to catch up, and hooking her arm through his, they continued on together.

"Sorry I sided against you with the whole Firebird thing," Pasha confessed timidly. "I hope you aren't mad at me."

Sonata patted his arm. “Not at all. We all have disagreements from time to time, and I understand why you did it.”

“You do?”

She stopped to admire a patch of baby’s breath dangling through the rushes.

“You’re a caretaker, Pasha. Your choice was motivated by the desire to do what’s best for the most people. You’ve experienced a lot of tragedy in your life, and it’s made you wary of trusting things to fate. You want to do everything in your power to protect the world from suffering.”

“But isn’t that what Pyro and Staccato want too?”

She folded her hands in front of her and trained her eyes on the path ahead. “It is. But Pyro and Staccato are old enough to know better. You’re still learning.”

He followed her into the valley where yellow acacia billowed overhead.

“Have you known Pyro long?”

“Since childhood. We were playmates. I know it may seem like we’re at each other’s throats all the time, but we’re really very good friends. Neither of us minds saying what the other needs to hear. I’m sure you know what that’s like. I mean, you and that friend of yours seemed awfully close. Have you been best friends long?”

Pasha smiled. Talking to Sonata was like talking to his sister; she picked up on everything.

"Since we were ten years old. We came to America a few months apart from each other. Both of us had lost parents to the Red Army; neither of us had ever been out of our home country before. We hit it off instantly."

Sonata put a motherly hand on his shoulder. "You're worried about her, aren't you? It's only natural you would."

Pasha hung his head low. "I do worry about her, and my mother, and my sister."

Sonata tried to look hopeful. "Well, the sooner we restore Voiler, the sooner they can join us."

"But when will that be? Before it was when I caught the Firebird, but if what Mother Genesis says is true, and I'm not meant to catch the Firebird, how can I help Voiler?"

Sonata crossed to the edge of the pond where several lotuses churned in slow, spiraling eddies. "You could always take back the throne."

Pasha gaped at her. "You mean become king?"

"Of course!" She shrugged as though it were no big deal. Pasha rubbed the side of his face and shook his head.

"I hate to break it to you, Sonata, but I never planned on taking the throne. Staccato said the choice was up to me; he said I didn't have to do that."

"He said you didn't have to, but have you ever considered why you should?"

"I haven't, because there aren't any good reasons. I couldn't be a king, I mean have you seen my record? I'm a wanted criminal! I have warrants! Who puts a bootlegger in a seat of government?"

Sonata set her hands on her hips. "From what I hear, it happens in America all the time."

This made him laugh. Sonata took him by the arm and sat with him upon a bench.

"Pasha, you did what you had to to survive. You only joined the Breadwinners to save your mother. You were twelve, a little boy. But forget your past for a moment and consider what you could do to help Voiler if you were king."

Pasha drew a deep breath. "I don't know, what could I do?"

"Well, for starters, Ursa is currently under Draconian rule. After King Bruin died, stewardship fell to Karkinos. But once the Land Lock was placed, Karkinos was forced to relinquish his management of Ursa, and the position fell to Draco. But if an heir to the throne surfaced, Samael would be forced to release Ursa. A steward would no longer be needed."

Pasha shut his eyes and considered for a moment. "Okay, so there's that. But what about afterwards? How do you know I wouldn't be a terrible king?"

"Pasha, you're the type of person who likes to be in control so you can prevent bad things from happening. As king, you would have ultimate control. You would have the power to ensure your people were safe."

Pasha chuckled. "Just because I'm a little controlling doesn't mean I'm a person who needs to be in control."

"You're very stubborn, aren't you?"

Pasha nudged her playfully. "From what I hear, it runs in the family."

Sonata smiled and tousled his hair. "Very funny, cousin." She looked him seriously in the eye. "Will you at least think about it? I mean, you can brainstorm an idea without the intention of carrying it out, can't you?"

Pasha heaved a sigh and shoved his hands into his pockets. He glanced her over. She seemed so earnest, so hopeful. He would hate to disappoint her. At last he threw back his head.

"Alright. I'll think about it."

Sonata gave him a one-armed hug. "I appreciate that, Pasha."

He held up a finger. "But I do have one condition. If I'm gonna give this actual consideration there are things I wanna know. Things about Voiler, the people, the history. I can't rule a country in a world I know nothing about."

She nodded her head. "That's very true."

"Yesterday, when Cicada was reading Pyro's newspaper, it said the C.O.N. tattooed the birth names of their victims on their arms. What does that mean? Why would they do that?"

Sonata shut her eyes as though preparing herself for an

unpleasant conversation.

"There's an old Fay saying that the only way the devil can find you is if he calls you by name. So, a long time ago Fay used to give their children two names to protect them from evil: their birth name, and a Fay name. The birth name was kept secret, and was only known by the family. Other than immediate kin, only husbands and wives were allowed to use each other's birth names in private as a gesture of intimacy. The Fay name was what you were called in public."

Pasha rubbed his chin. He had never heard of such a tradition. A sense of dread pooled in his chest as he realized how much he had to learn about this place.

"So, could any name be a Fay name? Like John, or James?"

Sonata leaned back and let the sun shine on her face. "Well, the original idea was that a Fay name had to be somewhat outrageous-sounding. Though, what was outrageous centuries ago might very well be in vogue these days. Anyway, it's difficult to tell Fay by their name alone."

"So, people still do this?"

She threw up her shoulders. "Some do, but it's mostly tradition now. Melodious and I are the only members of the group without a Fay name. Of course, there are still some Fay who remain heavily devoted to the old ways, and trust me, there are a lot of old Fay customs. Take Skelter for example."

Pasha scratched his head. "Skelter is a Fay? I thought he was an ordinary human like me."

"No, you're right. Skelter isn't Fay by birth. But he comes from a Fay upbringing. It's a lifestyle. Intermarriage is common in Voiler, especially amongst mermaids and two-leggeds." She shook her head. "Non-mermaids that is. Female mermaids who marry non-mermaid men can only produce mermaid daughters. The sons are born ordinary men, but they grow up in a home where magic is a part of their daily lives.

"Now as for what you read about the C.O.N., it's like I said, birth names are very sacred. It's considered a great insult for someone to use a Fay's birth name without their consent. The C.O.N. will often torture victims with Fay names in order to find out their true names so they can tattoo them on their arms as a way to demean them."

"That's terrible!"

Sonata frowned. "I know. As if it weren't enough to cause someone bodily harm, but to humiliate them as well, it's monstrous."

At length they returned to the camp. Sonata checked the time.

"Well, we have the whole day ahead of us. What do you say we let Harpagos and Scheherazade stretch their wings?"

Pasha lit up. Ever since yesterday he had been dying to get back in the saddle. "Absolutely!"

And together they made their way towards the corral.

***

Pasha and Sonata were only gone a couple of hours. As they

made their way back to the glen, Pyro came running out to meet them. His hair was wilder than usual and his braces fell off his shoulders. Sonata gave his disheveled appearance a once-over.

"What happened to you?"

Ignoring Sonata's question, Pyro seized them both by the shoulders and fell to his knees in gratitude.

"Thank goodness you're back! Why did you leave?"

Sonata rolled her eyes. "Really, Pyro! What's happened now?"

"We can't get her under control! She's driving us crazy!" He led them back towards camp.

"Who?"

"Who do you think? The ray of destruction! Cicada got bored so I chucked her a book and told her to start reading, and now she's taking everything apart!"

As Pyro finished the sentence, they came upon the glade. It looked as though a tornado had ripped through the valley, destroying every mechanical object it could find.

Sonata gaped in horror. "What book did you give her?"

Pyro picked up a heavy volume carelessly tossed aside. He placed it in Sonata's hands.

"*Advanced Mechanics Vol. XI*? Why would you give her this?"

"I dunno! It was the first thing on the shelf! Obviously, she likes to read since she had her hands all over my newspaper, so I thought it'd keep her occupied for a while! After that I don't know what happened!"

Pasha scanned over the wreckage once more. The wheels of the wagon had been removed, the coffee maker had been deconstructed into exactly twenty-one pieces, and the back of the radio was lying face-down with the circuit board exposed.

Pasha rubbed his chin. "So, you gave her a book on mechanics and she started disassembling everything?"

Sonata rolled up her sleeves. "You know when toddlers reach that stage where they get into everything?"

"Yeah."

"That's what we're dealing with now, only worse. Instead of a toddler we have a young woman with an accelerated learning ability." Sonata marched towards the canopy with a look of determination. "I told you to keep an eye on her, Pyro! Where was Mother Genesis?"

Pyro bumbled after her. "I dunno! Something about an annual meeting with the United Arboreal Timbers of the Southern Copse."

Pasha cocked his head. "The what?"

Sonata waved an impatient hand. "That would be the sylphs' general assembly."

Sonata pulled back the canopy. Her wheelchair was missing. Something fuzzy was trembling inside the tea kettle.

Sonata gasped. "Cello!"

She lifted the lid of the teapot where Cello had taken refuge. At the sight of Sonata, Cello's whiskers seemed to unwind with relief. He climbed up into her arms and hid his face in her shoulder.

Sonata shook her head back and forth in disbelief. "Where was Skelter in all of this?"

"Climbing up some coconut tree, no doubt! You know Skelter, every time we visit any place tropical he slinks off to pick fruit. Haven't seen him all day."

Sonata groaned into the back of her hand. "Well, I must admit Skelter would've been helpful at a time like this. He's always so good with children. Where is everyone now? Where's Staccato? Where's Melodious? Where is *she*?"

Pasha gestured to a trail of screws and bolts. "Something tells me we should follow the hardware."

They tracked the string of screws and bolts to a clearing where Staccato, bereft of his staff, was hanging suspended inside a net meant for big game. Melodious was feeling around for discarded parts and gathering them into a basket. As soon as the three entered, they both turned to Sonata.

"Where is she?" she demanded.

They pointed to the treetops. With her hands on her hips Sonata strode to the bottom of an aspen tree and craned her neck towards the canopy. Pasha joined at her side. High up in the branches, Cicada was fiddling with Sonata's wheelchair.

"Cicada Sycamore! You get down here this instant, and you

bring me my wheelchair!"

Sonata's authoritative tone didn't seem to register with her. Cicada looked down at them and grinned.

"Oh, you're back finally! It was boring without you two!"

"You come down here now!"

"Alright!" She lingered a moment, unfixing Sonata's wheelchair from the fork in the tree.

Sonata turned to Melodious, Staccato, and Pyro. "And none of you could contain her?"

Melodious shrugged. "In all my years of learning to cope with my blindness, never have I allowed myself to look upon it as a disadvantage. Today, I may have reconsidered that."

Sonata pivoted around to Staccato. "Staccato?"

"She took my staff!"

"Oh pish-posh, we all know you're one of the few miraculous in history who don't need a staff to wield the full extent of their powers!"

Staccato huffed. "You didn't let me finish!" He rolled to his side. He was clutching his right arm. The sleeve had been torn.

"I sprained it after chasing Cicada and falling down into the gorge. Now, I realize I'm not completely useless. I would summon my staff back, but I don't know what she did with it!"

Sonata clicked her tongue and, reaching up, set about healing his injury. Pasha furrowed his brow.

"Do physical injuries affect the use of your powers?"

Staccato leaned his head back and sighed. "They can if they're bad enough. Despite what people may think, moving objects without touching them does require some physical strength. It's sort of an extension. Ow!" He cringed as Sonata pressed harder.

"Sorry." She sighed. "You damaged it pretty bad. I'm afraid it might require multiple cleanses."

Cicada floated towards them with Sonata's wheelchair in her arms. To their surprise, everything seemed to be intact.

"And just what have you been doing with my wheelchair?"

"I've been waiting to show you all day. Pyro gave me this really swell book. Once I finished, I thought your wheelchair could use a few minor adjustments."

Sonata looked aghast. "A few minor adjustments?"

Before Sonata could protest, Cicada forced her into the chair and pulled out the footrest.

"I noticed you struggling with your left wheel last night, that's because the bolt was crooked. I also noticed your break was getting a bit rusty, but when I went to oil it up, we only had Smithfield's. For optimum efficiency *Advanced Mechanics* recommends using a lubricant with organic compounds. So, I added a little bee pollen to thin it down. You should find it rides much smoother now."

Indignant, Sonata rolled ominously towards Cicada's face. She paused. She looked down at her wheels. She steered herself back and forth.

"Wait a minute. That actually is much better!" She glided backwards, a smile replacing her scowl. "This is wonderful! Great Northern Star! It hasn't been this cooperative in years!"

"I took the liberty of installing a few upgrades." Cicada reached behind Sonata's wheelchair and pulled out a collapsible attachment. "It's a desk!"

Sonata's face lit up. "Oh my! Cicada, this is fantastic!"

"Oh! I almost forgot." On the corner of the tray was a little paper circle. Cicada pushed on the center, and it dropped down accordion style.

"It's a cup holder, or a pencil holder, or whatever you want it to be."

"Cicada, this is so thoughtful of you! I . . . Thank you! Thank you so much!"

Staccato cleared his throat. "Can I have my staff now, please?"

Cicada struck her forehead. "Oh, yeah! That's what I was supposed to be doing!"

"Cicada, that was two hours ago."

"I know, I know! I got so caught up in Sonata's wheelchair, I forgot."

She retrieved the staff from the top of an elm where it was camouflaged amongst the branches. "I mended your armillary sphere. I'm not sure if you noticed, but there was a crack forming near the seam which was causing the nucleus to leak. Anytime a container splits open it has to be mended immediately, or else the power can drain. It had already diminished a considerable amount."

Staccato swished the staff towards the knot at the top of the net. The cords came loose so fast he surprised himself when he collided with the ground. For a moment, he lay there pinching his arm in pain. Sonata fluttered down beside him in a state of worry.

"Staccato, are you alright?"

Wincing, he examined the tip of his staff. "Extraordinary . . . It takes years of study to learn how to properly handle a miraculous staff, and yet she's done it in one day!" He sat up and stared at Sonata. "Do you think . . . could she be developing faster than the average rate for an esperite?"

Sonata shrugged. "Mother Genesis did contribute her with the purpose of aiding us. Perhaps that's why: Cicada is gifted."

"Gifted? She's a downright prodigy!"

Pyro looked as though he would explode. "Prodigy? Have you seen the camp? She's torn up everything!"

"Not tearing up," corrected Sonata, "improving."

Pyro leaned back against a tree with his hands on his hips.

"Oh, so I suppose the wagon is better off without the wheels then?"

Cicada floated between them. "Oh, they're just drying. I gave them a new coat of paint with weather-resistant seal. They should be ready to put back on by tomorrow morning. And I only took the coffee maker apart to clean it. As for the radio, the capacitor needs replacing. Oh, and I have your chakras, Pyro."

Pyro's eyes bulged. He felt his holsters. They were empty. Cicada held them out, and he snatched them from her hands. Cicada ignored his attitude.

"See? Nice and sharp now!"

"Hmph! Taking my chakras . . . Ouch!" Pyro drew back his finger. He had cut himself on the edge of the blade. He stared down at the weapon in amazement. He gave it a quick toss into the tree tops and retrieved it in his right hand. "Blazes! I reckon this would chop down a tree if I weren't careful!"

Sonata reached for his finger and healed the cut with a teasing smile. "See?"

An enormous grin illuminated Pyro's face in a way that made his freckles beam.

"Alright, I'll say it! Cici's a genius!"

Chapter 24:

Skelter's Secret

Although it had taken Cicada an entire day to take the camp apart, it took only an hour to put it back together. By evening, everything was quiet again. Mostly because Sonata had used her powers to put Cicada to sleep. While they awaited dinner, Pyro sat with Pasha and taught him an old card game from Aries called Lava.

Pyro pinched a cigar between his teeth. "Sure you don't want to join us, Reverend?"

Melodious settled into his chair as he whittled away at a woodblock.

"I would if you had not accidentally burnt up my braille playing cards the last time we played."

Pyro's cigar drooped. "Right, sorry about that."

Pasha laid down a card. "Why are you always calling him 'Reverend' or 'Preacher Man'?"

Pyro blotted the ash from his stogie. "Because that's what he is, or at least, he used to be back when he lived in Malaria."

"Bavaria," corrected Melodious. "Like you, Pasha, I did not grow up in Voiler. My family moved to the Other when I was still a baby. After Draco seized Lake Hercules from Sagittarius, we were forced to leave our home. My parents decided it would be safer for their children to grow up in a world without ophidians."

"How did you end up back here?"

Melodious's shoulders tightened, and his jaw set. "Some ophidians from the C.O.N. mistook me for an escaped rebel. They slaughtered my entire congregation, my wife and children as well."

Pasha knit his eyebrows together. "I'm sorry, Melodious. That must've been terrible."

Melodious patted Pasha's head with his enormous hand. "I have peace, my friend. Trials produce perseverance."

Footsteps echoed down the path as Skelter reemerged from the woods. Three gargantuan sacks overflowing with fruit were flung over his shoulder. Pyro threw down his cards.

"And where have you been all day?"

Grinning, Skelter jerked his thumb over his shoulder to indicate the fruit.

Pyro rolled his eyes and nodded. "I see, you and your fruit."

Skelter nodded heartily as he partially emptied one of the bags on the stumps. There were two coconuts, a bunch of plantains, a grapefruit, a papaya, and several others which Pasha did not recognize. Swinging the remaining sacks over his shoulder, he headed back to the woods.

"I hope you're going to eat all that before we leave," Pyro called out. "The wagon doesn't need any more weight to carry."

Smiling, Skelter threw him a thumbs up and disappeared beyond the trees. Pasha looked back at Pyro with a cocked eyebrow.

"Gee, Skelter must really like fruit."

Pyro nodded and dealt out the cards again. “He has some strange habits, that’s for sure. Of course, lots of it’s old Fay traditions, like the whole vow of silence thing.”

“Skelter can actually talk?”

Pyro nodded his head. “He can. You’ll hear him every so often in his sleep if he’s having a nightmare. Used to shout all sorts of things when we were imprisoned together in Algedi. See, the belief is, if you speak no evil, evil will never speak ill of you.”

The thought made Pasha’s head spin. He rubbed at his temples. “How many Fay traditions are there?”

Pyro inhaled and shut his eyes as though the thought of numbering them were exhausting.

“Too many, that’s for sure. Just when I think I know ‘em all, Skelter comes up with a new one I’ve never even heard of before.”

“It must drive him crazy to not be able to communicate.”

Pyro slapped down another card and scoffed. “Drives the rest of crazy as well. We hardly know anything about him because he won’t tell us. Not even his last name, or where he comes from. All I know is, whatever happened to him before he showed up in Algedi near about destroyed him. Something to do with the C.O.N., but that’s hardly surprising.”

Sonata poked her head out the back of the wagon.

“Has Skelter returned yet?”

Pyro put out his cigar. “He just went back into the woods.”

"Will somebody please tell him dinner is ready?"

Pasha rose and stretched. "I'll go." He jogged towards the woods, cupping his hand over his mouth and calling out Skelter's name. But he couldn't find him.

He noticed a trail of fruit leading down the hill. It had to have dropped from Skelter's overfull sacks. Gathering them into his arms, he followed the path down to a bit of rocky coastline overlooking the sea. He spied Skelter standing along the edge, dropping heavy stones into the bags and tying them up. Pasha stopped behind a grove of palm trees and watched. What was he doing?

Something small and shimmery drew his attention to the ocean. Pasha shielded his eyes towards the setting sun and looked out over the water. A small mermaid, no bigger than Katya, was timidly peeking out of the waves to observe Skelter. Moments later, she was joined by another mermaid child. Soon there was an entire flock of them, all too afraid to raise their heads higher than the bridges of their noses.

When Skelter glanced up and saw the collection of mermaid children, he waved and smiled. With considerable effort, he dragged the first sack to the edge of the rocks and rolled it into the water. Pasha watched as one by one the mermaid's little eyes scrunched up with smiles, and they dove into the water. The pieces came together. Because of the curse, the mermaids in the water didn't have access to things growing on land like coconuts and bananas, so Skelter had taken to delivering them to them.

Pasha smiled to himself. With his hands in his pockets, he strode down to the beach where Skelter was struggling to hoist another sack. He cleared his throat.

"Need a hand?"

***

Somewhere in the wee hours of dawn, Melodious shot into the glade with urgent news. Staccato rolled over as Melodious jostled him awake.

"What? What's wrong?"

"You need to turn on the radio, now!"

Pyro kicked off his covers and sat up. "Tongs and Torches, Mel, can't it wait two more hours?"

"There has been an attack in Alshain. Two hundred Fay, dead."

Pasha drew up and rubbed his eyes. They had been in Alshain a week ago. He'd exchanged three-quarters of his paycheck there for American dollars and posted it to his mother.

Staccato bolted upright. "What? Was it the C.O.N?"

Melodious nodded his head. "Authorities say they were looking for someone. Torturing people for information. So far no one knows who."

Pyro smacked his pillow. "It's us, obviously! They're looking for us! They know Pasha showed up in Alfbern Hall. It was only a matter of time before they started picking through the rebel network."

Melodious dragged a hand across his forehead. "They say the

damage is so bad everything has been put on halt. Even the mail. Countries all over Voiler are sending aid to help get the city back on its feet."

Pasha raised up in his bed. "I posted my paycheck to my mother from Alshain. She can't go without it, she won't be able to pay rent!"

Staccato held up his hand. "Calm down, Pasha. I'm sure everything is fine, and if it's not we'll find a way to take care of it." He bent over his knees and hung his head in his hands. "I suppose it's best if we leave Cortijo Del Mar immediately before they track us down."

Chapter 25:

R.R.

When Faina laid the money in Mama Lydia's hand, she expected her to be pleased. Instead her sweet, soporific eyes radiated alarm.

Faina twisted the ball of her foot against the floor. "What's the matter?"

Anya glanced up from the piecework. At the sight of the money her eyes grew large, and she stared accusingly at Faina. Faina looked down at her feet. At first, Mama Lydia showed no sign she'd heard Faina. After a moment or two, she turned towards Anya and Katya with a forced smile.

"Anya, sweetheart, would you mind helping Katya get ready for bed?"

Anya nodded like a good child. "Of course, Mama Lydia."

Taking Katya by the hand, she led the girl towards the washroom. As she passed, she tossed her faded blonde hair and threw Faina another questioning look. Faina ignored her. Once the door shut, Faina focused her energy on appearing calm.

"Isn't it enough?"

Mama Lydia tried to smile. "Yes, actually, more than enough." She sank her teeth into her bottom lip and brought herself to look Faina in the eye. "Darling, where did you get this money?"

Faina was silent. She glanced down at the floor and wrung her fingers individually until they popped. When it was clear she wasn't going to answer, Mama Lydia pushed her bangs back and heaved a sigh.

"I know Pasha likes to pretend I don't know about the Breadwinners, but I—"

"Oh, I know. I know you've known all along." Faina's voice was apologetic.

At length, Mama Lydia rubbed a hand over her mouth and motioned for Faina to sit. Faina watched, unblinking, as she leaned on her elbows and steepled her fingers to her lips. She shut her eyes and knit her forehead together. Mama Lydia remained like that for such a long time, Faina wondered if she was ever going to say anything.

"I know Pasha was the middleman between you and Klokov. However, Pasha is not here. Tell me you haven't been bootlegging for that mobster."

Faina opened her mouth to answer, but Mama Lydia cut her off with one final warning.

"Don't lie to me. Have you been selling to Klokov?"

Faina's breath caught behind her pallet. Her shoulders drew together.

"Yes." Her voice was small and quiet.

Lydia fell back against the chair, hands covering her eyes, and flew off in a Russian rant. Faina could not help but be reminded of Pasha and his tangents in Ukrainian and Polish. At last, she stopped and took a breath.

Faina gathered the courage to speak. "You've done so much for me Mama Lydia, and I know money is hard to come by. Bootlegging is a booming business, and nobody pays better than Klokov. You and Anya don't make very much. We haven't received anything from Pasha yet, but I knew if I kept selling to Klokov, my paycheck could keep us afloat."

Mama Lydia gaped at her with desperate confusion.

"Why is it that you and Pasha always take it upon yourselves to care for everything? You are children! Helping is one thing, but what you two are doing is dangerous, not to mention illegal! It is not necessary for you to risk your lives. That is my job, okay? I am the parent."

Glass shattered and the window broke apart into a million shards. Faina and Mama Lydia leapt to their feet screaming. Katya and Anya burst out of the washroom and shrieked while Mammoth bellowed and growled.

Soon, the ruckus was over. Mama Lydia held Faina close to her chest behind the kitchen wall. She motioned for Anya and Katya to stay back. Together, Faina and Mama Lydia peered into the sitting area.

A brick had been tossed through the window. Faina dared forward, but Lydia jerked her back by the shoulder.

"*Nyet*, let me!"

When nothing more happened, Lydia crept towards the clutter, head down. A note was tied to the brick. With shaking hands she unfolded it. Trying not to stutter, she read aloud.

"*H—hand over your son. - R.R.* Who is R.R.?"

Anya threw her hands up and turned to Faina.

"What have you done now?"

Faina squinted at her. "Why do you always think everything is my fault?"

Lydia held up her hand. "Girls! Girls! Enough!" Anya and Faina fell silent for a moment or two. Then, with a lowered voice, Anya crossed her arms.

"It's obviously the Breadwinners."

Faina shook her head. "No, it couldn't be. Klokov said they don't harass family members. He wouldn't even ask me anything about Pasha."

Lydia rubbed the space between her eyebrows. "I would not count on the word of a thug."

Chapter 26:

The Library in the Grotto

According to the laws issued by the Ecliptic Council, all wars and quests must cease during the Christmas season and may resume the week after. Having been a government official himself once, Staccato was never one to take the law lightly. So, the company resolved to spend the remainder of the year in Larame, the capital of Pisces, and the halfway point to Cetus. The two-day journey in the yellow gypsy wagon was hardly tolerable due to Cicada's restlessness. Her behavior seemed to shrink the caravan until everyone was on edge and the only escape was sleep.

When Pasha awoke from his nap, he found her pacing back and forth across the ceiling.

Pyro groaned from the lower bunk. "Cici, lay down! You're making everyone nervous!"

Cicada crossed her arms like a child. "I'll go crazy if I have to lay down one more minute! There's hardly any room to breathe in here!"

"Aw, fire and brimstone! It's a two-day trip! You're overreacting!"

Cicada stopped and glanced down at Pasha. "Am I overreacting?"

Pasha rubbed his face. "Yep."

She tapped at her chin. "Why do you think that is? I mean, I guess Pyro's right, it is only a two-day trip. And everyone else seems to be tolerating the journey. Is it possible I'm . . . ."

Pasha tuned her out as she began pacing again. Ever since they left Cortijo Del Mar, Cicada had developed a habit of wondering aloud. Skelter turned over in his Murphy bed and slammed his pillow over his ears.

Pasha sat up on his elbows. "You know, if you shrank you'd have a lot more space to explore."

Cicada ground to a halt, her eyes widening. "That's a perfect idea!" Her body trickled down until it was only a few inches high. "Now I can pace all I want!"

Cello poked his head out of a drawer. He watched Cicada darting back and forth with predatory instinct. Unable to control himself, he sprang forward and batted her with his paws. Cicada shrieked.

"Hey! I am not a lightning bug!"

Pasha scrambled over the bunk and grabbed Cello. "Maybe only shrink down a couple of feet."

Pyro clapped his hands and laughed. "You're officially my hero."

Pasha chuckled as he laid back on his bed and stretched. "How far away are we now?"

"Take a look out the window. We're pretty much there." Pyro glanced back at the sliding door of Sonata's little cabinet bed. "In fact, we should probably be waking up Sonata soon."

As Pasha pulled back the curtains of the window and looked out at the beach, his eyes crossed.

"Am I seeing what I think I'm seeing?"

"What? You mean the pink sand? Pisces is famous for it."

Strips of colorful buildings stood on the horizon, mostly pink and orange. They crowded together on rocky cliff sides and crystal canals. It was as vibrant as a summer's day, and yet for all its color, there was something lonely about the stillness of the place.

Cicada pointed to a rosy smooth stoned castle sitting amongst acres of tropical gardens.

"There's the Placide, the palace where the royal family lives."

"*Lived*," corrected Pyro. "They were all trapped in the water when Samael placed his curse."

"That's right. The entire Barbos family, even Queen Calliope."

Pasha looked down at his feet. Cicada was only three days old and already she knew more about the world than he did.

Pyro narrowed his eyes and sat up. "Where did you learn that?"

Returning to her normal size, Cicada reached behind her trunk and produced another heavy book she'd stashed away.

"From *Peridot's Peerage*. It's a genealogical record of Voiler's landed gentry. I bought it from that bookstore near our last stop."

Pyro scratched at his chin curiously. "Is that the latest edition?"

"Of course, they print a new one every December."

Pyro thrust out his palm. "Let me see it."

Cicada slapped the copy down in his hand. Pyro leaned against the headboard and thumbed through the pages. He turned a suspicious eye on Cicada.

"You can have this back later."

Fearing another fight might break out, Pasha grabbed Cicada's wrist and towed her up to his bunk. He gestured out the window.

"So, what else did you read about Pisces?"

Before Cicada could answer, Pyro gave a cry of alarm. "Ballistics! That conniving little ash heap!"

Pasha and Cicada peered at him over the bunk. Pyro jerked his head out from behind the pages and scowled.

"What are you two looking at?" He shooed them away with his hand. Rolling their eyes, they returned to their conversation.

"You were saying, Cici?"

"Well, its capital, Larame, means 'tears of love.' It's highly appropriate, considering their culture is founded upon the virtues of brotherly love. In fact, Pisces is often described as having a utopian quality."

The sound of tearing paper echoed below the bed. They dipped their heads over the mattress and found Pyro stuffing a set of ripped papers beneath his pillow. He wrenched around, pretending nothing had happened.

"What?"

Pasha looked at Skelter, who rolled his eyes, advising them to ignore Pyro's behavior.

They descended to the beach below. The wheels weighed into the sand. The Placide lay within walking distance. They filed out of the wagon, eager to stretch their legs. The sun sank into the horizon of clear water. The sky was as pink as the ground, and its reflection turned the sea a similar shade. The heavens, the waters, and the land were scarcely distinguishable from one another. Lined up against the edge of the tropical coppice was a row of bungalows. Pyro gazed at them wistfully.

"Please tell me that's where we're staying."

Staccato pulled a pen and a piece of paper from under the driver's seat and scribbled out a message.

"That's the idea. But I wouldn't want to barge in without informing Queen Calliope of our arrival."

Pasha reeled around to look at him. "How are we gonna do that?"

Staccato rolled up the parchment. "The old fashioned way. Pyro, bottle!"

Pyro reached into the back of the wagon and produced a whiskey bottle with an inch of liquid left at the bottom. Throwing back his head, he downed the last bit and handed it to Staccato. Staccato slipped the paper inside, filled the bottle with sand, and corked it.

"Melodious? Would you care to do the honors?"

Melodious strode forward and took the bottle. "Point me in the direction."

Pyro took him by the shoulders and turned him towards the water. Everyone stood back as Melodious pitched the bottle seventy-three yards across the waves. It sank down into the blue. They stared at the water, waiting for something to happen. Bubbles formed on the surface. The top of a head emerged. Two eyes peered out at them. Staccato waved a hand, and lifted his staff in greeting. Without breeching any further, the mermaid pointed to the Placide. Staccato nodded, and the mermaid disappeared. A sparkling, orange tail flipped up behind her. Staccato placed a hand on Sonata's shoulder.

"Sonata, I need you to stay in the—"

Sonata threw back her head and groaned. "I've been in there for hours!"

He kissed the top of her head. "And another five minutes isn't going to kill you."

Sonata plopped down on the edge of the wagon while Staccato led the others towards the Placide. They wandered through the broken gates of the garden and past an outdoor pavilion covered with bright mosaics. At last they entered the flooded foyer. Shattered glass floated along the corridor from the broken bay windows. Pasha stared up at the high ceilings with seashell chandeliers in awe.

"So, I guess the castle flooded during the Land Lock?"

Staccato waved a hand. "Oh no, they're always like this. As

you know, mermaids have a land form, and a sea form. Therefore, they build most of their dwellings half inside the water and half outside."

They followed him down a slippery stairwell. Lichens leeched onto the swampy steps. The mermaid was waiting for them in the pool at the bottom of the hall.

"Queen Calliope will be with you shortly."

She vanished. Pasha figured it was safer for the queen's guard to see visitors first. Something long and colorful undulated beneath the waves at the back of the passage. He looked closer. It was an entire procession of mermaids, their tails sparkling like a rainbow. Two guards breeched the surface and held their heads high.

"Presenting Her Majesty Queen Calliope Barbos of Pisces."

They swam aside to make way for their ruler. From the depths of the water a gorgeous mermaid issued. Her hair was curly and cropped close to her head which seemed to highlight the stately contours of her face. She had an aristocratic look about her with high cheekbones and an elegant jawline. Her black skin was shining from the salt water. Instead of a jeweled crown she wore a wreath of flowers in her hair. She was prettier than any painting of a mermaid Pasha had ever seen.

Staccato bowed low on one knee, which was difficult to do on the wet staircase. The rest of them followed his example. A genuine smile appeared on Calliope's lips, as she caught Staccato before he slipped in the water.

"Don't fall now. Propriety isn't worth all that, not for you, old friend." She tossed her head and laughed. "*Bondias, mon cher*!"

She threw her arms around Staccato's neck, and they exchanged kisses on both cheeks. Physical affection seemed to be a trademark of the mermaids. They were always touching people, even strangers. What's more, it always felt genuine. Pasha listened as Staccato and Calliope conversed in their strange language.

"*Comen vu? Bien*?"

"*Wi, bien, bien.*"

He couldn't tell if they were speaking Spanish or French. It sounded like a little of both. He finally decided it was a Voilerian language.

"So what brings you all to our waters this evening?" Calliope inquired in English. "Surely, you're not looking for the Firebird. It is the season of brotherly love after all! You know what the Ecliptic Council says, Staccato. But then, I know you to be more of a rule breaker than you would have people think."

Staccato laughed awkwardly. "Oh, I don't know about that."

Behind him, Pyro and Skelter covered their mouths and snickered. Without giving himself away, Staccato conjured a pebble to fly up and hit the backs of their heads.

"It is that very law which has led us to your shores. That, and avoiding the C.O.N. We're in need of a place to stay until the New Year. Larame happens to be the halfway point to our destination."

Calliope winked. “All of you are always welcome in my kingdom for however long you need to stay. I would offer you the guesthouses, but I am afraid there is no way of opening them until the curse breaks. You see, the keys are stored under the water, and since they are mermaid forged they cannot be taken from the sea, according to the rules of the Land Lock. Until we can find a way to open them you are welcome to settle yourselves in whatever place you find suitable.”

“Our caravan will do fine, thank you. During our stay we planned to devote some time to finding a remedy for the curse.”

Queen Calliope fell into a look of hopelessness. “You may try your best. You can check the libraries in the Placide, but I wouldn’t get your hopes up. I have reason to believe they’ve been raided by the C.O.N. at least once. If there ever was any such book that told how to break the Land Lock, it is gone now.” She looked back to the horizon. “I must go. Send for me should you need anything else and enjoy your stay in Pisces.” She dove back into the depths, her servants and attendants following her in pairs of two.

Staccato ushered everyone back up the steps and into the dripping foyer. Trying to maintain a straight face, Pyro cleared his throat.

“So, uh, Staccato, exactly what rules have you been breaking?”

Skelter gave a snort, and he and Pyro fell into a fit of laughter. Staccato rolled his eyes.

"Hold your tongue, Pyro."

With his hand placed under his chin, Melodious followed Staccato at the head of the line.

"Do you really think we will be able to find a way to break the curse?"

Staccato hung his head. It was clear he had little hope in doing so.

"We can try, Melodious, but at this stage it feels as though it would take a miracle."

Melodious smiled, causing the bristles at the end of his mustache to turn up.

"Now, Staccato, there is no reason to lose hope. Everyone knows there is no such thing as an unbreakable curse. It is impossible."

Pasha pricked up his ears. "There are rules to curses?"

Staccato sighed. "Even magic has some order to it, Pasha, like everything else in the world. All curses are conjured with a catalyst: a person, object, or event that breaks the spell. As a rule, the criteria for the catalyst is often very specific, arbitrary, or unlikely. This enables the curse to last long enough to create significant damage."

Melodious tossed his head to one side. "Think of *Dornrösichen*," *Sleeping Beauty*, "and how a hundred years passed before a prince came along to wake the princess with a kiss."

"Or *Macbeth*," added Staccato glumly, "when the witches prophesied Macbeth would fall when Birnam Wood came to

Dunsinane."

Pyro skipped ahead to catch up with them. "Or Fluffy the Opaque when he was freed from the Five Flaming Furies by a humpbacked seraph who rode around in a bucket with a cockatrice under each arm."

Everyone halted to stare at Pyro, who scratched the back of his neck.

"You know, because Queen Pommelblossom said that was the only way the curse could be broken . . ."

At last, Staccato shook his head. "Pyro, Pasha has no idea what you're talking about."

"I thought everyone knew *The Ballad of Fluffy the Opaque*."

Pasha had to duck his head to keep from laughing. "It's a ballad?"

Pyro threw back his shoulders and looked expectantly at Skelter. "Maestro, if you plea—"

Before Skelter could unstrap his violin from his back, Staccato snatched the bow away from him.

"Skelter, I swear, I will throw that thing in the ocean if either of you start up a rendition of *Fluffy the Opaque*!" And he stormed off ahead of them.

Skelter inched his fingers towards the strings.

"And no plucking either!"

***

Later that night, Pasha dreamt his mother was stroking her fingers through his hair and calling his name. He couldn't see her, for he had his eyes closed, but he knew the touch of her graceful fingers.

"Wake up, Pasha, my love." She was bending down to kiss his cheek when he felt whiskers brushing against his nose. He opened his eyes. It was Cello, standing on his chest purring. Pasha laughed and stroked his spine.

"Hello, Cello."

He closed his eyes again but Cello kneaded his sharp, needle-like claws into Pasha's abdomen. Pasha shot up like a spring trap and pried Cello from his lap. All was quiet. Unfazed by the disturbance, Cello wandered over to the window and stuck his head between the curtains. A bright light was surging somewhere on the rosy beach. He pawed the glass and chirruped. Pasha glanced back at the copper tea kettle Cicada nested in. A faint glow ebbed from the spout, suggesting she was asleep. Pasha scratched the back of his head. If it wasn't Cicada creating the light outside on the beach, what could it be? Intrigued, he peered out the window for a better look.

A silent, incandescent light rolled past the panes. Pasha's breath caught in his throat. It was the Firebird, moving as he had never seen her before. She wasn't racing but slowly drifting. She didn't burn but lazily pulsed as though sleepwalking.

There was no time to waste. Pasha threw back the covers and scaled down the ladder. As his feet were about to touch the floor, Pyro twisted in his sheets, scaring Pasha so bad he nearly fell backwards onto poor Skelter. Tiptoeing around Melodious, Pasha sprang for the door and dashed out into the night.

He drew round in circles, searching the sky, but she was already gone. Growling, Pasha pulled at his hair and kicked the sand. If it hadn't been for the obstacle course lining the floor of the caravan he might not have lost her.

He was about to flop hopelessly down on the ground, when he noticed a thin trail of scintillating golden light hanging over his head. Pasha arched his neck for a better look. It was a perfect outline of the Firebird's flight path, and it continued snaking off into the distance. Fearful it might somehow fade away, Pasha jumped to his feet and ran alongside it.

The trail led him up the rocks, down into crevices, and through a series of caved tunnels. Somewhere in the distance someone was humming the tune of *The Blind Man*. He walked on through the narrow stone tunnel until he reached moonlight. At the exit, a staircase unfolded before him into a glittering pool. Something was splashing around inside.

Pasha stopped at the bottom of the steps, transfixed. A mermaid glowing with a soft amber light was awaiting him at the edge of the lagoon. She reclined atop a crag. Her waves of sunny hair draped into the ebbing pool of water. Her skin was honeyed and warm from sunshine. Her gilded scales scintillated with sparkling light.

When she lifted up her eyes, the irises were pure, metallic, gold. At the sight of Pasha, she ceased humming. She did not look at all surprised to see him. A sweet smile warmed her lips.

"Hello, Pasha, my love."

Pasha couldn't remember how to speak. The air prickled with an eeriness, and she didn't appear entirely there, or perhaps he wasn't entirely awake. She rose and slid into the water, her hair trailing behind her sun-browned shoulders like a cape. The glowing light never shrank from her silhouette. Pasha had yet to see a glowing mermaid. Esperites glowed, but did mermaids glow as well? She submerged to the tips beneath her eyes, which peeked out and stared at Pasha as she glided forward. After a moment or two, she lifted her head and rested her chin on the edge of the pool.

"I'm not scaring you, am I?"

Pasha cocked his head. It was an odd thing to say. He glanced off to the side.

"Uh, I don't think so."

She bit her bottom lip and giggled.

"Perfect!" She clapped her hands and beckoned him forward. "Let me have a look at you!"

Before he could consent, she was turning his head about by the chin, and cooing over his eyes and nose as though he were six years old.

"I would ask how you know me," he murmured, her hands

squeezing his mouth, "but everyone here seems to know who I am before I introduce myself."

The mermaid clicked her tongue as she released him. "Well, you can thank the rebel network for that, darling. Ever since the Firebird showed up all the Fay know who you are. Funny, I thought you might be afraid to come near the water after you almost drowned in Stella Real."

He knelt closer to her. "Well, this is a lagoon, it's a little different. Hey, speaking of the Firebird, you wouldn't happen to have seen her drifting by recently, would you?"

The mermaid shrugged and coolly examined her nails. "Oh, I did, but I'm afraid you won't have any luck catching her now. She's gone."

Pasha fell back on his haunches, exasperated. "What do you mean 'gone'? Where did she go? How do you know?"

She waved her hand casually and leaned her head back. "Oh, what does it matter? Do you want my help or not?"

Pasha squeezed his eyes shut as though his head hurt. "Help with what? I wasn't aware you were offering me help."

She shoved her hands on her hips in a sassy attitude. "Well, why else would you be here?"

Pasha opened his mouth, then closed it. He rubbed his left eye with the back of his hand.

"Look, ma'am, all I know is one minute I'm sleeping in my

bed, and the next minute I'm following a golden light through a cave looking for the Firebird."

"And it led you to me! Ta-da!" She turned her back and bent forward. "Now hop on!"

Pasha stared at her with his eyebrow raised. This woman had to be insane. What was she doing? When he didn't move, she glared at him over her shoulder. She struck her forehead.

"Of course, what am I thinking, you need the olives first!"

Pasha sighed and cradled his head in his hands. The mermaid reached out for his arm.

"Pasha? Are you alright, darling?"

He brought his head up to meet hers. "Who are you?"

She stared at him for a moment, then broke into an impassioned smile.

"I'm Eve!" She grabbed his hand and shook it convulsively.

"Okay. Why are you here, Eve?"

Gasping, she reached forward and slammed a hand against his mouth.

"We dare not speak of it here!" She withdrew mysteriously into the water, glancing back and forth. Pasha continued to gape at her. Perhaps being trapped in the water for so long had messed with her brain. She waved her hands towards a squat tree hanging over the lagoon.

"Well? Go pick some of the olives!"

Pasha hesitated. Annoyed, Eve hunched her shoulders.

"Pasha, what are you waiting for? You want my help, don't you?"

Pasha looked at her doubtfully, then forced an awkward smile, trying not to hurt her feelings. "Can you actually help me?"

Eve beckoned him forward impatiently.

"Come here, I'll tell you a little secret."

Pasha crept forward on all fours, and allowed her to put an arm around his shoulders. She cupped a hand over her mouth.

"I know how to break the Land Lock!" Only she did not whisper this, she yelled it. Pasha jumped back, startled. Eve didn't seem to notice his apprehension. Instead, she sat there grinning like a schoolgirl.

"Isn't it exciting?"

Pasha eyed her up and down. "Really?"

She nodded her head, as though she couldn't contain herself.

"You'll let me show you?"

Pasha scooted forward. Even if she was crazy, even if she ended up being delusional, what could she possibly do to harm him?

"Alright. Show me."

"Splendid! But before we go anywhere you must eat one of the olives. We wouldn't want you drowning, after all."

Getting to his feet, Pasha made his way to the olive tree and plucked a handful of the berries. Eve beckoned him closer.

"Let me have one too," she begged. Pasha placed it in her open mouth. Eve shut her eyes and hummed with satisfaction.

"Mmm, you have no idea how long I have craved these," she exclaimed between mouthfuls. "They're called Siren's Breath, olives of the merfolk. They grow on coastland. You can eat them right off the vine, no brining necessary." She dusted her hands off. "Right, come along, love."

Pasha lowered himself into the pool. "Where are we going?"

"To a secret place hidden beneath the Placide." She wrapped his arms around her neck. "Hang on tight, and let me do the swimming."

As soon as Pasha was settled, Eve sprang back and plunged down into the deep. They took off at a fair speed, traveling along the craggy reef where creatures like violet pincushions bristled in stony crevices. Colorful tubes waved in the current like trees drowned in a hurricane.

"The C.O.N. can't harm us down here. They know better than to enter the sea where the mermaids would rip them apart. " Eve emphasized this last part with a twinge of violence.

She babbled on, and soon the underwater kingdom of Pisces appeared in the distance. Pasha couldn't tear his eyes away from the magnificent architecture ahead of them. The reef was abundant with blue archways and windows where mermaids slept in their seashell beds. Stunning, turquoise statues hovered from the hanging porticos and pavilions. Pink banners rippled in the tide with orange fish printed into the design.

As they swam past the storied buildings towards the sea floor, Pasha felt like they were flying. Eve carried him down a shallow roofed tunnel and through a labyrinth of mosaics until finally they reached a staircase leading to an underground grotto.

It took Pasha's eyes a moment to adjust after breaking the surface. The grotto was lit with floating spheres of soft light. The high ceiling of the wide circular room was capped off with a skylight where water flowed over the top. Two small staircases on opposite sides led towards long hallways. It was like being at the bottom of a well. Painted lunettes and murals crowned the archways.

As Pasha lifted himself out of the water, he shivered in the frigid air. Eve furrowed her brow.

"You're cold, aren't you? Well, don't you worry." She swung herself onto the first step. The golden scales of her tail became nothing more than ripples of light dancing upon bare human legs. Her seashells were now part of a long white dress that appeared from nowhere. Without so much as a stagger she got to her feet and walked over to the large fire pit at the center of the room. Pasha was baffled.

"How—I mean . . ."

"All mermaids can grow legs and walk on land, silly!" She giggled and pulled a lever attached to the side of the pedestal. A torrent of blue fire came streaming up through the large bowl of aquamarine coals. Pasha felt as though his head would split in two.

"I'm only teasing, Pasha." She frogmarched him to the edge of the fire pit. "Yes, I know there's a curse shackling all mermaids to one form or the other right now, but Samael holds no power over me."

When he began to ask why, she held up a finger and shook her head.

"You'll find out why in time, and that's all we'll speak of it."

When Pasha was warmed, he followed Eve down the left hallway and into an ancient library. The tapestries hanging from the ceiling told stories of courageous mermaids in shell-encrusted armor. Peculiar artifacts like spears constructed from fish bones slept inside moldy display cases. Gargantuan books with decaying spines stuffed the tight wedges of the wide shelves. Pasha had to fight a sneezing fit to get closer to the texts. Eve smirked knowingly.

"You're allergic to the damp, aren't you?"

Pasha wrinkled his nose and nodded.

Eve transferred a heavy volume from the shelf to a reading easel on the podium.

"In that case, the sooner we get out of here the better. This is the book that's going to solve all your dilemmas."

Pasha read the title. "*A Guide to Curse Breaking* by Cirseas Verity-Gardner." He flipped open to the first page. "There wouldn't happen to be anything about catching the Firebird in here, would there?

Eve threw up her hands. "Oh, forget about the Firebird! There are much more important things you need to be concerning yourself with."

"That's what Mother Genesis told Staccato, but he didn't believe her."

Eve smiled fondly. "That doesn't surprise me. Staccato has never been able to take other people's advice. He has to learn things on his own. He's a very clever man, but terribly stubborn."

Pasha inclined his head. "You know him?"

"I do." She flew through the pages. Dust sparkled in the light. "Mother Genesis was right. Despite what Staccato says, catching the Firebird isn't your greatest assignment. This is what you should be focusing all your efforts on." She pressed a finger beneath a heading. "*Enchanted Weapons in the Wrong Hands*. The first things it mentions are ophidians and mermaid objects."

Pasha leaned forward and read aloud. "*The Land Lock is a curse hostile ophidians have long aspired to achieve. First discovered by alchemist Sheal Ashur in the third century A.D., the Land Lock would confine mermaids to a single form. If in her oceanic form at the time the curse is placed, the mermaid would become a prisoner of her own habitat. If in human form, she would become restricted to her terrestrial configuration. Because a spell of such magnitude has never been cast, no one is quite certain how to break it. Of the many theories, the most compelling one to date is the Allegra Shoal Theory, proposed nearly a century after the Land Lock's conception. Shoal predicted the curse would only ever be cast in a time of great political upheaval when an heir would be supplanted from the throne. To reverse the effects of the curse, a baptism of royal mermaid blood must take place. The unlikely specifics of such a catalyst are consistent with the classical laws of cursing, being just absurd enough to allow for considerable time to pass before the plague is lifted, thus causing a heavy amount of damage to the mermaid population.*" Pasha looked up from the text, baffled. "What do they mean by 'baptism'?"

"It's when a mermaid enters the sea and transforms for the first time after learning how to walk. Pasha, you realize what this means, don't you?"

Pasha gaped back at her with an empty expression on his face.

" . . . No."

"Pasha, your grandmother was a princess of Karkinos. You know how mermaid genetics work, don't you?"

Pasha thought back to what Sonata had said about mermaids intermarrying with two-leggeds.

"In unions of mermaids and non-mermaids, female mermaids only pass on their mermaid genes through female children."

Eve nodded her head. "Exactly . . ."

The revelation exploded inside him. Why hadn't he put it together before? His grandmother, Queen Evangeline, had been a mermaid.

"Mama and Katya are mermaids!" He struck his forehead with the heels of his hands. "My grandmother was a mermaid and my grandfather was a two-legged! Ugh! I'm such an idiot!"

No wonder Katya always knew what he was feeling; if she was a mermaid she was also an empath. As for her crazy notions and premonitions? It wasn't psychosis, she was probably using her powers of psychometry to find out things no one else knew. Sonata had even explained to him mermaids carried more copper in their blood, which explained why the doctor found excessive copper in Katya's tissues! Could it be that without access to her mermaid form, the copper was causing the Kayser-Fletcher ring? To top it all off, Sonata, his mother's first cousin, was a mermaid! He rubbed his fingers through his hair and groaned. All these signs, and he had never put them together!

Eve squeezed his shoulder. "All you have to do is submerge them in the ocean. Then they'll transform into mermaids and the curse will be broken."

"I have to tell the others!"

She grabbed him by the hand, and led him back down the hallway. "Come, I'll return you to the surface."

***

Pasha ran through the chilly midnight air across the pink sand, soaking wet in his pajamas.

"Sonata! Pyro! Staccato! Anybody!" He swung open the door

to the caravan, tripped over Melodious and landed sprawled in the middle of the floor. Pyro stretched and rubbed his eyes.

"Flaming bollocks, Pasha! What is it?"

Cicada swarmed out of the spout in her tea kettle, dousing everyone with her bright light.

"Why are you wet?"

Sonata knocked from the inside of her bed. "What's going on out there?"

Above him, Staccato stuck his head over the side of the loft where he slept. He took one look at Pasha, strung out on the floor, soaking wet in his pajamas, and cocked an imperious eyebrow.

Pasha was panting. "Why didn't you tell me my mother and sister were mermaids?"

"I thought that was an obvious conclusion, given that your cousin is a mermaid."

"Well, Sonata said her father and Evangeline had different mothers. I assumed Evangeline was a two-legged."

"Surely, that isn't why you came bursting in here, drenched, and screaming like mad?"

"No, I know how to break the Land Lock!"

Chapter 27:
The Miraculous Aunt Poppy

When Faina made her weekly visit to Aunt Poppy's apartment for tea, the last thing she was expecting was to be handed a compact of face powder.

"Aunt Poppy, what is this for?"

Aunt Poppy's eyes bulged from behind her coke-bottle glasses. "Don't tell me you haven't thought of trying to cover up those bruises?" Her two black cats, Ink and Iseault, wove behind her like a braid as she crossed to the kitchen.

Faina fingered the sore spots on her face where she'd fallen after running from the police the previous day.

"Are they really that bad?"

Aunt Poppy leaned against the table and cocked a hand on her hip.

"*Malyutka*," little one, "you keep this up any longer and people are going to think you have landed yourself a man."

Faina flipped open the compact and dabbed at the cut on her collarbone.

"Without Pasha, I'm having to steal twice as much. We need the money."

"Isn't he supposed to be wiring you cash from his new job?"

Faina slumped down in her seat and groaned. "He's probably halfway to California laughing it up with some choice bit of calico."

Aunt Poppy shook her head and rummaged through a drawer in the kitchen.

"Oh, now don't try to go fooling me, silly girl. I know better. Pasha is in Voiler with my nephew, Staccato Nimbus."

Faina's mouth fell open. She wasn't sure which question to ask first.

"Did you say Staccato Nimbus was your nephew?"

Aunt Poppy gave a jolly bob of her head. "That is right. I am his father's sister."

She took the broom resting against the stove and jabbed it once into the floor. The wood peeled itself back like birch flesh as the figure of a bronze owl with its wings outspread split from the handle. The broom had transformed into a staff. Aunt Poppy gave it a flourish and the tea set floated up from the table.

"Who do you think taught Staccato all his tricks?"

Faina blinked as though she were seeing Aunt Poppy for the first time.

"You're a miraculous?"

Aunt Poppy tilted the head of her staff into Faina's cup. Tea flowed from the beak like a spout.

"I am, indee—Ink! You get down from there at once!"

Faina jumped and turned in time to see Ink hopping up on the counter, his nose inching towards the uncovered butter dish. Faina watched, leaning forward in her chair, as Aunt Poppy enchanted the feline to float up in the air and drift gently to Faina's lap.

"You naughty boy! Now you just sit there with Faina and keep your nose out of trouble!"

Iseult swaggered forward and planted herself proudly at Aunt Poppy's feet, as though to remind everyone that she was the well-behaved pet.

Faina eyed Aunt Poppy up and down. "So, you aren't Poppy Potemkin, you're Poppy Nimbus."

Aunt Poppy held up a crooked finger as she laid Faina's cup and saucer upon the table.

"Well, we had to change our name in order to fit in in the Other. After my father died, my parents migrated to Lake Baikal. I was just a girl then. Mother thought it was best to avoid all the political hubbub taking place in Voiler at the time. We went to Siberia and studied the endangered unicorn population. Nobody really lives there you see, so we could live our lives without being bothered. Jessant, or Jesse as we called him, Staccato's father, was already grown and married by then, so he stayed behind in Aquarius. But I was frequently called upon to visit once it was discovered we had another miraculous in the family."

She toddled into the kitchen and fetched a hand mirror. With a wave of her hand, it drifted towards Faina. It was made from blown glass, and the frame was decorated with hazel and honeysuckle.

"What's this for?"

Aunt Poppy merely smiled.

"This is a calling glass. Hold this out in front of you, and slowly begin turning as you repeat Pasha's name. Do it until you see him appear. Now go on, say it."

Ink hopped out of Faina's lap with a thud as she stood. She held the calling glass at arm's length, and slowly spun around, never taking her eyes off her reflection.

"Pasha . . . Pasha . . . Pasha . . ."

As her tongue portioned out the final chant she could hear someone laughing. She stopped. Her reflection was gone. Someone's hand eclipsed the glass. There was a colorful tornado of yellow interior, and Pasha appeared smiling back at her.

"Faina?"

Faina let out a shriek and stumbled backward. The calling glass flew into the air. Aunt Poppy lunged for it and caught it before it hit the floor. Pasha couldn't stop laughing. Aunt Poppy handed her back the mirror and pulled out a chair.

"Perhaps you should sit down."

Faina nodded and lowered herself to a seat. Pasha struggled to catch his breath.

"Did I scare you?"

"Yes!" The mirror rippled at the volume of her voice.

"Shhh," hissed Aunt Poppy. "You don't have to yell."

Faina pressed a hand to her lips. Pasha's face was clean, his skin no longer mottled with cuts and bruises.

"What are you doing? What's it like there? When are you coming back?" All the questions came spilling out at once.

"It's amazing here, you would love it. I'm not ready to come home yet, but I need you to do something for me. It might help me get done sooner."

"Anything! What do you need?"

He explained the Land Lock Curse to her. "I need you to help me break it."

Faina's heart skipped. Finally, he was going to come back and take her to Voiler!

"Yes! Yes! How do we do it?" The mirror was rippling so violently it distorted Pasha's face.

"This is gonna sound crazy, but I need you to get my mother and sister to submerge themselves in the ocean." Pasha fumbled for an explanation. Frowning, he said directly, "They're mermaids."

"Mermaids?" Faina's jaw dropped.

Pasha looked impatient. "Yeah, my grandmother, Queen Evangeline, was a mermaid."

"Does that make you a mermaid?" A fascinated grin was growing on her face.

"No, Faina, I'm not a mermaid! I can't even swim! It's complicated. Now pay attention! This is very important. You can't tell Mama what's going on."

"Then how exactly am I supposed to pull this off? It's the middle of winter here, they can't just go for a swim in the Hudson!"

"Yeah, that's where things get a little tricky. You might have to push them."

Faina stared at him, horrified. "Push them? Let me get this straight. You want me to lie to your family, take them on a little ride, then push your poor mother and sister off a dock?"

Pasha bit his lip. "I told you it would be crazy."

Faina threw up her hands. "Ugh! Pasha!"

"Faina! You have to do this, everything depends on it!"

"And what happens after I push them in the water?"

"They'll turn into mermaids and join me in Voiler."

Faina ground her jaw together. It was all she could do to keep from taking the calling glass and dashing it against the table. "You mean they get to come, and I don't?"

"Trust me, Faina, you'll be safer in New York with your uncle."

Faina's eyes lit up with wet rage. "My uncle is dead!"

Pasha stumbled back as though burned by a hot stove.

"W—what?"

"He was shot outside the bank a few days after you left. The police think it was the Bowery Butchers, but they don't know why."

Pasha's face was full of panic. Tears formed in his eyes. For six years the Chevalskys and the Dalkas had been like one large family. Pasha's sister was Faina's sister, Faina's cousin was Pasha's cousin. Uncle Matvei had loved Pasha, and Pasha had looked up to and respected him. Seeing Pasha cry put a deeper ache inside Faina's heart, and she too fell to sobbing.

Finally, Pasha managed to get the words out. "Ma's taking care of you?"

Faina had to take a deep breath before she could speak. "Yeah."

Pasha rubbed his forehead with his free hand and muttered to himself. "If she leaves, you and Anya have no place to go . . ."

Faina's jaw ached as her muscles grew taught. "There is one place," her voice was almost mocking. "Take us with you!"

"Faina, I can't do that yet. Not until I catch the Firebird. It's just as dangerous here."

"It's just as dangerous, and yet you want your mother and nine-year-old sister to join you?" She set the calling glass down on the table, thrust back the chair, and walked away with her arms crossed and her back turned.

"Let me explain," he called after her. "My mother and sister will be safe in the ocean. The C.O.N. can't reach them there. You and Anya don't have that kind of protection. We're being hunted down by the C.O.N. as we speak. Samael has already killed two hundred people trying to locate me. Until our situation improves you have to remain in the Other."

Aunt Poppy cleared her throat. "Anya and Faina can stay with me until you have caught the Firebird. Faina can even bring her dog."

"Thanks, Aunt Poppy," replied Pasha. "Faina, will you please come back and listen to me?"

Faina snorted and plodded back to the mirror. Pasha resumed his instructions.

"You can tell Katya. Let her help you. She may think of a way to convince Mama, you might not have to push her at all."

Faina continued to glower at him without moving a twitch, but Pasha pushed out his lower lip and stared into her eyes. At last, Faina heaved a dramatic sigh and threw up her hands.

"Fine."

"Thank you, Faina! I owe you everything!"

"You can say that again! Now hurry up and catch that bird so you can come back and get me!"

"I will, I promise!"

He gave her a weak, longing smile. He really did miss her. Faina's shoulders lost their rigidity, and her expression softened.

"I'll see you soon." There was nothing in Faina's voice that sounded certain, but every bit was hopeful.

"See you soon." He pressed his fingertips to the glass, and Faina pressed hers back. Pasha's face was replaced with her own reflection. He was gone. After staring wistfully at the glass where his face had been, Faina remembered where she was. She was standing in the dark of Aunt Poppy's apartment. She fell back into the chair and dissolved into tears.

"What am I gonna do? I can't push Mama Lydia off a dock!"

Aunt Poppy tilted Faina's chin up and pinned a stray hair behind her ear.

"Hush, my dear. Dry your tears and listen to me. There is no rush, despite what Pasha says. This must be carried out with discretion. You have time to come up with an idea. You just have to remain calm. In the meantime, you need to get Katya and Mrs. Chevalsky out of New York."

Faina sniffed and rubbed her eyes with her sleeve. "Out of New York? Why?"

"Don't you see, Faina? It is not safe for them here. That brick was a warning. Next, they will try to force Pasha's whereabouts from Mrs. Chevalsky by means of violence, or else draw him out by putting his family in danger."

"But I don't understand. It can't be the Breadwinners. But who else would wanna know Pasha's whereabouts? I can't think of any gangs with the initials 'R.R.'"

Aunt Poppy shrugged her shoulders. "Perhaps it is not a gang. It could be an individual, someone gone rogue. They must expect you to know them." She stared into Faina's eyes, prompting her to think.

Faina rolled through lists of names in her head. "Nothing rings a bell."

Aunt Poppy dusted off her hands and faced Faina with a hard stare.

"Well, that is no matter. What is important is that you get the Chevalskys out of the city as quickly as possible, and then we can think about the Land Lock." She scanned her over. "Do you still have Leo's pistol?"

Faina nodded her head.

"I trust you know how to use it."

The look of severity wearing on Aunt Poppy's features sent a chill running down Faina's spine. It was then that the darkness dawned on her. Every life of the household was now in serious danger.

***

Faina returned to the apartment late that evening to find Anya and Katya busy with piecework. Faina looked about, confused.

"Where's Mama Lydia?"

She could tell by the hardened ridge along Anya's shoulders she was in for a scolding. Anya folded her piecework and tucked the needle in the top of the cloth. Without a word, she patted Katya's head and led Faina by the arm into the hallway. Faina shook her head.

"What's the matter?"

Anya tightened her arms across her chest. "Mama Lydia started a new job today. She'll be working nights from now on."

Faina glanced between the kitchen and the hallway. "What new job?"

Anya sighed and dropped her voice lower still. “When she saw her pay from the factory wasn’t stretching far enough, and that your illegal income was bringing in more money, she went down to the Cherry and landed herself a job as a waitress.”

Faina clenched her teeth. “You mean the speakeasy in the drugstore on the Bowery?”

Anya nodded, her lips pursed together. “That’s the one.”

“She can’t go back to another speakeasy! Who gave her that idea?”

Anya drew her mouth tighter still and screwed up her eyes. “You did!”

Faina took a step back. “Me?”

“Yes, you! You and Pasha both actually! That’s how you justified working for Klokov, isn’t it? You said bootlegging paid better than any other job. So, she went down to the Bowery and got herself hired as a waitress. Oh, and from now on you’re to stay home and supervise Katya. Mama Lydia said so. You may not go down to the Foxhole for any reason, and you can only leave the house to run errands and walk Mammoth.”

Faina threw her arms in the air and stamped her feet. “But I can’t stay in the house tomorrow! I have someplace I gotta be, and I promise it has nothing to do with bootlegging!”

“Tell that to her! I’m not covering for you anymore! You’re gonna get yourself killed!”

Chapter 28:
A Friendly Favor

Faina and Katya watched the revolving doors of Spiegel Automotive across the street. Mammoth sat at their side. Motorcars spun slush on the asphalt like blackened eggs. It was early evening. Anya was still at the factory and Lydia had left for work. Faina had spent an entire night concocting a plan for getting the Chevalskys out of New York and into the bay. So far she had only come up with a solution for the first half, and it required a car.

"Now, remember Katya," she smoothed Katya's collar, "you can't tell your mother about any of this. She can't know we were here, and she can't know about the mermaid thing."

"Oh, I know." Katya hugged Faina's knees and propped her chin against Faina's hip. "You know what I love about you, Faina? You always tell me the truth. Grown-ups always lie because they think I can't handle things."

Faina squeezed Katya's hand. They waited several more minutes. At last, there was a glimmer as the doors rotated. Faina's mouth fell open. It was him, Roman Schegelov, all grown up, and sporting a smartly-tailored coat. He was even more handsome than he had been as a boy, and he still had those dimples! His jaw had squared and set, and his shoulders had broadened with muscle. It had been four years. He would be twenty-one now. Faina practically drooled as he swept off his fedora and ran a pocket comb through his wavy, bronze hair. He lit a cigarette and leaned coolly against the brick wall. Katya tugged on her sleeve.

"Faina! Is that him?"

Faina forced her eyes away. "Uh, yeah. That's him. Roman Schegelov."

"He's awfully handsome." Katya giggled.

"I know." Faina struggled to swallow her giddiness. She handed Katya Mammoth's leash. "Stay here. I'll be right back."

The road cleared. Determined to hide her jitters, Faina threw back her shoulders and put forth her most feminine swagger. To her delight, Roman's eyes swiveled her way.

"Well, well!" She cocked her hands on her hips and eyed him over. "Roman Schegelov! Look at you, all grown up!"

She could hardly keep from melting under those sleepy blue eyes scintillating with mischievous boyhood. The light of recognition came into his eyes.

"Faina? Leo Spichkin's kid sister, is that really you?"

She posed like a movie star. "The one and only!"

"You sure ain't a kid anymore." He popped his eyebrows and puffed on his cigarette. Inside she was squealing. She looked back at the car dealership.

"You can say that again. So, I hear you're selling tin lizzies to mobsters like Klokov these days."

He shrugged. “I’m an associate of an associate. You still a woman at large, or have you put your life of crime behind you?”

“Oh, I have my fun still. A little bootlegging here and there . . .”

He crossed his ankles and chuckled. “So, you’ve come a long way from your days as ‘The Kissing Cat Burglar’?”

Faina placed a strategically bashful hand over her lips. “You still remember that?”

“Of course I do, how could I forget?” He held out his hand as though reading the headline of a newspaper. “‘Thieving Little Girl Steals from Families and Kisses the Boys to Keep Them Quiet.’ That’s quite a story.”

“Well, I’ve certainly changed my game since then.”

“You were one bold little girl. If I remember correctly, I didn’t have to become one of your victims to get a kiss from you. You remember that?”

Faina slapped a hand over her mouth and laughed out loud. “Oh geez, not that story! I can’t believe I did something so embarrassing! Leo was furious, but who could blame him? His ten-year-old sister grabbing his unsuspecting friend and kissing him! You nearly jumped out of your skin!”

He leaned closer and smirked. “Well, I might be less jumpy now that you’re older.”

Faina smiled in a way that pushed her lower lip forward in a flirtatious manner.

Roman inhaled his cigarette. “So, what are you doing up here in the Bronx, anyway?”

“I came to see if you might do a favor for an old friend’s little sister.” She batted her eyes and turned out her ankle.

“For Leo Spichkin’s sister? Anything!” He checked his watch. “Let’s see, how about in fifteen minutes you meet me down at the Kosmo and we’ll discuss it over a cup of coffee?”

Faina glanced back at Katya who nodded and threw her a thumbs up.

Faina twisted a strand of hair around her finger. “Sounds like a plan.”

“Great!” He put out his cigarette and tipped his hat. “I’ll see you then!” And he disappeared through the revolving doors.

***

Once Faina had settled things with Roman she moved on to the next phase of her plan. After dropping Katya and Mammoth back home, she headed for the drugstore on the Bowery. Inside it was quiet but Faina knew better. A life-sized aluminum advertisement for cherry cola hung near the back of the store. In the picture, a woman with large melting eyes sipped from an ice cream float. Faina pressed the cherry floating at the top of the glass. A bell rang within. A panel slid open in the woman’s face and a pair of suspicious blue eyes squinted down at her.

"Password?"

"Rhapsody in Blue."

The advertisement rolled back like a sliding door. A smooth-looking man with a white trilby motioned her inside and shut the ad behind her.

Faina fidgeted with the collar of her coat. "I need to speak with a woman who works here. Lydia Chevalsky."

The man nodded with his cigar between his teeth and directed her to an empty table in the corner.

"Wait right here, she's in the private room."

Faina's head swiveled. "Private room?"

Her apprehension didn't appear to register with the man. He turned and blew his smoke away from her.

"Yeah, she'll be one minute."

Faina's eyes traveled along the back corridor where several curtained booths ran along the wall. Every now and then, a woman with rouged knees would scamper from the folds of drapery carrying a drink tray. Once a phantom hand reached out and snatched playfully at a waitress. Her stomach turned. Finally, Mama Lydia emerged from one of the larger booths, staggering in a pair of high, strappy heels. Someone caught at the back of her skirt. She ripped it back with such violence she tripped out of her shoes and fell against a pillar.

They had dressed her in a tight, shimmery number that hugged her hips and fringed at the knee. Her dark tresses were piled beneath an oversized feather headdress. Her blush stain was smeared so heavily on her high cheekbones she looked as though she'd been slapped. Faina froze. Horrible guilt clenched her heart. This was all her fault.

The man who had let Faina in tapped Lydia on the shoulder and gestured to her at the table. Lydia's mouth fell open as she spied Faina. She drew in her arms and strode towards her with several authoritative clicks of her heels.

"Faina, what are you doing here?" She pulled out a chair and huddled close. One of her fake eyelashes was coming unglued.

"I—I needed to speak with you. I had a phone call from Pasha. He wants us to leave New York and join him in Atlantic City right away." Her voice was strained.

Lydia shook her head. "Atlantic City? Wh—"

"He says we're going to start over. He got a job working for a motor company, and he's already got an apartment picked out."

Lydia fixed her gaze on Faina with suspicion. "An apartment? He's sixteen."

"The company provides boarding for young employees, it's part of a startup program. The thing is, it won't be ready until Pasha finishes training in Tampa."

Lydia raised an eyebrow. "Tampa? As in Tampa, Florida?"

"That's where the headquarters are. In the meantime, Pasha says to go ahead and move into a hotel in New Jersey. It's already paid for."

Lydia glanced around the bar. "Sweetheart, why couldn't you have waited to tell me this at home? You didn't need to come down here, you shouldn't be in a place like this."

"Because we don't have much time. A friend of mine has offered to drive us to the Hudson Terminal Friday. A motorcar will be awaiting us in Hoboken. So, I thought you might wanna turn in your notice today. Anya and I are gonna stay behind for the first week. Aunt Poppy has asked us to feed Ink and Iseult, and her chickens while she visits her nephew in Astoria. She even agreed to pay us. Once that's done, we'll come join you."

Lydia stared at her with reluctance. Faina could tell she was annoyed Pasha hadn't spoken to her about it, but that wasn't unusual for Pasha. At last, she sighed and managed a faint smile.

"Well, I suppose I will have to find time to pack."

Faina waved a hand. "Don't worry about it. I'll take care of everything, you just hang onto your scales—uh, I mean tails! I mean hats! Hats is what I meant!" She forced an awkward giggle. Lydia raised an eyebrow.

"Well, in that case, I have only one request." She patted Faina's knee. "Next time Pasha phones, tell him I said if he doesn't cough up the truth about why we are staying at a hotel in New Jersey, I am selling all his baseball equipment."

Faina batted her eyes in surprise. Mama Lydia didn't suspect

Faina of lying, only Pasha. She had managed to pull it off, after all.

"Will do, Mama Lydia!"

Chapter 29:

The Siberian

Friday night, Roman parked outside the tenement house in a polished, hunter green Cadillac. Faina's eyes bulged as she trailed her fingers over the hood of the car.

"*Blin*!"

Roman glowed with pride. "Swell, ain't it?" He took Katya's suitcase and held the door open for them. "You two ladies look like regular 'It Girls', if you don't mind my saying. Clara Bow better watch out."

When they pulled up outside the drugstore, Mama Lydia was nowhere to be found. She said she would wait for them on the sidewalk. Faina bit at her nails as Roman put a comforting hand on her shoulder.

"Maybe she popped inside for a minute to get outta the cold."

Minutes ticked by. Drunken couples swaggered down the street. Sirens wailed in the distance. At last, Faina opened the passenger door.

"I should see what's keeping her. Wait here."

She shoved her trembling hands into her pockets. Her fingers enclosed around the handle of Leo's pistol. She sought out the secret entrance as before and pressed the cherry. Again the man appeared and let her inside.

"Do you know where Mrs. Chevalsky is? I was supposed to

pick her up fifteen minutes ago."

He gestured to the private booths. "She's running a little behind."

"A little behind? She handed in her notice three days ago, this is supposed to be her last night!"

The man shrugged. "She's serving a very important client."

Faina was too nervous to be timid. She cocked her hands on her hips and stamped her foot.

"Who?"

"The Siberian."

Faina's hand flew to her throat. "The Siberian? As in Protasio Puskov? The Bowery Butchers' Protasio Puskov?"

Protasio Puskov was mothered by an Italian and sired by a Siberian. His father had done time in the gulags under the reign of Tsar Nicholas II. Protasio earned his moniker by inheriting his father's signature violence.

The man tipped his cigarette. "The very same."

Faina shuddered. So, they had come for her just as Aunt Poppy had warned. She had to do something. She had to get inside that booth.

A showgirl brushed past her in a long trailing gown, headed backstage. Faina was struck with an idea. She grabbed a giant prop fan another woman had cast aside and hid her face. When no one was looking she snuck behind the curtain and headed for the dressing rooms. A rack of costumes awaited her in an empty hallway. Faina tossed the fan aside and fished through dazzling sequined numbers. Once she had found something that suited her, she ducked into a deserted dressing room and changed.

Faina shimmied into a pink gown hemmed with enormous boa feathers. She tucked the pistol into her garter. The cold metal burned against her skin. Without looking she took the jewelry hanging from the mirror and threw it over her neck. Once she had let down her hair, she began rummaging through the vanity for a pot of rouge. Her eyes snagged on a clear prescription bottle. The label read Amobarbital. A sleeping barbiturate. Her fingers seemed to trip over themselves as she hurried to unscrew the bottle. She poured the contents onto the dresser and crushed them into a fine powder.

When at last she finished, she swept the contents back into the bottle and tucked it into the bodice of her dress. She folded her clothes into a compact little pile and tucked it under her arm. An even bigger fan was sitting on a wicker chair in the corner. She snatched it up and headed for the door.

Outside the kitchen, waiters lined up covered trays on a long banquet table. Faina removed the cover from one of the platters and replaced the freshly cooked dinner with her folded clothes. A bottle of half-finished champagne sat in a bucket at a vacant table. Faina removed the cork, poured the crushed barbiturates into the liquid, and gave it a good shake. With the tray and the bottle in hand, she marched towards the booth where Lydia was held captive.

As she approached the curtain she was startled by a terrible slamming noise. Mama Lydia cried out.

"Where's the boy?" demanded a booming voice.

Faina felt as though her spine had become the pincushion for a thousand needles. She set her teeth together and forced herself through the curtain. Five unsavory men sat around the table. Lydia was at the far end flanked by a swarthy man in a pinstripe suit. This was the Siberian. With one hand he held her by the scruff of her hair, and with the other, he coiled his fingers into a fist. Faina scanned the room and picked out the spare muscle. She jerked her thumb over her shoulder and made her voice as bubbly and as feminine as possible.

"You gentlemen are wanted back at headquarters by Mr. Boiko." She knew enough about the Butchers to be aware this name carried some weight. As the two brawny men hastened out of the booth, Faina set the tray on the side table and turned to the Siberian.

"Sounds like things are getting much too serious back here." She set the champagne on the table and plucked a cigarette holder from the measly man seated on the right. She climbed onto the table. "You boys could use some fun."

The Siberian cocked a heavy eyebrow. "And who exactly are you?"

She turned and made her eyes wide.

"A compliment from Mr. Boiko, of course."

The others did not seem willing to protest. One man leaned towards her on his elbows and held out a lighter.

"Would you like me to light that for you, Miss?"

Faina's eyes grew as round as the pearls draped around her neck. She hated cigarettes. Leo used to drive her crazy with his Lucky Strike addiction after they moved to New York. But how would it look to refuse him? An idea struck her.

"No thank you, darling. I only smoke Chiestans." A brand of cigarettes she had made up on the spot. "I just needed something to gesture with."

"Chiestans?" The man on the left sneered. "Never heard of 'em."

She tossed her hair over her shoulder. "I'm afraid they're awfully hard to come by in the U.S. I have them imported from Spain from time to time, but I'm all out just now."

The measly man raised his highball. "I see, a woman of class."

Faina turned to the Siberian. His hand was still curled in a fist. She crossed her ankles and sat up tall, pursing her lips in a frown.

"What's the matter, Mr. Puskov? Can't you lighten up a little?" She gestured to Lydia, who was staring at Faina in frozen terror. "Give the lady a break. Didn't your mother ever tell you? You catch more flies with honey."

She popped off the table and reached for a bottle of vodka. She poured a glass and handed it to Lydia.

"Here, sweetheart. Take a swig of this. Dulls the pain."

With trembling fingers, Lydia took the glass by the stem. She opened her mouth to speak, but Faina stopped her with a fierce jerk of her head. She set aside the bottle and retrieved the champagne concoction from the sideboard. Swiveling around to the measly man, she batted her eyelashes.

"For the rest of us, how about something bubblier? A tipple for the smart-looking gentleman in the glasses?"

He draped a dopey grin across his face and held out his glass. "Yes, please!"

Faina bent low behind him and poured the bottle over his shoulder. Meanwhile, she slipped his gun from his pocket. His head turned. Faina swiped off his glasses and slid them over her nose. With a twirl, she dropped down on his opposite side and propped her elbow on the table.

"What do you think? Do I look as handsome as you?" The gun was shoved up under her skirt.

"You're a doll, that's for sure."

She replaced the spectacles crookedly on his face. Without asking, she topped off the next man's flute. Before he could protest, she tipped the glass to his lips and poured so quickly he nearly choked. Again she fished a firearm from his pocket and tucked it next to the other in her hosiery. By now her legs felt like lead. Once the man had guzzled his drink she dabbed at the corners of his mouth with a dinner napkin.

"Sorry about that hon, got a little over-excited."

She glanced over at the measly man whose posture was already decomposing. Faina rose to her feet and braced herself to face the Siberian.

"Aren't you gonna sit down, Mr. Puskov?"

The Siberian's eyes narrowed. "I'm in the middle of conducting business."

"So I've heard. You're looking for that Breadwinner, aren't you? Pavlo Chevalsky?"

He remained silent. Getting this man to talk wasn't going to be easy.

"Well, have I got news for you." Faina set aside the bottle and seated herself next to Lydia, propping her ankles on the sideboard. "I've got a cousin up in the Bronx with Blue Devil connections. He says he saw the *peirogi* slipping out of an apartment on Belmont. Apparently, he's staying with an Italian."

She reached around and gave Lydia a pinch. Receiving the message, Lydia threw back her head and covered her face in a dramatic display.

"No! Not my Pavlo!" She turned to Faina and pointed a finger in her face. "You! You horrible, snitching rat!" She gave Faina a wink.

The Siberian's stony face split into a grin as he seized Lydia by the wrist and pivoted her around to face him.

"So, he's been hiding out in the Bronx, has he?" He didn't seem to notice the other two men were practically unresponsive. The one in the glasses was dipping his head onto the table.

Faina's face fell in horror as the Siberian drew a pistol from the inside of his suit jacket and cocked it into place.

"Well, he'll come running back when he hears how his Ma got her brains blown out by the Butchers."

Faina drew Leo's pistol from her garter and fired straight into the Siberian's chest. Lydia jumped and screamed. The man on the left side of the table rocketed from his chair and immediately fell over into a coma. The Siberian crumbled against the wall, struggling to dam the flow of blood from his heart and lungs. Faina dropped the gun, snatched her clothes from the covered tray, grabbed Pasha's mother by the wrist, and dashed towards the exit.

Outside the booth, the Cherry had fallen into pandemonium. Showgirls screamed and waiters ducked behind tables. No one paid attention to the two women bolting up the stairs and out the door.

At the sight of Faina and Lydia, Roman jumped at the wheel. Lydia dove into the back seat while Faina flung open the passenger door.

"Step on it, Roman!"

He wrenched the key in the ignition. "What happened? Why are you dressed like that? What's the emergency?"

"I shot the Siberian!" As the words departed from her lips the cold weight of reality settled upon her shoulders. She had killed a man. He had attacked her guardian, a mother, and so she shot and killed.

Roman pounded on the gas. “You what?” His voice cracked.

“I’ll explain it all later, in the meantime get us out of New York!”

As they careened down the Bowery, two black Rolls-Royces picked up after them in a chase. Roman swerved right onto Broome Street.

“Faina, unless we lose these guys real quick I can’t drop you off at the terminal. It’s too dangerous.”

“What about the ferry?”

“That might be our best bet. We’ll slow them down by crossing into Breadwinner territory.”

Without halting for traffic, Roman veered onto Elizabeth Street. Horns blared in their wake. One of the Rolls-Royces took the turn too hard and toppled over on its side. Faina fingered her neckline with apprehension. At the intersection of Elizabeth and Canal, Roman swung left and drove right past the Foxhole. Shots fired. Lydia and Katya screamed and ducked down to the floor. Pedestrians threw up their purses and hats and ran screaming down the boulevard. Breadwinners poured out of the old brewery, guns drawn, hats pulled low. Some piled into vehicles waiting on the curbside and sped after the Butchers.

As they drove beneath the shadow of the El Train, a horrible popping noise set their teeth together. Their ears pierced with the scathing sound of tires skidding across the pavement. Faina dared to look in the rearview mirror. The tires of the Rolls-Royce had been shot out. The car rolled across the square in shatters, stopping short of the sidewalk.

Faina squealed. "They took them out! The Breadwinners took them out! We're safe!"

Roman raised his eyebrows. "For the time being."

Roman managed to get them to the ferry terminal without picking up any more followers. They decided it was best if Faina drove the Cadillac into New Jersey. Roman would have the car waiting at the exchange place sent back. Faina changed back into her normal clothes, and Roman walked Faina to the ticket booth.

"Thanks for helping me tonight, Roman. You ended up saving our lives."

"It was nothing. I remember getting into some pretty dangerous scrapes with Leo back in the day."

"Well, I know he'd be thankful too."

Roman smiled. There was a long pause that made Faina's arms and forehead tingle. His blue eyes fell upon her lips. As he drew forward she felt herself lean in magnetically and kiss him on the lips. His gold hair brushed against her cheek as she pulled away. The prickling in her skin dulled to a heady burn. It had lasted a good moment, and yet it was over too soon.

"Be safe," she advised.

Roman tipped his hat. "I would say try to stay out of trouble, but I know you too well."

Her lips stuck in a smile. She gave him one last sassy look over her shoulder before returning to the car.

Faina sat in the driver's seat and tried to act as though nothing had happened. She was worried they might have seen her kiss Roman, but Lydia had her eyes covered, and Katya was still frozen with fear. She shifted the car into gear and followed the directions to the platform.

"Are you okay, Mama Lydia?"

Lydia waved a faint hand. "I have been beaten, held captive, interrogated, and had a gun held to my head all in the same night. I am not okay, but I am alive."

"What do the Butchers want with Pasha anyway? Did they say?"

Lydia drew a heavy breath and pinned her forehead against the cool glass of the car window. "Something about hassling his own kind. I took it to mean the Breadwinners."

"But that's not right. The Breadwinners and the Butchers are rivals."

"Rivalries are never permanent, Faina. Either one gang succumbs to the other or they all start marrying each other. How long did you think a gang like the Breadwinners would last? Sure, their ideas about excluding women and children from violence are admirable, but it is a disadvantage when you put them up against gangs who are willing to do anything. How do you know the Butchers haven't infiltrated the Breadwinners? In terms of violence, they could easily overpower them. That's how Capone is taking over Chicago."

Faina stared up at her through the rearview mirror with a cocked eyebrow. "Gee, Mama Lydia. You sure know a lot about this kinda stuff."

Lydia leaned over the seat and hugged Faina's neck with an amused smile. "I know a lot more than you kids think, that's for sure." She kissed her cheek.

Chapter 30:

Flight to the Bight

When it came to driving, Faina had some experience but was by no means a skilled driver. Furthermore, she did not quite know where she was going. She followed the coastline where the luxury of street lamps was unfortunately bound to run out. Fewer and fewer cars littered the highway as they pressed on. Stone buildings gave way to tall shadows of thin, black pine trees.

An hour into the drive, they spotted two yellow headlights trailing behind them. As Faina was glancing into the rearview mirror, a deafening shatter split the air. The side mirror exploded into a thousand shards. Screams flew up from the back seat.

Faina flattened her foot against the gas. Heads pitched against the seat as they swerved around a corner on two wheels. Spatters of bullets hit the back windshield. Katya and Lydia ducked down with their arms over their heads, screaming and sobbing. Glass spat all the way into the front seat. Faina had cuts on the back of her neck from the spray of shards. She took every turn which came across their path, hoping to shake their pursuers.

They flew down a slope until the vehicle bounced to a level position. Faina slowed the car. The other headlights had disappeared. It grew quiet again. There were no street lamps, and the road became sickeningly confusing. Their visibility reduced to an unendurable ten feet of relentless black asphalt spinning before them like a wheel. For all they knew, it was an optical illusion, and the pavement was moving while they stood still. Faina's imagination overworked itself to its own detriment. Every stray branch was a man with a gun. Every noise was a bullet loaded into a chamber.

The motor thrummed beneath them. They listened for wheels, gunshots. Nothing. Faina picked back up to a normal speed. Perhaps it was over now.

Two round lights switched on ahead of them. A second car was parked on the side of the road, camouflaged by the lampless street. The driver turned the ignition. Faina slammed the car to a stop, seized the gear, and threw the vehicle into reverse. Bullets fired through the windshield. Faina screwed her eyes closed and shielded her face with her arm. She did not take her foot off the pedal.

The firing stopped. The car climbed onto the road, its headlights shining in their faces. Faina pushed the stick forward and raced past the Rolls-Royce in the opposite direction. Their hearts shoved into their throats as they scaled out of the valley and back onto the main road.

Trees thinned. In the distance was a gray shipyard and the eternal depths of the sea. It was almost over. The end was in sight, but so were two armed vehicles in the rearview mirror. Buildings rose up around them as the countryside closed. They entered the narrow streets of the harbor, headed for the sea.

Lydia was clutching her chest.

"Faina, what are you doing?"

Faina didn't answer. She accelerated down the hill. Her eyes were riveted to the docks. They were going so fast now, at times they could feel the car being lifted off the ground. Faina crashed through a pile of barrels, showering the car with splinters. The dock stretched before them like a runway. There was only one way to go: forward. She kept her foot on the gas.

Faina forced Lydia's screaming out of her mind. When they were a few feet from the edge, Faina threw open the door and tossed herself out of the front seat. The car pitched forward, eclipsing the sky. It hurtled nose-first into the water. A massive tidal wave billowed over the dock. In a single moment, Faina spotted a dinghy moored below deck. As the water came crashing down she slid herself into the boat and covered herself with the tarp. When she looked up again, the car had been swallowed by the water.

Faina laid out on her stomach. There was a tear in the tarp where she could see out into the water. Bubbles rippled in the place where the Cadillac had sunk. She swallowed and gasped for air. What if Pasha had been wrong? She waited for a sign. Had she just become responsible for the death of the woman who loved her like a mother, and a child whom she cherished so dearly?

A light materialized far beneath the waves. It throbbed for a moment or two, then swelled. It bled through the bay, sweeping beneath the dinghy and casting green light on Faina's chilled face.

Somewhere, there was a choir of otherworldly voices, disembodied and harmonious. Silhouettes of beautiful women with long fish tails eclipsed the water. She could see the outline of the butchered car below the surface. Triangular blades of glass drifted from the windshield in a slow churning motion.

Two shapes emerged from the mangled wreck; two mermaids—a woman and a child. They were safe! They had transformed! Faina was so relieved she actually laughed aloud.

As suddenly as the light had appeared, it vanished, and the world seemed darker than it had before. Headlights scanned across the dock. Dogs barked in the distance. Faina huddled, frightened, beneath the canvas. She couldn't keep her mind from recalling all the monstrous things she'd heard about the Bowery Butchers. She envisioned herself tied to a chair, a gun pointed at her temple, a man slapping her face until her skin felt numb.

The engine of a motorbike popped down the road. There was a susurrus roaring sound far on the horizon. She listened and strained her ear. Was it thunder? No, it was too long for thunder. Almost like a stampede. She felt the tide begin to drain. The boat was sinking lower beneath the dock. The sound was coming from the ocean. She peered out of the tear in the tarpaulin. The tide was plowing out of the horizon line, barreling towards her. Faina clung to the bench of the boat, waiting for the waves to consume her. At the last moment, the water shot up into the air.

The water climbed upwards and around her like a barrier. She peeled back the canvas. Her eyes followed the walls of water high above her head. It was like being at the bottom of a long tube. The webbing of white foam against the seawater had the look of marble. The tiptop of the harbor was visible above the space where the tube opened. Water climbed up the hill, chasing back the cars, and anyone who dared approach the dock. Faina was safe from the tidal wave; she was safe from the Bowery Butchers.

Half an hour passed inside the strange oceanic cyclone. Faina laid back on the floor of the boat and gazed at the beautiful stars sewn into the sky. All about her, she could hear mermaids singing in the distance. Even the cold had evaporated.

Eventually, the watery enclosure died away, and the music faded off. Faina rose up out of the boat. She couldn't help but feel she was being watched. As she turned around, she was startled to find a lone mermaid, peering over the edge of the boat.

"Go home now, child. You are safe."

Chapter 31:

Opening the Floodgates

Pasha was too impatient to eat, too anxious to sleep, too tense to do little else than spend his time alone with Harpagos in the stables of the Placide. What was taking Faina so long? It had been a few days since he had given her the instructions on how to break the curse. What had gone wrong?

It was all very frustrating. When Pasha told Staccato about Eve, who was somehow not subject to the rules of the curse, Staccato was dumbfounded. Stranger still, he almost seemed frightened.

“That’s impossible.” Those were his very words.

“You’re the one who encouraged me to believe in the impossible! I’m telling the truth!”

“I’m not saying I don’t believe you, Pasha. I don’t doubt your story. Whatever happened is beyond our comprehension. No mermaid in Voiler should have been immune to that curse. There must be something more at play that we’ve yet to understand.”

His lack of answers irritated Pasha. Staccato hadn’t been willing to accept things beyond his comprehension when Mother Genesis said it. Pasha supposed it didn’t matter to Staccato, as long as the problem was solved. Mother Genesis had been right about him having tunnel vision.

Pasha sighed and laid his nose against Harpagos’s downy muzzle. The pegasus nickered and bumped Pasha with his forehead.

"I can't sleep, Harpagos." Everyone had gone to bed hours ago. "But I guess I'm keeping you up."

Harpagos bent his head lower so Pasha could stroke behind his ears. Pasha laughed and hugged the horse's neck.

He was beginning to feel sleepy when a distant and thunderous roar cried out from the horizon. He turned and gaped out the door. The tide receded back at an alarming rate, as though it were being sucked up through a straw by the clouds.

Pasha ran from the stables and dashed onto the beach. Water drained from the rosy sandstone houses and dripped from the balconies of the Placide. Waves flushed down tiled staircases. Garden waterfalls disappeared.

There was a clamor from inside the caravan as Sonata threw open the back door and careened down the ramp in her wheelchair. A kimono was thrown over her nightgown, and she had her prosthetic legs in her lap.

"Out of my way, boys! It's happening!"

"What's happening?" yawned Pyro, irritably poking his head out the door.

Cicada zipped outside, blinding them all with her garish light. "The curse, it's breaking!"

Staccato hustled out the side door in his robe. "Did someone say the curse is breaking?"

Skelter was stepping out the back to join them when Melodious exited the front, relieving the wagon of his weight and catapulting lanky Skelter face-forward into the sand.

Melodious tilted his head towards the waves. "Someone tell me what is happening."

They watched the water scuttle back from the pink shore. There was a strange bubbling noise. The stillness split open like a porcelain shell. An enormous tidal wave mounted in the distance.

Staccato's eyebrows rose. "Get to higher ground!"

Melodious hightailed it to the porch of one of the bungalows. Skelter shimmied up a palm tree. Pasha climbed to the roof of the caravan with Pyro following after him. Cicada floated a foot or so higher, but Sonata remained rooted to the spot in her wheelchair. At the sight of Sonata pinning herself to the beach and hurriedly trying to attach her legs, Pyro turned and ran back.

"What do you think you're doing?" He grabbed the handles of her chair and wheeled her around.

"Pyro, let go!"

"It could be a false alarm! What if it's high tide?"

Cicada floated overhead. "It can't be high tide. Tides occur in a distinct pattern based on the alignment of celestial bodies, making them easy to predict. Given that neap tide has already passed and Larame adheres to a diurnal pattern, we aren't due for a natural surge for another twelve hours."

Pyro clenched his teeth. "Will you butt out?"

Sonata tugged on her wheels; so far she had only managed to get one leg on. "You heard the woman, it has to be the curse! Now let me go!"

The tide swept around them and before Pyro could stop her, Sonata dove from her chair into the brine, still holding onto the other leg. Thousands of mermaids rocketed up from the water. They laughed, they trumpeted on conch shells. Many came tumbling onto the sand, their tails falling away in place of legs. The mermaids who had been trapped on the land came flooding in from the countryside, jumping into the ocean with celebration.

Staccato cupped a hand over his mouth. "Pyro! The undertow!"

But Pyro was already losing his footing. The pull of the current was too strong, and he was swept under. Staccato's eyes swelled. Pyro was lost in the foam, hidden in the frenzy of wild waves.

Sonata reemerged with a tail, her skin shining, and Pyro's arm thrown over her shoulder. She dragged him back to the shallows and deposited him in the surf.

"I told you!"

She dove back under the water, showcasing her beautiful sea green scales. Pasha's jaw dropped. With a little water the prosthetic legs had transformed into a prosthetic fin. The surface was smothered in aquamarine stones which matched her scales almost perfectly.

The crowd hushed as a bubbling mass surged up from the depths. Queen Calliope appeared in an amphibious chariot drawn by strange, horse-like creatures with fins on their necks.

"My fellow mermaids," she sang out, "on this day, the curse placed on us by the C.O.N. has been broken!"

Everyone cheered and splashed until the Queen held out her hand for silence. She gazed across her crowd of subjects and spied Pasha atop the garish, yellow wagon. She stretched out an arm, radiating a gracious and irresistible warmth.

"Pasha!"

Pasha glanced back at Cicada. "Me? Is she talking to me?"

"Come here, sweet child."

Cicada nudged him forward. Pasha climbed down from the wagon and approached the edge of the water with an overwhelming sensation of awe and fear. He could feel the crowd trailing him with their eyes. The Queen's strange horses pulled the chariot closer. In the sloshing waves, he stood in the shadow of the Queen with his head bowed respectfully.

She gestured to him with her flowery trident. "Pasha, today you and your friends have done a great service for mermaids everywhere. We honor you as a hero, and recognize you as the true King of Ursa! All hail King Pasha!"

The crowd echoed with a resounding "Hail!"

Pasha was blushing. Too much was on his mind right now. Humbled as he was, he did not feel like standing in front of a crowd at the moment.

Calliope lowered her voice. "Your mother and sister are safe. Soon they will be here, and you will be together again. Come, let us celebrate!"

An evening of feasting and music followed. The night was resplendent with flashy colors, and sweet-smelling air. Mermen beat steel drums with impassioned energy. Their beaded dreadlocks had a timpani of their own as they swung to and fro in the excitement. Melodious joined in on his accordion. Mermaids stamped and twirled to the music, performing something akin to a salsa, a samba, and a hula. Perfumes of citrus, garlic, and spices sizzled from kitchens. They hung in fragrant clouds around bright platters of pineapples and fish, which Skelter eagerly trailed all night. The gates of the Placide were thrown open, inviting the revelers into the sultry gardens.

When a spare moment became available, Pasha approached the Queen. She was conversing with Staccato.

"Your Majesty," Pasha said, "with all due respect, I don't deserve credit for discovering how to break the curse. It was shown to me by a mermaid named Eve."

"*Wi*," yes, "Sonata told me the story of how you came to the library in the grotto, and I find it very perplexing. We've looked for your friend, but no such mermaid matching your description has been found in Pisces."

"But somehow she was unaffected by the curse; maybe she wasn't normally in the water."

"Pasha," Staccato interjected. He seemed eager to put a stop to the conversation. "What you're suggesting is impossible."

At this remark, Pasha had to grind his teeth together to keep from exploding.

"She knew you!"

Staccato wheeled around, his eyes wide.

Pasha clenched his fists. "I told her about how you were afraid to listen to Mother Genesis, and she laughed and said you were clever but stubborn."

Staccato's cheeks paled. One might have thought he had seen a ghost.

"Think!" Pasha persisted. "A young mermaid with gold hair, gold eyes, and a gold tail!"

"How old was she?" Staccato's voice was dark.

"Young. About Sonata's age."

The color flooded back into Staccato's face, and he shook his head.

"No. I don't know any mermaids who fit that description."

Pasha exhaled through his nose. Calliope must have sensed his tension for she stepped between them.

"Even if you did have help, Pasha, it still doesn't diminish your heroism. You alerted Staccato, and you got your mother and sister to the ocean, breaking the curse once and for all. And your friend, the one in the boat—"

"My friend in the boat?"

"The girl with the black hair and the freckles, the one who brought your mother and sister to us. She is to be honored as well. They were in very great danger. I will let your mother and sister tell you the story when they arrive."

Pasha's breath stole away.

"Relax," Calliope assured him. "They're all fine. All three of them. They were not harmed, I assure you. My people protected them, they saw no harm came to the girl."

Staccato slapped Pasha heartily on the back, trying to suck him out of his morbid ruminations. Sonata appeared at his elbow.

"I'll take him. Come with me, Pasha, I'll help get your mind off things."

He floated lifelessly after her. She took him to a quiet place outside the pavilion where the waves lapped against the long stone walkways. Nearby, the strange horse-like figures glided across the surface.

Sonata seated him on a bench. "Stay here for a while in the quiet. Let it clear your mind." She crossed to the railing where the horse-like creatures gathered for attention. Pasha studied them with a curious eye.

"What are those things?"

"Oh, these? These are kelpies." She beckoned him over. "They're sort of like amphibious horses."

The smallest turned its triangular head towards Pasha and blinked its enormous eyes.

"Go on, give him a pet."

Pasha ran his hand down the bridge of its green nose. It felt like seal hide.

"Are there other creatures like kelpies down in the mermaid kingdoms? I mean, creatures I've never seen?"

"Oh, yes. But not just in the mermaid kingdoms, all around. There are unicorns, orricks, and well, there's an entire world out there for you to discover."

"That's a little scary."

"Scary? Pasha, you shouldn't be scared, you should be excited!"

"I am excited, it's just, well . . . Staccato, Mother Genesis, Queen Calliope, everybody keeps telling me I'm a king. It's a lot of pressure. To be honest, I do kinda wanna reclaim the throne, but all I can think about is how much I don't know. Kings aren't just born, they're bred. It's sixteen years too late for me."

He was expecting her to be disappointed; instead, she looked thoughtful, understanding, even.

"You're right about one thing, kings aren't just born. But it's never too late to learn, and we'd be there to help you."

"But a king is responsible for so much. I don't know if I can make decisions for the good of an entire people." Pasha exhaled and slumped over the railing. Sonata patted his arm.

"Pasha, right now Samael is making your people suffer. They need you." She leaned back against the banister and tilted her head towards the stars. "He's created a lot of poverty in Ursa."

Pasha scrunched up his eyebrows. "How so?"

"For one, he's forcing people with natural abilities to apply for licenses in order to practice their careers legally. It's costing people an exorbitant amount of time and money. People like caims."

"What are caims?"

"They're a sort of doctor who heals using spiritual power, magical healing. In Ursa, no one can heal without a license. Were I to treat so much as a paper cut I could be heavily fined."

"Hasn't this been brought to the Ecliptic Council's attention?"

"Samael was threatened with the idea, and so to get around it he created new jobs without licenses. Do you remember how I said people in desperate situations sometimes sell their blood to ophidians?"

Pasha nodded.

"Ophidians have this thing they call *saignants*—a person, usually a young woman, who is hired as a living vessel to drink from. It's usually done at parties or other large gatherings. The ophidians consider it an ancient art form, a cultural tradition. It's a practice that dates back centuries in their country."

Pasha's face was growing pale and sickly. "Wh—what do you

mean exactly?"

"It's sort of like a human platter. The person lays out on a dining surface, and a chef uses a variety of sutures and blades to make small incisions in the veins so the blood can flow freely, but slowly. Usually, they're disrobed."

Pasha's knees trembled. Sweat gathered on the back of his neck. "But how can they get away with that? It's dangerous! People could die like that!"

"It's all very regulated. They're very careful about how much blood is lost. They never go beyond a pint, which isn't much to go around at a party, so they're usually served with appetizers arranged on the body. They're paid quite handsomely."

"Are you okay with this or not?"

Sonata blinked her eyes at his outburst of passion.

"I'm not! I'm only explaining how they manage to get away with it."

Pasha could hardly contain his shock. "And people actually sign up to do this?"

"Well, it's like I said, the pay is above and beyond excellent in a time where money is hard to come by."

"Just how many people find themselves in this position?"

"I don't have an exact number, but I know it's a pretty significant sum."

Pasha threw back his shoulders. "What else has he done?"

"Let's see, we've covered a few of the permissible atrocities. Would you care to hear about the more illicit affairs he's getting away with? The ones the Ecliptic Council doesn't know about?"

Pasha nodded. His eyes drew tight in a defiant line.

"I didn't get to finish telling you about the caims. Do you know why the ophidians are so eager to get rid of them?"

"Because they use magic, and you said Samael wants to get rid of all magic."

"There's more to it than that. You see, ophidians have their own medical physicians they like to use. Do you remember the bodies you came across in the kitchens at Alfbern? Do you know where they came from?"

Pasha steeled himself.

"When caims aren't available, people have to go to physicians provided by the ophidians. When a patient is in need of surgery or extreme medical care, the ophidians often kill them and tell the family they died during the operation. That's where they get their food from."

Pasha turned a greenish color and clutched the railing until his knuckles turned white. But there was more in his face than sick revulsion, there was also anger.

"How has the Ecliptic Council tolerated these people for so long? This can't be permitted to continue any longer!"

"That's why we need you, Pasha!"

Pasha's knees straightened. His mouth snapped shut. Sonata

had put an entirely different spin on things. Before, giving up the throne had seemed like the most responsible choice, but now he wasn't sure.

Footsteps echoed behind them, and Pyro appeared at the top of the stairs.

"Pasha! There are some people out here that would like to see you." He winked.

Pasha's face lit up. He dashed up the steps and followed Pyro back to the pavilion where his mother and sister waited.

Unfortunately, his excitement was short-lived. At the sight of his mother, his heart sank. Tears streaked down her face. Her shoulders rose and fell with uneven gasps. Calliope and a few of the other mermaids tried to calm her.

He bolted towards her. "Mama!"

"Pasha," she squealed, practically tripping to get to him. She flung her arms around his neck, her lips fluttering in unintelligible sobs. He took her by the hands.

"Shhh, it's alright, Ma. Calm down. What's wrong?"

She looked him in the eye with her swollen, tear-stained gaze.

"Faina! Faina and Anya! We have to go back for them! They are in terrible danger!"

Chapter 32:

The Russian Rogue

To avoid recognition, Faina skipped the subway and hopped a freight train back to Manhattan. She arrived at Orchard Street shortly before dawn, exhausted and whiplashed all over. A crowd had gathered outside her tenement building. Her body stiffened as an indescribable cold rinsed down her spine. It was an effort to move forward.

A chain of police officers rippled against the throng like reeds on the edge of a pond. The front door was punctured with row after row of bullet holes. Neighbors screamed and cried. Faina swallowed. Despite the icy snowfall sticking to her cheeks, her forehead broke out into a sweat. She powered her way to the front of the line and peered down at the wreckage.

Anya's body was slumped coldly against the door, undisturbed. The bullet that had passed through her was embedded in the plaster over her head. Her blood stained the entry in thin fluid layers which darkened by degrees. It painted the snow like watercolor. The whites of her eyes had faded to the shade of newsprint, and her complexion was tinged with anemic blue. She had been dead for some time. It was a shell, it wasn't even Anya. Most frightening of all, it looked as though it had never housed a soul.

Faina didn't even realize she was screaming until the cry was long out of her throat. Soft, comforting hands enclosed around her wrists and pulled her back from the crowd. It was Aunt Poppy.

"Faina! Come away, my darling."

She folded Faina into her shoulder. Faina squeezed her eyes shut, feeling she could never open them again.

"Shhh, it is okay." Aunt Poppy stroked her hair. Within the bustling clamor, Faina could hear Mrs. Borsuk regaling the police with everything she'd seen.

"I heard yelling at the front door. Two people arguing, Miss Dalka and a young man. He was asking about someone, I couldn't hear who. Next thing I knew, Miss Dalka was ordering the young man to leave . . ."

Upstairs Mammoth was barking from the window. He sounded as though he would rip someone apart. Nearby an officer reported to his superior.

"We've got four witnesses, more or less reporting the same incident with a few minor differences. The one detail no one seems to be arguing is the identity of the killer."

"Who was it?"

"A boy named Anastas Sippenhaft. Big fella, son of a couple of anarchists taken into custody back in 1919. Apparently, he was looking for information concerning a recent tenant, a kid named Pavlo Chevalsky."

Faina lifted her chin from Aunt Poppy's shoulder. Her eyes widened in horror.

"What did they say?"

Aunt Poppy grabbed her by both hands. "Never mind that, Faina. Calm down, let's get you inside."

But Faina refused to move. Her skin burned with hatred. Her lips curled over her teeth.

"It was Anastas!" Her chin thrust forward, and the muscles in her neck became as stiff as steel.

Aunt Poppy pinched her shoulders, her gaze growing still firmer.

"Faina . . ."

Before Aunt Poppy could stop her, Faina tore herself away. She sprinted blindly down a maze of slummy alleyways, ignoring the throbs of pain every step sent shuddering through her body. She bolted through chilling, emptied-out buildings, past shifting, unsavory figures until at last, she came to Anastas's tenement building. Rats scurried over broken beer bottles in the gutter. Bullet holes riddled doorways. Scorch marks blackened the bricks. She slalomed around brown puddles of alcohol and excrement. Arching her back, she shouted at the endless number of cracked, filmy windows.

"Anastas!" Her voice echoed back to her from the cool brick walls. She doubled over, hands hanging on her knees. She drew in another deep breath and straightened herself.

"I'm giving you one last chance to deny it! Do you hear me?"

Before anyone could answer, someone wrapped their arm

around her lower waist and pressed the barrel of a gun into the small of her back.

"You don't have to yell. I'm right here."

Anastas rested his chin on her shoulder as though any minute he would whirl her around and sweep her into a dance.

"Face me," ordered Anastas, calm but threatening.

Faina turned. The tip of the gun was barely peeking out of Anastas's pocket. He smirked down at her.

"Now, I'm gonna put this away, but I wouldn't move if I were you."

He gestured with his eyes towards a car parked behind them. Vadim was pointing a pistol at her from the back seat. Anastas sheathed his revolver and, pulling her even closer, set about tying her wrists together with some rope from the inside of his coat. He motioned to Vadim, who opened the car door.

"Get in."

He resumed aiming the gun at her. Faina allowed him to escort her to the vehicle. She was surprised to discover a member of the Bowery Butchers sitting behind the wheel.

"You've been working with the Butchers this whole time."

Anastas nodded. "I have."

He looped her bound arms around his neck and dragged her into the back seat so she was sitting in his lap. Faina couldn't fill her lungs with enough air.

"It was you who threw the brick through our window! You set the Siberian on Pasha's mother!" The pieces stuck together like some perverse puzzle. "'R.R.' . . . The Russian Rogue! Your fight name!"

"You're just now figuring that out?"

Faina ignored him and shook her head. "You killed my family. Uncle Matvei, and Anya, you killed them both!"

There was an odd mixture of guilt and defense in his face, as he lowered his head and turned his eyes away from her.

"To be fair, I didn't shoot your uncle. That was an accident. Bukowski was given orders to bring your uncle to headquarters without seriously injuring him. The plan was to interrogate him. But Bukowski lost his nerve once your uncle started to shout. That was never meant to happen."

"What did you want with him? He never did anything to you!"

Anastas ground his teeth together.

"I wanted to know where Pasha was hiding!"

"Uncle Matvei didn't know anything! What about my cousin? What about Anya? Are you gonna tell me that was an accident too?"

Anastas's shoulders hunched. Again he looked away from her.

"I wanted to know where you had been all night. I heard you shot the Siberian. I was worried. But Anya refused to tell me anything. Said it wasn't any of my business. Told me to leave immediately or else she would tell Klokov I'd been harassing you again."

Faina's eyes bore into him, demanding he finish the story. "Go on, it obviously doesn't end there!"

Anastas grew stiffer. He scratched the side of his face. "I never liked Anya's attitude. She was always stubborn, stuck-up. I was angry she wouldn't tell me where you were, and I didn't like her giving me orders. I lost my temper with her. I threw her up against the wall and told her if she didn't tell me where you were, I'd knock her teeth out. She started screaming. Lights came on in the building. I knew if I let her go she would run her mouth, so I did what I had to do."

Tears flooded Faina's gaping eyes. He said it as though it were all so trivial.

"You always find a way to justify yourself, don't you?" She choked with sobs. "You don't even think you did anything wrong! What kind of person are you?"

He ran a knuckle down her cheek. "Come on now, Kitten, don't cry."

Faina snapped her head away. "Don't touch me! Let me go!"

"Don't be sore, Faina." He pulled her closer. "We've got a lot of chatting to do, and it will go a lot smoother if you cooperate."

They pressed against the seat as the engine roared, and the car started up. Faina was too scared to cry now.

"Where are you taking me?"

Anastas patted her cheek. "You'll find out when we get there." He put his head down close to her ear. "In the meantime, how about a little kiss? You know, you never came sneaking around my house during your stint as the Kissing Cat Burglar. I believe I'm overdue."

It would have been wiser to wait until they were out of the car to fight back. It would be easier to get away once they were outside the vehicle. But Anastas had stirred the incendiary temper inside her.

"Overdue?"

"That's right. You owe me one."

Faina's nostrils flared, her lips curled back, and before she could stop herself she had spat in Anastas's face.

"That's all I owe you."

A shadow crossed Anastas's eyes so deep that a chill ran over Faina's shoulders. A cry knocked from her lungs as his fist shot up and closed around her throat. He forced her head back against the window.

"Don't disrespect me! I'll bash that giant nose of yours right back into your skull! You hear?" His scream made her ears itch. Faina struggled to coil away from him, sobbing uncontrollably.

***

Anastas didn't bother her again until they reached the abandoned warehouse down by Pier 39. Faina was marched inside at gunpoint, and taken to a wide, dusty room on the second level. It was even more chilly down by the water, and the inside of the building was icy. A single chair sat poised in the middle of the floor. Anastas dismissed the Butcher thug who had driven them and instructed him to return in an hour. Only Anastas's brothers remained.

"What do you want with me?" Faina's voice was hushed and

numb.

Anastas swirled her around by the shoulders and again placed her arms around his neck.

"Tell me where Pasha is hiding."

"Why? None of this makes sense! He didn't steal the money, you set him up."

A shudder ran along the fault line of muscle in Anastas's neck. A wave of intensity flushed down his features.

"You really don't know why?" He rolled back his sleeves to reveal one of the deep, green bruises from where Klokov had flogged him. "They beat me with chains, Faina! I couldn't so much as lean against a wall for days! And it's Pasha's fault! He's spent the past six years humiliating me, turning everyone against me! I've had enough! When I find him, he'll die knowing he brought his misery upon himself. I will beat the flesh off his skeleton!" Faina squealed as Anastas reached up and pinched her chin. "And you're gonna tell me where he is!"

"You're crazy." She wrenched herself away.

Anastas roped her back by the scruff of her neck and tilted her head up appraisingly. "Come on, now, it doesn't have to be bad. If you give me what I want there's no reason to go rough on you. In fact," he ran a finger under her chin, "I could be very gentle."

An idea struck in Faina's brain. Without a word, she closed her eyes and tilted her head up invitingly.

"Atta girl," he snickered, closing in on her.

The moment Faina could feel his breath on her nose she pulled his neck down using her restraints and sank her teeth into his shoulder. Anastas cried out. Blood trickled over her teeth. As he moved to throw her off, she kneed him in the groin. Anastas dropped his hands from her hips. Faina swung round to his back. With her bonds up around his throat, she pulled back with her entire body weight, choking him. Anastas gagged, clawing at his neck.

A shot fired into the rafters, and Faina screamed. She fell back on the floor, taking Anastas with her. Vadim closed in on her, pointing a gun at her face. Her heart was beating against the inside of her chest. Her eyes darted towards Alexei who was hanging back in the shadows. His feet turned in slightly, and he tried not to look at her.

"Alexei," she pleaded. "Alexei, please, don't let them do this!"

Alexei took one look at his brothers and stepped back.

"You were always such a sweet little boy," she persisted. "Do you remember when I used to come visit you at the orphanage?"

Alexei opened his mouth, but Vadim whipped the side of Faina's face with his gun.

"Don't talk to him!"

Faina stared up at Vadim in helpless wrath. There was nothing she could do. Her lip pushed out, and she wept. Anastas slipped out of her hold, rubbing the front of his neck. He got to his feet, looking somewhat out of breath, and gestured to the chair.

Vadim tossed her roughly against the seat and fastened her ankles to the legs. Anastas pulled Alexei aside.

"Don't be such a putz."

Alexei pushed him off. "I'm not a putz!"

Anastas held his gaze for a moment, then turned back to Faina with a sneer. He lit a cigarette and strode towards the chair.

"You had your chance, Faina. You chose this." Without warning, he struck her across the face so violently she could feel the bruise swelling up on her jaw immediately.

"Where's Pasha?" He smiled slightly and leaned down to wipe the trickle of blood off her lip.

Faina pressed her lips together, trying to withhold her tears. When it became clear she wasn't going to answer, Anastas seized her by the throat, tipping the chair back. She could feel his fingers pinching into the delicate bends in her throat.

"I said, where's Chevalsky?"

Faina gagged through her sobs. "I . . . don't . . . know. . . ." She winced at the scraping in her esophagus.

Someone gave a suppressed whimper. Anastas dropped the chair back on its legs and swiveled around to face Alexei.

"Go wait outside!"

This time Alexei did not fight. He rushed out the door.

Something silvery flashed in the shadows from Anastas's pocket. Instinctively, Faina pinched her eyes shut, afraid to look. There was a click as he unsheathed a folding knife. A sharp point pressed gently into the flesh beneath her chin. Faina began to hyperventilate as she craned her head away.

Anastas's breath was like vinegar, his voice hot and sticky on her neck. His words dragged sickeningly through her ears.

"Don't lie to me." He sank the triangular tip into the soft pith of her left cheek. "Is he in New York?"

Faina whimpered in reply. He slashed the knife across her face, splitting open a fine thread of blood. Her scream pinched their ears. Anastas recoiled and laid a heavy slap across her mouth to shut her up. The knock nearly rendered her unconscious. She went limp as he held her by the scruff of her hair.

"Nice dress, by the way." He took a drag on his cigarette and knelt down at her feet. "Don't you think so, Vadim?"

Vadim scoffed, sizing her up. "Better than her brother's trousers."

Anastas snickered as he casually dug a gash into the side of her calf. Faina let out a scream. Vadim backhanded her in the side of the temple. Faina's head fell back in a swoon.

"What'd you do that for?" snapped Anastas.

Vadim threw out his hands. "What? What are you yelling at me for?"

"She can't answer questions if she's unconscious!"

Faina's eyes fixed on the end of Anastas's cigarette. Tears

distorted the light into kaleidoscopic fragments.

Outside, Alexei let out a scream. Anastas and Vadim jumped to attention. With a deafening crack of snapping wood, the door broke down. An enormous, hairy monster stood on the threshold and barked.

Faina lifted her head. It was Mammoth!

The boys scuttled to their feet in terror. Vadim reached for his gun, but Mammoth was too quick. He jumped forward and sank his teeth into Vadim's arm, forcing him to drop the firearm. Mammoth dragged him to the floor.

Alexei stood in the doorway, terrified, with his arms down by his side.

"Alexei, your gun," Vadim hollered. But Alexei stared at him wide-eyed.

"Shoot, you idiot!"

But as Mammoth turned his attention towards the youngest Sippenhaft, Alexei turned away and ran as fast as he could. Anastas reached into his jacket and pulled out his revolver. Faina shrieked.

"No! Don't shoot!"

Anastas adjusted the compartment. With the cigarette still hanging from his mouth, he raised the gun. Faina felt her chest stiffen, her tears dried up.

"I said, no!"

She felt herself manipulate a phantom force of her will, like a third arm. The glowing embers ebbing from the end of Anastas's cigarette exploded in a blossom of red inferno, lighting his clothes on fire. Anastas was sent screaming. He tossed the revolver aside, and he and Vadim fled the warehouse like burning scarecrows.

Mammoth snapped at their heels as they ran out the door, chasing them a little way before he decided they'd gone an appropriate distance. He let loose a few warning barks as if to say, "And don't come back," or, "Stay out, you heathens!"

Faina lowered her head and burst into tears. Mammoth tiptoed to her side and licked the tip of her nose. Faina struggled with her restraints. The rope scraped raw patches on her wrists. She shivered as the cold leaked through the walls of the warehouse. With nothing left to do, she began screaming for help.

Chapter 33:

Rescued

By the time the sun had risen, Faina was drifting in and out of consciousness. Mammoth's hot breath fell upon her lap as he strived to keep her warm. She had ceased trying to struggle free when she lost the feeling in her fingers. Now they were so stiff, she could hardly bend them.

She had lost her voice hours ago screaming for help, which had yet to come. It hurt to move her swollen jaw anyway.

Even the movement of her eyes seemed to take some kind of effort, as if unsticking them from the frozen tears hauled up in the corners. The right eye was swelling shut. From the hole in her stockings, she could feel her skin drawn tight with exposure. She had tried to unleash the fiery power that had saved her before but she didn't know how. She didn't know where to begin.

Noises came from outside. Faina's voice faded in a brittle trail as she tried to gasp. She listened close. Footsteps on the stairs. Whispering. Faina was seized with terror.

"They've come back." The last of her tears seemed to unthaw and came pouring down her face in horror. "They're coming to kill me."

She was delirious. There was a metallic tumbling as the latch of the door was unlocked. Mammoth stood erect and at attention. He sniffed the air and relaxed. He wagged his tail as though he recognized the intruder.

Faina's head lolled back as she felt faint once more. Somewhere in her dreamy state, she could hear everything unfolding around her. Someone calling her name. Mammoth barking. Heavy footsteps.

Someone dropped to their knees at her side. Fingers unlaced the ties around her wrists and ankles. Someone was lifting her up, cradling her, pressing their warm fingers against her scarred cheek.

"*Nyet*! No! Pyro, *vona mertva*!" The voice was frantic with thick breaths of sobs. She welcomed the hot tears falling upon her face.

"Calm down," said a second voice. "I can't understand you."

"*Mertva*," the first choked. "Dead! *Moya* Faina *mertva*!"

"Relax, she's not dead. It's going to be fine."

For a fleeting moment, Mammoth floated through her mind. What if he wandered away? She dug her hands into the waves of dreaminess and paddled desperately towards consciousness.

"Mammoth . . ." she muttered, unable to open her eyes.

A breath of joy caught in the voice of the one holding her. "Yes, Mammoth is right here, Faina." He placed her hand on Mammoth's warm, furry back. "See? He was a good boy to find you. He saved your life."

A burst of warmth blossomed next to her. Someone put their hand on hers, and the heat traveled up her skin. She felt herself floating back to the floor. Her eyes fluttered open. A face loomed over her, fuzzy and imperceptible, but slowly things grew clearer.

"She's waking up," they gasped.

A wave of ecstasy flew through her.

"Leo?" she whispered. Tears welled up in her once again as she found the strength to reach out and touch his face.

"No," he corrected her gently. "No, Faina, it's Pasha."

"Pasha?" The words echoed back. She began to see it, as though the suggestion had unlocked the reality. His face was breaking through the smoke. The large brown eyes. Bushy eyebrows forever knit together with anxiety. The tooth she had knocked crooked when they were kids.

Her smile recoiled into a sneer, and the sneer melted into a look of hurt and abandonment.

"They hurt me!"

Pasha looked as though she had slapped him in the face. Tears of guilt streamed down his cheeks.

"*Prosti*! I'm sorry, Faina! It's all my fault! I made a mistake, I should never have left you here alone. I'm gonna take you away from here. We're gonna go somewhere far away, just like I promised. I'll never let anything hurt you, and I'll never ever leave you again, I promise!"

He pressed his nose against her cheek and cried, washing her face with the comfort of warm breath and heated tears.

There was a wave of tranquility as another presence entered the room and knelt down beside them. She pulled at Pasha's shoulder.

"Let me see her."

She felt herself being propped up towards the third entity.

"I'll kill Anastas," Pasha muttered through clenched teeth. "I'll tell Klokov to save him for me! That way I can put the bullet in his head!"

"No, Pasha, stay here. Vengeance isn't important now, it will do nothing to save Faina. She needs you by her side."

Pasha pulled Faina closer. "Can you heal her, Sonata?"

Sonata smiled confidently as she turned her attention to Faina's eyes.

"Of course I can."

A hand was laid against her forehead, and Faina felt the pain shrinking from her body. Exhaustion overwhelmed her as Pasha lifted her up in his arms and carried her through the door.

Chapter 34:
Waking

The smooth sound of waves breaking one over the other escorted Faina gently from her dreams. Before she opened her eyes, she felt the softness of a pillow against her cheek. She felt the hug of a mattress against her body. Blankets draped over her. Her feet were bare. The flesh of her knee brushed against fresh-smelling linens. A gull was hollering yards away.

She slid her eyes open. There was a blurry picture of a window framing a pink coast and blue sea. Her eyes closed. She tried again. She focused on a large, sunset-colored butterfly sipping away at a bright, yellow hibiscus in a flower box on the windowsill.

She looked down at herself. She was dressed in her favorite pink nightgown with the flowers embroidered on the sleeves. Where was she?

Her eyes popped, and she furrowed her brow. Something heavy weighed in her pocket. She slipped her fingers beneath the fabric. Her hand enclosed around something small, flat, and cool. A smile brightened her sleepy eyes. It was the lucky penny.

Someone grunted across the room. Pasha was slumped over in an armchair, asleep. His head was thrown back and his mouth hung open.

Faina smirked and took in her environment. It was a small, one-room bungalow. Brightly colored walls in all manner of tropical hues surrounded her. The beach was at their doorstep. A jar of freshly picked daffodils and honeysuckle sat on the table.

Mammoth was asleep in front of the fire. The front door was open just a hair. The dazzling, yellow paint of the gypsy caravan shone through the gap. Fragrances of bacon and butter drifted past her nose, followed by the alluring scent of coffee.

Pasha groaned as he stirred to life. Faina turned her head towards him without raising up from the comfortable bed.

"Pasha?"

Pasha lifted his face, half-confused. He was bright-looking, healthier, if not a little sleepy. His clothes were fresh and clean. She hadn't seen him without a bruise or scrape since they were twelve years old. She tossed a pillow at his head.

"Pasha, where are we?"

Pasha lit up with attention. His face cracked open with a grin. Ignoring the question, he jumped forward, shouting her name. He grabbed Faina in a hug and pressed her face so tightly against his chest she couldn't breathe. Sobs of guilt wracked his body. Tears soaked through the shoulder of her nightgown.

Once she had wriggled her head out from his grip, she felt the healing power of her friend's embrace. Everything sank in at once, and tears squeezed from her eyes too.

"I'm so sorry, Faina! I should have listened to you and come back for you sooner."

"It's alright," she assured him softly. "You were just trying to protect me."

"And I failed."

"I'm alive, aren't I?"

She felt something fluffy on her leg. Mammoth was poking his giant, furry head between them.

Faina and Pasha laughed as they broke apart. She invited the dog atop the bed. Faina peeled back the blankets to look at her legs. The worst of the injuries lingered, but most of the cuts and bruises had disappeared or faded. Pasha read her thoughts.

"Sonata healed you. Some of the injuries were too serious to completely absorb, but I think she managed to cure most of them."

Faina was speechless. She touched her cheek where the cuts and bruises had been. Pasha laughed softly.

"No scars on your face either."

Faina scooted closer. "How are Katya and Mama Lydia?"

Pasha drew a long exhale through his nose. "They're pretty torn up about Anya. Mama is blaming herself."

"But are they okay?"

He gave a weak smile. "They're great. You should see Katya. She has a golden tail, and Faina, her eyes have turned gold too! The ring around her iris is gone. She looks healthy! And Sonata says she never had Wilson's disease or psychosis. In fact, she's a really powerful empath."

Faina's eyes closed as she smiled with genuine satisfaction. "That's so wonderful, Pasha."

She glanced back at him. He was now looking serious. His eyes burned with intensity.

"So, Anastas did this to you?"

She nodded. As all that had passed flooded back to her, she fell back against the pillows, exhausted with grief.

Tears dripped from Pasha's eyelashes that he hastily wiped away with the heel of his hand.

"Ma said you struck some kinda deal with Klokov to let you continue to sell in my absence."

"I did for a while. But she made me stop. Did Klokov find out about Anastas?"

Pasha sighed and laid down beside her, sandwiching Mammoth between them.

"Alexei ratted out his brothers. With everything that happened—the murders, the double-crossing, then kidnapping you—the Breadwinners have put a price on his head. As far as I know, they haven't found him yet. Anyway, Klokov pardoned me. To make up for it, I asked to be released from the Breadwinners without penalty. He obliged."

A smile rose to her lips. "I see."

Pasha stared, grinning at her without saying a word. Faina raised an eyebrow and covered half of her face.

"What are you looking at me like that for?"

Pasha hid his face in the pillow and laughed. "I'm just so happy you're alive!"

Faina surged across Mammoth, wrapping her arms around Pasha and scuffling his hair. Pasha chuckled and grabbed her hand.

"Alright now, silly! No horseplay until you get your strength up."

Faina giggled, refusing to listen, and pretended like she was going to bite his hand. Pasha playfully locked her arms behind her back and pinned her in a backwards hug. They both laughed until their sides hurt.

When they finally caught their breath, Pasha's face became stony again.

"Faina, what exactly happened in the warehouse?"

The smile faded from Faina's lips. She told Pasha the whole story. When she got to the end, she looked down at her palms. She had almost forgotten about the strange phenomenon with Anastas's cigarette.

"Pasha, something happened to me inside that warehouse . . ."

Pasha cradled his face in his hands, unable to hear any more. She nudged him to look. He peeked one eye open.

She stared at the fireplace in a state of intensity. Nothing happened. Pasha lifted an eyebrow.

"Uh, Faina?"

"Shhh! Wait!" She extended her hand. She dwelled on the anger, the unholy bombardment of fear that had nearly drowned her. Her eyes squinted up in concentration.

Pasha reached out and lowered her hand.

"Maybe you should lie back down."

"But Pasha—"

He placed his hands on her shoulders and pushed her back towards the mattress.

"Faina, you've been through a lot in the past twenty-four hours."

Her neck burned and prickled. She kicked up from the blankets.

"You're not listening to me!" A flame careened out of the fireplace and balled up in her hand. Pasha jumped back and fell off the bed. Faina took one look at her palm and burst into a peal of excited giggles.

"See? I did it! I told you!"

Slowly, Pasha's head appeared at the footboard. "Faina . . . you—you just made fire jump into your palm!"

"I know! It's crazy! It's like I can control it with my mind or something!"

"But you're terrified of fire!"

Faina snorted and kicked her legs as though it were the funniest thing in the world. "I know!"

Pasha climbed back onto the bed, his eyes trained on her palm.

"Faina, you know what this means, don't you? You must be an igneous!"

Faina tilted her head. "A what?"

"It's what Pyro is! A person who controls fire."

"But he can generate fire, I can only manipulate it."

Pasha shrugged his shoulders. "Maybe this is only the beginning. Maybe you have to work your way up."

Faina yawned and the ball shrank. Her eyes bulged.

"Where did it go?"

Pasha smirked. "I think it would work better if you weren't so tired." He patted the pillow and gestured for her to lay back down. "Come on, there will be plenty of opportunities to ask Pyro about it later." He pulled the covers back over her. "By the way, Aunt Poppy packed all of your stuff for you."

"Where is Aunt Poppy now? Is she still in New York?"

Pasha nodded his head. "But not for much longer. She's decided to move back to Voiler. She has some property in Stella Real. But all your clothes are over there in that trunk. You're gonna need something to wear to the Christmas Ball."

Faina's eyes lit up. "A Christmas ball?"

"Yeah, every Christmas, Pisces throws a ball at the Placide, and everyone is invited. You're supposed to dress up."

"Is that where we are? Pisces?"

Pasha tapped his forehead absentmindedly. "Yeah, in the capital, Larame." He patted her knee. "I hope you don't mind having a tropical Christmas."

She smiled. "Any Christmas is a good Christmas to me, you know that."

"You're gonna love it here, Faina! I can't wait for you to get to meet everybody . . ." Pasha was speaking a mile a minute. He was his old self again, that excitable ten-year-old boy. At times Faina found herself struggling to keep up with him. But even though she was tired, she was happy to see him so joyful.

At length, he stopped himself. "I'm wearing you out, aren't I?"

"Me? Worn out? I don't think that's possible." But her body betrayed her as she fell back into the covers and curled up. "Pasha, what about Anya's body?"

She glanced up at him. He had grown stiff and did not answer.

"Pasha, what about her funeral?" The words swelled with pain as they tripped off her tongue. "I'm the only one left to bury her. How do I do this?"

Pasha's head hung low; he refused to meet her eyes.

"Aunt Poppy is taking care of it."

His tone made it sound as though it were not something she was to be involved in.

"When is it?"

Pasha fiddled with his hands in his lap. "Faina, you can't go back right now."

Faina felt a burning tension prickle down her forehead.

"What do you mean? Pasha, Anya was my cousin, the last of my family. Are you telling me I can't bury my own cousin?" She could feel the volume of her voice rising like a temperature.

In a moment, Pasha was clinging to her hands.

"Faina, you can't, it's too dangerous. You shot the Siberian. If the Butchers found out you were in town they'd kill you!"

Faina wrenched herself away from him, her vision clouded with a sluice of fiery tears.

"She was my cousin, Pasha! Like my sister!" She was screaming with sobs now.

Pasha braced his arms around her like a straitjacket.

"I know it hurts, Faina, but it's for your own safety!"

Exhausted, she buried her face in her hands and allowed Pasha to pull her head against his chest. She stopped fighting him.

"She'll be buried next to your uncle. Once things are settled between the Breadwinners and the Butchers we can go back and visit the cemetery, okay? It's gonna be alright."

"But my whole family is dead, they are all dead! My parents, my brother, my aunt, my uncle, and now my cousin! I'm completely alone now!"

Pasha shook his head as he lowered his voice.

"No, Faina. You're part of my family, remember? Family is

people who love you, and we all love you! You aren't alone. We won't ever let you be alone! You hear me? Thieves' Honor!"

He wiped at her tears with his thumb, and Faina's breathing slowed. She closed her eyes, still clinging to him.

Chapter 35:
The Half-Igneous

Faina's bouts of grief and melancholy were somewhat curtailed by her urge to explore the world of magic surrounding her. Pasha soon found he could slow her tears by taking her flying, or hiking through the woods to find magical creatures. Though he often worried she might overexert herself, he enjoyed watching her rise again. Every day she went swimming with the mermaids. Whenever Pasha fretted, Sonata always reminded him, "There is no better medicine than sunshine, salt water, and the company of mermaids."

When he couldn't venture past the shallows, Pasha followed Faina along the shore and over rocks. When she wore herself out, they laid on the sand together. Pasha would watch in fascination as the sun nurtured new freckles to blossom from her skin like phototropic flowers. Every day she waxed stronger and shined brighter.

Naturally, the other members of the company took an immediate interest in Faina's abilities. In no time at all, Pyro was observing her. She couldn't breathe fire, and she couldn't generate it, but she could certainly interact with it. This explained why she was always causing fiery accidents.

"Well, there is no question about it," said Staccato one day over lunch. "She obviously possesses Voilerian origins." They had all congregated outside at the table. "What do you think, Pyro?"

Pyro hastened to finish off the last bits of his sandwich.

"From what I've observed, I believe Faina is half-igneous."

Pasha lifted an eyebrow. "What does that mean?"

"There are three types of igneous. The first is full-blooded igneous, like me. Full-blooded igneous are the product of two igneous parents. We can generate fire with our bodies. We can breathe fire like dragons. Our lungs are resistant to smoke inhalation. We're invulnerable to extreme cold, and lastly, we can't be burned by fire unless it's administered by our own hand."

Pasha glanced at the pink, fleshy scar running up Pyro's forearm.

"And as you know, if we get wet, we can't light up again until we're dry. Moving on, we have the second type, usually known as half-igneous. Half-igneous are the result of one igneous parent and one non-igneous parent. Generally, they can't generate fire with their bodies, but they can manipulate it. Rather than being cold-resistant, they're susceptible to cold. For example, I can't contract hypothermia. Faina on the other hand nearly died from hypothermia."

"In other words," interjected Faina, "half-igneous are less powerful than full-blooded igneous."

"Not true. Half-igneous have an advantage over full-blooded igneous. Full-blooded igneous temporarily lose their powers when wet, but a half-igneous can continue to manipulate fire even when they're soaked."

"But what about my brother? If I'm half-igneous, shouldn't he have been too?"

"Typically half-igneous' powers aren't awakened until later in life. You're sixteen years old, and you're only now discovering your powers. Without prior knowledge of one's own gift, it can take even longer. Sorta like Katya and Mrs. Chevalsky. It's likely your brother died before he had a chance to discover his abilities."

"So, I can manipulate fire, but I can't generate it, and I can't breathe it?"

Pyro shrugged. "Well, it is possible to master some of the powers of both half and full, but it takes training, and it's very rare. That's when you become the third type, a chief."

Faina sat back, looking stunned. "So, you're saying one of my parents was an igneous?"

"They would've had to be. That's the only explanation. Igneous distribution isn't like miraculous. It's purely genetic. It can't just show up randomly in a bloodline. Did you ever see your parents do anything weird with fire?"

Faina looked thoughtful. "Well, my mother liked to bake, but I don't remember her ever flambéing dinner with her bare hands."

Pasha snorted and almost choked on his food.

"What about your father?" Pyro continued.

"No." A look came across her, as though her mind had opened a box of old anomalies. "There were a lot of strange things about my father, though. He wasn't Russian, he was from Ireland. When he met my mother in Yekaterinburg, he only spoke English."

"Wait." Cicada held up a hand. "If your father was from Ireland, how come your last name is 'Spichkin'? I mean, I only know what I read in books, but that doesn't sound very Irish to me."

Faina's eyes nearly crossed. "You're right! That makes no sense."

Staccato smoothed his waistcoat. "Well, there is one thing that can help us. Your father's name should be recorded in the immigration files in Libra. Pasha's mother was the only Voilerian immigrant to ever go unrecorded."

"That's ridiculous!" Pyro beat his hand on the table. "You don't really think every person to ever immigrate to the Other is registered on some stupid government list, do you?"

Staccato crossed his arms. "Having served on the Ecliptic Council myself once, yes, I do."

"That's a load of shrapnel! It's not like it's difficult to get to the Other! And it's not like all the gateways are being supervised!"

Staccato sniffed. "That's what you think."

Pyro rolled his eyes and shook his head. "There's no way. It would be impossible to monitor every way in and out of Voiler. With a fair bit of magic, you can make them at home! I bet there are entrances you don't even know about!"

Pasha's eyes darted back and forth between the arguing pair. "What are you talking about?"

Staccato straightened his collar in a dignified manner. "Every resident of Voiler who migrates to the Other is recorded by the Branch of Exodus. It's international law."

Pyro shook his head. "The only reason anyone would ever migrate to the Other is to get away from the C.O.N. And if there's an official Ecliptic Council register of migrants lying around in some government building, they would be out there hunting Fay like rabbits!"

"They are," reminded Melodious from the end of the table, "which is exactly why people do everything in their power to avoid registering. If the Ecliptic Council is going to keep a record of every Fay who migrates to the Other, then people should have the option to keep those records private, lest they end up like my family."

Staccato pinched his temples. "I'm not saying it's a good idea. If I believed everyone who left Voiler should be slapped down on a list, I wouldn't have kept the whereabouts of Pasha's mother a secret."

Melodious folded his hands beneath his chin and turned away. "No, I don't suppose you would have." He said this with such obvious contempt, Pasha couldn't help but wonder if Melodious was less at peace than he let on.

Staccato stared at Melodious in shock before retaliating in an almost threatening tone.

"What exactly is that supposed to mean?"

Melodious shrugged in a passive-aggressive manner. "Only

that there is always an exception."

"An exception for whom?" Staccato's voice was quiet but nonetheless challenging.

"Those carrying a title."

Staccato's face dropped in surprise. It was almost as though he had been expecting Melodious to say something else. Before he could make a retort, Sonata threw up her hands between them.

"Personal politics aside, it's worth a try! Though I wouldn't get my hopes up. Not many Voilerians settle in Russia. Over half the country is completely remote. That's why Lydia was sent there in the first place."

Faina leaned forward on her elbows. "But it's still possible, isn't it?"

Staccato threw up his shoulders and smirked. "Well, anything is possible. Sonata is right, it wouldn't hurt to check the records. Of course, it will be some time before we can do that. Our main priority right now is to catch the Firebird. Once that's done, we can start looking into the archives."

A thought occurred to Pasha. "Sonata, can't you figure out who Faina's father was using psychometry on something he touched? I'm sure Faina has something that belonged to him."

Sonata bit her lip. "I'm afraid it's a little more complicated than that. Unless I knew her father personally, it's unlikely I'd be able to discern his identity just by reading an object. I might be able to tell you how he obtained the item, what his feelings towards it were, or if it passed through a war or something."

Pasha shrugged. "But at the very least you might be able to offer up some clues."

"Very true. Do you have anything of your father's, Faina?"

Faina stared dismally at the tabletop. "If I do, it's with Aunt Poppy. She's supposed to bring the rest of my stuff when she comes back to Voiler. I'll see what I can find. It's like Staccato said, I guess it's worth trying."

Chapter 36:

The King's Counselor

Pasha stood on the porch of his bungalow and watched his mother float through the waves with Katya in her arms. The sky blushed with rosy sunset. Katya's gilded eyes fluttered with sleep as Lydia's lips moved in rhythmic patterns. She was singing.

Her eyes snagged on Pasha. Smiling, she beckoned him to come join them. Pasha edged back and shook his head. Laughing, Lydia cupped a hand over her mouth.

"There's nothing to be afraid of, darling!"

Sorry to disappoint her, he made up another excuse.

"I'm not feeling up to it right now, Ma."

Lydia nodded and went back to lulling her youngest to sleep. As Pasha sank down into the nearest rocking chair, he realized how embarrassing it was that his mother was a mermaid, and yet he couldn't swim. His head drooped between his shoulders.

"Something bothering you, Pasha?"

Staccato was standing at the bottom of the steps, his staff cocked over one shoulder. Pasha forced himself into an upright position and put on a cheerful smile.

"Not a horseradish!" He paused awkwardly, playing back the phrase in his head. He pinched the space between his eyebrows. "Uh, sorry, Russian expression. I mean, no, nothing is bothering me."

Staccato chuckled and leaned forward on his staff. "It's alright, *ya ponyal tebya*." I understood you. Pasha's eyes snapped open.

"You speak Russian?"

Staccato shrugged with a false air of modesty. "Picked it up from Aunt Poppy. Like you, I've always had a penchant for languages. I understand you speak four."

Pasha motioned for Staccato to join him on the porch. "I do."

As Staccato made it to the top of the stairs, his eye was drawn to the set of paintings drying against the wall.

"Are those your mother's?"

Pasha nodded his head with pride, standing up. "Yeah. She was an artist back in Russia. When I was little I was always covered in paint because she was always covered in paint."

Staccato bent down for a closer look. He appeared to be utterly absorbed.

"Well," he muttered, "it runs in the family, you know. Her mother was an artist. A glassblower."

Pasha leaned against the railing with his hands in his pockets.

"You must have known Evangeline pretty well, seeing as you were best friends with her brothers, Javaid and Thessalos."

Staccato nodded his head and brought himself to smile. "I was very close with the Soters. The girls, Estella and Evangeline, called me the family pet." He snickered. "When I was eighteen years old, Thessalos gave me a position as his personal advisor, and so I went to live at the palace, Alveare."

Pasha's mouth fell open. "You were eighteen years old?"

Staccato stood and dusted the knees of his trousers. "That's right. I was the first two-legged advisor to a mermaid sovereign in Voilerian history, as well as the youngest."

Pasha flopped back in his chair, dumbfounded. "Well golly, I officially feel under-accomplished."

Staccato laughed and took the seat beside him. "Well, I was an obnoxiously ambitious young man. And the King was a young man too. He received a lot of criticism for taking me on. People accused him of playing favorites, for we were friends first, Theo and I. That's what we called him, Theo. No one ever called him Thessalos. Anyway, I suppose it was a little unfair."

Pasha shook his head. "Not at all. If you're looking for someone to fill the position of most trusted advisor, why wouldn't you choose your most trusted friend?"

Staccato flexed his lip thoughtfully. "That's very true. I've never thought of it that way. See, Pasha? You're already thinking like a king."

Pasha smiled bashfully and leaned forward with his elbows on his knees.

"How did Sonata's father, Javaid, become king when he's the second-born child? Did Theo abdicate?"

A glimmer of reluctance passed through Staccato's pale eyes.

"When Evangeline . . . when Theo's youngest sister died, he

could hardly bear it. He doted on her. I suppose it was because she was the youngest. Or perhaps because she was the sweetest."

"What else was she like?"

Staccato narrowed his eyes in thought. "She was . . . a little off-the-wall," he stopped himself. "Well, in a good way. Eccentric would've been a better word. You know how artistic types are. But she was very warm, very affectionate. She loved to tease and play pranks, and she was always laughing." He smiled fondly. "She looked up to Theo, much like Katya looks up to you, and he treated her with just as much love and affection. So, it took a toll on him when she died, as you can imagine."

Pasha waited for Staccato to explain. He took a breath and massaged the bridge of his nose.

"After that, Theo couldn't go on any longer, and he passed the crown onto Javaid. Mermaids are easily affected by strong emotions, as you probably know from your mother and sister. And Sonata, of course. Really, Pasha, if you want to know more about how to be a benevolent ruler, you needn't look any further than Sonata."

"If all mermaids are as compassionate as Sonata, then Katya should rule, not me—or better yet, Mama. Shouldn't she be first in line anyway?"

Staccato folded his hands beneath his chin. "I don't believe I've told you this yet, Pasha, but shortly after your mother was born, King Bruin created a bylaw preventing any mermaid from inheriting the throne. You are his first non-mermaid heir, so the title passes to you."

Pasha furrowed his brow. "Why would he do that?"

Staccato pressed his fingers together as though trying to repress a bitterness.

"Bruin was a bit of a tyrant. He was never actually meant to become king. He was the youngest of eight sons. When his whole family was assassinated by the C.O.N. during his brother's coronation, he struggled to fill the position. Furthermore, he was wracked with grief. At the time, Samael used Bruin's weakness to manipulate him and turn him against the Fay. He even became a follower of Primal Instinct."

This was all new to Pasha, who stared at Staccato in disbelief.

"But he married a mermaid!"

Staccato shook his head. "Bruin and Evangeline were not in love. It was an odd business, your grandparents' marriage. Normally, mermaids abhor the idea of marrying for political advantage. Love is one of the highest and most respected virtues amongst their kind. But Atergatis, Estella and Evangeline's mother, feared Bruin's instability would threaten the alliance between Karkinos and Ursa. So she pressured Evangeline to marry him. I believe Samael encouraged Bruin with a similar argument. Though he was no doubt secretly hoping to break the two kingdoms apart by forcing them to marry. Bruin had a reputation for being a scoundrel, and we all knew the marriage was doomed from the start.

"Shortly before Evangeline discovered she was expecting, Bruin stole the trident, Sea-Splitter, from the Soters—the very weapon Samael later used to curse the mermaids. Theo put an end to the alliance, and as a result, Bruin and Evangeline's marriage was automatically annulled. Naturally, Bruin still wanted to see the child, but Evangeline refused. In retaliation, Bruin wrote a bylaw banning his own daughter from ever ascending the throne. Once you become king, Pasha, you will have the power to change that law."

Pasha looked out over the water. Katya was asleep in Lydia's arms now, her hand curled under her chin. Staccato observed them from the corner of his eye. Out of habit, he began humming the scale again, but quickly stopped when he became aware of himself. Pasha couldn't help but notice he was embarrassed. He cleared his throat.

"You never explained to me how my grandparents died."

Staccato's eyes dilated with surprise, as though he hadn't been expecting the question.

"It was most unfortunate how your grandmother died." He cleared his throat. "Evangeline became . . . unstable while she carried your mother, started having delusions." He fidgeted with something stuck to the arm of the chair. "The doctors thought she had puerperal psychosis, mania caused by the onset of childbirth. She became convinced Bruin was possessed by some kind of evil, and that perhaps if she talked to him in person she could cleanse him, or something.

Anyway, when your mother was born, the C.O.N. attacked Polaris. The city became a war zone, and that's when Evangeline ran off to try to reason with Bruin."

Staccato took a long pause. Pasha feared he might not go on. He felt sorry for asking him now. He should have realized it would be a sensitive subject for Staccato, considering he had known Evangeline. Pasha fiddled with his hands, thinking of a way to end the conversation.

"I see, so the C.O.N. killed her."

"No. Bruin killed her."

Pasha gaped at him in alarm, unsure of what to say. Staccato ground his teeth and shut his eyes as though struggling against his own prejudices.

"I shouldn't say that. It was clearly an accident. She fell on his sword. That's how she died. And Bruin fell in battle later that day."

Pasha opened and closed his mouth. In a way, it frightened him to think such a grisly tragedy could happen in his own family. But it certainly hadn't been the first.

"Are you sure? I mean, how could you tell if it was an accident?"

The line of Staccato's expression grew harder, and he stared forward with his shoulders set.

"Well, she was in the forge. The sword was lying on a table with the hilt against the wall. She had one leg over the anvil, as though she had tripped backward, and the blade was coming up through her chest."

Pasha was overcome with a dreadful realization. He covered his eyes in shame.

"Staccato, I shouldn't have asked. I'm so sorry."

Staccato softened and shook his head apologetically. "Don't apologize. You have every right to know how your grandmother died." He stood, his shoulders sagging a little.

Pasha stared up at him, eyes full of regret. "But I didn't know you were the one who found her."

Chapter 37:
Season's Greetings

Xylophis carried a telegram on a polished tray through the fustily bedecked halls of Apophis Manor. He sauntered past bell jars of zoogenic skeletons, luxe vases, and crystal chandeliers. He promenaded through vast archways draped with veils of the finest black chiffon. He swaggered on until he arrived at a posh parlor musically accompanied by the clinking of wine flutes.

Samael was lounging on a spacious, velvet couch between two lovely women. They hung on his honeyed words like butterflies.

Xylophis bowed as his master's heavenly blue eyes drifted upward in an examination of his presence. With an unhurried gesture of his bejeweled arm, Samael removed the telegram from the tray and scanned the first few sentences. He snapped the paper shut and crammed it into the inner folds of his robe. Not wishing to appear gauche, he smoothed over the gesture with a smile the texture of buttermilk.

"My apologies, ladies, I have business to attend to." He kissed each of their hands. On the second woman, he lingered. "I did so enjoy your thoughts on LaFitte vs. Mizusawa. I wholeheartedly agree it was one of the court's most despicable fallacies."

The woman put a hand to her chest. Her eyes radiated with a chaste intensity as though she had been touched by the hand of God.

Xylophis shadowed his master into a hallway, where Samael's

sangfroid waned.

“I hope this is worth it, Xylophis.”

He ripped open the paper and absorbed the message with impassioned eyes. His frigid countenance softened to flesh. He grinned with ironic delight.

“So, it’s true?” Xylophis stared at his master, awestruck. “The heir of Ursa really is alive? Bruin’s child lived after all?”

“If it weren’t true, the Land Lock wouldn’t have broken yet.” He sighed and swept a hand through the ends of his silky hair. “There’s no use fretting. Curses aren’t meant to last, as we both know. Though I had been hoping for a couple more decades.”

Xylophis dropped his shoulders and rubbed his chin. “But how did they figure it out? We destroyed every known copy of the reversal!”

Samael clicked his tongue and ran his hand along the edge of the windowsill.

“The details don’t matter. We must strive to look at the positives. Every misfortune has its opportunities. At least we know who this boy is now, which means we can deal with him faster. Make preparations for my leave at once.”

At this request, Xylophis stared at his master with such questioning, it was a wonder Samael didn’t slap him.

“Your leave? You mean you want to journey all the way to Larame?”

Samael looked him over with scathing eyes. “Yes, and be quick about it. I wish to meet this ‘Pasha’ in person. Get me something fast. The Hermes should suffice.”

“But Your Majesty, the flying restrictions—”

“Do you think I care about flying restrictions, Xylophis? Honestly! If we fly, we can cut the trip down to two days.” He made to rejoin the party in the parlor, but Xylophis trailed after him.

“Are you certain, Your Majesty? I mean, it’s so close to Christmas!”

Samael ground to a halt and swept round to face Xylophis with stinging contempt.

“Indeed it is. Shall we dress the dragons as reindeer? Do you think the children would like that? Or is it a bit much?”

Xylophis regarded him with confusion, his lips fluttering in a silent stammer.

Samael rolled his eyes. “It was a joke, Xylophis.” He put a pained finger to his temple and drifted down the hall. “My wit is utterly wasted on you, isn’t it?” He turned into the study. Xylophis hastened after him in a flurry of swishing robes.

“But why such haste? You know how the Fay are. They forgo all sense of urgency this time of year. It’s the law of the Ecliptic Council. ‘During the season of peace on earth, all wars are obligated to stall until just before the New Year.’”

“Which is precisely why we mustn’t lose our sense of urgency.

Their guard is down. They're all lying around some accursed tree on a beach in Pisces singing Christmas carols! What better time to strike, I ask you?"

Chapter 38:
Battle of Wills

The screen door of the bungalow swung open with fury as Pasha marched out of Faina's cabin and onto the front porch. He slammed it behind him, almost hitting Faina in the face.

"Pasha Chevalsky, you come back here right now!"

But Pasha wasn't listening. "Where's Staccato?" he thundered, as though Faina were willing to answer him.

"It doesn't matter!" She stomped her foot. "He already said I could go with you to chase the Firebird!"

"Well, I'm gonna tell him you can't! You've been through enough already! You're gonna stay here in Pisces while I catch the Firebird, and that's final!"

Faina thrust an irate finger in his face. "You can't tell me what to do! Even if you could, I hardly think you're the best person to be making decisions about my safety!"

"What's that supposed to mean?"

Faina hiked her hands on her hips. "Does this sound familiar? 'Stay in New York, Faina! It's safe there!' I've been shot at, targeted by thugs, thrown into the back of a vehicle with my family's murderer, and left to freeze to death in some shady warehouse!"

Pasha tore at his hair. "That was New York! This is Pisces! You can swim around with the mermaids all day and pet jack-a-lopes!"

Faina crossed her arms. “That’s not what you said before! When you first got to Pisces you said it was too dangerous for me here!”

Pasha faced her and looked her squarely in the eye.

“Look, I didn’t say it was ideal, but it’s clearly the better option! Why am I even arguing with you about this? You’re not going!” He vaulted over the railing and set off to find Staccato.

“If anything happens, I can protect you!” Her voice broke. “We can protect each other!”

Without looking over his shoulder, Pasha tossed his hand up. “I don’t need protecting, Faina.”

“Pavlo Ruslanovitch Chevalsky, if you tell Staccato not to let me come, I’ll never speak to you again!” She screamed her words. Birds flew out of their nests.

Pasha paused and bit his lip. She didn’t mean it. She would get over it. It was for her own good, after all. He continued on, ignoring the slam of Faina’s door.

***

When Pasha found Staccato he was making his way back from the Placide with a telegram. Pasha pleaded with Staccato. He insisted if anything happened to Faina he would die. But Staccato didn’t appear to be showing him much sympathy.

“Pasha, Faina is a grown-up young lady who is perfectly capable not only of lending her assistance, but of making her own decisions. It wouldn't be fair for me to deny Faina employment simply because you don't approve."

Pasha eyed Staccato with a raised eyebrow. "What if you were in my place and it was Sonata?"

Staccato snickered and shook his head. "Nice try, but I am Sonata's guardian. Furthermore, she too is old enough to make decisions that not even I can stop her from making. Now, I understand why you're upset, but I'm afraid you're going to have to get over it. Besides, Faina may be safer amongst people qualified to protect her. In the long run, she may be better off. Now if you'll excuse me, I've received some distressing news."

Pasha looked down at the telegram in his hands.

"Sorry, I didn't realize it was urgent."

Staccato frowned and leaned on his staff. "Quite alright. I'm afraid the C.O.N. showed up outside Cortijo Del Mar a few nights ago and began torturing sylphs for information. Three of them were taken to Crux. Now that the Land Lock has been broken, the mermaids were able to drive them back, but so far they haven't been able to retrieve the hostages. Infiltrating Crux is no easy task, after all."

"Why? What's Crux?"

Staccato's eyes overflowed with a sinister dread.

"It is a place of utter darkness," his voice became thin and pale, bordering on tremulous, "a place of suffering. A place so redolent with black magic and liliths it is sometimes referred to as the Devil's

Throne."

"What are liliths? You never explained."

"Non-Fay women who devote their souls to the breeding and manipulation of dark magic. You see, magic should only ever be harnessed by those born with the power. If a non-magical entity tries to possess magic it becomes dark, it becomes sorcery or witchcraft. It isn't something to be taken lightly. It is more powerful than you can imagine, and Crux is overrun with it. Pray you never find yourself in such a godless place. There are sights there that would send a warrior to his knees. Now, if you'll excuse me, I have matters to attend to." Staccato swept inside his cabin with an air of gloom.

Defeated, Pasha walked back to the cove in front of his bungalow and plopped down upon a rock far above the water's edge. No sooner had he sat than someone was waving a gingerbread cookie shaped like a seashell in his face.

"Want a cookie?" asked Katya with her mouth full. She rested her chin on the top of Pasha's head. Pasha smirked and took the cookie between his teeth.

"Thanks," he muttered.

Humming, Katya laid herself out on the rock with her head in her brother's lap. She looked up at him with her shiny eyes.

"What's the matter with you?"

Pasha scoffed and wiped a bit of icing from the corner of her lip. "Don't you know already?"

Katya surrendered to an incriminating grin. “Well, kinda, but Mama says it’s polite to ask.”

Pasha leaned back and snorted. “Thanks for the gesture.”

Katya sat up and faced him. “It’s Christmas Eve, you and Faina can’t be mad at each other on Christmas Eve.”

Pasha stared her down with a skeptical eye. “I think she’s a lot madder at me than I am at her.”

Katya put her arms around his neck and hung playfully from his shoulders. Her salty hair brushed his knees.

“Just tell her you’re sorry! You can’t stop Faina from coming with you. And if you’re together you won’t have to worry about what could happen to her while you’re away.”

Pasha lowered himself onto his elbows and stared overhead.

“That’s true.” He bit his lip. “But do I really have to apologize? I mean, Faina knows I’m trying to protect her.”

Katya latched onto his bent knees.

“You were being bossy. If you’d said the same things to me in front of Mama, she would’ve told you to stop. Take Faina some gingerbread cookies. You know they’re her favorite, and she never stays mad for long.”

Pasha smiled and nodded his head. “You’re right.” He stopped and stared at Katya throwing herself at his knees like a ram. “What are you doing?”

Katya crumpled into his lap, giggling. “I wanna play!”

"You wanna play, do you?" Rolling forward, he snatched Katya around the waist and threw her over his shoulder. "I suppose you are overdue. Come here, little fish!"

***

It took some time, but Pasha finally found Faina in a tree overlooking the gardens of the Placide. It was no surprise to him that her nose was buried in a copy of *A Christmas Carol.* She read it every year.

She was so absorbed in her reading, she didn't notice Pasha scaling the tree until he was right below her.

Her shoulders stiffened. "Go away, Pasha. Find your own tree."

"I brought you cookies." He reached into a pocket of his satchel and held them up to her as a peace offering. Her eyes lingered on them for a moment, then she sniffed and forced herself back into her reading.

Pasha snapped the head off of a brightly decorated reindeer shape. "You're gonna let me eat all of these?" When she didn't reply, he sighed and stuffed them back into his bag. "You should know, your wish was granted."

An eye fluttered above the pages to look down at him with vague interest.

"Staccato says you can come along."

Her voice was bitter. "But you don't want me to come."

"Faina, you know it's not that I don't want you to come. I just don't want you to be in danger. But I've come to realize I can be a bit controlling . . ."

She glowered at him. "A bit?"

" . . . And a little bossy."

"A little?"

"I'm very bossy and very controlling, okay? You're not a baby, you're not my little sister, and I can't make you do anything. So, I'm sorry. I'll try to do better."

Faina closed her book, set it down in her lap, and smiled. "Thank you!"

"So you forgive me?"

"I forgive you." She pushed his cap down over his nose. "Now give me your guilt cookies."

Chapter 39:
Samael Introduces Himself

On the night of Christmas Eve, the bay throbbed with music as mermaids all around the capital filled the evening with Christmas carols. Floating orbs of light, like the ones in Polaris, hung suspended across the coast in accordance with an old Pisces tradition. Spinning fairy lights, crafted by esperites, oscillated around lanky trunks of palm trees. Silver shells hung in sparkling clusters from branches. Pasha and Faina enjoyed the spectacle from the porch with blankets and coconut-flavored hot chocolate.

As was their tradition, they engaged themselves in a highly competitive game of poker. In place of money, they wagered gingerbread cookies and Christmas candy. In the end, it didn't matter who won, for they always shared their winnings with each other.

After beating Pasha for the fifth time that night, Faina pressed her cards to her lips.

"Hey, do you remember when Pyro said full-blooded igneous can only burn themselves if they do it intentionally? It made me wonder—"

"Whether or not Pyro gave himself that scar on purpose?" Pasha took a sip of his hot chocolate. "I've been wondering the same thing." He laid down a card.

"But why would you wanna give yourself a burn scar?"

Pasha yawned and stretched, snuggling into his blanket. "I

don't know. Pyro doesn't seem to share a whole lot about himself. He does some strange things. Last week, Cicada bought this record book about the Voilerian gentry. Pyro took it, ripped out an entire section and gave it back to her."

"Now that's just crazy."

They each took turns laying down a hand. After several moments had passed, Faina smiled with a mischievous glint in her eye.

"Do you think Pyro and Sonata have a thing going?"

Pasha rolled his eyes. "Faina, not again."

Mammoth groaned as if to agree with Pasha. Faina was always coming up with ridiculous pairings, as though she were surrounded by book characters. Faina shrugged her shoulders.

"What? I mean, haven't you noticed?"

"That they're always bickering with each other? Yes, a telltale sign of a happy couple."

Faina snickered. "Alright, wise guy, but seriously, think about it! It's like in the pictures. Two people who can't stand each other fall passionately in love!" She placed the back of her hand against her forehead and pretended to faint. "'Oh darling, I hate you! I love you! I love you! I hate you!'"

Pasha chuckled but remained unconvinced. "Faina, they're complete opposites. They're fire and water!"

Faina leaned forward with a juicy look in her eye. "But you know what happens when you mix fire and water?"

"What?"

She wiggled her eyebrows. "It gets steamy!"

Pasha snorted and hid behind his cards. Faina gave him a playful nudge.

"Admit it! Sonata is secretly a pyromaniac!"

Pasha could not contain himself any longer. He burst into uncontrollable laughter. The two collapsed in a fit of giggles until their sides ached.

As they caught their breath, something red streaked over the roof. Faina sat up.

"Pasha! Did you see that?"

Pasha waved his hand carelessly, too comfortable to get up. "It's probably just Pyro setting off some tricks for Christmas Eve."

Faina shook her head. "No, it was different. It was bright red!"

"Santa Claus?" he joked.

She swatted at his shoulder. "Come on!"

She dragged him to his feet and led him around to the back of the cabin. She scanned the trees and sighed.

"I don't see it now."

Pasha rolled his neck, eager to settle back into his comforter. "I'm telling you, it was probably Pyro."

Faina shook her head and towed him into the woods. "Pasha, it could be the Firebird! We have to make sure!"

They ran down the path, kicking up pink sand and ducking

beneath heavy palm fronds. They peered down the leafy thickets and waited. A hurricane of sizzling ash trailed across the road.

Faina squeaked. "There she is!"

Without hesitating, they took off. The sand soon gave way to a mulch-laden path, and the rocks and twigs hurt their bare feet. At the bottom of the hill was an ancient-looking stone wall, twenty feet high, and covered in mermaid ruins. The Firebird alighted at the top of the edifice and looked down upon them teasingly.

Faina tossed her hands. "Great! How are we gonna get up there?"

As the Firebird turned to preen under her wing, the light of her plumage fell across a narrow, stone stairwell carved into the rock. Pasha and Faina exchanged glances. They tiptoed to the bottom and began climbing.

"Is she still there?" Faina whispered, unable to see around Pasha's backside.

"Yeah, she's still there."

"Perfect! I have an idea!"

The Firebird watched them from the far end of the wall, swishing her tail all the while. Once at the top, Pasha and Faina laid out on their stomachs, holding very still. Faina handed Pasha a matchbook from her pocket.

"Light this for me."

Pasha's eyes glazed over. "Faina, you're an igneous. You still need me to light a match for you?"

Faina gritted her teeth. "Just do it!"

Rolling his eyes, Pasha did as told. Faina kept her eyes concentrated on the little bloom. She cupped her trembling hands around the flame with reluctance. It rolled into her palm like a tennis ball.

Pasha's eye darted between Faina and the flame. "What are you gonna do?"

"Something Pyro taught me. I'm gonna trap her."

The Firebird tilted her head, as though amused by their game. Faina released the ball so it spun across the surface like a penny, stopping short of the Firebird and igniting a wall of flames around her. The Firebird looked back at Faina, unimpressed, and passed through the blaze. Pasha stared at Faina dryly as the fire evaporated.

"You really thought that was gonna work, didn't you?"

Faina gave him a shove. "Put a sock in it, Pasha."

Something sparkled in the corner of Pasha's eye. He turned his head towards the valley below. His mouth fell open in awe. He smacked Faina's shoulder hurriedly.

"Faina, look!"

A pale, incendiary light burned in the ruins of an old temple. For reasons neither of them could explain they were compelled to go near it. Without a word, they made their way down the other side of the wall, mesmerized by the brilliance sifting through the palms.

Behind them, the Firebird squawked, but they didn't seem to hear her. They floated down the path. The Firebird swooped down and sliced right under their noses, near enough to touch, but they did not react. The strange light captivated them.

They ascended the staircase hand in hand and drifted, possessed, beneath the archways. As they drew closer, they became infused with indescribable ecstasy. The light seemed to be changing forms, taking on a more recognizable shape. A hand extended from the silvery radiance. A hood peeled back from a face. The light vanished, and with it, all feeling of hypnotic obsession died on the spot. An unbearable darkness fell upon them.

A slippery voice reached towards them. "Good evening, Your Majesty."

In place of the light stood a beautiful man with marmoreal skin and a cupid face shining behind a black veil. He was wrapped in a marbled, silk robe of black and silver. He had an aura of supreme grandeur that chilled them to the marrow.

Pasha grabbed Faina's arm and made to back away, but something heavy strung around their ankles and they tripped backward. Pasha felt his pulse quicken as massive pythons entangled around their legs.

The man removed his gloves one finger at a time. "I advise you not to struggle. They won't bite without my consent, but if you keep on writhing like that they'll tighten their grip, and they've been known to crush bones."

The serpent advanced up Pasha's waist, pinning his elbows to his sides. "Who are you?"

The stranger raised his eyebrows in surprised amusement. He turned to one of his servants, a man with hair so blonde it easily stood out from behind his veil.

"I don't believe I've been asked that question before, Xylophis." He sniggered and circled around to Pasha's head, folding his hands behind his back and leaning down to examine his face. "Which tells me a lot about you, Pasha. You see, everyone here knows me. Hasn't Staccato taught you anything? Come! Who am I?" He swatted Pasha's ribs with his gilded walking stick.

Pasha wheezed through the pain. "You're Samael, aren't you?"

"Precisely." His sculpted lips peeled into a sneering grin. Pasha stared up at the cruel face. Not a single blemish or wrinkle marred his complexion.

"But . . . I don't understand. You were friends with my grandfather over thirty years ago. You'd have to be at least—"

"Oh, my people don't age like other races. We're far too superior for that." He admired the smooth texture of his hand. "I'm seventy years young, and have many more years ahead of me."

He turned his attention to Faina, who ignored the snakes and glared up at him with blazing contempt. His glorious blue eyes swept over her skin.

"I wasn't expecting two of you."

He pinched Faina's jaw and turned down her face. His eyes bounced from one to the other.

"Your sister? Is this the mermaid who broke my curse?" He eyed her legs. Pasha felt panic rise in his chest.

"She's not a mermaid! She's a two-legged! She doesn't have any powers!"

But Samael wasn't listening. He barked at his attendants, "Soak her! Xylophis, do you have my ax?"

A host of veiled servants stormed her with buckets of sloshing salt water and emptied them over her body until she was spitting and coughing. Samael knelt at her feet, clutching his weapon with a violent tenderness. Faina was trembling in the cold, but her eyes stayed pinned to the hands wringing the ax handle.

When nothing happened, Samael's lips wrinkled into a scowl, and he tossed the weapon aside. "If you aren't a mermaid, what is your purpose?"

"She's nothing of interest to you!" Pasha pulled against his restraint, and it pressed deeper into his skin.

Samael regarded Pasha in silence for a moment. His lips slid into a smile.

"If she's no use . . ." Samael shrugged. He rolled his neck and his jaws hinged open. His eyes rolled over into black voids. Any remaining light in Faina's face fell away in terror. He motioned for his servants to bring her forward. Faina screamed as she was dragged across the stones and thrown at his feet. He placed a bony hand on her head and pushed it back to expose her white, freckled neck.

Pasha screamed. "No!"

Samael hovered over his victim, frozen. His eyes rolled back into baby blue, and he crouched over Faina, laughing. He dropped her unceremoniously.

"Tell me, Pasha, are you indeed the heir of Bruin?"

"I'm told so."

Samael's eyebrows rose. "You have a skeptical nature, don't you?"

Pasha threw him a cutting glare. "Why would you think that?"

"The way you answered me now. If I had asked you if you were Pasha, you wouldn't respond with 'I'm told so.' People would think you had amnesia. You aren't really sure if you're Bruin's heir, are you?" He touched the tip of his cane thoughtfully to his lips. "I wonder, however did Staccato convince you to come along on this endeavor? After all, it must have been quite a culture shock discovering there's a whole other world out there, one full of magic. Most of your kind would have shrugged Staccato off as a madman. What persuaded you to believe him?"

Pasha and Faina exchanged wary glances. Faina shook her head, but Pasha shrugged.

"There were phenomena, miracles, things which defied

explanation."

Samael remained impassive. "I see, you mean prophetic dreams and all that?"

"Well, yeah, as a matter of fact. There was this dream where I was looking up at the North Star—" Pasha stopped. He narrowed his eyes. "How did you know that?"

Samael stared at him for several moments without answering. Laughter broke over him. Reddening, Pasha's face contorted into a scowl.

"What's so funny?"

Samael dragged a hand across his eyes almost apologetically. "What do you know about miraculous? Aside from being able to move things without touching them, that is."

Pasha glanced sideways as he tried to recall the powers Staccato had first listed.

"They have the ability to cast illusions, interpr—" He froze. His eyes grew wide. "They can interpret and induce dreams!" Pasha couldn't believe how foolish he had been. "You're saying Staccato put dreams in my head? Dreams that led me to believe I had some kind of destiny? That I was Bruin's heir?"

Samael folded his hands and frowned in sympathy.

"Don't feel ashamed, Pasha. What with growing up in the Other, you were an easy target for Staccato. It could've happened to anyone of your upbringing." He crouched beside Pasha and put a consoling arm around his shoulder. "You have a right to be angry, but you certainly aren't the first person Staccato's exploited in the name of the greater good. It's in his nature; he's an ambitious man, a former politician for heaven's sake! Lying is a part of his job."

Even though everything Samael was saying made sense, Pasha still didn't like the feeling of his arm around his shoulder.

A challenging spark ignited in Faina's eyes. "Don't listen to him, Pasha! Samael is only giving you half the story. He wants you to doubt yourself. I'm sure Staccato has a perfect explanation for all this."

Samael rose to his feet. "You're right about one thing, my dear. There are two sides to the story, but can you honestly say Staccato has given you both? Has he told you of the prejudices my people have suffered at the hands of the Fay? The international rights denied to my own country?" He returned his attention to Pasha. "Listen, Pasha. I know luring you into my midst and shackling you with pythons isn't the best way to win your approval. But I didn't see how I could communicate with you any other way. Staccato obviously wasn't going to let you anywhere near me. I've wanted to meet you for some time, to keep Staccato from taking advantage of your ignorance. I can't possibly hope for you to trust me, but—"

"Why would we trust you?" demanded Faina, growing bold. "I mean, you associate yourself with snakes, of all things! Why don't you just feed us a poisoned apple and hop on your flying broomstick while you're at it?"

Samael furrowed his brow and shook his head, as though disappointed with her.

"I see the Fay have already infected you with their prejudice. My dear girl, you must liberate yourself from this predisposed way of thinking! Snakes are merely the beginning. You've been taught your whole life to fear the serpent, that he is the most loathsome of all the beasts. You fear what you do not understand—"

Faina rolled her eyes. "In case you haven't noticed, I'm not afraid of snakes."

"But you allow your preconceptions to define them as evil. Open your mind, for once! Snakes are beautiful!"

Samael extended a graceful hand to one of the wiggling adders on the ground. It wound itself lovingly around his arm as though it were the trunk of a favorite tree. He held it out to her.

"Look at its color, how brilliantly this one shines! Here, run your finger along his scales."

With her elbows still pinned to her sides, he took her finger and brushed it along the smooth, opal discs.

"Feel how smooth he is? This one has just shed his skin, and so he sparkles more than the others. I ask you, how can something so beautiful be bad, truly?" He stroked her hair and pinned a curl behind her ear. "Only ugly things are evil. Think of Cinderella and her ugly stepsisters."

Faina wasn't fooled; in fact, she appeared unnerved. Samael released the serpent to the ground.

"I believe I have a way to resolve your dilemma." He crossed between them. "You'll be headed to Cetus once the holidays are over. Are you familiar with the legend concerning the lava which runs through the Heart of Fornax?"

Pasha struggled to maintain a comfortable position. "Doesn't the Firebird drink from the lava to get strong?"

"She does, and were you to drink it, you too would be given power. It is said that he who drinks from the Heart of Fornax will receive everlasting knowledge. Pasha, you would know truth from a lie, good from evil. Never again would you have to worry about whom you should trust, for you would already know. And you would know who you are, whether or not you are Bruin's heir or Staccato's pawn."

A glaring fireball rippled silently over the temple, leaving a wake of smoke and ash. Samael's mouth fell open as he craned his neck.

"The Firebird! Xylophis, my mask!"

A servant placed a triangular mask in his hand, and Samael fitted it over his mouth and eyes. The pythons still entangled them.

"I'm afraid I must leave you here. But think about what I said."

He swept his dark cape around him, and in a flurry of billowing robes, they disappeared.

Once they were completely out of sight, the snakes went slack.

Releasing their prisoners, they slithered away into the shadows, where they vanished. Pasha couldn't bring himself to move. Breathing was like trying to pump air into a punctured tire. In one moment, his understanding of the world had eroded like a sandcastle in a hurricane. He was lost. His head fell into his arms. Faina placed her hands on his cheeks, forcing him to look up at her.

"Pasha? Pasha! Listen to me! Don't let Samael get into your head! Don't do it!"

Pasha gave an empty nod, not really aware of anything Faina had said. He was sure it was comforting, whatever it was. But there was little anyone could do to suck him out of his misery.

Footsteps echoed behind him. Someone was running up the stairs. A light from the end of a staff poured over them.

"Are either of you hurt?" Staccato helped Faina to her feet, checking her over for injuries.

Pyro strutted beneath the archway, rubbing his hands together. A fine stream of smoke billowed between them.

"Alright, what's the damage? Did he take a nip at ya? Wait until I get my hands on him, the torchin—"

Faina shook her head.

"We're fine. Just a little wet. He didn't hurt us."

Staccato was aghast. "He didn't?"

"No, it's a long story, I'll explain later. Right now, we have to go after the Firebird!" She pointed in the direction where the fireball had flown overhead.

Pyro grabbed ahold of Faina's arm to keep her from running off. "That wasn't the Firebird. That was me. We did see the real Firebird though. That's how we found you! One minute I was sitting in my cabin, next thing I knew she was beating her wings on my window! Funny. It's almost like she was trying to lead us to you, to save you."

Staccato shook his head. "That's impossible. The Firebird is impartial. She does not show favoritism. Any help she shows Pasha would have to be given to Samael as well."

Pyro scoffed. "Well, she sure ain't doing him any favors, that's for sure! But our birdie seems to be keeping an eye on Pasha."

Ignoring Pyro, Staccato bent over Pasha and hoisted him to his feet.

"Great Northern Star, Pasha! Are you sure you're alright? You look positively sick!"

Pasha flailed his arms like a startled pigeon. He stumbled backward, trying to put as much distance between him and Staccato as possible. Staccato stared back at him, his gray, bushy eyebrows knit together. Pasha was so breathless with anxiety he could hardly get his words out, and his shoulders rose and fell in erratic patterns.

"My dream, the one about Polaris falling . . . did you use your powers to plant that in my head?"

Staccato's eyes widened for a split second. The silence which followed confirmed Pasha's worst fears. Pasha stared at him, open-mouthed in shock.

"Well, did you?"

Staccato didn't move, but his entire posture seemed to tighten like a nervous cat's spine. Pyro shifted to the side and rubbed at the nape of his neck. Finally, Staccato blinked and coughed into the back of his fist.

"Pasha, what you must understand is—"

"You did! You planted that dream inside my head and you pretended to have read my mind and interpreted it!"

Staccato held up a finger defensively. "I never pretended to have read your mind."

Pasha thrust out his hands in disbelief. "But you manipulated me! I didn't tell anyone about that dream! I never spoke of it out loud! Then you came along and interpreted the whole thing like it was my cosmic destiny that I should come along and help you!"

Staccato opened his mouth to say something but stopped halfway and sighed instead. He dragged the heel of his hand over one eye.

"Pasha, I know what it looks like, but—"

Sonata came flying up the steps. "Nobody ever waits up for me! Is everyone safe?"

At the sight of Staccato and Pasha facing each other with such obvious tension, she stopped short and glanced from one to the other.

"What's going on? Pasha, why are you upset?"

But Pasha ignored her. "What about the blizzard in Central Park? That never really happened, did it?" Pasha tangled his fingers through his hair as his head spun with a new horrifying revelation. "And Katya!" He turned and scowled at Staccato as though he were the most despicable villain to ever walk outside the pages of a storybook. "You filled her head with your poison too, you sick, conniving *nehidnyk*!" Scoundrel.

Before Pasha could process what he was doing, he found himself charging at Staccato. Pyro grabbed ahold of his wrists.

"Hang on there, Pasha, old pal, let's not get carried away!"

Pasha was practically spitting as he clawed for Staccato. "Katya is fragile! She's only a little girl! How could you?"

He must have struck a cord with Staccato, for he now stared at Pasha with the sincerest conviction. He lowered his eyebrows.

"If I suspected for one moment putting a dream inside your sister's head would be harmful to her well-being, I would never have done it!"

"Then you have terrible instincts!"

For a moment everything went silent. Finally, Staccato threw up his hand pleadingly as he pinched the bridge of his nose.

"Pasha, from the moment I saw you, I knew it wasn't going to be easy to convince you of the truth. You were visited by the Firebird twice and yet you were still unwilling to accept its existence. So, I did what I thought was necessary to win your confidence."

"By lying to me! You thought you could win my confidence by lying to me!"

"I never lied to you, Pasha. Manipulated you, maybe. But all I did was show you the truth the only way I knew how. You were so stubborn, so close-minded, so determined to cling to your own bitterness that you left me no choice."

The muscles in Pasha's neck drew tense and hot, like the overworked gears of a machine.

"You're actually defending what you've done? You're not sorry?"

"I wouldn't go so far as to say I'm not sorry." If this was true, it was strange how even when Staccato was penitent, he carried himself with a sort of respectful dignity. "I'm sorry I have upset you, and I'm sorry for any distress I may have brought you."

Pasha eyed him over with a scowl. "I bet you are, because I'm done!"

Staccato drew back as though he had been shoved. "What do you mean you're done?"

Pasha pushed past him towards the archway. "I quit!"

Shocked by his declaration, Pyro and Sonata threw up their hands and voiced their pleas. Faina ran after him, latching onto his elbow and towing him back towards the stairs.

"Pasha, let's stop and think about this for a second!"

Shaking his arm free, Pasha spun round to face her. "What's to think about? He used me! I'm nothing but a means to an end! Nothing gets between Staccato and what he wants! Not the truth, not other people's feelings, not basic human decency!"

Faina took ahold of Pasha's shoulders. "Fine, forget about Staccato for a minute. There's still an entire world out there that needs your help! In a matter of weeks, hundreds of people have died so Samael could find out where you were staying. The C.O.N. blew up bridges, held hostages, tortured innocents, all in the hopes Samael could have five minutes to corrupt your way of thinking."

Pasha felt his defenses lowering. An encouraging smirk tugged at the corner of Faina's mouth.

"So your profound, prophetic dream was a ruse." She shrugged as though it were nothing. "Two things remain true: First, you're the only other person who can catch the Firebird, and second, Samael is an evil man who must be stopped."

Sonata came forward out of the shadows, her expression pitiful.

"Listen to Faina, Pasha. I know it wasn't right what Staccato did, but he only did it because we wanted you here that badly." Her hands folded over her heart.

Pasha faced her with a curious look in his eye. "Wanted?"

Sonata descended the stairs and took his hands beseechingly in hers.

"Catching the Firebird and taking back the throne isn't the only reason why Staccato brought you here. He brought you here because I asked him to. We—that is, Mama, Papa, Aunt Estella, and I—wanted you here. You, your mother, and your sister are the missing pieces of our family. It was time for you to come home. You see, even if you choose not to become king, even if you choose to give up the Firebird, we still want you in our lives. But please, don't quit. Don't leave. Stay, for my sake."

Pasha's shoulders fell back into their natural position. He took one look at his cousin's hands and sighed.

"If what you say about bringing our family together is true, I'm happy to do whatever you want."

A delighted smile filled Sonata's cheeks as she pulled him into an affectionate embrace.

"Oh, thank you, Pasha!" She released him and held him at arm's length. "And please, do forgive Staccato. He doesn't see you as a pawn. He genuinely cares about you, as he cares about all of us."

Pasha's eyes wandered cynically towards Staccato, who was standing a few steps behind on the landing, watching and saying nothing.

"Sure he does," scoffed Pasha, "like a fisherman cares about the hook that snares the fish." He tore himself away and made his way back to the cabin in solitude.

Chapter 40:
The Prince of Sheratan

The company arrived in Cetus the day before New Year's Eve in a ship called *the Hoku-Pa*. Katya and Lydia stayed behind in Pisces with Queen Calliope. As the ship approached Port Baleen, Pyro was adamant Pasha and Faina come on deck to see the volcanoes. Cicada came along too, though Pyro had not invited her.

On the horizon, the air was so dense with white vapor it looked as though the clouds had descended upon the earth. A strip of terracotta peaks divided the land from the sky. The shore was lined with chains of black, smoldering mountains dripping with viscous trails of lava. The image reminded Pasha of dark chocolate cakes drenched in cherry syrup.

A loud wailing noise reverberated through the bones of the ship.

Pasha swiveled in place. "What was that?"

A massive figure breached beside the boat like an island rising from the bottom of the sea. Pasha instinctively grabbed Faina and yanked her back.

"Watch out! It's a volcano! A volcano floating up from the water!"

Faina clutched Pasha's arm in fright. Mammoth hopped up and down, barking. Pyro, Sonata, and Skelter looked at each other and snickered. Pasha's ears burned scarlet.

"Alright, what is it this time?"

Pyro covered his mouth, unable to control his laughter. Melodious shook his head from side to side, frowning.

"Give the boy a break, Pyro. There were plenty of things about the Other that seemed foreign to you."

Sonata helped them to their feet and beckoned them towards the odd creature floating alongside the boat.

"It's a leviathan." She ran her her hand along the shallow, bumpy, caldera-like crater.

Pasha peered over the railing, ready to spring back at any moment. A sleepy eye materialized from the foam. It was almost smiling. Now Pasha understood. The leviathan was an enormous, whale-like creature with a smoking, volcanic blowhole!

Faina cocked an eyebrow as she leaned forward for a better look. "It's a what?"

"Leviathan," explained Cicada, "an aquatic marine mammal that blows lava from its spout. They helped create the Phoenix Islands."

Pasha held up a hand. "You mean these things sneezed and a ring of islands appeared?"

"Yep. That's pretty much it."

Sonata nudged Faina closer. "Go ahead, pet him."

Faina ran a hand across its head. The leviathan shut its eyes and hummed until steam whistled from its spout like a tea kettle.

Faina threw back her head and sang with laughter. “This is the most amazing thing I’ve ever done!”

After a brief spell of pets, the leviathan submerged back into the water and went on his way.

Pyro gestured to the string of volcanoes surrounding them. “If you think that’s amazing, feast your eyes on the Igneous Arc!” His pride gushed like the calderas themselves. “It begins here off the coast of Phoenix, continues up through Taurus, and then—”

Cicada burst with enthusiasm as she finished Pyro’s speech. “Then it wraps its way up the coast of Aries, extending all the way into Cassiopeia’s western waters!”

Pyro waved her away with a short huff. “Thank you, Cicada.”

“No problem!” Of all the things Cicada had learned so far, she had yet to master sarcasm.

“As I was saying, all of Aries’s coastline exists within the Igneous Arc. Our kingdom accounts for the highest number of land volcanoes in all Voiler, every one of them active.”

Cicada bubbled back into the conversation. “Wrong! Mount Hika was deemed dormant two years ago.”

Pyro was beginning to resemble a volcano himself. “Don’t you have somewhere to be? Aren’t you supposed to be preparing to save our hides or something?”

“You’re not in danger yet.”

Faina leaned into Pasha’s ear. “Someone’s about to be.”

Pyro threw out his arms. "Well, when are we going to be? The only reason your mother dumped you on us is because you're supposed to save our lives, or some nonsense! I've traveled across an entire continent, and now an entire ocean with you constantly interrupting me, constantly breaking into my things, and it better be for something!"

Cicada tossed her glittering hair over her shoulder. "Excuse me, but you're not exactly the most pleasant person to be around."

"What are you talking about? I'm delightful! You, on the other hand, are downright irritating!"

Sonata's hands flew to her lips. "Pyro! Don't say that!"

Melodious held out his arm. "Now, now, you two. Let us try to settle down. Skelter, why don't you play some music?"

Skelter was about to put his bow to his instrument when Cicada's light boiled bright red. She was putting off a glare now. Pasha slapped a hand over Faina's eyes and squeezed his own shut.

"Irritating?" Cicada clenched her fists. "You know what's irritating? How touchy you are! Snatching books out of my hands and ripping out the pages! I read those papers you stashed under your pillow! You tore them out because you don't like being a—"

Pyro pointed a threatening finger in her face. "Don't do it! Don't you dare!"

"A prince! You hear that, Pyro? Prince! You're a prince! The Prince of Aries! Prince! Prince! Prince!"

Pyro's muscles twitched. The veins in his neck strained. "Don't use that word! I am not a prince!" Sparks flew from his tongue.

Pasha peeked open an eye. "You're a prince?"

Cicada folded her arms across her chest. "He sure is! Prince Pyro Scorch Anomaly the Third, second-born son of King Ignitus and Queen Bravery, first in line for the throne!"

Pyro flushed from head to toe. Smoke billowed out his nose as he exhaled. "I am not first in line! If you paid any attention to those bloody books you'd know I rebuked that title twenty-two years ago! So they ought to stop printing my name in that garbage!"

Sonata rolled her eyes. "Calm down, Pyro. It's just a genealogy—"

"No! I will not calm down! I've written that Mr. Peridot fifteen times now asking him to take my name out of those stupid records, and I'll be burned if he prints so much as a greeting card when I'm done with him!" He turned to Cicada one last time. "And as for you, unless you want to find yourself floating back to your mother in a mason jar up the Eridanus, don't ever call me 'prince' again!"

Cicada snorted. "Shows what you know. The Eridanus flows away from Cortijo Del Mar, not towards it!"

Staccato popped his head above deck, looking quite bewildered. His eyes darted around the chaos.

"What is going on up here?"

Without a word, Pyro turned and stormed past Staccato

towards his cabin. Sonata sighed and shook her head.

"Oh dear, I better go after him." She flurried down the stairs in Pyro's wake, leaving Staccato awaiting an explanation.

"So, Pyro is royalty." Pasha shrugged. "You learn something new every day."

Staccato rolled his eyes. "Pyro and his drama!"

"So you knew?"

Melodious sat on a barrel and chuckled. "Well, of course he knew! Everybody knows!"

Staccato wrinkled his nose with a bitter laugh. "For the love of stars! If it weren't for his parents, we wouldn't have the funds to operate."

Pasha rubbed his chin. "Oh, yeah! You said Aries covers a large portion of your finances."

"A little deal I made with them when I bailed Pyro out of federal prison in Capricornus nearly seven years ago."

The floor shook as Skelter raised his hand and hopped up and down.

"Yes, and you too, Skelter. They'd fund the resistance, and I'd pull some strings to have him released."

Faina's eyes sparkled with intrigue as she turned to Skelter. "You and Pyro went to prison?"

Skelter leaned against the railing, trying his best to play the rebellious bad boy he was not. Staccato shook his head.

"It's a long story. But I wouldn't advise you to go probing him about it just now. He'll tell you in his own time."

But Faina could not quell her curiosity. "But why is Pyro so ashamed of being a prince? He's certainly proud of his country, and his parents must be nice people if they help fund the resistance. Why did he rebuke his title?"

Staccato glanced over his shoulder and sighed. He crept closer and dropped his voice. "It's because of his older brother."

Pasha lowered his chin to his chest. The pieces came together.

"He died during the Sheratan Hostage Crisis, didn't he?"

Staccato nodded. "Arson was quite a bit older than Pyro. He devoted a considerable amount of time to taking down the C.O.N. and made a lot of enemies in the process. The Hostage Crisis was an act of revenge towards the Anomalys. Pyro and his younger sister, Candescence, were amongst the captives. In exchange for their freedom, Arson surrendered himself to the C.O.N. and was killed. Pyro was never the same after Arson's death. He felt responsible for what happened, and refused to take the throne."

Faina put a hand to her lips. "Poor Pyro."

Staccato blinked several times as though to put out a bad memory. "It's rather a personal story. Don't go repeating any of this back to Pyro. I should see how he's doing. We'll be in Port Baleen soon. Remember, don't say anything!" He headed back down the stairs but took one last look at Cicada. "That means you, Cici." He disappeared.

Pasha faced Cicada with an admonishing stare. "You shouldn't have done that. It wasn't very nice."

"Nice?" Cicada huffed. "What about the way he treats me?"

Melodious offered her a weak smile. "We are not saying Pyro is justified, my dear."

Pasha bobbed his head in agreement. "But you didn't have to go and spill his personal information. That was a little below the belt."

Cicada threw her hands on her hips and craned over Pasha. "What would you have had me do?"

Pasha shrugged. "I don't know, it was pretty funny when you blinded him that one time."

It wasn't long before they found themselves drifting into port. A magnificent floating city emerged through the fog. It was like entering an enormous terrarium. The broad, cylindrical buildings of glass panels reached for the sky. Bushy rooftop gardens fanned outwards across the heavens. Rows of onion-domed apartments hung over the canals like Christmas ornaments. At least one side of every building was smothered from foundation to eaves in a lush carpet of herbage. All of this was presided over by a mirrored glass tower shaped like a tentacle, rising above the horizon line to stand sentry with the calderas.

Cicada's vivid eyes glowed with interest. "The entire kingdom runs on sustainable energy, mainly solar power. That's why it looks the way it does. Cetaceans are all about the protection and conservation of nature."

"It's amazing!" Pasha leaned over the railing. "I've never seen anything like it."

An entire coterie of important-looking mermaids gathered on the docks. Scrolls of black tattoos stamped their skin. Waves of dark hair cascaded over their bare shoulders, often with a sun-bleached strand or two. King Lahar stood at the front, crowned with a wreath of pine needles. Gauntlets of purple and blue paua encased his wrists. His face was broad, and the intricate tattoos adorning his cheeks seemed to emphasize its muscular structure. When the company made their way from the gangplank, his arms and smile opened.

"Welcome, friends! Staccato, my brother!"

He pulled his old companion into a bear-like embrace. Pasha bent towards Cicada's ear.

"Just how many royal connections does Staccato have?"

Cicada sucked her teeth. "Too many to count. He has a knighthood in three different countries, you know."

Pasha's eyes swelled. "Three?"

Their conversation was cut short by introductions, and soon they were following their escorts to Tiaki, the Cetacean palace. The company would be staying in the state guesthouses overlooking a private beach. At the sight of their accommodations, Pasha and Faina's mouths hung open.

"*Blin*!" Faina rubbed her eyes. "Mermaids sure are swell hosts!"

Pasha had to remind himself to blink. "Tell me about it."

The guesthouses sat on two levels. There were four cabanas on the top and four on the bottom. The houses were bow-shaped with panels of geometric windows flanking the two far sides. The front doors were triangular with matching knobs. The apartments on the lower level were mermaid-friendly and opened upon a sparkling, blue canal. Inside, the spacious beds were ensconced in glass gables affording them a view of the stars. If they desired privacy they need only pull on a lever, and the gable would be shuttered. Pasha and Faina's cabins sat right next to each other, just like back home.

When Pasha finished arranging his belongings he found Pyro, Staccato, and Lahar unwinding on the front porch. Staccato relaxed with a cup of coffee while Pyro and Lahar smoked pipes. Lahar's eyes overflowed with a sense of adventure as he faced Pasha.

"Are you ready to see Fornax?"

Pasha's limbs stiffened. "Are we going now?"

Staccato set aside his cup and shook his head. "Not until tomorrow night."

"But that's New Year's Eve."

"Precisely! A luckier day there never was, and I think we could use a bit of luck, don't you?"

Pasha tried his best to appear laid-back. It shouldn't have been difficult, considering he was sitting in a rocking chair with a seaside view, but Pasha had a proclivity for working himself up.

"Just out of curiosity, how do we get inside a volcano when it's too dangerous to go near it? Wouldn't the heat kill you?"

Lahar drew his pipe away in a thoughtful manner. "Fornax isn't like any volcano you are accustomed to, Pasha. It flows with a special kind of magma we call Ichor. It cools very quickly. It's only at its hottest temperature when it forms as a moving body of liquid. So, when the lava splashes down from the falls it cannot burn you, it just feels like hot water. We in Cetus harvest Ichor for a variety of purposes, including medicine, fragrance . . . if you travel to the hot springs you can even bathe in it."

Pasha recalled what Samael had suggested in Pisces. He rubbed the back of his neck and cleared his throat.

"Can you drink it?"

Lahar shrugged his shoulders. "Depending on where you reap." His curls shook with a jovial laugh. "I don't suppose you've heard the legends about drinking the Ichor which runs through the Heart of Fornax, have you?"

Pasha looked down at his feet. "'He who drinks from the Heart of Fornax will possess all knowledge, and know good from evil.' That's why the Firebird drinks it."

Staccato scanned Pasha from the corner of his eye. "How did you know that?"

Pasha coughed, his voice growing quieter still. "That was what Samael said."

Staccato's eyebrows rose far up his forehead. As he was opening his mouth to say something, Lahar unknowingly interrupted him.

"If you make it to the Heart of Fornax tomorrow night, perhaps we will know for certain if the legends are true."

Pasha drew back in surprise. "You mean no one has ever journeyed to the Heart of Fornax before?"

Lahar shook his head. "Not since its creation, many centuries ago. When the ancient Cetaceans first prophesied about the Firebird, they hoped to earn her blessings by building a nest for her in Fornax. There she would be protected and could drink the blood of the mountain to grow strong. The road to the Heart was designed with traps to challenge the strength of those who pursued her, so only the worthy may hope to win her favor."

"Do you know what kind of traps?"

Lahar leaned on his elbows and shook his head once more. "The challenges were created to play with your mind, alter your perception of reality, perhaps even drive you mad. Some even say black magic was used."

As soon as there was a break in the conversation, Staccato grabbed Pasha by the arm.

"Pasha, may I speak to you in private for a moment?"

Pasha gave an obedient but curt nod as he stood and followed Staccato around the corner. Staccato was in such a state of urgency he nearly threw Pasha up against the wall.

"You said Samael was the one who told you about the legend of drinking the Ichor. What else did he tell you? Did he tell you to drink it?"

Pasha hesitated and glanced off to the side. Staccato gave him a shake.

"Well?"

Pasha stared up at him in alarm, offended by his impatience. "Yes. He said if I drank from the Heart of Fornax I would have everlasting knowledge, and I would know who to trust, you or him."

Staccato's face grew pale. "I don't suppose I have to convince you of why listening to anything Samael says is a bad idea."

Pasha gave a brusque sigh. "I don't suppose so."

Staccato narrowed his eyes and held him at arm's length. "Pasha, don't you think now would be a good time to let go of your grudge?"

Pasha pressed his lips together, as though doing so would keep him from popping off.

"I don't know. When do you think would be an appropriate time to get over being manipulated?"

Staccato made a hissing noise as he clenched his staff and bore down on him with scowling eyes.

"Several days ago."

Pasha stared at Staccato a long time before answering. "I guess you and I have different standards." And without another word, he walked away.

Chapter 41:
Fornax

The tolling of the bells from Ambergris Square measured the tenth hour of the final day of 1924. The cloudy breath pumping from Fornax eclipsed the twinkling stars by degrees until a breeze off the water brushed them away. Framed against the evening sky, the flumes of burning lava seemed brighter than ever.

King Lahar and Queen Opal led the way to the volcano with a procession of mermaid sentinels. Meanwhile, the younger mermaids showered fragrant flower petals in their wake. They weaved in a line, stern-shouldered, grave-faced, and silent. Pasha felt his heart thrum boldly against his chest. This was it. The time had come. Everything had led to this moment.

He recalled the day when the Firebird had first come to them, when Anastas had stolen the loot from their secret hiding place. How far away that moment in time seemed now.

They halted at a door made from larimar. Somewhere beneath the island, mermaids were opening the chamber. Pasha took a timid glance at Faina. She caught his eye and gave his hand a reassuring squeeze. A folded paper passed down the line of bodyguards. It was placed in the hands of the King. He scanned the writing.

"The door should open momentarily."

The crackle of the torches seemed loud in the silence of their patience. No one stirred. A red salamander scurried along the ceiling over Pasha's head. It examined him with curious eyes. Melodious stood predictably calm. Not even the boisterous Skelter or Cicada thought to fidget. Pyro's structure was tense with a rigid urge to fight. But the gravity lining each eye bordered on frivolous compared to the petrous faces of Sonata and Staccato. The pair locked eyes on the door with a dutiful vengeance.

At length a shudder ran through the seam of the floor, undulating beneath their feet until a crack appeared in the wall. The door rolled away. King Lahar stepped aside and bowed his head.

"Our prayers go with you, my friends, as well as our hopes and strength. May your hearts be fortified with courage and your heads sobered with the knowledge of truth. Should you find yourselves trapped or in need of assistance, Staccato will summon me, and we will do everything within our power to reach you. Know that this power is limited, but know also that Cetus has never taken kindly to limits. You know the task you undertake, my friends. You may now enter Fornax."

And with Cicada lighting the way ahead of them, they journeyed into the cunning furnace.

By the time they reached the bottom of the stairs, they were too far to see the light of the entrance. The surrounding rock glowed with veins of magma, illuminating their path in a scarlet light. Behind Pasha, Skelter trembled.

"Are you alright, Skelter?"

Skelter forced himself to nod.

Sonata reached out for his hand. “Skelter has a phobia of the dark.”

“And small spaces,” added Melodious. Skelter’s palm glowed with a soft green light as Sonata did her best to absorb his anxiety.

Cicada bobbed through the line. “In that case, I’ll be sure to stick close.”

Skelter offered her a grateful smile.

Staccato turned to prod them forward. “Come along now. The sooner we reach the Heart, the better.”

They meandered for some time through the underground tunnels and winding staircases. As they passed beneath the first archway, Staccato’s mouth fell open.

“Something tells me we’ve reached our first challenge.”

They gathered over the threshold into a vast chamber. Everyone gasped with horror. Their bodies were no longer subject to gravity. Everyone was leaning at such a severe forward angle that by all physical evidence they should have been falling over. Yet, they remained upright.

Pyro waved his arms as if to test the air. “What in the blazes is happening?”

Sonata took a step forward and found herself closer to the floor. “We seem to have come to a point where the laws of gravity no longer apply.”

To their left was an upward slope leading to a doorway. On the right was a downward slope also leading to a doorway. They scattered about the room in exploration, finding themselves in all sorts of angles.

Pasha, who was hesitant to move at first, was startled as Pyro nudged him on the shoulder.

"Woah, mate! Check it out!"

As Pasha turned to face Pyro, his jaw dropped. Pyro, who was known for being quite small in stature, was now towering over him.

"How is this possible?"

"I dunno, but I think I could get used to this."

Faina seemed to enjoy testing these new limits. She climbed down one of the stairs and reclined so acutely backward she appeared to be laying down.

"Could it be some kinda magic?"

Staccato shook his head. "No. An illusion like this could not be sustained by magic over such a long period of time unless it was dark magic. But if it were black magic, we'd be experiencing a severe sense of dread, so we can rule that out."

Melodious seemed befuddled, and Pasha supposed he had every right to be. After all, he couldn't see how they were are all hanging around like bats.

"You mean to say we are all leaning in different directions as we speak?"

Staccato rubbed his beard. “Sonata is leaning approximately forty-five degrees towards the ground without falling over. Skelter is hovering parallel with the ground. Pyro, who is ordinarily five feet and seven inches, is taller than Pasha, who is six feet and two inches. And Faina, well, now she’s swinging from one of the beams and her body is being pulled towards the ceiling.”

Melodious chanced a step forward. His body was gradually lowering itself nearer to the floor. “We are traveling downhill.”

“No, this is even ground.”

“Correction, my friend, you only think you are on even ground. The obstacles in the volcano were made to alter our perception of reality. What the architects of this chamber weren’t counting on was a blind man.”

All the while Faina had been creeping towards the lefthand slope which led upward. The moment Faina set foot on the incline, she was swept off her feet. Pasha flew to the edge.

“Faina!”

Faina reached out for a ledge on the wall and caught herself. Pasha’s senses turned upside-down. She was being sucked uphill. Without stopping to figure out why, Pasha thrust his arm into his backpack and pulled out a rope.

Sonata bit her nails. “Can you throw a lasso?”

Cicada rolled up her sleeves. “He doesn’t need to.”

The esperite flew up the hill and held out her hands to Faina.

Faina let go of the ledge and hung onto Cicada's arms. Pasha watched, breathless, as Cicada struggled to tow Faina back down the hill. When she was close enough to touch, Pasha reached out and grabbed Cicada's waist, giving them one last pull back to earth. They collapsed to the ground.

Faina breathed a sigh of relief. "Thanks for that."

Cicada glowed, as though grateful to have a purpose. "That's what I'm here for!"

While Pasha admonished Faina for her clumsiness, Melodious folded his arms and scratched his chin. He laid down on his stomach and reached a hand up the slope.

"This is not uphill. It is downhill. Despite what your eyes are telling you, everything about this room is a lie. Staccato, walk across the entrance one more time."

Staccato did as told and leaned forward like before. "Alright, now what?"

"Can't you feel it in your muscles? If you walk forward, you can feel them working the same way they would if you were climbing uphill."

Sonata made her way ahead of Staccato. "Melodious is right! If you close your eyes, you would never know the difference!"

Pasha turned in a circle, taking in the curious space around him. "So all of this is an optical illusion?"

Melodious stood and dusted himself off. "Exactly!"

"In that case, the way out must be . . ." Pasha trailed off. The remaining door lay at the bottom of the incline to the right of the room.

"Well, there's one way to find out!" Pyro picked up a rock off the floor and rolled it down the slope. It slid right back in the opposite direction and halted at Pyro's feet.

"We have our answer."

Pasha fished the rope out of his bag. "Just in case . . ."

They anchored one end of the rope around a jagged rock and clung to it as they made their way down, or up, the slope. Pasha's thighs ached, just as Melodious had predicted. It had all been a trick of the eye.

With a flick of his staff, Staccato untied the rope and wound it back into Pasha's backpack.

As they passed through the doorway, they found themselves in a wide room where seawater drained into a massive lake. On the opposite side, sitting atop the wall, was a wide corridor. There was no boat, no bridge—just water, and the high wall had no ladder.

"Well, that's discouraging," remarked Pyro dryly.

Faina shrugged. "Okay, so you won't be able to light up. That doesn't mean you won't be useful."

Cicada appeared deep in thought. Her eyes stuck to the corridor ahead of them.

Pasha furrowed his eyebrows. "What is it, Cici?"

Without answering, she drifted across the water and into the corridor beyond. They watched her in curious silence. At the first pillar, Cicada stopped and rubbed her chin. She gazed up at the ceiling once or twice. Floating, she passed through the archway and into the passage. As soon as her head inched past the column, a storm of arrows came shooting out of the walls.

Pasha jumped. "Cicada, look out!"

But the warning was unnecessary. Cicada became translucent like a ghost. She observed the arrows passing through her body with a tranquil but inquisitive eye. When the barrage had ended, she plucked one of the arrows from the ground and sailed back across the lake. She placed it in Pyro's hand.

"I'm afraid you'll have to stay dry. The moment anyone passes those columns, wooden arrows shoot all the way down the corridor. You're going to have to burn them up. You can't do it if you get wet."

Pyro snapped the arrow in two and groaned. "She's right."

Faina's eyes darted between them. "But after he's destroyed the arrows, then he can come, right?"

Cicada shook her head. "They reload."

Pyro threw up his shoulders. "Guess I'm out."

Faina bounced on her toes. "But couldn't I do it? You throw me a light, and I can manipulate it."

"You're not strong enough yet. It takes a lot of power to fry something so quickly, it disintegrates."

Staccato heaved a heavy sigh. "It's not too late for you to go back."

Pyro shook his head. "Nah, I think I'll wait here, you know, for when you come back."

Pasha stared anxiously into the water. "How deep do you think it goes?" He rubbed the back of his neck. "I mean, what if we can't hold our breath that long?"

Sonata reached into her backpack and produced an olive branch.

"You're in luck."

Each of them, except Pyro, took an olive and ate it, while Sonata prepared to ease into the water. She stopped and tossed an expectant look at Staccato. His mouth slipped into a wry smile.

"What are you looking at me for? I'm not going to stop you."

Sonata beamed. Turning around, she slipped into the lake, allowing herself to transform. Her prosthetic fin replaced the artificial legs at the end of her tail. Sonata swiveled it back and forth, testing it.

"Alright, last one in is a blobfish!"

She grabbed Staccato by the wrist and wrenched him headfirst into the water. Everyone roared with laughter. Seconds later Staccato resurfaced, rubbing his eyes and spitting water.

"You've been waiting ten years to do that, haven't you?"

Sonata kissed his head and glided ahead of him towards the middle of the lake. "Poor Staccato! You're always such a good sport."

Melodious reached out a hand. "I will need a guide to help me swim."

Skelter and Cicada each took a hand and led Melodious into the water. Faina took a flying leap into the pool, driving Pyro up against the wall.

"Careful now! I won't be of any use wet!"

Faina mumbled a hasty apology and waved Pasha forward. "Well, what are you waiting for?"

Pasha groaned and took a single, nervous step towards the edge.

"Come on, Pasha," urged Faina, "you can't be afraid now."

Sonata cupped a hand over her mouth. "Exactly! Not after swimming all the way to the library in the grotto!"

Pasha tucked his arms around his torso. "I wasn't exactly the one doing the swimming."

Faina trod towards the rim of the pool and held out her hands. "Come on, you son of a mermaid!"

Pasha dropped down to his knees and put his arms on Faina's shoulders.

"Just because my mother is a mermaid doesn't mean I'm a mermaid."

He allowed Faina to drag him forward. The moment his legs dropped into the water, his muscles tensed and he scrambled up Faina's neck.

"Hey! Hey! Not so fast! Ugh! Pancake, Faina!"

Pyro burst into laughter. “Did you just shout ‘pancake’?”

Pasha moaned and hid his face in Faina’s shoulder. “That’s a Russian expression, isn’t it? I can’t keep them straight anymore.”

Faina giggled. “Afraid so.”

Cicada cocked her head. “You all shout ‘pancake’ as an expression?”

Pasha shrugged as though it were very simple. “You know, like *chort*.”

Faina clicked her tongue and put a hand over Pasha’s mouth. “They don’t know what *chort* means either. In Russian, pancake is ‘*blin*.’ It’s like when English speakers get frustrated, they say a word that sounds like another word. *Evfemiszm*.”

“Euphemism,” corrected Pasha, still clinging to her shoulders.

“Whatever! Look, it’s like when English speakers get angry and yell ‘shoot,’ or ‘shucks,’ as opposed to—”

Staccato held up a hand. “Alright, Faina, we get it. Now come along, you two.”

Before Faina pushed away from the wall, she gave Pasha a reassuring pat on the hand. “I’m not gonna let you drown. Thieves’ Honor.”

Pasha released a quiet whisper of a laugh in reply. With his arms around Faina’s neck, they paddled towards the center, Pasha kicking his legs.

Sonata threw back her shoulders. “Alright everyone, heads

down, tails up!"

Faina tipped them head over heels into the depths of the pool. Nine feet below them, at the very bottom, sat the next archway. Together they followed Sonata's undulating wake through the door and made it to the other side. Everyone kicked off from the bottom and swam to the surface. They made it look so easy! Even though Pasha was not in any want of air, he gasped like a dying man the moment they broke the surface. Everyone stared at him in alarm as he threw himself to the side of the pool, scrambling like mad to get out.

When everyone had composed themselves, they climbed the stairwell leading to the corridor. Pyro waited patiently on the opposite side.

"Are you all through yet?" His voice echoed in the long chamber.

Sonata peeked over the top stair. "We're here!"

"Alright, those arrows shouldn't trigger until you walk past that column."

"Let us know when you're ready!"

He held up a finger. "Give me a moment."

Pasha watched as Pyro charged himself up. His fists became engulfed in flames. They pulsed two or three times, then swelled in size. Sonata turned to prepare herself for the walk. Pyro waved his hands in a passion.

"No, Sonata! Let Melodious do it, his reflexes are faster than yours!"

Exasperated, Cicada plowed ahead of Sonata. "For goodness' sake, I'm the one who can ghost! I'll do it!"

Staccato's voice was terse as he addressed the group.

"As soon as Pyro's flame appears, everyone needs to run to the other side as fast as they can. Cicada, on the count of three." He extended his staff, ready to deflect any arrows that made it through Pyro's blaze. "One . . . two . . . three!"

Cicada breezed past the column, triggering the flood of arrows. A torrid stream of fire rocketed over their heads, charring the projectiles.

Staccato waved them forward. "Go!"

They sprinted beneath the searing carapace. Black ash rained on their heads, but Staccato urged them to keep going. At last, they reached the other side of the long hall, the arrows burnt into nonexistence, no one hurt.

Pyro's voice rang breathless across the room. "Is everyone alright?"

Staccato glanced at each of them. "We're fine! You did well, Pyro!"

"I'll be here waiting when you get back."

No one wanted to leave Pyro behind, but there was no other alternative. They pressed on, traveling deeper and deeper into the bowels of the mountain. The walls began to shrink and constrict.

Eventually, the ribbons of lava running along the pathway faded. The light from Staccato's staff dulled to a barely perceptible pulse.

"It would seem we have reached a point where all light must go out. It's a spell of darkness."

Faina fidgeted at Pasha's elbow. "But I thought you said magic couldn't last that long on its own."

"Yes, but this is dark magic. I can feel it."

Pasha glanced at Cicada. Her glow had diminished, and she was beginning to look gray and transparent. She stared down at her hands.

"I'm feeling a bit faint."

Staccato turned to the esperite in alarm. "She has to go back! This darkness could kill her!"

Pasha scratched his head. "Don't esperites eliminate darkness?"

"This isn't regular darkness, it's black magic. There's no way she would survive. Cicada, you have to go back."

Cicada put a hand to her heart as though the mere suggestion had stung her.

"But Mother told me I was to assist you on your journey to catch the Firebird."

"And you have, Cicada, you've been a big help."

Faina nodded. "Yeah, Cicada, if it wasn't for you I'd be dead."

Sonata laid a hand on her shoulder. "We'd be shish kebabs if you hadn't figured out the next corridor was booby-trapped."

"Go on, Cicada," encouraged Staccato, "we'll be back out in no time. When we return, we might need your help again."

Cicada sighed. "Alright. See you on the other side." She drifted back down the hallway, growing brighter in the distance.

They pressed on. With every step, the space around them grew darker. Skelter shook behind Pasha's shoulder. He could feel Sonata's soothing presence, but Skelter could not compose himself.

Pasha turned around, squinting through the darkness. "He's not calming down, is he?"

Sonata sucked her teeth. "If the fear becomes great enough there is little I can do. The best I can hope for is to take the edge off, but he's so overwhelmed I don't even think I can manage that."

Staccato urged them forward with a gentle hand. "In that case, it's best we hurry."

The walls grew so tight it became impossible to deviate from the path. Skelter was unraveling fast. Pasha could catch a trace of his tenor voice in the way he was hyperventilating.

There was a clamor at the end of the line. Pasha could feel the brush of Staccato's figure as he turned towards the back.

"What was that?"

Sonata's voice resonated with alarm. "Skelter's fainted."

"Then I'm afraid you must go back."

"Me?"

"You and Skelter together."

"But I can't revive him! He has to do that on his own."

"No, but someone has to drag him out, and you can soothe him when he awakens. Pyro and Cicada are waiting behind for this very reason. They can help you get back."

Sonata was silent for a moment. Pasha heard her sigh. "Alright."

There was a shuffling noise as she dragged Skelter backward out of the tunnel. As for Pasha and the rest, they went on their way.

There was little opportunity for the tunnel to get any tighter without disappearing. It remained this way for another quarter of a mile when at last the traces of lava reappeared, and Staccato's light bobbed back into existence.

"We're reaching the end," he declared.

The walls opened. They could move their elbows again. No one was more relieved than Melodious, whose sheer size had almost prevented him from completing the journey.

One by one they flooded into an enormous passage with a single convoluted walkway over a pitch-colored pond. The exit lay on the other side.

Faina glared down at the water, unimpressed. "All we have to do is cross this pond?"

But Staccato's face was heavy with dread. "It's a reflection pool."

"I can see that." She made to dip the toe of her boot in when Staccato grabbed her by the shoulders and yanked her back towards the edge.

"Don't touch it!"

"Why not? You said it's just a reflection pool."

"That's not what you think it is. In Voiler a reflection pool is an enchanted body of water that reflects your guiltiest memories and fools you into believing you can alter the outcome. I should know, they're forged by miraculous. It tempts you to jump into the water."

"And what happens if you fall in?"

"Unless you're pulled out in time, you drown, unable to draw yourself away from the visions. The object of this challenge is to cross the pond without letting it distract you."

"Can't we close our eyes?"

Pasha's eyes glazed over. "Faina, you can't just cross that by closing your eyes. Look at the path, it's all over the place. You'd have to keep your eyes open to know where you were going."

Melodious stepped forward. "I will escort each of you. The pool cannot affect me with my impaired vision, and my senses are strong enough to navigate the path."

Staccato gave an anxious nod. "I think that's best. Take Pasha and Faina across first, that way I can intervene if need be."

Melodious held out his hand to Pasha. Swallowing, Pasha took it and stepped onto the walkway.

The first few steps were quiet. He kept his eyes pinned to the doorway on the other side. Visages of glaring fire and black smoke clawed at the corners of his eyes.

"Do not look down." Melodious's voice was heavy like concrete.

But even with his eyes focused on the goal ahead of him, Pasha could still catch glimpses of the scenes unfolding beneath.

"Pavlo," a strangled voice cried. "Pavlo, my son! Look at me!"

Pasha found his head drawn downwards. Melodious tightened his grip.

"It is not real, Pasha! Look away!"

Not real? What was Melodious saying? Nothing could've been more genuine. Pasha pulled back, wrenching his head over his shoulder to look into his father's face.

"Papa!"

His father was standing under the cypress tree, his wrists bound, a thick coil of rope draped around his neck. Melodious tugged Pasha along. The other end of the rope came down with a jerk. Pasha's father soared upwards like a marionette, choking and kicking. The noose made scathing red scratches around his throat. Pasha dug his heels into the path, but Melodious picked him up and slung him over his shoulder. Pasha was shouting as he reached for his father.

"Papa! *Nyet*! Pa—"

He froze. He wasn't staring at his father, but at Staccato on the other side of the pool. Melodious had set him down on the stones. They had made it across.

Pasha blinked and rubbed his eyes. There was an unmistakable thread of sympathy in Staccato's expression as he met Pasha's gaze.

"It's alright, Pasha. It wasn't real."

Pasha wrenched his head away in shame, refusing to acknowledge Staccato. His ears and neck burned.

As Melodious carried Faina over, it was all Pasha could do to keep from running across the path to comfort her. Pasha's worst memory was the murder of his father. But Faina's nightmares numbered too many to count anymore. Several times, Melodious had had to stop while he and Staccato ordered Pasha not to move. But Faina's screams were unbearable to listen to.

Finally, it was Staccato's turn. He was panting before Melodious even made it back across. Staccato laid his trembling hand in Melodious's and followed him to the walkway.

It wasn't long before his brow was sweating. His steps were tentative and fragmented like a spooked horse. As his gaze drew downward, his eyes seemed to fade into a colorless shine.

What happened next, Pasha would no more have expected than a train plowing through the wall. With a violent twist, Staccato wrenched himself from Melodious and lunged for the pool.

Pasha and Faina cried out. Melodious swiveled and dove for Staccato, seizing him from behind.

"*Nein*, my friend! Stay focused!"

But Staccato was putting up a tremendous fight.

"Let go! She needs me!" He wrestled his arm back and elbowed Melodious in the face.

Pasha sprang forward. "Hang on!"

"No!" Melodious was adamant. "You won't be able to resist! Stay there, both of you!" He was clinging to Staccato's wrist. With his free hand, Staccato swung his staff into the side of Melodious's head. Melodious recoiled with a shout as Staccato threw himself into the pond.

Pasha and Faina watched helplessly. Their jaws hinged open as Melodious dove in after Staccato. Their heads disappeared beneath the deep for what felt like an agonizing passage of time.

Pasha and Faina stared at the spot where the two men had vanished. At last, a hedge of bubbles rippled at the surface and Melodious reemerged with Staccato. His head was rolled back in half-consciousness.

Faina and Pasha helped drag Staccato to the shore. He was breathing, but his brows were furrowed. His fingers shook with fricative patterns.

Faina pressed a concerned hand over her mouth. "What's wrong with him?"

Melodious sighed and shook his head. "He is still hallucinating. He will be alright, but I am afraid the visions will last him another hour or two."

Staccato arched his neck as if fighting to stand. "I'll break it! I'll break that blasted thing! I will!"

Seeing Staccato in such a state, Pasha could not help but abandon his resentment.

"What's he seeing?"

Melodious hesitated. Pasha couldn't tell if Melodious was in the dark, or if he knew and was deciding whether or not he should share.

"There are some people who prefer to bury their wounds, telling no one, hoping that in time they will forget. I believe Staccato is one of those people."

Staccato gave another twitch, his voice low this time. "She needs you . . . we need you, please."

Melodious lifted Staccato and threw him over his shoulder.

"Come, we must carry on."

They filed through the arch.

On the other side was the final chamber. A sealed doorway awaited them on the far edge of the wall. Instructions had been carved into the entry. Pasha stepped forward for a closer look.

"They're in Ukrainian!"

"No," argued Faina, "they're in Russian."

Melodious smoothed his mustache. "I would venture to say they are in every language." He laid Staccato on the ground and ran his hand along the carved letters. "Brail . . . German brail."

Pasha scratched his head. "Brail, Ukrainian, Russian, and German? How is that possible?"

"These instructions are meant to be universally understood. No matter who you are, or where you come from, the text will appear in your native language. Go ahead, Pasha. Read it in English please, so we can all understand."

Pasha cleared his throat and read aloud.

"*Congratulations, you're almost there*
Beyond the archway is one last lair
but if you desire to get through
you must journey two-by-two
Any more would fail the test
and it won't accept any less
If you find yourselves at odds
it's best to choose peas in pods
So nines and sevens, fives and threes
one of you shall have to leave
If heads or tails is a must
choose the one your heart most trusts."

He eyed the text up and down. "Funny, I wasn't expecting that to rhyme in English."

Faina cocked her head and raised an eyebrow. "'Peas in pods'?"

Melodious dusted his hands. "Only two at a time may enter. Seeing as Staccato is in no state to go anywhere, we are odd numbered. Pasha, you have a choice to make."

Pasha glanced at Faina. The instructions had said to choose the one you most trust. It wasn't that he didn't trust Melodious, but Faina was his best friend. Still, this was a dangerous expedition. What if he chose Faina and there was a fire-breathing dragon on the other side? What if she got injured? What if she died?

Pasha glanced back and forth between the two and stammered. He had promised Faina that he would quit babying her, but could he live with himself if anything happened? He had to make a choice.

"I choose Faina."

Faina raised her eyebrows in disbelief. "You want me to come with you?"

"You're my best friend, aren't you?"

He led her by the arm to the archway. They stood on the crescent-shaped threshold.

"You will have to face each other," advised Melodious.

They did as he suggested.

"Now, if I am correct, clasp hands and the door will turn."

The moment their palms touched, the door rotated. Pasha gave a shudder. It shut closed behind them.

They were inside a vaulted chamber. At the center of the room was what appeared to be a low-slung alter draped in velvet. As they drew nearer, they realized it was a bed. Lying in the middle of the pillow was a crystal vial of pale, silver liquid. Attached at the neck was a yellowing tag with instructions written in scrawling ink. Pasha lifted the bottle in his hands and squinted at the directions.

"*The doors of the heart cannot be thrust*
without a final test of trust
Whoever has joined you on this side
by these rules must abide
One of you must drink this juice
to let the locks of Fornax loose
Lay down here and close your eyes
to let your companion claim their prize
As soon as you begin to dream
the doors of Fornax will break their seams
But if you wish to get out alive
a bond of trust has to thrive
for those who seek cannot leave
without the one who waits and dreams
and the one who sleeps can never wake
unless the voice of the seeker has spake."

Faina seized the bottle from Pasha's hands and pulled out the stopper. "Well, bottoms up!"

"Faina, no!"

Faina stared at him with glazed eyes. "What? It's obvious what has to be done. There's no other way."

"But what if it's lying? What if it's poison?"

"Pasha, only you can catch the Firebird. There's no point in me going in there. It has to be you. We don't have a choice."

"Yes, we do! We don't have to do this!"

"Pasha, we've come all this way, invested all this time, risked our lives in the process. You're willing to sacrifice all that just because you're afraid this is a trap?"

"I'm not willing to sacrifice you!"

Faina sighed and dropped her shoulders. She turned back towards the door in defeat. "Well, I guess there's only one thing to do."

Just when she had him convinced she was about to see reason, she ran to the other side of the altar, unplugged the bottle, and downed the contents.

"No, Faina, no!"

Pasha vaulted over the table and wrenched the bottle from her hands, but it was too late. She had drunk it all, every last drop. Pasha's heart constricted in his chest. He was finding it hard to breathe.

Faina smirked in triumph. "Now move out of the way."

She brushed Pasha aside and laid herself down on the altar. Pasha grabbed ahold of her shoulders and scanned her eyes for any signs of oncoming death.

Faina rolled her eyes. "Will you relax? I can't fall asleep while you've got a death grip on my arms."

"Faina, why did you do that? That was a stupid thing to do!"

"If this is supposed to be a trust exercise, you're failing miserably. Why are you always so anxious?"

Pasha's eyebrows stretched in disbelief. "Because I'm always trying to keep everyone alive! Because I always feel like the person with their finger in the dam! I've spent my whole life trying to take care of everybody!"

"Because you won't trust anybody to take care of you! That's why I'm laying on this altar right now, so you don't have to!"

Her eyes fluttered. She was losing energy.

Pasha's voice broke as he covered his eyes. "*Chort*, Faina, why are you always so reckless?"

Faina rolled her eyes. "This stuff is kicking in fast. There isn't much time, so, Thieves' Honor?" She held out her hand.

Pasha forced an exhale and squeezed it.

"May I, Pasha Chevalsky, rot inside the Heart of Fornax if I ever forsake Faina Spichkin."

Faina closed her eyes. "And may I, Faina Spichkin, never wake up from this sleep if I ever forsake Pasha Chevalsky."

Her muscles went limp. Her breathing slowed. She was finally asleep.

Pasha jumped as a cranking noise echoed through the chamber. The wall rolled aside, revealing the passage which led to the Heart of

Fornax. The golden Ichor dripped in streams down the wall. Pasha took one last look at Faina, sleeping soundly, and carried on into the heat.

Chapter 42:
Midnight

This was it, the center of the volcano. Everything was washed in crimson light. Thin wooden beams jammed between the wall and ceiling. How had it managed to stay up for all these years? It didn't look very secure.

Overhead was an enormous mass of tangled brambles: the nest of the Firebird. Jutting out from the far wall was something akin to stairs. Pasha crept up the winding steps, striving to make as little noise as possible. He reached the top.

The nest was empty. The Firebird had yet to arrive.

Pasha sighed and looked down at his watch. The minute hand was just striking midnight. It was now 1925.

A noise echoed from the other chamber. The door! Pasha swiveled around to look back through the last archway.

Faina was still. Had the door moved? He couldn't tell.

All was quiet.

Then, a slithering voice snaked through his ears.

"Oh, look, something to toast the New Year with!"

"Leave her, Xylophis! As long as the girl sleeps the door remains open!"

Pasha drew a pistol from his belt, bolted through the entry, and aimed the gun at Samael.

"Touch her and you die!"

Samael threw up his hands in mock defense and slipped on a sickening smile.

"Don't fret now, Pasha. Xylophis here has been advised not to lay a finger on your friend. You see, as long as she stays alive and asleep, we're not subject to the rules of your little game. In fact, Xylophis, you may leave now. You've played your part, but the rest is between His Majesty and me."

Xylophis glanced uncertainly at his master, then staggered back through the archway.

Pasha kept the focus of his pistol on Samael. His eyes scanned Faina. Her holster was empty. His attention flew up. Samael withdrew her gun from his sleeve and returned Pasha's gesture. They were locked and mirrored, standing over Faina's body, each with a pistol aimed at the other. They began circling.

Pasha gritted his teeth. "How did you get in here? The mermaids would never open the passage for you. How did you do it?"

Samael shrugged. "It was simple really. In fact, why don't you chance a guess?"

Sweat was running down Pasha's temple. "You waited for us to open it for you."

Samael waved. "Go on."

"You had a spy, someone on the inside, an ophidian undercover, maybe."

"A lilith actually, but you get the idea. I'll finish the rest. When the door opened, the C.O.N. attacked the island. The chamber couldn't be shut while you were inside, so the mermaids tried to bar us from the entrance. Obviously, they failed. The first task was simple enough for a person with heightened awareness. I'm sure it was a breeze for your giant blind man."

Pasha nodded. "Yeah. Melodious had no trouble at all."

"Mr. Krüner is like us. We too can see what others cannot. We can perceive with more than just our eyes."

"And the lake? What about Pyro? He should have stopped you."

Samael snickered. "It didn't exactly help that he was standing on the edge of a pool."

Pasha eyed the bruise spoiling Samael's delicate features.

"It takes more than a little water to finish off Pyro." Pasha gestured to the injury. "I see you didn't count on that."

The simper was snatched from Samael's immaculate lips.

"Yes, quite the spitfire, isn't he? But it doesn't matter, I won out in the end. As for your mermaid companion, the accursed esperite, and that mute clown, they were easily overtaken."

"And Staccato and Melodious?"

"A blind man and a delirious miraculous? There was little they could do to interfere."

Samael clicked the pistol into place, a glaring hatred burning in his eyes. They froze as a whistling sound echoed down the passage.

They glanced back at the Heart. The Firebird had arrived.

Samael took one look at Pasha and fired the gun. Pasha ducked to the floor. They bolted for the door. At the threshold, Samael shoved Pasha aside and stretched open his arms. Pasha could not believe what he was seeing. The Firebird seemed to be flying straight for Samael's hand.

Pasha raised the pistol and fired. Samael staggered out of the way, straight into one of the support beams. It snapped in two. Pasha had missed.

The Firebird pulled herself upward, fleeing out the vent. The floor gave a shudder as the walls around them collapsed in an avalanche. Everything went black in a cloud of dust.

When the ash finally settled, Pasha found he was alone. He had been cut off from Samael. He had been cut off from the Firebird. The ceiling had collapsed so low he couldn't raise himself any higher than his knees.

He looked back at the door. It had been destroyed. He was completely walled in.

"No!"

He crawled to the place where the exit had been. He clawed at the rocks. "Faina! Faina, wake up!"

He put his ear to the wall and listened. He heard nothing. He yelled until his voice grew hoarse. "Faina? Faina, you have to wake up! Wake up now!"

After several minutes had passed, he laid down on the floor and resolved to wait. What had happened to Samael? Was he killed in the avalanche? Or was he, too, stuck on the other side? Could he have escaped? Was he out chasing the Firebird, free of competition?

His mind went over the numerous times the Firebird had saved him. Was it possible she would rescue him yet again? It was hard to believe she was as impartial as the prophecy said. But then who was he to deserve her attention? He had never been special before. Why should he hope for anything different? Why should he hope for anything good?

Two hours dragged by.

When Pasha's voice felt strong enough, he tried calling for Faina again, but he never received a response. She couldn't hear him. She would be stuck on the other side in eternal sleep unless Pasha could awaken her with his voice.

The thought made his bones ache. Now, not only would he die, but surely Faina would perish as well. Tears welled up in his eyes.

Wiping the moisture from his face, Pasha looked down at his shoes. A faint light remained in the room. He lifted his head and looked about. Where was it coming from?

A trail of glowing Ichor seeped through the cracks in the stones. According to legend, one drop of the golden liquid sliding down his throat would give him everlasting knowledge.

Pasha gave vent to a bitter sigh. What knowledge could he

possibly gain in his present situation? The knowledge of how many hours he could last trapped inside a caved-in volcano? He shook his head. A thought occurred to him. With everlasting knowledge, perhaps he could figure a way out.

He stored the idea away. It was only a stupid legend, after all! But hadn't he dismissed the Firebird the same way? Here he was in a place where magic was a part of everyday life, where dragons and curses were fact, not fiction. Who was he to question the legend of drinking the Ichor?

Even if the legend wasn't true, it couldn't hurt. According to King Lahar, Ichor was harvested for all sorts of purposes. If you could bathe in it, how harmful could it be? Even if the legends were only legends, the worst thing that could happen was nothing.

He thought of Faina rotting away in the next chamber. For her sake, he had to give it a try. He had to find a way out.

That was it. His decision was made. He crawled beneath the slow-dripping trickle. He tilted his head towards the stream. Pinching his eyes closed, he opened his mouth and awaited the drop. He could smell a fragrance like citrus juice.

The moment the liquid hit his tongue, Pasha gave a start. As the flavor melted into his mouth, his muscles relaxed. The taste was as heavenly as the fragrance. It slipped down with pleasurable ease. He pressed his lips to the cleft in the ceiling, eager for more. When at last he'd had his fill, he laid back, satisfied, and waited for something to happen.

He held his fingers over his face. Nothing. He focused on his toes. Nothing. Anxious for something to change, he stared down at his hands again.

The light grew dim. He blinked. The outline of his hands was growing fuzzy. A heavy weight dropped in the pit of his stomach. His throat went dry. His forehead began to sweat. He was going blind.

Terror overwhelmed him in icy hot waves. His muscles shrank into thin, tight cables. No matter how hard he breathed he couldn't get air into the depths of his lungs.

He groped for a stone and hurled it against the wall. An anguished scream scraped the back of his throat.

There was nothing to do. He threw himself against the floor, with his hand thrown over his stomach. It was still.He tapped his fingers to the base of his throat, feeling for the phantom obstruction blocking his airways. His pulse throbbed against his fingertips. Something about it soothed him. He slipped two fingers down to his sternum and felt the beat of life pumping through him. Soon he dissolved into tears, which dissolved into sobs. Finally, he wore himself out and fell asleep.

Chapter 43:

A Second Chance

Pasha awoke several hours later to a clanking, shuffling sound overhead. He opened his eyes. Total darkness.

So he hadn't dreamed it, he really had gone blind. He could hear rocks shifting and tumbling away.

"Pasha! Can you hear me?"

It was Faina! She was awake! She was alive! Her voice was panicked with sobs.

"He's not responding! What if he's dead?"

A sound like laughter burst from the back of his parched throat. "No! Faina! I'm alive! It's okay!"

Already his other senses were heightening. It sounded crazy, but he could smell her. It was difficult to describe. It wasn't as though Faina had a particular fragrance about her, like an odd, natural perfume. It was more of a familiarity, as though he could smell the freckles singed into her cheeks, smell the countless hugs she had buried him in, smell the past six years of their friendship in one grateful breath.

"Pasha?"

There was light! Was there? He was blind, how could he tell? Perhaps he wasn't completely blind. Maybe there was still something left. A smile forced its way into his mouth as a familiar hand touched his face. Arms encircled him. He was wrenched into an embrace, and his nose was buried in a thick mass of messy hair.

Faina's voice was dense with grateful tears. "I thought you were dead! When I saw the Heart had collapsed I knew you must be trapped inside!"

"But how did you wake up?"

Pasha could smell a faint stain of indigo as Staccato's voice floated into the mix.

"The instructions said she could only be awakened once you told her to. She didn't have to hear you. You just had to say it."

Faina let go. She held Pasha at arm's length. "Something's wrong. What's wrong with you?"

Pasha's shame smothered him. How foolish he had been to lose hope and drink the Ichor! If only he had waited a couple more hours, he would still be able to see.

"It's your eyes! There's something wrong with your eyes!" He felt her hand brushing back his bangs. "You've gone blind again, haven't you?"

"Step aside." There was a crunching noise as Staccato made his way through the debris. With a rough jerk he tilted Pasha's head back. There was a subtle sensation of bright light pouring into his eyes as his eyelid stretched open.

"It's happened before," explained Faina from behind. "He has panic attacks and he loses his sight for a little while. It always comes back though."

Staccato sounded suspicious. "How long has it been since you could see?"

"About six hours. I was asleep for most of it."

A growl rose in Staccato's throat. "This isn't anxiety."

Pasha felt as though the floor of his stomach had disappeared. Staccato's voice was harsh and grating.

"You drank the Ichor, didn't you?"

This time, Pasha remained respectful when he answered him. "Yes."

"And now you're blind."

"What? You mean permantly?" Faina shouted the words so loudly it echoed off the walls and hurt Pasha's ears. Staccato sucked his teeth.

"No, it's only temporary."

Hope drowned Pasha like a tidal wave. "What did you say?"

"I said, it's only temporary! Why, I don't know. No one has ever successfully journeyed to the Heart of Fornax to study its chemical properties. Anyway, your pupils are showing some stimulation. It should wear off in a couple of hours or so."

A sigh of relief rippled through Pasha's body.

"Shame," said the voice of Melodious from the other side of the barricade, "would have been nice to adopt a protégé." He reached through the opening and patted Pasha on the shoulder. "But I am glad you are not harmed."

But something was still distracting Pasha. “So, you didn’t know I would go blind?”

Staccato gave an irritable sniff. “No. But even if I had, would it have stopped you? I told you not to listen to Samael! I told you not to drink the Ichor! You were a complete fool to disobey me! Now, I believe I know you well enough to trust this wasn’t over some lust for power. You obviously panicked. You thought no one would come to your aid, and so you decided to drink the lava in hopes that its ‘all powerful knowledge’ might inspire some kind of solution.”

Pasha nodded. Staccato had guessed it all.

“Let this be a lesson to you. It is essential that you develop some kind of faith! You doomed yourself before anyone had a chance to rescue you. You were so convinced you were beyond saving that you caused yourself more trouble than if you had simply had a little patience and trust, specifically trust in me!”

Pasha bowed his head. “I realize that now.”

Staccato jerked him forward by the back of his collar.

“I am not your enemy! You may not be able to understand everything I do, but believe me when I say it is for your own good!”

Pasha winced as Staccato squeezed the back of his neck. He felt like a kitten being carried in its mother’s mouth.

“I’m sorry, Staccato! I really am!”

There was a deflating noise as Staccato heaved a sigh, and dropped him to the ground. “All is forgiven. I think you’ve learned your lesson."

Pasha rubbed the back of his neck and tried not to groan. "So what's happened? Where's Samael? Did he die in the avalanche?"

"I'm afraid not. Samael was fortunate enough to escape. The rockslide formed an alternative exit on his side, and he got out. The Firebird is still at large. War is being waged outside these walls as we speak."

Pasha nodded. "But he hasn't got the Firebird?"

He could detect a smile in Staccato's voice. "He hasn't got the Firebird."

"Then I still have a chance!" Pasha staggered to his feet. Faina had to grab him to keep him from falling over.

"Yeah, but you're not exactly in fighting form at the moment."

Melodious helped them through the opening. "We can hold Samael off until his sight returns."

Pasha's thoughts drifted back to the others. His heart pounded. "How is everyone else? Are they alive? Are they okay?"

Staccato led them over the broken stones. "Everyone is fine. Pyro put up a good fight, despite not being able to light up, and Cicada was able to save Sonata and Skelter by blinding their attackers."

"And you and Melodious?"

There was a touch of smugness in Staccato's voice. "We're alive, aren't we?"

The palest of shadows moved in front of Pasha's eyes. He

grinned.

“Well then, let’s go catch the Firebird.”

Chapter 44:
To Catch a Firebird

The first sunrise of 1925 was stained with black and red. By the time the company had retraced their steps to the entrance of the volcano, Pasha had regained a third of his sight. Staccato and Sonata draped Pasha and Faina in a space blanket to conceal their identity and escorted them back to the guesthouses.

Outside, the earth was shaking with cannon fire. The bay resounded with musical bellows, and the sound of thunderous tails slapping the water.

Pasha tilted his head. "Leviathans?"

Faina laughed. "Yeah, nothing scares away a bunch of ophidians like flaming whale snot!"

Staccato and Sonata hastened Pasha up the stairs, Faina in tow. Inside, Mammoth was barking and growling. They crossed the threshold and the door slammed shut. The curtains scraped against the rod as Staccato drew them closed. Sonata pushed Pasha into a chair.

"Both of you stay here! One of us will return in an hour and then we can set out for the Firebird. Lock the door behind us, and don't do anything rash!"

Pasha heard the door slam. He listened to the footsteps echo down the stairs until they disappeared amongst the cannon fire.

His eyes scanned the room for Faina's messy shadow. "We aren't really gonna listen to them, are we?"

"Are you kidding? Of course not!" The legs of her chair scratched the floor as she pushed back from the table. "You're gonna need some kind of cane." Drawers bounced in their hinges as Faina rummaged through the kitchen. "Ooh! This might work! Look what I found!"

Pasha stared at her with a dry glower. "I can't look, remember?"

"Oh, yeah, sorry. It's a broom! I'll just unscrew the head from this handle, and *voila*!" She bounded across the room and placed the rod in Pasha's hands. "Will this work?"

Pasha stood and poked around with it. "I guess so."

Faina clapped her hands together. "Okay, okay! Now we gotta test your eyesight! How is it so far?"

Pasha stood back and looked at her. Colors flowered back into the picture. He could see where her boots ended and her jodhpurs began. She thrust out her hand.

"How many fingers am I holding up?"

"Come closer."

She held her hand a foot from his face. Pasha squinted his eyes.

"Uh, six?"

Faina threw up her hands. "Since when do I have six fingers?"

Pasha rolled his eyes. "You have two hands, don't you?"

"I only held up one! Whatever, just stay close." She grabbed Mammoth's leash and buckled it to his collar. "Alright, let's go!"

Pasha grabbed his makeshift cane and followed her out the door. She led them down the path towards Ambergris Square where a good portion of the action was taking place.

Pasha struggled to keep up with his cane. "Where are we headed exactly?"

"To fetch Harpagos from the stables. I figure if you're gonna catch the Firebird, you need a pair of wings."

Pasha could feel the heat hitting his face as they bolted past a blurry stream of fire.

"Staccato!" Pyro hollered, not seeing Pasha and Faina running through the street. "Watch out for the fury!"

Pasha did not need twenty-twenty vision to discern the grayish, red-eyed figure tearing up the pavement with his hands as he ran full-speed through a crowd of people. His sheer momentum was tremendous. What's more, his strength was nowhere near relative to his size. He swiveled round and raced towards Pasha and Faina. Faina grabbed Pasha's arm, trying to tow him out of the way, but there was no time. As the fury leapt towards them, Mammoth shot into the air and sank his teeth into the fury's shoulder.

The fury let out a strangled cry as Mammoth wrestled him to the ground. Faina clapped her hands.

"Good boy, Mammoth!"

Desperate to get away, the fury managed to scramble out from beneath Mammoth. With nowhere else to go, he ran into the ocean where an army of armored mermaids greeted him with the flash of tridents. That's when Pyro spotted them.

"*Oi*! What do you two think you're doing out here?"

Faina whistled for Mammoth and dragged Pasha off towards the stables before Pyro could stop them. Pasha's vision was strengthening fast. The color of Faina's eyes came into view, and the contours of her expressions. He was almost back to normal.

The stables were deafening with the shrill brays of horses and pegasi. At the sight of Pasha, Harpagos kicked up his heels.

Faina unlatched the stall. "Are you sure you can see good enough to fly?"

Pasha mounted Harpagos bareback. "Even if I can't, Harpagos can." He reached out a hand for Faina. "Hop on."

"I can't, I have Mammoth. You're gonna have to go alone."

Pasha made to dig his heels into Harpagos's side. "Be careful then."

Faina balked at him. "Aren't you gonna beg me to go back to the cabin and hide until it's all over?"

Pasha shook his head. "Not while you have Mammoth."

Faina's face split into an enormous grin. Outside, a large, fiery figure streaked across the sky like a meteor. Faina held open the door of the stall.

"Well, what are you waiting for, Breadwinner? Go!"

Harpagos charged out of the pen, beating his wings against the fresh morning. They lit up into the air, shooting past the horizon like a falling star in reverse. They sped across the coast with determination until the Firebird was in sight. They soared after her into the valley below.

She wasn't far out of reach. They hovered over the treetops. Carefully, Pasha brought himself to a low standing position on Harpagos's back. It'd been years since he'd pulled such a trick, but he had to catch her! Mother Genesis had to be wrong! He reached out his hand.

Out of nowhere, a knife spun through the trees and cut Pasha in the side of the head. Harpagos snorted and kicked, clearly spooked. Pasha was sent flying. He grasped for Harpagos's mane but it was too late, he was already falling.

The wind was knocked from his lungs as Pasha hit the ground. He had landed on the top of a cliff. He tried to move, but his muscles seemed to cramp defiantly. His head fell back, and he winced in pain.

A hand seized his throat. He opened his eyes. His vision was perfect now. Samael stood over him, close enough that he could see his eyes through the veil.

"Of all the sinners in the world, why do I end up with the one saint for an adversary?" Samael stretched his jaw. Fangs unsheathed themselves from pink gums. "You can always depend on a corruptible man to do themselves in. That's what made warping your grandfather so enjoyable. It keeps me from getting my hands dirty. You, on the other hand, I'll just have to finish off myself!"

As Samael was lowering his teeth towards Pasha's neck, a rock flew up and struck him in the side of the head. Pasha dropped to the ground.

"Stay back," warned a familiar voice.

Pasha swiveled around. "Ma?"

Lydia stood at the edge of the woods, struggling to lift a long-hilted sword. She ran at Samael, her wrists shaking with the weight of her weapon.

Pasha was screaming. "Mama! No!"

He staggered to his feet and ran after her, but Samael reached her first. He snatched Lydia's wrist. The weapon fell from her hand. He wrapped his fingers around her neck.

Pasha halted, his eyes wide with terror. Samael glanced from mother to son, grinning.

"Who would have thought after thirty-five years I'd finally get to see the baby?"

Pasha's mother was shaking. "I do not care what you do to me, but you will not touch my son!"

Harpagos reappeared, landing next to Pasha and stamping his hooves. Pasha put out a hand to steady him.

"Let her go!"

Samael rolled his eyes and addressed Pasha's mother. "Your son is a perfect Mama's Boy, by the way." He backed her towards the edge of the cliff where the bay ran shallow and the rocks ran deep.

Pasha fell to his knees. "Please don't! Don't hurt her! I'll do whatever you want!"

Samael smirked. "Quite a devoted son you have. Shall I accept his offer?"

Lydia shook her head. "You started this with me. I am the heir; I am the one you want."

Samael sucked his glistening teeth. "That all changed when you spawned this little charmer. See, you're not really a threat anymore. He is."

He hurled her off the cliffside.

"No!"

Pasha leapt onto Harpagos, rammed his heel into his side, and tore over the cliff. His mother's hair billowed around her as she soared down the bluff. Behind him the Firebird whistled and sang, but Pasha didn't care, he just wanted to save his mother.

Harpagos dove down and looped beneath the falling woman. Pasha reached out his arms and caught his mother around the waist. Gasping for breath, Lydia hooked her arm around Pasha's neck. He pulled her onto Harpagos's back.

A rapturous shout interrupted their rejoicing.

"She's mine!"

They turned their heads. Samael wrapped his arms around the Firebird with jubilation.

Pasha's face fell. A violent light glared in Samael's eyes. The long, trailing sleeves of Samael's robe caught fire. Flames advanced up his shoulders and burnt his skin.

With a terrible cry, he released the Firebird and smacked at the blaze. But the Firebird turned right back around and plunged after him, lighting his ponytail on fire.

Pasha couldn't believe what he was seeing! The Firebird was attacking Samael! In an instant, Pasha was reminded of how the tail feather had burned Anastas's hand. The Firebird really had been on his side! Or perhaps she was on no one's side. Maybe she was never meant to be caught. Either way, the prophecy had been wrong.

Samael batted the bird away, his clothes smoldering. He hastened to his pegasus and took off across the bay. Along the seawall, a retreat was in motion as C.O.N. members fled in countless directions. Pasha and Lydia flew towards the dock where everyone had gathered and was staring out at the ocean.

The Firebird dropped low over the water, drifting past the leviathans. She was headed directly for Pasha. Her body illuminated with a pale light. It swelled larger and larger until everyone was forced to shield their eyes. Any remaining enemy within the touch of the glow vanished into cloudy vapors.

The Firebird was transforming! Feathers peeled away from the light surrounding her until a translucent woman took her place.

Everything went quiet. There were no cannons, no war cries,

just the lap of the sea against the rocks and the gulls calling in the distance.

The woman's face radiated a comforting warmth as she stood smiling at Pasha. Her golden hair glistened like the sunlight off the waves. Shoulders browned with summer peeked out from her white gown.

Pasha squinted. "Eve?"

Eve threw back her head and laughed. "Pasha, you silly thing. Don't you know who I am?"

Pasha stepped closer. Those hands, they were his mother's! Those golden eyes, they were his sister's! Etched in the lines of her face was his own, and the faces of the family he loved.

"Evangeline!"

Eve's smile was so broad it pinched her eyes.

"That's right!" She wrapped her arms around Pasha, who couldn't help but laugh as she held him close.

When Evangeline caught sight of his mother, she stopped. Her eyes stared at Lydia with sharp pain.

"Lydia . . ." Her pearly tears fell onto the dock like rain.

There was no sense of estrangement in his mother's expression. It was as though she had known Evangeline her entire life. Her eyes filled with longing as she stumbled forward and found herself in her own mother's arms.

Scintillating traces of light fell around them like snow. "Look how beautiful you are! Look at your beautiful family!" She went on whispering soothing sounds into Lydia's ear, things Pasha could not hear. So many questions struggled inside him.

"But you're the Firebird? How is it possible?"

Evangeline looked up. "Didn't Staccato tell you about my mirror?"

Pasha stared at her, aghast. So there was more information Staccato had withheld from him. He shook his head.

"While I was carrying your mother, I created an enchanted mirror from legend with the power to purify souls. When the C.O.N. attacked Polaris, I took the mirror to Bruin, hoping to cast out whatever evil Samael had buried inside him. I tried to make him look, but he pushed me away. That's when I tripped over the forge and was impaled by the sword, Sarmentum. The mirror fell and shattered to the ground. In the final moments before death, I saw my reflection. My spirit was transfigured, and I became the Firebird."

"But how was it possible?"

"The mirror is capable of a great many things, Pasha; not even I know all of its powers. When the mirror was shattered, the forces divided amongst the shards. Whatever piece I found myself staring into had the ability to transform my spirit."

"So you didn't die?"

She shrugged. "My body died. But my soul was given a new earthly form. I was given a second chance. I decided to do everything in my power to stop Samael and restore my heir to the throne. Only when I was caught could I cross into Paradise."

"So that's why Mother Genesis said you wanted to be caught by Samael. You wanted him to catch you in hopes you could kill him yourself."

"Exactly."

"But what about the legend? What about the prophecy? What about the wish?"

Evangeline's shoulders rose and fell. "Some legends are merely that: legends. Cetus's prophecy about the Firebird was partially true—Samael did catch the Firebird, just not in the way he was hoping. I'm afraid I'm not very good at granting wishes."

A million things flooded into Pasha's mind. "What about what happened in Karkinos? You were waiting to save me. How did you know I would end up there?"

Evangeline covered her eyes, half-embarrassed. "Oh, that. You see, when I discovered you would be returning with Staccato, I quickly realized I had made a terrible mistake."

Pasha furrowed his eyebrows. "Mistake?"

"Pasha, I don't know if you're aware of this, but your mother was never meant to leave Voiler alone. She and I were to start life over together, for our own safety. Both our deaths were to be falsified. A secret gateway was built in Karkinos. It was just for the two of us. For safety reasons, a default was put on the entry, a loop, if you will, so no matter where Lydia and I were coming from, we would always end up in the safety of my own kingdom. Unfortunately, the gateway was forgotten after my death. Not even I thought about it, and I knew how to break the loop. You are my descendent, Pasha. So when you first entered Voiler, you were automatically transported to the gateway in Stella Real. Knowing you could easily drown, I waited for you. And once you'd been saved, I broke the default to prevent your mother and sister from experiencing the same predicament."

Pasha stroked his chin. "You saved me from being flogged by Klokov. You brought Faina and me those jewels after Anastas stole from us."

Evangeline's nose wrinkled as she laughed. "Pasha, I've always been watching over you, my love. You, and your mother, and your sister, and . . ."

She froze. Her smile fell and her eyes dilated. She glanced anxiously around the crowd.

"My time is running short." She brushed a stray hair from Pasha's forehead. The phantom gesture was a perfect replica of his mother's. "Take back the throne, my darling; you're strong enough, you're capable enough, and the world is in need of a heart like yours."

The wind rose up from the sea. She reached out for Lydia and Pasha's hands. "We'll be together again someday. You'll see."

Her features receded away in the morning light. Pasha panicked.

“Wait, Evangeline, you never explained how you came to me in the grotto! I still have so many questions.”

Evangeline’s smile was resistant to fade. “You’re clever, Pasha. You’ll figure it out in time. Besides, the dead tell no tales.”

The breeze urged against them like a hurricane, squalling Pasha’s bangs across his forehead, pressing his clothes to his chest. Evangeline looked out over Pasha’s shoulder. Her eyes fell upon Staccato, and she was gone.

Chapter 45:
Evangeline's Dying Wish

Several days later, once the aftermath of the battle was cleaned up, Pasha found himself looking out over the bay from the end of a dock in Ambergris Square. Off in the distance, his mother and Katya dove through the waves. Their sun-kissed faces disappeared beneath the white foam. Two tails—one pink, one gold—lashed out behind them.

Letters were written to senators, appeals were made to the Ecliptic Council. It would be a long process. There would be legal battles, lawyers, and judges. It all sounded quite grueling. And yet, Pasha was glad because it would buy him some time—time to learn things, time to get to know the world around him, this world that was a part of him, a part of his mother, a part of his past.

He was startled by the sound of someone strolling down the dock. He turned. It was Faina. She was wearing a breezy dress and a matching cloche. She had Mammoth on a new leather leash.

"Mind if we join you?"

Pasha gestured to the spot next to him. "Not at all. I was hoping you would show up soon. Been shopping, have we?"

She nodded and pulled back Mammoth's fur to show off his new collar. "Got Mammoth a new wardrobe."

"Oh boy, look at you, Mammoth!" He massaged Mammoth's neck, and Mammoth thumped his leg with vigorous delight.

"Would you believe it? Ever since the battle of the Firebird, everybody has been asking me what kind of dog he is, and where they can get one. King Lahar said he'd like to raise up a whole unit of them for the military!"

"Oh, I can believe it. You're quite the ferocious beast, aren't you?" Pasha scratched Mammoth behind the ears.

"Only if someone messes with his pals." Faina sat next to him, taking off her shoes and letting her feet hang off the edge of the dock. "I still can't believe your grandmother was the Firebird the entire time!"

"I know, it's pretty wild."

"I'm still sort of confused about how that works. Was she a ghost? If she never really had to be caught, why was her soul put to rest after Samael caught her?"

Pasha brushed his hair back and sighed. "Sonata tried to explain it to me as best she could, but the fact of the matter is, there's still a lot we don't know. In Voiler, ghosts are a real but rare phenomenon. Not a lot is known about them, except for this thing called Moram Mortem, or delayed death. For some unknown reason, a soul is detained until a very specific event or set of circumstances occurs, kinda like a catalyst in a curse. That's what Sonata believes happened. She thinks maybe the catalyst in this case was seeing Mama for the first time, or me, Evangeline's heir."

Faina rubbed her hands up and down her arms, as though the

idea unnerved her somewhat. "Did you ever find out what Evangeline meant by 'the dead tell no tales'?"

Pasha swung his feet back and forth and nodded. "Except for ghosts, the only people who can communicate regularly with the dead are miraculous. But the dead often possess knowledge the living can't handle, sometimes divine knowledge. So lots of times, instead of directly sharing information, they have to put the person on the path to discovering things themselves. That's why Evangeline took me to the library in the grotto instead of just telling me how to break the Land Lock. Oh, and that's another thing. No one knows for sure how she appeared to me in her human form instead of as the Firebird."

Faina stared into the water, thinking hard. It was a lot to process. Pasha himself was still struggling to wrap his head around it. At last she looked up at him.

"How do you think Staccato felt about seeing Evangeline's ghost? I mean, it had to be pretty traumatizing, seeing as he was the one who found her body."

Pasha sighed and gave the dock a slap. "Beats me. We'll probably never know." There was an edge of bitterness in his voice. "I have a million questions I wanna ask him right now. If my mother was so important, why did she get dumped in an orphanage in Siberia? Couldn't someone have cared for her? And since she was an orphan, how come she knows *The Blind Man*, and how gypsies teach horses to fly? And if Staccato was only waiting for a male heir to be born, why didn't he take us back sooner? Why couldn't he have taken us when I was born? I could've been taught how to rule! My father wouldn't have been murdered! I would never have had to become a Breadwinner!"

"I thought you and Staccato patched things up."

Pasha hunched his shoulders. "That was before he began avoiding me like the plague. It's like the moment I began asking questions I became diseased, or something."

A moment of silence passed between them where the sun warmed their cheeks and shoulders. A breeze rippled through their hair, and Pasha laid back on the dock just breathing, enjoying the sun.

Faina peered at him over her shoulder. "And how are you, by the way?"

He peeked open an eye and squinted in the late morning sunlight. "Me?"

"Yeah. Lots of big things coming your way. You officially made up your mind to become king."

"Yeah, well, I kinda had to, didn't I?"

Faina swung her feet back and forth, tracing a wave with her toe. "I was afraid you'd say that."

"Say what?"

She shrugged and took off her hat. "I know you, Pasha. You're only doing this because it was your grandmother's dying wish. That has you written all over it: obligation, duty, all that jazz."

Pasha lifted himself onto his elbows. "So you think I should call the whole thing off? You don't think I should take the job?"

"No, I didn't say that at all. I just wish you'd do it for the right reasons."

"So you *do* think I should be king?"

"Absolutely I do!"

He raised himself into a full sitting position and leaned forward to get a look at her face. "Why the absolutely?"

She turned to meet him with an eyebrow cocked. "Pasha, I've known you how many years now? We've grown up together! You're my best friend! If anything makes you happy, it's helping other people. Nothing upsets you more than watching the world suffer. You never fit in with the other Breadwinners. You stuck out like a sore thumb, and you know why? Because everyone could see how much it pained you to strike another person who was just trying to earn their daily bread. Someone like you. You never swore unless you really meant it, you never spit unless you were trying to look tough. You were just Pasha. Sweet and gentle Pasha. Now that might make you a terrible street fighter, but think what kinda king that would make you."

Pasha looked up at his friend with the sun shining behind her. She was wearing that smile she always wore when she had gotten her point across. Faina was right. The dread that had been anchored to the fate of ruling a country was all of a sudden lifted. He began to see everything in a new light.

"You know everything, don't you?"

She shrugged and smirked. "Pretty much."

She splashed him with her foot, and they laughed. Together they leaned back, taking in another of those sunshine-filled breezes. At length, Pasha sighed and stretched.

"I guess pretty soon we'll be finding out more about the mysterious Faina Spichkin. Staccato said when we go to the Ecliptic Council, we'll check the migration records for your father."

Faina shrank a little and turned her head to look off in the opposite direction. "Oh. That."

Pasha leaned forward with a concerned expression lining his eyes. "What's wrong?"

She sighed and stared down into her lap. "It's just, I know it sounds silly, but . . . I thought I was lost and alone before, losing my parents. Then I lost my brother, then my uncle, and finally my cousin. But for some reason, not knowing where my father came from, and that he was keeping secrets, makes me feel more alone than ever."

It broke Pasha's heart to see her so disappointed and feeling alone, especially when it wasn't true.

He put an arm around her. "What do you mean you're alone? As much as I've bossed you around, treated you like a baby, driven you crazy with my controlling behavior, how could you possibly think you were alone?" He squeezed her shoulder. "You're a part of my family, my mother's family, my sister's family, my family. And you're stuck with me whether you like it or not!"

A smile bled into Faina's features.

"Thieves' Honor?"

"Thieves' Honor!"

And with that, they sat back and basked in the sunny afternoon with many jokes, many laughs, and lots of love.

The End

Eager for more of Pasha's adventures? Here's a preview of The Glassblower coming out in 2019!

The Letters

It was Samael's long held belief that the devil had it easy when it came to luring souls into eternal condemnation, for human beings constantly condemned themselves. Not only did this make the job simple but it was also amusing. More often than not a man's virtue was the very vice which did him in. Conviction becomes wrath, chastity turns to pride, and love? Love was the most dangerous of them all. Love could make anything permissible. Ah, the beauty of human nature.

It was this very principle that came to mind when Samael searched through the box of paints excavated from Evangeline's studio. It had been lifted during The Land Lock when the kingdom was abandoned. At the time, searching through stolen boxes had seemed a hopeless endeavor. It was hardly the first time he'd scoured the artifacts in search of information about Evangeline's enchanted mirror. The former queen of Ursa had crafted her looking glass thirty-five years ago. Its power had enabled the dying woman to preserve her soul in the manifestation of The Firebird. It was The Firebird that had brought her grandson, Pasha Chevalsky, to Voiler, the world where magic continued to thrive. Magic was, in a way, what Samael sought to cleanse Voiler of. Likewise it was now what Pasha was fighting most to protect.

With Pasha's arrival into Voiler he could take back the throne Samael had stewarded all these years. Until The Firebird had appeared, Samael was sure the line of Northstars were dead. After all he'd seen to it himself. It was he who had orchestrated the assassination of the king and the first seven princes. And in the end it was he who had manipulated the youngest prince, Bruin, into breaking the alliance with Karkinos.

He should've known better than to believe the headlines all those years ago that Evangeline's infant daughter had died shortly after the mother. It was too convenient. And now Samael stood to lose everything. His power would reach only as far as his own miserable country of Draco. It would extend no further than their pitiful chain of horned mountains. That is, unless he stopped Pasha. Unless Samael found a flaw in the legality to prevent Pasha from ascending the throne, the kingdom of Ursa would slip from his administration.

Unaccustomed to being outsmarted, Samael had collected an arsenal of unfavorable publicity to rely on. Yet he feared attacking Pasha's character wasn't enough.

The thought circulated through his mind as he stood amongst the crates of Evangeline's belongings in the library of Apophis Manor. His most trusted servant lingered nearby as always. "This may come as a surprise to you, Xylophis," Samael pressed his fingers to his chin, "but I actually prefer doing things legally. I'm certainly not above resorting to tools such as blackmail or bribery. But corruption often leaves a trail. We must present innocence," here he stopped to pour a decanter of fresh human blood into his wine glass, "even when there is none." He tipped it to his lips. "In the meantime we must also focus our efforts on collecting and destroying the shards of that bloody looking glass before it is used to destroy us. Now that Staccato knows of the fragments' power, it's only a matter of time before the resistance figures out what it's for and starts looking for the pieces."

He removed a box of paints from an old crate and blew the dust from the cover. It was useless. The boxes had been in his possession for ten years. During that time countless excavations had turned up absolutely nothing. They hadn't found one shard, not one bit of information concerning the mirror. It had all been lost. Still, Samael pressed forward, removing the lid and rummaging through the calcified tubes of pigment with little expectation.

His nail snagged on a slip of material. He drew back in frustration. Samael's eyes traveled to the floor of the box in search of the thing which had caused the pain. Then he saw it. He saw it for the first time: an aged loop of ribbon cropping up from the seam where the bottom of the box met the side.

The lavender blue of Samael's eyes illuminated. It was a false bottom. Breathless, he slid his finger through the loop of the ribbon and lifted the panel from the container. There, stuffed into the hidden space, was a worn leather diary. It didn't even have a lock. Samael flipped to a random page, and holding it up to the pale cylinder of lamp light, read to himself. As usual, Xylophis was insufferably restless.

"Your Majesty? What is it? Is it about the mirror?"

Samael ignored him as he continued to devour the entry. After he had crossed the halfway point, he could hold back no longer. Arching his lovely neck, he parted his artistic lips and let out a delighted peal of laughter. Xylophis was impossible.

"Dear Cobra, I beg of you, My Prince, what is it you've discovered?"

Samael held the letter lovingly to his chest. "Oh, Xylophis, I love it when people do my job for me!"

CPSIA information can be obtained
at www.ICGtesting.com
Printed in the USA
LVHW040852180620
658260LV00004B/775

9 780998 042909